ANNABELLA

and

CAMBERMERE

Aileen Armitage is half-Irish, half-Yorkshire by birth. She began writing when failing sight forced her to give up work in the outside world and in 1998 she was the winner of the Woman of the Year Award. Aileen is married to the writer Deric Longden.

ANNABELLA
and
CAMBERMERE

Aileen Armitage

Pan Books

Annabella/Cambermere

Annabella first published 1996 by Severn House
Cambermere first published 1997 by Severn House

This edition published 2001 by Pan Books
an imprint of Macmillan Publishers Ltd
25 Eccleston Place, London SW1W 9NF
Basingstoke and Oxford
Associated companies throughout the world
www.macmillan.com

ISBN 0 330 39755 9

1 3 5 7 9 8 6 4 2

A CIP catalogue record for this book is available from
the British Library.

Printed and bound in Great Britain by
Mackays of Chatham plc, Chatham, Kent

ANNABELLA

Chapter One

It was a few days after Laura Sutcliffe arrived at Aspley Hall that cousin Anna announced that she was dying. The discovery, one sun-soaked June morning, filled Laura with shock and horror. It was cruel, so bitterly unfair. To be seventeen and abruptly wrenched from life was unutterably saddening.

"Are you sure?" Laura asked her cousin in disbelief.

"There is no doubt of my condition," Anna replied as she lay curled on the chaise longue. "It is beyond cure, a canker eating away deep inside me. I feel so sorry for Papa. My death will grieve him deeply, only child as I am. He will be alone in the world, with only Nanny to care for him." A tear welled unbidden.

"How long have you known?" Laura asked, kneeling beside her.

"I've only just learned. Even Papa does not know yet."

"And Miss Oliphant? Does she know?"

Anna shook her head weakly. "Nor do I intend to tell her yet. You know how she fusses over me as it is. Time enough for her to learn, and Papa too."

Of course Uncle Reginald could not know, Laura thought; otherwise he would not have sent for her to come here to Aspley Hall to be Anna's companion. Only last week he had received her, open-armed and genial, and bade her to behave discreetly and in a ladylike manner so as not to unsettle his delicate daughter. Laura remembered with remorse how she had privately scoffed at the notion of Anna being delicate. Overpampered,

1

certainly, but no invalid as Uncle Reginald seemed to believe. But that was a week ago.

Laura was still shaking at Anna's revelation when one of the underhousemaids came into the drawing room to poke up the fire and add fresh coal. Despite the heat of the day, fires were always lit in Aspley Hall, for Uncle Reginald had left instructions that Anna was always to be kept warm. For some reason he always believed her delicate and in need of nurturing like some rare bloom.

The maid came to stand before Anna, small and neat and aglow with life, and Laura admired the aura of liveliness about her, regretful of Anna's inevitable decline. The girl cocked her dark head to one side.

"Miss Oliphant's looking for thee, Miss Anna. She said she wants to take thee for a walk on t'moor since it's so fine and sunny."

The corners of Anna's lips quivered. Laura pitied her. It must be difficult for her to fight down the terror of approaching death.

"Please tell Miss Oliphant I shall not walk out today, Dora. I prefer to rest here awhile."

The girl bobbed a curtsy and left. As her footsteps died away along the corridor, Laura counted the seconds until the housekeeper's agitated footsteps would replace the silence. She would inevitably come hurrying, anxious and a little perturbed that Anna should decline to go out, for nursery habits of obedience to her commands died hard.

Laura looked at the mantelshelf to watch by the glass-domed clock there how long it took Miss Oliphant to come. Above the clock a gilt-framed mirror tilted at an angle where she could see Anna's reflection, small and vulnerable as she lay curled on the chaise longue. Laura saw her stretch cautiously and raise her weight gingerly on her elbows. With extreme care she lowered her legs to the carpet, then hesitated.

"Do you think that if I stand I might test fate too

far?" Anna asked. "Perhaps I will find I am weaker than I realize."

It really was a pity, for Anna's hollow-eyed face really was quite attractive, oval and pale and framed by a cloud of fair curls that fell past her shoulders. Her eyes were almost as blue as her father's though not so penetrating, calm almost despite her dread. At all costs, Laura resolved, she must be brave and maintain a placid acceptance of fate for Anna's sake. It was not going to be easy, for every inch of her still quivered with shock.

Still there was no sign of Miss Oliphant. Cautiously Anna levered her weight off the chaise longue and stood up, closing her eyes. After a few seconds she opened her eyes.

"I feel no nausea or faintness, Laura. I feel quite steady, except for the fluttering of my heart. Perhaps death is not quite so close as I had thought. I only hope that it will not be too lingering and painful when it comes."

The figure in the mirror was slim and graceful, the cream day gown fitting closely enough to reveal the small breasts and diminutive waist.

Pity stabbed Laura. What did it matter how beautiful Anna might have been if the grave was soon to enfold her charms? She gazed sadly at the pathetic little figure and reflected how deceitful it was that no sign betrayed the canker gnawing away within.

Laura was so deeply engrossed in this reflection that she was startled when Miss Oliphant suddenly erupted into the drawing room. Keen blue eyes looked up into Anna's, searching her face, and her reddish hair bristled under her cap.

"Now what is all this, Anna? Dora says you will not go out. Are you not well?"

Anna lowered herself onto the chaise longue. "Nothing to worry about, Nanny. I simply prefer to sit and read."

Miss Oliphant's short figure straightened, the thin hands smoothing her dark skirts as if she still wore a starched apron. When she spoke, impatience edged her voice, emphasizing the faintly Scottish accent she had long ago overlaid with more standard English.

"Now listen to me, Anna. I am not Nanny but Miss Oliphant, if you please. It is now five years since your papa decided I was no longer your nanny and high time you remembered it. And second, you must recall that your papa left clear instructions when he went to London that I was to exercise my discretion as to your daily routine. Warmth and rest were essential, he said, and also moderate amounts of exercise. I was to take advantage of fine weather to ensure that you and Miss Laura obtained good lungfuls of fresh moorland air. Your daily regime is my responsibility, Miss Anna. I am accountable to your father. Just because Miss Laura is here is no reason to defy him."

"I know his instructions," Anna replied quietly.

"Then why do you defy me?" The tone of authority in her voice was daunting. Seeing Anna made no move to rise, Miss Oliphant returned to the attack, more coaxingly this time.

"Now come along, Anna, we can't have you sitting about moping on a lovely day like this. Miss Laura will come with us. I'll ring for the maid to fetch your coats and outdoor shoes. Now be a good girl and get ready, or it will be time for lunch before we reach the moor."

She was crossing to ring the bell beside the fireplace. Anna raised one languid arm to stop her.

"No, Nanny. I have made up my mind. I shall stay here."

Miss Oliphant crossed the room with quick, neat steps and laid a hand on Anna's brow. "You *are* ill, Anna, aren't you? Your forehead is quite hot. I thought it was unlike you to cross me," she said vexatiously. She hated illness, regarding it as a presumptuous invader that dared to disturb her ordered regime.

"Is it one of your sick headaches, Anna? You haven't suffered an attack for so long now that I hoped that old trouble was gone," she inquired, the concern evident in her lowered tone.

"No, Nanny. I have no headache."

Miss Oliphant lifted Anna's hair to inspect her neck. "You have no spots, have you?"

Anna shook her head feebly.

"Have you any pain? A stomachache, perhaps?"

"Not a pain, exactly, but an uncomfortable feeling as though I have cramp."

Laura started. The canker was at work. Anna could not have long now.

Miss Oliphant was quick to make a diagnosis. "That's it, a stomachache. The plums we had for dinner last night, I'll be bound. I remarked at the time that you should not have had a second helping." She stood back, satisfied. "Then you rest here, Miss Anna, and I'll go and make an infusion of senna pods for you. We'll soon have you right again."

She bustled away, relieved at having discovered a course of action with which to resolve the problem. Miss Oliphant was always thus, Laura noted, momentarily nonplussed and only happy when she could take positive steps to deal with a problem. No wonder Uncle Reginald was so highly satisfied with such a capable housekeeper. Anna was barely nine years old when her mother died, and Uncle Reginald was so often away in London in the Houses of Parliament, helping the queen to govern the country, Miss Oliphant said.

It took Miss Oliphant a full half-hour to reappear with a cup of hot senna tea. When she had gone, Anna sighed.

"If my days are numbered, then there are matters to be attended to. The new gowns for which I have been measured last week must be canceled; my pretty cat, James, must be accustomed to a bed other than mine at night, and my few belongings must be disposed of."

Laura was helping Anna in the phrasing of her last

6

will and testament when Miss Oliphant came back. She looked at Anna critically.

"You do look rather pale and that's a fact, Anna," the housekeeper murmured thoughtfully. "I hesitate to worry your father when he is so occupied with important matters, but I think he would consider it remiss of me not to call in the doctor. I'll send the coachman to fetch Dr. Sheard."

Anna cast a stricken look at Laura. "There is no need, Miss Oliphant, truly."

"Perhaps not," Miss Oliphant reflected, "but we'd best be on the safe side. Your papa would wish it."

When she had gone, Anna turned to Laura.

"I debated whether to tell her of the dreadful symptom, but I knew it was no use. I cannot avoid the doctor's examination and she would send for him all the more quickly if she knew."

"What symptom?" Laura inquired.

Anna shook her head.

Laura was puzzled. "Anna, how do you know you are dying? Hasn't the doctor already been to see you?"

Anna shook her head again.

"But you were well yesterday, talking of your new gowns and the collar you proposed to buy for your little cat. How is it that today you know you are dying but no one else knows?"

"I know, and that's all," Anna said quietly. "There can be no doubt. And now everyone else will learn of it too. It is so humiliating, so degrading. I wonder if all those who suffer from a nauseating final illness feel the same sense of being besmirched. I feel utterly degraded, putrefying under the attack of a hideous thing within me. I shall become an object of disgust and loathing. Death will indeed come as a merciful release from such degradation. Poor Papa! He'll be so shocked when he learns of it, and he will be so desolate once I am gone, for I have neither brothers nor sisters to console him in his grief."

The shadows of the elm trees in the grounds of Aspley Hall lengthened across the floor of the drawing room before Miss Oliphant ushered in Dr. Sheard. The old man smiled and drew Miss Oliphant to the window. Murmured words floated across to Laura, and the mention of stomach pain and possible appendicitis as she was leaving.

Appendicitis, she had not thought of that. She remembered Anna telling her of a child in the village, the daughter of a hand in one of the Braithwaite mills, whose appendicitis had flared suddenly into peritonitis and whose death had followed swiftly. Perhaps that was Anna's illness too. In a few more moments Dr. Sheard would confirm it.

He came out of the room, rubbing his thick-fingered hands together across his ample stomach and smiles spreading across his plump face. His was an intriguing face, one chin falling below another, three in all, till the final one rested quiveringly on his stock.

"No need for alarm . . . a glass of sherry as a tonic . . . no bathing or riding . . ." Laura heard the deep voice of the doctor intone.

Miss Oliphant's voice whispered something in reply that Laura could not hear, but she did catch the doctor's murmur of "rather late." So they had realized that Anna was in the last stages of illness. It was confirmed. She was dying.

The doctor turned to Miss Oliphant. "I shall prescribe a sleeping draft for her and you may pour her a dose should she feel at all uncomfortable. But do not fret. In a day or two she will feel quite well again."

Comforting words to ease the doomed victim's mind, Laura reflected as Miss Oliphant ushered him out. An opiate to alleviate the agony that must come. She had noted his hesitation, his obvious embarrassment at referring to the pain Anna must endure. Feeling uncomfortable, he had said, as if choosing milder words could lessen its intensity. There was no hope for Anna now.

Sorrow flooded her. She went back into the drawing room.

The maid, Dora, brought more coal. When she had done she came to Anna.

"Will there by anything else, miss? Shall I bring tea up?"

"When Miss Oliphant comes," Anna replied, making a stern effort to control the tremor in her voice. "And bring me the writing box from the desk, please."

When Dora had gone, Anna dipped her pen in the inkstand and wrote carefully, in neat copperplate script.

"The last will and testament of Anna Braithwaite," she wrote. Laura reminded her to add the date. Anna chewed the tip of her pen. "All my clothes and my jewels I leave to Laura Sutcliffe, my cousin. Dear Laura, I'm glad I have you in whom to confide. You are so buoyant and optimistic, so sure of yourself that you make me feel a dim little shadow by comparison. I daresay you will not care for my gowns overmuch for you consider my taste too subdued, but I know you will like my jewels. The seed pearl necklace I inherited from Mama and my Whitby jet brooch with its matching earrings I know you've always admired. You at least will have mellow memories of your little cousin whenever you wear them."

"Oh, Anna!" Laura protested.

"It will not take long to dispose of my few belongings. My gray mare I cannot bequeath to anyone, Papa having bought it for me. It would be best to leave him to do with her as he feels best." As Anna laid aside her pen and sealed the document, Dora returned with the tea tray laid for three.

"Where is Miss Oliphant?" Anna inquired.

"In t'library, miss, reading. She says she'll be along shortly."

Laura felt annoyed. The housekeeper should be here, ministering to her declining charge and not idly reading.

The evening sun glowed low between the elms, casting a glorious golden radiance across the parquet floor, and outside all was peace save for the song of the birds. Laura listened sadly, wondering how much longer Anna would hear their song and at the same time bitterly resenting that nature continued to pour her blessings on the earth, unaware of Anna's tragedy. At last she heard footsteps, and Miss Oliphant came in.

Usually Miss Oliphant walked with a positive tread, with an air of decisiveness about her. Now she stood uncertainly, pink and tight-lipped, by the small table in the window alcove, her fingers clenching and then relaxing their hold on the red-backed book she carried.

She laid the book on the table and came hesitantly toward Anna. For a moment she stood there, her fingers clasping and unclasping in the folds of her gown, and at last she spoke. Her voice was tight and hard, as though she was having to force it out.

"Anna, my dear, we must talk," she said jerkily. Pity for her filled Laura.

"Do sit down, Nanny, here by me."

She sat stiffly, her normally alert eyes clouded now with doubt and apprehension. "Not Nanny, Anna, I have told you. Miss Oliphant, or Emily even, if you prefer."

Laura wondered at her condescension, allowing Anna to make use of her Christian name. As it was, the thought occurred to her that the familiarity came a little late, a consoling gesture to make Anna's last days as happy as she could.

"Anna, I feel it incumbent upon me to talk to you of a matter which gives me cause for embarrassment," she said in a rush of words. "There are matters one avoids discussing in polite society, but I feel for once one must contravene the proprieties in order to save you from alarm."

Laura rose swiftly. "Then I'll leave you," she said, but she was puzzled. Whatever Miss Oliphant had to say could be no more alarming than what Anna had discovered this morning.

"Yes, that would be best," the housekeeper agreed.

"Miss Oliphant, I know already. I am dying," Laura heard Anna say before she closed the door.

There, she had said it, and in a tone of such quiet calm that even Laura was surprised. Her cousin undoubtedly had courage.

Despite her anxiety, Laura could not resist eavesdropping.

"Rubbish. You are, how shall I say, temporarily indisposed, that is all," she heard the housekeeper say firmly. "What is happening to you is perfectly normal. We all of us undergo it. It is a sign that we have reached maturity at last, and we should be proud of it." There was a pause, and then Miss Oliphant added softly, "Do you understand, Anna? You are a woman now."

"A woman, Nanny? A woman destined to die?" Anna's voice was shrill.

Miss Oliphant gave a short, brittle laugh. "Not yet, my dear. The doctors in all the medical books pronounce this indisposition as normal, the result of girls growing faster than boys. They call this phenomenon a cicatrization of an interior wound."

"A wound?" Anna leaped on the word.

"A wound of a woman's internal system, which is the whole basis of her womanhood. They say she is invalided by a wound of love. I'm afraid I express myself badly, my dear. I feel it may be wiser for you to read for yourself for the details are complicated. My explanation might only confuse you. Here, I'll leave the book for you. Read it, and afterwards you may discuss it with me if you wish."

Laura backed away quickly. As Miss Oliphant laid her hand on the knob Anna stopped her.

"Is there a name for this malady, Miss Oliphant?"

The housekeeper hesitated. "There is a medical name for it, but in common parlance it is usually known as the flowers, or the curse." Quickly she stepped out and closed the door behind her.

The curse! Laura gasped. So Anna's fatal illness was no more than that! She wanted to laugh, to giggle uncontrollably with relief. What a ninny her cousin was, to think she was dying!

But then, Laura reflected more soberly, Anna must have been kept in ignorance all this time. At seventeen, only a year younger than herself, the shock must have been dreadful.

Dora came up to remove the tray as Laura rejoined her cousin. Dora had the country-fresh look that predicted a long and healthy life.

She stifled a yawn and then grinned apologetically at Anna. "Sorry, miss, I'm fair tired out, up at five and all." Anna seemed unaware that Laura had returned.

"Dora, have you heard of the curse?"

Dora almost dropped the tray as her eyes grew wide and her mouth dropped open, and then she began to giggle nervously.

"What on earth makes thee ask, miss?"

"I want to know. Have you?"

"Well, of course. I'm fifteen, tha knows."

"Have you . . . suffered from it?"

Her eyes rounded again in surprise. "Aye."

"And you recovered?" Anna sounded hopeful.

"Aye."

"Have any of the other maids suffered from it, do you know?"

The eyes narrowed now. "Aye, all of them I should reckon. All girls do, don't they, miss?" She addressed Laura, who nodded. "Will that be all, miss?"

"Yes, you may go. And thank you."

Anna turned her blue eyes on Laura. "Is it true, Laura? Dare I hope that I may live? It is difficult to shake off the belief I have had for a whole day now that death is inevitable. But Dora's words do seem to confirm Miss Oliphant's." She reached for the red book.

The Gentlewoman's Guide to the Upbringing of Children, it said on the cover, and inside a slip of paper marked the spot Miss Oliphant evidently intended Anna to read, and she turned to it eagerly. Three pages were ragged at the edges, the result of having been at some-time firmly glued together and later cut open. Laura watched while Anna read eagerly.

"There," she said when Anna had finished. "Are you content now?"

"It says it usually occurs at the age of thirteen or four-teen, and I am now just past my seventeenth birthday." Anna blushed violently. "But what it says here cannot be true."

"What about?" asked Laura.

"About babies. Hitherto I have never questioned the arrival of a baby into a family. Once I was taken to visit an orphanage and saw the wistful little faces of children who, so the matron said, were hoping that some day a father and mother would come to choose them. Some-how I suppose I believed that parents went to choose a new child just as they did a piece of furniture or a new carriage."

Laura laughed merrily. "What utter nonsense, Anna! Surely Miss Oliphant has enlightened you before now? Heavens! I knew all about it years ago."

"Perhaps you did, you living on a farm too, but I knew nothing, until today."

Laura's face registered incredulity. "Nothing at all? Had you never even heard whispers?"

"One of the maids once hinted at strange rituals in bedrooms. From what I gleaned from her, for she was unusually reticent on the subject once she had aroused my interest, I had vague mental pictures of a gentleman and a lady in the privacy of their room, sitting opposite each other in cane-bottomed chairs and performing some unimaginable ritual. That is, unimaginable until now. What the red book tells me filled me with disgust. Perhaps I have learned something I was not yet intend-ed to know. Perhaps I have read further than Nanny in-tended."

Miss Oliphant came back, and this time her manner was as brisk and capable as usual.

"Have you finished reading, Anna? Then let us all go down to dinner for you have eaten hardly anything to-day."

Only once did she refer to the subject at dinner.

"Did you understand all you read, my dear?"

"I think so."

"Are you content now?"

Anna sighed deeply, her childhood illusions of cane-bottomed chairs gone forever. "I think perhaps I might have been happier to have had some dreadful disease, as I believed. I can hardly believe it to be true, for it is so distasteful."

Blue eyes regarded her sharply.

"You must not think too harshly of men, my dear. I know how you have always disliked the company of gentlemen, ever since you were a child. Even your papa's colleagues. At times you seemed downright afraid of them, but really, there is no need to be so alarmed in male company, my dear. After all, one day you will marry, and marry well too, I'm sure. I would not wish you to think badly of men, that is all. They are only human."

She resumed her attack on the boiled beef with an air that indicated that this topic of conversation was ended, and both girls were too well-mannered to oblige her to continue a subject she evidently found embarrassing. It was true Anna was shy of men for she knew so few—a couple of uncles including Laura's father, now dead, old Dr. Sheard, the minister at the chapel, and the rest were not really people, but servants like Coker the butler and John the footman.

"One thing however," Miss Oliphant added. "Now you are a woman we must make plans accordingly. Now we must put up your hair and discard your white smocks. They are for little girls, but you're a big girl now. Let's see." She cocked her head to one side, looking in the

candlelight for all the world like some bright-eyed little
robin. "Yes, we could plait your hair and wind the plaits
around your head. We'll try it in the morning. What do
you think, Miss Laura?"

"Then can I have my hair washed tonight?" Anna
asked.

Miss Oliphant's eyes rounded in horror. "Good heavens, no! Not at a time like this! Next week, perhaps."

The girls lingered alone together after dinner as a
sleepy-eyed Dora cleared the table. Anna looked at the
little housemaid almost with fondness.

"You were right, Dora," she said softly. "I shall survive."

Dora sighed as she heaped up dishes on the tray.
"Aye, we survive. But it's a damnable nuisance, and no
mistake. Men have t'best of it, like me mam says. No
curse for them, no having babies every year, just t'fun of
making 'em. Or not making 'em if they've any sense, but
having fun just t'same. Women is just men's playthings,
she says, and I reckon she's right."

"Is she?" Anna's eyes were rounded.

"Aye, I reckon. She's had eight bairns in nine years,
two of 'em dead now, poor things. She blames
t'Croppers Arms, where me dad likes to have a drink.
When he's drunk there's no stopping him. I'll not get
wed. Not for a long while yet."

"Don't you like men, Dora?" Laura asked.

"They're all right. But they're after one thing, I know.
That lad in t'stables wanted me to go in t'barn with him
today, but I'm not daft. I knew what he were after soon
as he started to unbutton me blouse."

She gathered up the tray and left. For a time Anna sat
stunned. Today had been a day of revelation for her,
Laura knew, one discovery after another, but this latest
information was almost too much for her to digest. That
this ritual she now learned replaced the cane-bottomed
chair one was actually desirable to men was incompre-

hensible. With an effort she put the distasteful thought aside.

"I shall not call her Nanny, but Miss Oliphant, or rather, I'll call her Emily from now on. After all, I am a woman and entitled to a woman's privilege. My mother, if she were still alive, would probably call her Emily and so shall I. In my newfound status I shall become mistress of the house in Papa's absence, so it is time to establish that to Miss—to Emily. Till now she has maintained her dominance, but the time has come to reverse the roles."

Laura marveled at Anna's resilience, all thoughts of death forgotten, but that night as they lay in bed she could hardly sleep. Anna was restless, tossing and moaning in her sleep. Suddenly she awoke with a cry and clutched Laura's arm.

"I had the most terrible nightmare! I remember little of the dream, only that it was the same one I have endured many times before, although not lately." She clung, terrified, to her cousin. Laura soothed her.

"What frightened you, Anna?"

"Something grostesque and horrifying was pursuing me, some monstrous thing which I never saw, for it was always just around the corner, just out of sight, but I could hear its footsteps. They were distant and slow and growing closer and louder every second. Oh, Laura, it was terrible!"

"There, there, dear. It's over now."

"Just as it was about to appear around the corner and I was dying of terror, I woke up, the blood roaring in my ears. The deafening thud of my own heartbeat was the clumping, menacing footstep I dreaded."

She wept piteously and Laura spoke to her firmly. "Come now, Anna, you are a woman now and must learn to put childhood bogeymen behind you."

The fair girl lifted tear-filled eyes to the dark one. "It's the same dream I've had so often, over and over again, ever since I was a little girl. Oh, Laura, it frightens me so much! What does it mean? Why does it terrify me so?"

Laura shook her head helplessly. "Who can ever explain a dream? They're always meaningless. It's just that you've had such a day of worry, my dear. But the worry is gone now, and there's no longer any need to fear."

Reassured, Anna slept at last. But Laura lay awake far into the night, disquieted without knowing why. All she knew, intuitively, was that something threatened, something far more fearful and less tangible than Anna's mistaken idea that she was dying. And somehow Anna's ominous dream was a sign that presaged the danger's arrival.

Chapter Two

Emily Oliphant rolled up the last recalcitrant wisp of red hair into a rag curler and took a look about her bedroom before taking off her woolen dressing gown and climbing gratefully into the high bed. One final peep to see her charge was comfortable, and then she could rest.

Her carpet-slippered feet made no sound on the parquet floor as she opened Anna's door. Both Anna and Miss Laura were sleeping peacefully. Emily would be glad to be asleep herself. Such a tiring day it had been, one way and another.

She had committed it all to her diary as faithfully as she had done the events of every day of her life since she first came to Aspley Hall, so long ago. Over seventeen years ago, to be precise, just before Mrs. Braithwaite gave birth to Anna. Every night since then Emily had sat down to record the events of her daily life, at first in the attic bedroom she shared with another nursery maid, and then later, as promotion to nanny and then housekeeper followed, in the privacy of her own bedroom next to Anna's. A row of small diaries, closely written, now occupied a locked box in the bottom of her wardrobe. To anyone else they would seem remarkably uneventful, a record of childhood illnesses successfully nursed to recovery and of dismissed maids replaced by others. Apart from Mrs. Braithwaite's nervous illness, which had necessitated frequent stays at a sanatorium, and her subsequent death, little of import had occurred. Life had been fairly smooth and untrammeled since the day Emily Oliphant left the arms of her family to take up service.

"Harrowfield? That's a long way off," Emily's mother had said in alarm. "I'll never see thee, lass." Her Scottish father, with the mop of red hair so like her own, had bidden Emily to take the position and not let sentimentality get in the way. As long as Emily sent wages home regularly, he could afford to do without her company, Emily realized, and to be perfectly truthful she would miss him little in return.

Not that he was a cruel man—oh, no, that could not be said of him—but narrow and mean of spirit. He cared only for his own feelings, his disappointments and frustrations, and was incapable of registering the feelings of those about him. When his wife tried to speak of her problems, her inability to pay the tallyman for the blanket she'd needed for the newest baby, for instance, he waved her troubled face from his sight in irritation. A working man should be left in peace once he got home from the pit, he would roar.

"This house is full of wailing," he would complain as he sat by the grate in the one living room of their little cottage. "If not you, then it's the bairns. Too many howling creatures in this house!"

"And whose fault is that, I'd like to know," retorted his harassed wife. Time and again Emily had been obliged to watch her mother's distress and her father's anger. No one else's problems had the right to invade his private world of self-absorption. Over the years Emily's heart hardened against the self-pity of her father, and by extension she had come to believe all men were equally selfish and thoughtless.

But a good Christian upbringing forbade her ever to mention her parents save in the tones of honor and respect that the Commandments dictated. So her diary mentioned her mother but little and her father not at all. Now Mother was dead and Father remarried to a younger woman, there was no cause to mention him at all.

All Emily's feeling was transferred once she reached Harrowfield and Aspley Hall, to her new young mistress and later to Mrs. Braithwaite's beautiful golden-haired baby daughter. Emily had been nurserymaid then, under the jurisdiction of a very brisk and capable nanny. Then one day Mrs. Braithwaite sent for her.

"Nanny tells me she wants to marry, Emily. I know you are very fond of little Annabella. Would you like to become her nanny, if Mr. Braithwaite approves?"

Mr. Braithwaite, busy with his affairs of extending the mill and negotiating to buy a second, had no objection to the new nanny for his two-year-old daughter. But he had to the baby's name.

"Not Annabella, I tell you!" Emily heard him declare loudly to his wife beyond the closed door of the drawing room. "We'll have none of your fancy Italianized names here. There's nowt wrong with Anna—it's got a good, solid ring to it. Now let's hear no more of it. Anna Braithwaite, if you please."

It was not long after that young Mrs. Braithwaite went into a decline due, said the doctors, to her being too fragile to endure an uncomfortable pregnancy and protracted labor which were now taking their toll. Sorrowfully Emily recorded in her diary the strangely withdrawn behavior of her young mistress, alternating with uncontrollable bouts of inexplicable temper. Her sudden, capricious changes of mood made it wise to keep the little Anna from her, and this seemed only to distress Mrs. Braithwaite more.

"You're trying to keep my Annabella to yourself!" the woman would cry piteously. "You're trying to steal her from me because you have no child of your own!"

Blushingly, Emily had tried to avoid such conflict. It was illogical of Mrs. Braithwaite to accuse her of stealing the child's affections because of her own childlessness. After all, she was still only just turned twenty, young enough for a proposal of marriage to be still forth-coming.

But to tell the truth, Emily's thoughts always faltered at the thought of marriage. Flattering though it would be to be asked; in her inner ear she could still hear what a husband demanded of a wife. There was no privacy when a whole family shared one bedroom.

"Oh, no, Jock, please," she would hear her mother's voice plead. "Not again—not yet!"

And her father's voice, blurred as though with anger or with drink, would insist, and then would follow the grunts and moans Emily dreaded to hear, stuffing the sheets into her ears to shut out the noise. For as always it would end with her father snoring and her mother weeping quietly. Marriage as a state held little appeal for Emily. It may be comfortable for a man, but it was misery for a woman.

And not just women of the poor. Mrs. Braithwaite seemed no happier despite the Braithwaite wealth and comfort. No doubt the poor frail creature would have welcomed more of her husband's company, but he was always busy at the mill.

"First things first," he always used to say when she complained. "How am I to get on in the world if I stay at home all the while? Once the business is settled, I've to get cracking on getting a seat in Parliament."

Emily Oliphant turned over in her narrow bed and scolded herself for lying awake going over the past. It was past midnight already, and for years now her routine had been to sleep from ten until six, always with one ear cocked for any sound from the child. It was not wise to break a good habit. Life flowed more smoothly if one always followed a regular, unvarying routine. Poor child, she thought, I do hope those horrid dreams she used to have years ago are not going to return. The child had had a trying day.

Next morning Anna came down with Laura, still pale but at least no longer wearing the desperate, haunted look of yesterday. Truth to tell, Emily felt a trifle guilty that she had not guessed, that she had let the girl experience what she had not been prepared for. But then genteel people did not talk of unpalatable subjects. Still Emily felt a pang of guilt. Procrastination had become a habit, until at last she believed the girl was somehow going to avoid the normal indisposition of a woman. She eyed her charge.

"How are you today, Anna?"

The girl smiled faintly. "I am well, thank you, Emily."

"Perhaps we will forgo our walk today. Come, let us sew our samplers in the drawing room in the sunlight, and you can rest."

Laura looked reluctant. "I should like to write to Mama, if you will permit."

Emily watched Anna's fair head bent over the sewing frame and felt concern for the child. So fragile, so ethereal, just like her mother, and so innocent. She recalled a line from Shakespeare somewhere: "Chaste as the bud ere it be blown." That was Anna, pure and unblemished as the first rosebud in June, and that was how she should remain if Emily had her way. Far more ladylike than the pert Miss Laura seated at the secretaire.

For a time the two of them plied their needles in silence. Then Anna spoke without looking up.

"I saw John as I was coming downstairs this morning."

"John, dear?"

"The footman. He was talking to Dora in the vestibule. He was flirting with her, Emily."

Emily dropped her needle in surprise. "Flirting?"

"That's what Dora calls it. Actually, through the banisters I saw him pinch her—um—her . . ." Emily heard a suppressed giggle from Laura.

"Anna, really! What shocking behavior! And how very unladylike of you to observe and to comment upon it. I shall speak to Mr. Coker, to ensure he exercises a tighter control over his staff."

Anna bent her fair head dutifully over her sewing again. Emily began to regret her sharp tone to the girl.

"Come, let us go up to your room and see what we can do about pinning up your hair as I promised. I seem to remember I have a tortoise-shell comb in my drawer—it will do admirably until we buy you one of your own."

Anna sat quietly, her hands folded in her lap before the dressing table, while Emily combed the long fine hair. Through the mirror Emily studied the girl's face, serene now and uncommunicative. Emily blushed as she recalled what Anna had been about to say about John and Dora. One knew what part of the anatomy one of the lower orders was likely to pinch—thank heaven she had prevented Anna from saying it aloud! Really, it was most unlike her. Adolescence was a strange time indeed, bringing about changes in the personality. It would be wise to keep an even closer eye on the girl than usual.

"There now, what do you think of that?" A long thick plait of golden hair lay neatly coiled on the crown of Anna's head. Anna turned this way and that to inspect the effect.

"I look much older, Emily." Her voice was faint and rather dubious. Emily resolved to help Anna firmly over the threshold of womanhood she seemed a little wary of crossing. No time for weakness. Life must be squarely faced, and it was Emily's duty to strengthen her charge's personality. Mr. Braithwaite did not like feeble, ineffectual people.

"You look charming, my dear. Gracious enough to play the hostess at your papa's table when he entertains guests," Emily said reassuringly, and then saw Anna's stricken face through the mirror. "Not yet, of course, but in time. Perhaps when he is home for Christmas—that's six months away yet."

She looked around the bedroom, with its single bed with a rug beside it, the wide fireplace encircled by the brass-topped fireguard, the plain dressing chest, and the

carved mahogany wardrobe. "And I think it is high time
we changed the nursery into a bedroom fit for a young
lady. With your papa's permission, that is. I shall write
to ask him."

Anna smiled faintly. "Thank you, Emily. May I go
down to join Laura?"

Poor thing, she did look rather wan. "Of course, my
dear. I have plenty to do to occupy me until lunch, and
then Miss Pargeter is to come to tea this afternoon."

That was a pleasant prospect at any rate. Miss
Pargeter knew Aspley Hall and its occupants better than
most, having been Anna's tutor until a year or two ago.
With her, Emily could unbend a little and speak of what
was on her mind. In the absence of a close friend or an
employee of her own standing in the hall, she looked
forward to the retired schoolmistress's visits.

After tea the two ladies sat at table, a pack of cards
and a cribbage board between them. Anna and Miss
Laura had excused themselves and left the ladies alone.
Miss Pargeter's keen brown eyes looked up from under
arched gray eyebrows.

"Our little friend was very uncommunicative during
tea," she remarked dryly.

"Anna?" said Emily in surprise. It was amazing how
shrewd the schoolmistress was. Her perceptive eyes
missed nothing.

"Indeed, Anna. Miss Laura talks enough for two, but I
taught Anna long enough to know of her moods. Is it a
case of sulks at the moment? And for what, pray?"

"No, no, not at all," Emily said quickly, anxious to de-
fend her charge. "She has been a trifle indisposed lately,
that is all."

"Not the migraines again, surely?"

"No. But she has not had an easy time of it, this last
day or so. She is just becoming aware of what being a
woman entails."

Miss Pargeter snorted. "That is no pleasant discovery, to be sure. But it does account for her behavior."

"What behavior?" Emily's voice was sharp. Her charge's manners were beyond criticism as a rule.

"When I arrived, she was sitting alone in the window seat overlooking the stable yard, so engrossed that she was not aware of my presence. I had to speak first."

"Daydreaming, perhaps. Please forgive her. You know she welcomes your coming."

"Daydreaming, fiddlesticks! I could see what she was watching. One of the stable boys had pulled off his shirt and was sluicing himself under the pump. Young Anna's eyes were positively gleaming as she watched."

Emily stopped shuffling the cards suddenly. "Watching a *boy*! Disgraceful! I shall speak to her about it."

"It's natural enough at her age. I've taught enough village children over the years to know. Just keep a close eye on her, that's all. Your box this time, isn't it?"

Deftly Miss Pargeter discarded two cards and surveyed her hand thoughtfully. For a moment there was silence, then Emily put down a card.

"Ten. You don't think there is cause to worry, do you?"

"Fifteen for two." Miss Pargeter moved the peg in the board. "No, but one should exercise caution. After all, blood will out."

Emily's blue eyes rose to meet the other woman's. "She is of good blood on one side of the family at least. Admittedly Mr. Braithwaite is a self-made man of somewhat humble birth, but Mrs. Braithwaite was a lady. Anna inherits her ladylike manners from her mother."

"It was not of manners or breeding that I was speaking. Your turn to play."

"Seventeen. Then of what, may I ask?"

Miss Pargeter's smile was veiled with a knowing look. "Well, her mama was frequently—how shall I put it—indisposed? Anna may well have inherited the trait." She played a queen. "Twenty-seven."

"Mrs. Braithwaite was delicate, it is true. Thirty-one for two." Emily moved her peg up in line with Miss Pargeter's.

The schoolmistress leaned across the table and peered at Emily above her pince-nez. "Delicate? Now come, Emily. Though Mr. Braithwaite would not admit it and I know your loyalty to your employer, is it not true that the lady was periodically—unstable, shall we say?"

Emily flung down her cards. "Miss Pargeter," she said with a great effort at self-control, "we have been friends for many years, but I cannot allow you to imply that my late mistress was—was—unbalanced." There was a catch in her voice, and Miss Pargeter relented.

"*De mortuis nil nisi bonum.* You are right. We should not speak ill of the dead. Nevertheless, it would be as well to keep a careful eye on little Anna. I share your concern for her, Emily, truly I do."

It was as good as an apology, and Emily, coolly in command of herself once again, picked up her cards and resumed the game. During the next half-hour the schoolmistress's peg drew well ahead of Emily's and her feeling of triumph began to fade.

Miss Pargeter was counting up her final box. "Fifteen two, fifteen four, and two pairs are eight. That makes me the winner for this afternoon, I think."

With a sigh Emily gathered up the cards. She had not been concentrating as she should to outwit Miss Pargeter's quick brain. Her concern for Anna lay uppermost on her mind. She could not help referring to the subject again.

"Does Anna really seem unusually withdrawn to you, Miss Pargeter? Could it be that she feels outshone by Miss Laura, in which case it may soon pass?"

The older woman shrugged. "As I said, she was always a creature of moods, ever since her mother died. How old was she then?"

"Nine. It was eight years ago."

"Well, of course, there is also the fact that she is a Gemini."

"A Gemini?"

"Fifth sign of the Zodiac. Sign of the twins, which indicates a dual nature. Gemini children are usually sunny, charming children, but there is another secret side of them that no one will ever truly understand. So one expects occasional daydreams, when they withdraw into their own private world."

"I see." Emily had the profoundest respect for Miss Pargeter's knowledge of astrology, though her own practical nature told her it was all nonsense really. Still, the schoolmistress had just described Anna's character perfectly. And it was infinitely preferable to believe the child's remoteness to be due to her birth sign rather than to any inherited weakness. Emily's defensive mood began to soften and she began to feel more warmly toward her friend. So much more warmly that she let her amiable feelings overcome her usually sensible self.

"Do read the cards for me, Miss Pargeter. It is months since you last read them."

The schoolmistress's pince-nez slithered down her thin nose as her eyebrows rose. "I thought you did not approve, Emily, but if you wish it . . ."

Smoothly she shuffled the cards and laid out one row above another. Emily found herself leaning forward in curiosity as Miss Pargeter deliberated over them.

"Well, what do you see?"

"A change of circumstances, it seems."

Emily was shocked. "Not leaving the hall, surely? Oh, no, I could never do that."

"Well, as I've said before, the art lies in the interpretation, but I seem to see a change. And a man."

Emily felt her heart flutter. "A man?"

"Dark and disturbing."

"And what else?"

"It's hard to tell. Confusion, of some kind. No, it's no use. The cards fall in an unusually strange way—in pairs—I think I cannot have shuffled them properly after our game."

To Emily's disappointment Miss Pargeter swept the cards together and picked them up. Emily could not tell whether it was her imagination that the schoolmistress looked a little pinker and more flustered than usual as she put on her bonnet to leave. At the front door she paused.

"Do try and keep to your routine as far as possible, my dear," the older woman said, pressing Emily's hand. "It will be to your and Anna's advantage to undertake nothing out of the ordinary in the immediate future."

Emily laughed. "Change would be a fine thing, Miss Pargeter. We live a very ordered and uneventful life at Aspley Hall, but we are content to keep it that way."

As she lay in bed that night Emily Oliphant went over the afternoon's conversation in her mind. It was true that young Mrs. Braithwaite, beautiful and kindly as she was, had been prone to hysterical outbursts at times, which had always marked the prelude to a bout of the sickness, which meant another stay at the sanatorium. But the mistress had not been unbalanced as Miss Pargeter said. Fragile and easily disturbed, yes, but nothing more. Still, it would be wise to watch Anna lest she did develop a similar tendency.

But it was the thought of the cards that made Emily shiver. She detested change. Routine and familiarity were comfortable hooks on which to hang one's life. She sincerely hoped the schoolmistress's reading was inaccurate for once, and well it might be if, as she had said, the cards had not been adequately shuffled. But the dark man . . . Despite herself Emily felt the flutter of hope and anticipation again. At the age of thirty-two it was still not too late to hope. After all, she had once felt the sensation of a man's hands and knew what feelings they could arouse. . . . Hastily she brushed away the memory, ashamed of the guilty pleasure she still felt in recalling it.

In the bedroom while Anna climbed into bed Laura reread the letter to her mother by the light of the candle. "Dearest Mama, the journey here was uneventful and I am happy to see cousin Anna again." Laura smiled at the omission of a reference to Uncle Reginald, as she knew Mama would too. Laura was not overfond of her brusque uncle and was decidedly glad that business kept him in London. Mama believed him kind and considerate, but that was because he had been mindful of his duty toward his only sister when she was suddenly widowed, offering to take Laura into his household as companion to Anna.

"He makes the offer knowing that I cannot afford to keep you at school now," Mama had pointed out. "Saying that Anna needs a companion is his polite way of offering to feed and clothe you. We must not spurn his generosity."

Generosity! Laura snorted. He was a cold, unfeeling father, sparing little time for his only child. Not that cousin Anna captivated anyone's attention, for she was so meek and submissive she could be a positive bore at times. Then pity for her filled Laura as she recalled the girl's alarm yesterday. That priggish Miss Oliphant had caused unnecessary terror to the child out of oversensitive ignorance.

Laura glanced down the letter, wondering how much her mother would read between the lines.

"Life at Aspley Hall is still as quiet as ever. Anna rarely goes out, preferring to read or sew, and no one seems to call." She hoped Mama would not construe that to mean that Laura was complaining of boredom. Perhaps inside she did dread monotony after the carefree life at home on the farm while Papa was still alive, but she must not worry Mama. She would be missing her daughter, and it would not do to increase her anxiety.

"Anna is as happy to see me as I am to be with her." Not, perhaps, strictly true, for Anna had shown little emotion, but it would make Mama happy.

Sleepily Laura climbed into bed beside Anna's slim, curled figure to blow out the candle. Her cousin whimpered in her sleep, but at Laura's soothing touch she grew calm.

At breakfast next morning Anna was still listless. Emily made an effort to cheer her up.

"Another beautiful day, Anna. Would you and Miss Laura like a walk down to the village after breakfast? Fresh air, that's what you need, my dear." Emily's bright eyes took in the bowed form, the lacklustre hair. Laura guessed she was thinking that Anna must look more like herself before her master came home.

"Are you sure you gave your hair a hundred strokes of the brush last night, Anna? It does not shine today," she remarked in gentle reproof.

The girl nodded. "I did, but it needs washing."

"Of course. Come, help me sort your papa's mail, and then we'll go out," said Emily as she rose from the table. Anna followed in silence. Laura rose with a sigh. In the vestibule a neat pile of letters stood on the hall stand. Emily took them and led the way to the master's study and laid each one on his desk.

"R. Braithwaite, M.P." she repeated three times, and then held the fourth letter up in surprise. "Miss E. Oliphant, why, this is for me. It's your father's hand, Anna."

She broke the seal and scanned the contents of the single sheet of paper. Anna watched without a flicker of interest on her pale face. Emily's face brightened. "He's coming home!"

"When?" Laura asked.

"Good gracious, it's today! We must hurry and prepare. Ring the bell, will you, Anna? We must warn Cook and have his room made ready at once."

There was only the coolest of interest on Anna's face and no trace of hurry in her step as she did as she was asked. For the rest of the day Emily barely had time to notice the girls, the walk to the village forgotten in the flurry of activity to be ready for the master's arrival. It was nearing time for tea when the carriage returned from the station. The servants, headed by Coker the butler, lined up in the vestibule while Anna and Emily went out to the top of the steps to greet the master. Laura stood behind Anna.

He stepped down from the carriage, short and plump and smiling broadly at his daughter.

"Well now, and how's my bonny lass?" he inquired loudly, his arm about her slim shoulders as they mounted the steps together.

"I am well, Papa."

"You look a little peaky to me. Not enough fresh air, I'll be bound." He nodded to Emily. "Is that it, Miss Oliphant? Been moping without me, has she?"

"Of course she misses her papa, sir, but she is quite well, I assure you."

"And Laura. I'm glad to see you, my dear." Within the portals of the hall, the maidservants bobbed a curtsy and Coker advanced to meet his master. The brisk manner of the master seemed to Laura to bring a current of fresh air into the stagnant hall, rippling the usually torpid atmosphere. Even Anna's remote air seemed to dissipate.

"All's well, Coker?" Braithwaite demanded, and then, awaiting no answer, he went on. "Have my baggage taken to my room and bring tea to the drawing room. I want to talk to my daughter. And to you, Laura."

Coker turned to obey and Emily turned to leave also. Braithwaite stopped her.

"And you, Miss Oliphant. There is much to arrange." The urgency in his voice and the brightness in his hazel eyes indicated there was a matter of some importance to discuss. Laura felt a sense of excitement. Anna murmured an excuse and said she would join them in the drawing room in a few moments.

Miss Oliphant stood on the rug while Braithwaite reclined at his ease in a deep armchair. Laura felt sorry for the housekeeper. She could not sit until her employer bade her do so, but Braithwaite, careless as ever of the conventions, launched into the subject that was obviously claiming his interest.

"Miss Oliphant, I think it high time Anna left the seclusion of the country and came to live with me in London. Life is passing her by up here in the wilds of Yorkshire. I intend to take her back with me. Laura too, of course," he added as an afterthought.

Laura was dazed. This was wonderful news indeed. Miss Oliphant murmured, "I see, sir."

He spread his hands. "You must agree it is not good for the girl—both girls—to languish here when they could be meeting people and gaining new interests. Anna is no longer a little girl, you know."

Miss Oliphant shifted uncomfortably. Laura guessed that she was debating how best to put her misgivings to her master, for he was not a man to take opposition kindly. Always impetuous and demanding, he must be handled with caution.

Braithwaite grew impatient at her silence. "Well, Miss Oliphant, do you not agree it would be good for Anna? You need not fear that your services might be no longer necessary, for you will accompany her to London. Now do you like the idea?"

Hazel eyes challenged hers to argue. Emily lowered her gaze and replied with diffidence. "Sir, I would not presume to question your decisions, for I know you act always as you believe best, particularly for Miss Anna."

"Then why do you hesitate?" Laura could see her evasive answer had not fooled the master's shrewd mind. Eagerly he began to list the advantages to be derived from the move. "The girls will meet people of all walks of life, my colleagues in the House, people of wealth and even titled lords and ladies. They can advance themselves as they never could here. Think of it, visiting the grand houses in London and entertaining the gentry in Hanbury Square. It's a fine house, that of mine in the square, just by the park. All it needs is a mistress as pretty as Anna to act as hostess to my friends."

So that was it, Laura concluded from his words. He needed a lady to grace his table, to impress his London friends and perhaps to help him climb in the social and political world. Despite his love of his daughter, which Laura did not doubt for a minute, there was expediency in the move too. Reginald Braithwaite was no fool.

Emily spoke, softly and urgently. "Sir, I appreciate your reasons for taking the young ladies to London, but I would suggest that a little delay might be advisable. A few months, Christmas perhaps, but not just yet."

He eyed her shrewdly. "Your reasons, Miss Oliphant?"

Emily hesitated. Both she and Braithwaite seemed to have forgotten Laura, sitting listening breathlessly in the corner.

"I am waiting, Miss Oliphant."

Impatiently though, Laura could see by the drumming of his plump fingertips on the arm of the chair.

"Sir, she has been indisposed this week. An announcement such as you propose to make would upset her, I fear."

"Indisposed? Not ill, I hope?"

"No sir."

"Then the prospect of London should reanimate her, bring back the color to her cheeks. Now my mind is made up it were best done quickly. Where is that tea?"

Even as Emily crossed to ring the bell a tap at the door heralded the arrival of Dora, bearing a silver tray with tea and hot muffins. Braithwaite bit thoughtfully into a muffin and Emily poured the tea into thin china cups.

Laura watched her uncle smoothing the crown of his head with one plump hand while he munched. It was as though he was smoothing a crop of unruly hair where it once had grown, for now his pate was bald and shining, surrounded by a fringe of gray hair.

"Anna is a woman now," he said, disturbing Emily's

reverie. "That is another good reason why I must take her to London. There she will find a husband good enough for her, but here she'd find nothing better than a farmer. In London she could find herself a title even. She's pretty enough and biddable enough."

"A husband?" Emily echoed. Only then did Laura become aware of the white shape framed in the doorway. Anna had just come in.

"Aye, a husband. She's seventeen, old enough to be a wife and mother, so it's settled, Miss Oliphant. Next week we'll whisk the lass off to London and see what we can do about it. Tomorrow you can start about arranging the packing and everything."

Anna glided forward until she came into her father's view. Reginald Braithwaite smiled broadly. "Oh, there you are, lass. The tea is getting cold. Come, sit by me while Miss Oliphant pours it—another cup of tea for me if you please, Miss Oliphant. And one for Laura—I'd forgotten you were there, lass."

He sat back, basking in self-satisfaction and unaware of the gleam in his daughter's eyes. Laura saw it, but whether it was a glow of anticipation or fear in her cousin's eyes she could not tell. But knowing Anna's intense dislike of men, she could guess that if she had overheard the mention of a husband, that gleam could only be one of terror.

Chapter Three

Reginald Braithwaite stood at the parlor window on the first floor of his imposing villa and watched the nannies pushing perambulators across Hanbury Square. A credit to their parents they were, these plump, bonneted babies sitting gurgling at the sunlight while their older brothers and sisters walked sedately alongside in their high-buttoned boots and neat white smocks. A credit to those industrious citizens who had earned the right to live in this highly fashionable part of London near Regent's Park. Now farther east and south, beyond the infamous Tottenham Court Road and down toward the river, the children of the poor did not walk so proud and erect. It was a case of the sins of the fathers, if ever there was one. If only the poor would abandon their improvident and immoral way of life, they too could walk in the sun and prosper. As he fingered the gold watch chain stretched across his ample stomach, Reginald Braithwaite sighed at the shortsighted attitude of the poor.

Still, this last week he had been so occupied with removing his daughter and niece from Harrowfield to his London villa that he had had little time to think about the problem that had been filling his mind for the last few months. Now that Anna seemed reasonably settled in her new surroundings, there would be time enough to return to the matter. He pulled out the gold hunter watch attached to the chain and glanced at it. There was just time for a quick stroll around the square.

It was relaxing to watch the young people bowling their hoops in the sunshine. Braithwaite smiled indulgently at a boy who nearly cannoned into him as he pursued a wayward hoop.

"Easy there, lad, mind how you go," he warned him.

It was pleasant to stroll in the warmth of the early-afternoon sun, conscious of the impressive figure he made in his gray frock coat. A good piece of West Riding cloth that was, the best in England even if it had been woven at a mill not his own. Worsted, that was what he was known for, worsted sound and durable as any in the country. Why, it was now even used by Her Majesty's Army. Braithwaite smiled benevolently at a passing gentleman, although he was a stranger. He was pleased at his own acumen. Being the member of Parliament for Harrowfield had put him in a good way to further his own business. And it was quite legal, encouraged even, to use one's contacts in the House, always provided one could gain sufficient standing and esteem. In the last five years he had fared not so badly.

Luckily for Beatrice, as it turned out. His sister had been comfortably off enough in her neat little farm with only the one child, but her husband, William, had been careless. A farmer had no business to allow himself to catch cold like that, rapidly turning to congestion of the lung, and then to die suddenly, leaving a widow and young daughter unprovided for. But for a benevolent uncle, young Laura Sutcliffe could have been forced to go out to work now, instead of which she was leading the life of a lady. No wonder Beatrice's letters were full of wholehearted gratitude.

Braithwaite's brisk step had taken him around a complete circuit of the square, and there was still some little time to spare before young Lazenby was due to come. He would permit himself the indulgence of sitting for a while on one of the benches in the little garden in the centre of the square. From there he could admire his villa without making it obvious. The sight of the house always afforded him great pleasure, for it served as a continual reminder of his success. From lowly beginnings Braithwaite had risen to mill-owner and magistrate, and then back-bench member of Parliament with houses both in town and in the country. Before long, if he planned carefully, he could rise higher still. It was only a question of bringing himself into the prime minister's view, of making himself respected enough to be seriously considered for promotion. Braithwaite's plump face dimpled into a smile. He could see it now—a seat in the Cabinet, perhaps, entailing visits abroad and receptions for foreign ambassadors. Secretary for Foreign Affairs, that would be rewarding. Or, if they were astute enough to recognize his strong business sense. Chancellor of the Exchequer even. No position was too high to strive for.

Gazing with pride at the facade of his villa, Braithwaite's quick eye caught the sudden slight movement of a lace curtain at an upper window. The parlor—no doubt it was Anna, peeping furtively out to see her new surroundings. His thoughts lingered fondly on his daughter, pretty as a picture but so painfully shy. If only she could shake off that irritating aloofness and be more sociable, like himself. She was too much like her mother, unfortunately, timid and vulnerable. Pray heaven she did not become like her mother did at the end. Poor Edith. It was too painful to remember. A husband, that was what Anna needed, a strong and capable man to protect her, and one with position at that. Braithwaite's agile mind turned over the position once again.

That was why he had brought her to London, of course. To keep an eye on her, first, but to find a suitable husband also. To do that she must first impress the candidate he had in mind, and to impress she must be persuaded to mix in society. Here lay the difficulty. Since she arrived, admittedly only a week ago, she had stubbornly refused even to set foot outside in the square. And although he had suggested bringing some of his friends home to entertain, she had quietly declined to join them. But she must soon be brought to see reason, and as he was not an unreasonable man, he would not force her yet. Give her time, and then in a week or two she might prove more tractable. Here, Laura might prove useful, for she found no difficulty in mixing with people. If not, then he would have to exercise his parental will.

A shadow fell across Braithwaite's lap. He looked up in surprise at the tall figure blocking out the sunlight.

"Good afternoon, Mr. Braithwaite. I was just about to ring your bell when I saw you sitting here."

The low, vibrant voice of the young man startled Braithwaite. In his reverie he had forgotten Lazenby's visit. He blinked up at the figure silhouetted against the sun.

"Ah, Lazenby. You are very punctual, I am glad to observe. Let us go into the house."

As they crossed the square, the short rotund figure of Braithwaite trotting alongside the longer stride of the tall young man, Braithwaite could not help pointing with pride to his house.

"That is my house. My neighbor this side is a surgeon at one of the London hospitals, I understand, and I believe the gentleman on that side is a goldsmith."

Lazenby's lack of comment disappointed Braithwaite. He felt it was a mark of his standing to have neighbors of such a caliber, but to Lazenby it was evidently of little account. But then, the boy was a merchant's son and a graduate of Oxford University. Perhaps these symbols of status were taken for granted if one had the luck to be born into the bourgeoisie.

Braithwaite noted the younger man's coat, dark but threadbare at the cuffs, and his slightly stooped shoulders as he walked. He had the air of an academic all right, but by report he was capable and industrious. Lord Travers had spoken highly of him, which was recommendation enough, for the crotchety old peer was notoriously irritable and hard to please. If young

Lazenby had measured up to his exacting standards over the last four years, he would most likely suit Braithwaite well enough. All that remained was to discover if Braithwaite's requirements would be to Lazenby's liking. To judge by his appearance, he would be unlikely to reject the salary Braithwaite would offer.

"Ah, Depledge," Braithwaite addressed the butler, who opened the front door in answer to his ring at the bell. "Mr. Lazenby and I will take port in the drawing room."

"Very good, sir." Braithwaite watched approvingly as his butler took Lazenby's hat and walking stick with just the right air of obsequious respect. Braithwaite felt his butler, with a French-sounding name and a smart new uniform jacket, made just the right impression as head of a gentleman's London household. He beckoned Lazenby to follow as he entered the ground-floor drawing room.

It was a gracious room, light streaming in through the tall window to illuminate the horsehair sofa and deep leather armchairs, the potted palms in their gleaming brass containers, the embroidered tapestry fire screen standing in the center of the hearth and flanked by tall Chinese vases filled with pampas grasses. It was truly a gentleman's main room, and a gentleman of taste at that, thought Braithwaite. He had discreetly noted the contents of all the best London drawing rooms before furnishing his own.

"Please be seated," he invited the younger man, indicating an armchair facing the window. Seating himself opposite, Braithwaite could now watch Lazenby's every reaction while he himself remained master of the situation, silhouetted as he was against the light. It was a trick Braithwaite had learned long ago from his father, and old Braithwaite had known well how to turn every situation to his advantage. Between them, father and son, they had fought their way from comparative obscurity to becoming highly respected mill owners in

Harrowfield. Reginald Braithwaite watched young Lazenby closely as he spoke.

"Now, Lord Travers has probably spoken to you of his proposal, I take it?"

"That I become your private secretary when he moves to the House of Lords? Indeed, sir."

"How long did you work for his Lordship?"

"Since coming down from Oxford, four years ago."

The younger man's gaze was direct and unswerving, Braithwaite noted with approval. There was honesty and courage in the dark eyes.

"What did you study at university?"

"History and philosophy. I have a first-class degree."

Braithwaite nodded. Airy-fairy subjects they might be, but to have a first-class Oxford graduate as his secretary would be flattering to his position. But first he must assure himself of the young man's intention.

"Why are you and his Lordship parting company?"

The dark eyes did not flicker. "As you know, sir, Lord Travers has just succeeded to the title on the death of his father and must move to the Lords. He has a nephew recently graduated whom he would like to employ as his secretary."

"He is not dissatisfied with you?"

"I think not. He offered me the post if I wished to take it, but I would prefer to remain in the Commons. Part of my history studies included constitutional matters and I would prefer to work in the Commons, where legislation is initiated. His Lordship is content with the arrangement."

Braithwaite's eyes gleamed, for the young man had mentioned his own pet scheme. "Social reform? You are concerned with such matters, I take it?"

"Indeed, sir, and I understand you are energetic in this respect."

"That is so." Braithwaite sat back with a smile, undecided whether to recount a list of his achievements in social improvements in Harrowfield. It would be gratifying to recount how well-housed and schooled his millworkers and their families now were, due to his beneficence, but it would be more diplomatic to let rumor report it for him. "Aye, I'm a liberal man, Lazenby, both in politics and in outlook. I'm deeply concerned with improving the lot of the ordinary man."

"So I understand, sir, and so I should be happy to work for you."

Not so fast, thought Braithwaite. I have yet to be certain of you. Lazenby had not inquired as to Braithwaite's aims, so now was the time to tell him and see how he reacted. Braithwaite took a deep breath and fingered his gold watch chain.

"As you have rightly observed, Lazenby, I am energetic in my pursuit of social welfare. To this end I am now concerning myself with the plight of the poor in London."

"An admirable project, for their plight is desperate. How do you propose to help them, sir?"

Braithwaite was irritated. Lazenby was pushing too fast. He had said nothing about helping them. "We must walk before we can run, Lazenby. First we must discover the reasons for their poverty, and on that basis we can plan reform."

"The reasons are obvious, sir. Dirt, disease, lack of education, and thus of opportunity—"

"Yes, yes, I know. Poor housing and sanitation—I know all about that—but the causes go deeper. I feel perhaps the fault lies in the poor themselves. They lack ambition and the drive to work to improve themselves. I feel it necessary to make a detailed survey of the position and of their attitudes. We must have facts on which to base a judgment."

"Is it not perhaps rather sweeping to blame the poor man for his lack of energy? Circumstances have been against him for centuries, robbing him of the reason to struggle."

Depledge entered with a silver tray on which were a

decanter of port and two glasses. Braithwaite bit back his angry retort as the butler smoothly and dexterously poured the wine and served the gentlemen. Lazenby accepted the glass politely and sat back to sip and savor the wine. Damn him for his insolent coolness, thought Braithwaite. He was too confident of himself and his views. Perhaps he was not the right man, after all. Braithwaite wanted a secretary to whom he could dictate orders without explanation, not an intellectual whom he would fear to confide in lest his superior knowledge belittle Braithwaite's own opinion of himself.

But he must think carefully. Though he stood a little in awe of this poised young man who sat completely at ease, it would still serve him well to use the fellow. He could bring a coolly critical mind to appraise the poverty problem, setting forth arguments that Braithwaite could use to his advantage in the House. It was essential to catch the prime minister's eye soon, and what better way than over the subject of London's vice, which was known to be a matter of deep concern to the prime minister?

And there was Lord Travers. To reject his private secretary would damn forever the idea of broaching a possible alliance between young Lionel Travers and Anna. And this was the cause closest to Reginald Braithwaite's heart—to ally his money to the title and property of the Travers' family. Travers was evidently short of cash and his health was none too strong. To offer Braithwaite's wealth along with a fetching young bride for Lionel Travers would undoubtedly appeal to his Lordship, and if, as Braithwaite anticipated, Lord Travers did not live long, then Anna would very soon be her Ladyship, with estates in Kent and Rutland. Only then would Braithwaite feel that his life's work was done—from poverty to wealth and a title in one generation, that was a legacy for one's child of which a man could be rightly proud. Anna would be grateful when she realized at last what he had done for her.

Braithwaite made to regain mastery of the situation. "I should expect my private secretary to do my research among the poor for me, to collect and collate the results of his findings in a well-presented manner."

Lazenby nodded. "I am accustomed to such surveys and reports for his Lordship."

"In a highly confidential manner," Braithwaite went on. "My secretary will not divulge why he is there and for whom he is working."

"Understandably."

"He will live here in my house, with his own bedroom and use of my study. Thus I can supervise his missions to the areas of my work and receive immediate information."

"Very well. Who comprises your household, sir?"

Again he was taking the initiative. Braithwaite forced down an irritable reply and made an effort to be genial. "Myself, my daughter, Anna, my niece, Laura, Miss Oliphant, the housekeeper, and the butler and cook and the other servants, that is all. You would have little interruption."

The dark eyes for once showed surprise. "Your daughter, sir? I did not know."

"She has just come here from Harrowfield. She is seventeen and pretty and very impressionable, and therefore I would ask you to keep your distance from her."

It was abruptly said, and Braithwaite could see the surprise in the younger man's eyes. He had not meant to say so clearly that Lazenby must remember he was an employee, only to spare Anna from unnecessary embarrassment. To his surprise Lazenby's answer was cool.

"You need have no fear in that respect, sir. I care little for the company of ladies and particularly young ones whom I often find shallow and somewhat silly. I much prefer to immerse myself in my work."

Braithwaite was offended. Anna was not silly, or shallow, but he was not going to make the mistake of

leaping to her defense. Defensive statements always
conceded the other man's superiority, and he was not
going to give this overconfident young man the satisfaction. Attack was a far better weapon. He wanted this
fellow as his private secretary, but he resolved to lower
the salary he had intended.

"Well, no beating about the bush. I pride myself on
being a forthright and honest man. Your keep and
eighty pounds a year, that's what the job is worth if you
want it."

There was no hesitation. Lazenby put aside his glass
and rose, extending his hand. "Done, sir. I accept. When
shall I begin?"

As Braithwaite rose to take his hand, he was aware of
Lazenby's height and the firmness of his grip. Even as
he rang the bell for Depledge to show Lazenby out, he
was beginning to wonder if he had made the right
choice, but he quickly brushed the thought aside.
Braithwaite never made a wrong decision because he
calculated every possible result before committing himself. He'd never been wrong before, had he?

As he followed Lazenby out into the vestibule, Braithwaite clearly heard the rustle of skirts up on the landing.
Looking up, he could see no one.

"Anna, is that you?"

A moment's silence, and then Laura appeared at the
head of the stairs and began to descend. "No, Uncle, it is
I."

Braithwaite was disappointed, but held out a hand in
invitation. "Come and meet my new secretary, Mr.
Lazenby. He is to come and live with us shortly."

Laura came down, smiling in a way that irked Braithwaite, dimpling as she extended her hand to Lazenby.

"We shall be glad of your company, Mr. Lazenby,"
she said softly. Lazenby's dark eyes swept over her, taking in the lustrous dark hair and classical features. Laura
was actually blushing, Braithwaite noticed, and he felt

irritated. Really, Lazenby was right. Women were vain and shallow creatures.

Braithwaite watched Lazenby's firm, decisive step as he descended the steps and walked quickly away from the house. Well, the first step was now complete. Braithwaite would now be able to divulge the news to Lord Travers—casually, of course—that his ex-secretary was now assured of a new post. Not in the House, Braithwaite decided, but in the gentlemanly calm of the club he would tell Lord Travers. Then, over a congenial glass of Madeira, perhaps he could lead gently on to the subject of his daughter and young Lionel, and the advantages to be gained from their union.

It must be carefully handled, of course. One thing Braithwaite had learned during his years in London was that the gentry were best handled with tact and diplomacy. None of your direct, down-to-earth approaches as one would handle a business transaction in the wool trade. It had to be the hint, the subtle insinuation rather than a straightforward proposal, and Braithwaite knew he must take the utmost care to broach a matter so delicate and yet so important. Subtle finesse was called for, not a sphere in which a blunt Yorkshireman would feel at home, but he had pulled off tricky coups before now. He saw no reason to doubt that he could handle this one.

The opportunity arose soon, one evening at the club. Braithwaite loved the club, its stately appearance built, as it was, in the style of an Italian palace, solid yet quietly respectable furnishings, its impressive library, and distinguished members giving him the secure feeling of having arrived in London society, of being one of the respected establishment who represented the empire's strength. Impressive as the Athenaeum Club just up the road in Pall Mall, the Reform Club had a higher reputation for its once-aristocratic neighbor was reputed to be haunted now mainly by parasites and gentility-hunters, seeking instant fame and fortune. Braithwaite would have hated to be counted among that number.

Lord Travers was crossing the vast vestibule of the club as Braithwaite entered, evidently on his way to enjoy the delights of the club dining room, the best in town. A frown of irritation marred his classically high forehead as Braithwaite hailed him.

"Ah, your Lordship! I was hoping to see you. Would you care to take a glass of port with me after dinner?"

The right note of bonhomie without undue familiarity, thought Braithwaite. Lord Travers hesitated, one limp hand caressing a graying forelock.

"Ah, well, I do have some correspondence I must deal with after dinner, my dear fellow, but if it does not take long . . ."

"Capital! In the library then, at nine, say?"

He watched Lord Travers' shambling gait as he entered the dining room. Strange how the nobly born seemed always to be physically afflicted in some way, or to act as if they were—almost as if it were *infra dig* to appear healthy and normal. Lord Travers' son, young Lionel, had the same effeminate way of walking and a trace of a lisp. Sissified they might be, but they were aristocrats and thus entitled to respect, he supposed, but he could not help reflecting what a damned hard time they'd have had of it if they'd been born in a Yorkshire weaver's cottage instead of a stately mansion in Kent.

At nine Braithwaite went to the library. It was not easy at first to see Lord Travers in the vast room, but he found him at last, seated in an alcove in a deep leather chair, a glass of port already on the wine table at his elbow.

"Ah, your Lordship," said Braithwaite genially, pulling up a chair. His Lordship's eyes did not waver from the ceiling high above. "Admiring the frescoes?" he inquired.

"The Italianate marble pillars. Impressive, are they not? Reminiscent of the Louvre, wouldn't you say?"

Braithwaite did not answer. It would not do to confess he had never set foot in Paris, in fact nowhere outside England. He beckoned a waiter, trying not to notice that somehow his signal took seconds longer to attract attention than ever his Lordship's did.

"Port for his Lordship and me, please."

Lord Travers waved a desultory hand. "I have mine already. Now what is your problem, Braithwaite?"

Braithwaite spread his girth more comfortably in the chair, waiting until the waiter moved silently away. "No problem, sir. It is just that I have brought my daughter, Anna, up to town. There is so little to amuse her at my country home."

"Ah, I see. You wish to introduce her to London society. Well, there is no problem there once you have a suitable chaperon for her and carry out all the demands of etiquette. You have no wife, I believe?"

"She died eight years ago. You are very quick to perceive my dilemma, sir, and I should be glad of your advice in the matter."

An astute move, that. People were always flattered by seeking their advice. One could lead on later to the need for youthful companions for Anna, and to Lionel in particular.

Lord Travers' gaze moved down from the ceiling to rest fleetingly on Braithwaite's face and then to his glass of port. He picked it up and sipped languidly.

"I see no problem, Braithwaite. All you need is the services of a respectable lady, the wife of one of your colleagues, perhaps. What about Fortescue's wife? I'm sure she would oblige you." He put down his glass and picked up a sheaf of papers as if the problem was solved and the conversation at an end. Braithwaite felt disturbed. The interview was not going as he had planned. He coughed apologetically.

"I am sure your Lordship is correct, but if you were to see Anna, you would see that she is a sensitive, refined child. Very ladylike, you know, distantly related to Lord Whorton."

The papers sank a few inches, revealing a pair of blue eyes where mild interest now gleamed.

"Cedric Whorton?"

"Her second cousin, sir, through her mother's family. Anna has need of a lady of some distinction as her chaperon, I feel."

"Hmm." Lord Travers sat deep in thought. "My daughter, Gertrude, might be prevailed upon . . ." he murmured into his port.

"I should be so grateful," Braithwaite said with a smile. "Anna is a lady, and a wealthy young lady into the bargain."

"I'll let you know, my dear fellow. Now if you will forgive me, my correspondence . . ."

"To be sure, sir, and my grateful thanks." Braithwaite rose and made the slightest of bows, barely more than a low nod. One must not be servile, and especially when one had money to offer. Lord Travers' smile was brief before he disappeared again behind the papers. As Braithwaite turned to go, an afterthought prompted Lord Travers.

"Did you and young Lazenby hit it off, by the way?"

"He seems a capable young man. I have appointed him to begin work for me next week."

"Capital."

Braithwaite was not dissatisfied as he left the library. Travers seemed content about Lazenby and willing enough to approach Gertrude. The opening gambit had been made.

Etiquette. The word haunted Braithwaite as he gave orders to prepare a room in the club for him to stay overnight and sent a messenger to tell Miss Oliphant he would not be home. The social customs of high society were a morass to entangle the unwary and Anna was ignorant of their intricacy. He himself knew little of them beyond what he needed to know. He must order the bookseller to send him some books on the subject. Miss Oliphant would see to it that Anna was well drilled once she had the tools to do it.

"Your brandy, sir." The waiter laid a glass on the night table beside the bed and withdrew. Reginald Braithwaite pulled on his long flannelette nightshirt and tasseled nightcap, and climbed into bed. It was luxurious to sit there, sipping his bedtime brandy in the comfort of the feather bed and congratulating himself on his success so far. Now if only Anna was agreeable to Lionel Travers, all would be well, and there was no reason why she should not be. Dammit, the girl would be downright grateful she had such a provident and thoughtful papa.

As he nipped out the candle and lay down to sleep, Braithwaite forgot his daughter. Turning his mind instead to the research his new secretary was to carry out if London's evil dens of iniquity were to be wiped out, Braithwaite found himself musing over the sinful ways of whores and procurers. How could they lead lives of such depravity in these days of education and enlightenment, when the world was open to those who would study and work to better themselves?

Drifting thoughts of sleazy rooms and seminaked women tempting men to evil floated through his sleep-fuddled mind, awaking in him sensations that came infrequently nowadays, though nonetheless urgent for that. His plump fingers reached down under the blankets to ease the urgency, while his thoughts flew to Dolly Winthrop. He had not seen her for some months now. It would be wise to send her tomorrow a box of the sugar-coated bonbons she relished, along with a discreet note advising her that he would call on her that afternoon.

He smiled sleepily. A decorous and respectable lady was Dolly Winthrop, widow of an army officer and comfortably set up in a cozy little house out in Clapham, she understood Reginald Braithwaite well enough. In a position of importance such as his, in the public eye and eminently respected, she knew the tacit need for discretion. Plump and amiable, she would sit prim and demure behind the china teapot and pour his cup of tea with ladylike charm and politely trivial conversation. Then, the maidservant dismissed for an hour while her mistress talked over business matters with the visitor, Reginald Braithwaite's human needs would be quickly gratified. Neither referred to it afterward, nor to the two golden sovereigns he left discreetly tucked behind the clock on the mantelshelf. A trifle expensive perhaps, Braithwaite thought, but not too much for a man of his means who desired discreet satisfaction. He could be certain of Dolly Winthrop's silence. A lady eminently to be respected, was Dolly. Once again he congratulated himself on selecting his female company with such sagacity.

Yes, indeed, Dolly Winthrop was a lady of the utmost respectability and propriety. He was a lucky man.

Chapter Four

Anna dreaded the arrival of her papa's new secretary.

"All I know of him is that his name is Charles Lazenby and he is reputed to be both clever and handsome, but that does not interest me. He is a man, and I do not wish to have anything to do with him."

Laura, on the other hand, was eager for the young man's arrival, having had only the briefest of glimpses of him on his initial visit.

"Nonsense, Anna! We hardly ever see anyone, and it will be enlivening to have an intelligent man to talk with. Miss Oliphant has her limitations," she added with a mischievous smile.

"Well, I shall keep out of his way at least. You may do as you like," Anna replied.

"I shall, I assure you." Laura had not intended the proud toss of the head, but secretly she was growing a little tired of Anna and her shyness. If one gave in to her, the promised life of excitement in London would become deadly dull. Suddenly the front doorbell rang.

"There he is now," Laura cried, taking Anna's arm. "Do let's go down."

"No. I shall stay here."

"At least let's watch him over the banisters."

"You may, if you wish."

So, alone, Laura tiptoed to the head of the stairs.

"Do come in, Mr. Lazenby," Emily was saying warmly to a figure as yet invisible. Laura could see his portmanteau standing in the vestibule, vast and black and very masculine-looking. Then the new secretary entered.

He was tall, filling the doorway almost up to the lintel as he entered. But his face was in shadow, the sunlight streaming in behind him. His voice was kindly as he answered Emily.

"Thank you, ma'am. May I put my books down here?"

He placed a box on the hall seat and then straightened. Now, almost directly beneath her, Laura could study him, slim of body yet broad of shoulder, inclining to fair as he removed his hat, and reasonably young, in his thirties, she guessed. He had a slow, rather casual way of moving that seemed to exude self-confidence. As she shrank back from the balustrade, to avoid him seeing her, his eye caught hers. His look was so direct and penetrating that she felt he had touched her.

"Let me show you to your room, Mr. Lazenby, and afterward perhaps you would care to join Miss Braithwaite, Miss Sutcliffe, and myself in the drawing room. We take tea at four." Emily's voice was silkier than usual, Laura noted.

"I should be delighted, Miss Oliphant."

Laura fled before they discovered her, to the sanctuary of Anna's own little parlor her papa had allotted her, next to the main drawing room. There she listened to the passing footsteps as Emily led the newcomer to the staircase leading to the bedrooms on the second floor.

"A charming house," she heard Mr. Lazenby remark as they passed the door.

"Indeed, sir. Mr. Braithwaite takes great pains to maintain it as a fine house should be," Emily concurred.

It was only a few minutes until Laura heard her coming downstairs again, humming as she came. Mr. Lazenby's advent into the household was evidently a pleasant event for Emily. Laura pretended to be reading at the table as she came in.

"Ah, I'm glad to see you are perusing the books your uncle so kindly procured for you and Anna. There is so much to learn about etiquette in London society."

The door opened and Anna came in. Without a word she seated herself on the sofa and picked up another of the books, opening it where a leather bookmark hung.

Emily folded her arms primly. "I am glad to see you return to your studies, Anna. Have you fully understood the system of calling cards now?"

"Not yet, Emily. It is so complicated."

"Sit up straight, Anna. Your back is curved and it will stay like that if you slouch. Remember, back straight at all times. It is the mark of breeding."

Laura was about to retort that Mr. Lazenby evidently did not think so, for he had a slight stoop, but then thought better of it. Emily sat down opposite Anna and, taking the book from her, turned the pages.

"Let us go over it again," she said with patience. "Calling upon people of standing and leaving one's cards is the way to acceptance in the best circles, and your papa in his wisdom is well aware of it. You must try to understand for his sake, if only out of gratitude for his concern for you."

"But I do not wish to call upon people I do not know, Miss Oliphant. I would be happier left to read and draw in peace. Strangers make me nervous."

Emily's sigh was a mixture of impatience and well-meaning. "Anna, no more nonsense. Your papa wishes it, and you should be happy to oblige him."

"Yes, Emily."

Anna listened as she read slowly and with emphasis. "When driving, a lady should require her footman to inquire if the mistress of the house is 'at home.' If not, and it is a first call, she should leave three cards, one of her own and two of her husband's. In your case, of course, Anna, that means two of your father's cards. If not a first call, then the lady should leave one only of her husband's cards if his acquaintance with the master of the house is an intimate one and they meet frequently. If, however, they know each other but slightly, then two of his cards should be left. This, however, not on every occasion of calling. Is that clear, Anna?"

She shook her head gloomily, and Laura felt sympathy with her. There was far too much to remember, especially when, as Laura realized, she was not to be included in the tedious business at all. Emily's voice droned on.

"A lady should inquire if Mrs. Blank is at home. If the answer is in the affirmative, she should, on leaving, present two of her husband's cards, either silently to the manservant in the hall or leave them discreetly on the drawing-room table or on the hall table—never in the card basket, nor should she offer them to her hostess. Or she may send them in from her carriage outside with a message to say 'For Mr. and Mrs. Blank.' She should not leave her own card. I hope you are following me carefully, Anna."

"I was not listening." Anna confided later to Laura. "My thoughts were far away. I could not concentrate on what she was saying, for I did not want to hear it, and as I discovered long ago, when I dislike what is happening I have the ability to withdraw from it, as if into a world of my own. Emily's voice was prattling on, but to me it sounded only like the buzz of a bee outside a windowpane, irritating and meaningless. I let my mind drift to sunlit woods and splashing streams around Aspley, where I used to feel carefree and at peace in my starched smock and with Topsy, my favorite doll. She still has a place of honor on my pillow."

"Anna, pay attention! In a few moments we must go down to tea." Emily's tone was sharply reproving. "Mr. Lazenby will be waiting to meet you."

Her last words recaptured Laura's interest, but Anna raised a hand to her brow.

"What is it, Anna? Have you a headache? Is the heat

too much for you? I'll have the window opened in the drawing room."

"I'm sorry, Emily. I fear I shall be unable to join you for tea. Pray make my excuses to Mr. Lazenby and tell him I am indisposed."

The housekeeper sighed. "Then perhaps Miss Laura would be so kind as to take you to your room and stay with you for a while," she said. Laura felt disappointed, but dutifully took her cousin's arm and led her upstairs. Inwardly she believed Anna was shamming in order to avoid meeting a stranger, and regretted the loss of the opportunity of seeing Mr. Lazenby again.

Anna lay on her bed clutching Topsy. Laura, too, must have dozed, for when she awoke the shadows of the trees outside fell long across the room. The clock on the mantelshelf showed eight-thirty. Laura was again filled with a sense of disappointment. By now it was too late to go down to dinner. Laura woke Anna gently. "Splash your face with cold water from the ewer and we will go downstairs."

Having combed their hair and pinned it up again, they went down to the parlor. Anna sank into an armchair by the fireside. It was peaceful there with only the sound of the birds' evensong and a flowerseller's distant cry of "sweet lavender" to break the silence.

The peace was suddenly broken by the deep tones of Braithwaite's voice in the corridor outside.

"Come, Lazenby," he was saying jovially, "let us take a glass of brandy in the drawing room and I'll treat you to one of my best cigars. I rarely smoke, but this is a special occasion, so to speak. We'll talk more about your assignment over our brandy."

Charles Lazenby's murmured reply they did not catch. Muffled footsteps receded in the direction of the drawing room and they heard the door close. In a few moments more footsteps passed, probably Depledge bringing the brandy. Again there was silence until at last they heard a maid giggle.

"Not bad-looking, the new secretary, is he?" she confided to an unseen companion. "I could fancy him, couldn't you?"

"Not half," another girl's voice agreed. "Them nice slim fingers could slip inside my bodice anytime."

Laura laughed, but Anna's face remained expressionless.

"You going to turn his bed down?" continued the voice.

"Not yet; later I will, then maybe he'll catch me there."

A muffled shriek followed. "Ain't you the saucy one! But he's too good for the likes of you, Lizzie. I fancy Miss Oliphant has her eye in that direction."

More giggles followed. "He'd have to be hard pressed to take his chances there, if you ask me. What could a dried-up old stick like Emily Oliphant offer him? No, he'll have his eye on higher things than her, I reckon."

"Oh? Like who, then?"

Laura smiled at Anna. "Evidently the maids find Mr. Lazenby an interesting man," she remarked. "But I think he looks too refined to behave as they suggest."

"I think it's disgusting," Anna retorted. "I am sickened at the thought of Papa's new secretary harming a defenseless woman. Are all men the same, avid only to ensnare and betray women? I know Papa is not. For he at least treats men and women alike, with no evident aim to exploit the weaker sex. As I look back over the years, I can remember no occasion when he has made any distinction because of sex, always treating people with curt asperity if they are servants, and with blunt forthrightness when they are equals. It is true he reserves a kind of unctuous politeness for those higher-placed than himself, but he applies it equally to men and to women. Business rivals might accuse him of exploiting his workers in the mills or even his voters, for all I know, but he can not be accused of seeing the female sex as a race to be used or abused, of that I am certain."

Laura was mildly surprised at Anna's unusually spirited defense of her father, but made no reply. After all, she knew Uncle Reginald only slightly and felt herself in no position to agree or disagree.

Dusk was beginning to gather in the little parlor and it was nearing time for bed. An idea occurred to Laura. If she were to knock at Uncle Reginald's study door in search of a book to read, perhaps she would have the chance to see the young secretary again tonight after all.

"I'm going to bed, Anna, and I'll read for a little while," she told her cousin.

"Good idea. I'll follow you shortly."

There was no answer when Laura knocked at the study door.

By the light of the solitary oil lamp on Braithwaite's broad desk, with its piles of neatly arranged sheaves of paper, she looked along the rows of bookshelves, but could find nothing to take her fancy. Heavily tooled leather volumes of law and philosophy were not to her taste, nor would she have deemed them of special appeal to her uncle. Unable to concentrate on the task of finding a suitable book, she stood at the window instead and, lifting the lace curtain, looked out over the square.

The lamplighter passed by, touching into life the gas lamps circling the square and chasing away the shadows. A servant girl ran up the basement steps from a nearby house and scuttled along the street, tying her bonnet strings as she ran. Relieved from her day's work, she was probably hurrying home to her family or to her sweetheart, and Laura was mildly curious about her. Back in Yorkshire, once night had fallen around Aspley Hall, one felt isolated in a secure island of warmth surrounded by the wild dark moors, but here in London it was different. It was as though the world went on out there in the darkness, athrob with energy and activity, with secrets she was eager to know.

She turned away from the window and returned to the circle of lamplight on Braithwaite's desk. A map on the top of a pile of papers caught her eye, and she studied it diffidently. It was a hand-sketched road map of London. She recognized Hyde Park, which she knew to be not far away from Hanbury Square, and Buckingham Palace and the famous Piccadilly. A circle had been drawn on the map, enclosing an area marked "Soho."

Pinned to the map was a single sheet of paper headed "Memorandum." She ran her eyes down it casually, taking notice only when she realized it was a note from her uncle addressed to Mr. Lazenby.

"Attached is a sketch map of the area in which I wish particular investigation to be made," ran Uncle Reginald's peremptory hand. "Notorious dens of iniquity are said to be found here. Bear always in mind that your manner of investigation is for you to decide, but discretion must be maintained at all times. An incognito would seem advisable. Propriety must be observed; make no advances yourself but wait until advances are made to you. Your conduct thereafter I leave to your judgment."

How intriguing! The note had the conspiratorial air worthy of one of the cheap penny novelettes she occasionally contrived to read. She was curious as to the exact meaning of the note—dens of iniquity? She had hazy visions of Lazenby in gin parlors and gambling saloons where rich heirs to a noble family name lost their fortunes. And even worse places, perhaps. Places where, so rumor had it, designing women robbed men of their integrity and self-respect. Laura wondered if Mr. Lazenby was perhaps going to find himself out of his depth in such a milieu. She smiled mischievously. It would be interesting to watch his reaction over the next week or so.

"Make what observations and investigations you may," the note concluded, "bearing in mind that the further and more detailed your final report, the better my case will be for the betterment of these poor folk."

There was a light tap at the door, which startled her,

and then the maid, Lizzie, came in with a package in her hand.

"Oh, beg pardon, miss. I thought there was no one here. I was just going to leave this here for the master as he's still talking with Mr. Lazenby. It just came by special messenger."

At this late hour? Laura was curious as she laid the packet on her uncle's desk, for she had caught the whiff of lavender. By the delicate script addressing the package to "Mr. Reginald Braithwaite, M.P.," she was certain it was a woman's hand. A special messenger had brought it, so it must have been sent by someone in London.

Suddenly she heard voices and the door opened. She fell back in alarm on hearing Uncle Reginald's voice, but there was no way of escape. She retreated, her back to the desk, as he strode in.

"Come in, Charles," he was saying genially, waving a cigar that threw up a cloud of blue smoke, "come in and I'll give you the map I spoke of. Why, bless my soul," he said as he caught sight of her, "here is Laura. I told Charles Anna was not feeling well and so you were both unable to join us at dinner. Indeed, I thought you were in bed fast asleep now, young lady."

"I could not sleep, Uncle. I came in search of a book," Laura hastened to explain.

"And found none to suit you from all my collection?" Braithwaite remarked with amusement. He turned to Lazenby. "These cost me a pretty penny or two, I can tell you."

"A fine collection, sir," Lazenby replied quietly, but Laura could feel his eyes were still on her and not on the rows of books.

"If you would excuse me, Uncle . . ."

"But of course, my dear. Mustn't let the excitement of the capital overwhelm you, my dear. Moderation in all things is my motto."

"Yes, Uncle. Good night. Good night, Mr. Lazenby."

"Good night, Miss Sutcliffe. And I hope you will feel free to make use of any of my books that might appeal to you. Do you like poetry?"

"Poetry?" She could not help the tone of surprise.

"Poetry?" Braithwaite almost exploded. She saw his eyes, usually rather small for a big man, widen in horrified astonishment. "I would have thought books like these were more to your taste, Lazenby, law and philosophy and the like."

"There is much philosophy to be found in poetry, sir, philosophy distilled to its essence."

"No doubt, no doubt," Braithwaite rumbled, but Laura could tell he was mystified. "But let us not detain you, Laura. Good night, my dear."

As she reached the door, she remembered the package. "Oh, Uncle, a packet came for you this evening by special messenger. I put it on your desk."

"Indeed?" He picked it up and inspected the handwriting, then tossed it down again with an exclamation of annoyance. "I'll read it later. Good night, Laura."

She closed the door behind her and made for the staircase, still avoiding the stranger's eyes. As she passed an open window overlooking the basement yard, she heard the sound of voices and of giggling. Curiously, she looked out.

At that moment Anna came upstairs on her way to bed.

"What are you looking at, Laura?" she inquired.

The light of the gaslamp outside threw a pool of yellow into the yard, and in it Laura could see two dark shadows almost merged into one. One was the tall shape of a man, and the upturned face of the girl was clearly recognizable as Lizzie, now no longer wearing her starched cap.

"It's Lizzie, with a man," Laura said. Anna leaned forward to look out too.

"Leave off, Frank. You know I'm not that sort." Lizzie was giggling.

"Then you been leading me on all these weeks, Lizzie. I told you I'd marry you soon as I'm able."

"Then I'll wait till I have the ring on me finger, if you don't mind," she said archly.

"Come on, Lizzie, be a sport. You know you want to, and I promise you you'll like it."

There was some skirmishing, apparently of a playful kind, for although she slapped him he laughed and kissed her hard. They watched, curiosity mounting.

"Come on, Liz, let me." His voice was low now, barely audible but clearly urgent. For a few moments there was silence and then Lizzie winced. Another scuffle and then quiet again. After a few moments they could hear the young man beginning to pant. Lizzie, her back pressed against the yard wall, was starting to moan softly.

"Oh, I love you, Liz, I really do." Laura was fascinated by the shape of the shadow, the two figures now blended into one with the girl's head thrown back and her eyes closed. He was jerking his hips sharply backward and forward, thrusting against the maid's slim body. Suddenly it came to her what he was doing and she was amazed.

A stern voice called from the door below, the door leading to the kitchen quarters.

"Lizzie? Is that you? Come in here!" It was the butler's voice. Instantly the young man broke away from Lizzie, cast one startled look toward the open door, and ran to the basement steps. In seconds he was down the street and away.

"Lizzie! Do you hear me?"

"Yes, Mr. Depledge. I'm coming." They saw Lizzie's white, frightened face as she slowly crossed the yard below and vanished indoors.

Anna's face was pale as the two girls went on upstairs to the bedroom.

"Was that it, Laura?" she asked faintly. "Were they doing what I read about in Emily's book?"

"Yes," said Laura. "Didn't they have a nerve! Out in the yard where they could be seen!"

"It's disgusting," Anna said as she unfastened her gown. "They're no better than animals. They don't *like* doing it, do they?"

"Well, he does, I'm sure," Laura replied. "And I guess Lizzie must too, or she would not have let him do it."

Anna pulled on her nightgown and climbed into bed. "Well, I think the whole affair is disgraceful and I hope they are both punished."

"Lizzie too?" Laura asked in surprise.

"Well, not Lizzie perhaps. But the young man should be punished severely for using her so. Now I will think no more about it."

Laura was amused. "Can you put such an event out of your mind so easily? I'm sure I shall think about it half the night."

"No, I shall forget it at once. Long ago I learned I could detach myself from anything I disliked and withdraw into a private world of my own. Like when Emily rants on at me. I cut myself off. So I shall put this incident from my mind now and forget it."

Laura was climbing in beside her when she remembered the map and the memorandum in Uncle Reginald's study. Excitedly she told Anna of the new secretary's mission to uncover vice, for the betterment, as Uncle Reginald wrote, of the poor.

"Dear Papa," Anna remarked calmly, "so noble and kind and anxious to devote his life to the poor. So respected he is. I should be proud of such a papa."

The girls rose early and went downstairs to early-morning prayers. For anyone to miss the morning assembly of family and servants in the parlor before breakfast was regarded as either weakness or sinfulness. So they silently went to stand by Emily in the vestibule to await the sound of the bell. Mr. Lazenby joined them and said a cheerful "Good morning." Emily responded with a smile.

As the bell sounded, dead on the stroke of eight from the vestibule clock, the green baize door to the servants' quarters opened and Depledge came forth, followed by Mrs. Marker and the other servants. They stood in a neat line by the parlor door while Emily and the girls entered, followed by Mr. Lazenby. As they sat down by the chenille-covered table they heard Braithwaite's firm tread as he, too, entered.

He opened the great Bible on the table, adjusted his spectacles, and began to read. It was evident he enjoyed this moment from the slow, stately way he read, giving every word its due emphasis. The servants stood in a row by the door, motionless and silent as a line of waxwork figures. Then Laura noticed that Lizzie was not among them.

"Our Father, Who art in Heaven," Braithwaite's voice intoned deeply, and everyone joined in the servants' murmured words of the prayer. When they had done, Braithwaite removed his spectacles and laid them on the table. At this point, if he had no particular orders of the day to issue, he usually dismissed the servants and rang for breakfast. Today he glared in silence at the company. Miss Oliphant's face was bright pink. He deliberated for a moment, arching his fingertips into a steeple across his stomach.

"Last night," he said at length in great solemnity, "an incident was brought to my attention that has aroused my deep anger and shame. Anger because I will not tolerate sinful behavior in my household, and shame that the servant of a respected neighbor has been led into sin by one of my household."

The servants shuffled in embarrassment, all staring steadily at the floor. Only Depledge kept his head high, conscious of duty well done.

"I refer to the housemaid Elizabeth, whose wantonness has endangered the career of a young footman in the household of Mr. Williams. No punishment would be too severe for her wicked action, but I am a lenient man, as you know. I content myself with dismissing her and letting her go her way in peace, in the earnest hope that my clemency will evoke some measure of repentance and good intention in the girl, but I wish you all to take notice that I will tolerate no further misconduct of this nature. Attend to your work and strive for approval if you would prosper. Elizabeth will leave my roof this morning, and I wish none of you to talk to her while she prepares to leave. Now you may go."

"No! No! It's not fair!" Without realizing it, Laura leapt to her feet and glared at her uncle. She was aware of a circle of faces turned toward her in horror. Depledge stood poised motionless, and Miss Oliphant's jaw sagged open. Braithwaite, in contrast to the ring of white faces, grew red.

"Laura," he snapped. "Please sit down."

"But it's not fair. It wasn't Lizzie's fault. It was the young man—he pressed his attentions on her. It is not just for her to take the blame. Uncle, you could not be so cruel!"

"Be silent, miss." His voice thundered across the room. "I shall speak to you after breakfast. Depledge, go about your duties."

In silence the servants shuffled out, leaving Emily and Mr. Lazenby and the girls. Laura wanted to cry out, to protest again.

"Come," said Emily. "Let's go to breakfast."

As they were crossing the vestibule, they heard voices raised in argument above them. Looking up, they saw Lizzie, dressed in outdoor coat and hat and carrying a small tin trunk, marching down the stairs with Depledge behind her.

"Why should I use the back stairs, Mr. Depledge?" she was saying defiantly. "I ain't got nothing to be ashamed of and I ain't sneaking out the back when I ordered a cab at the front. I'm a good girl, I am, and I ain't being pushed out quietlike, as if I was a thief. So there."

"The cab is not here, Lizzie. Forgive me, Miss Braithwaite," Depledge said firmly, but they could see he was distressed by this disturbance in his usually smooth handling of the household. "Come down to the kitchen, Lizzie."

"I'll wait here till the cab comes," she said equally firmly, and banging the little tin trunk down on the floor, she seated herself upon it. "I ain't budging until the cab comes," she pronounced.

Depledge took hold of her arm and she glared at him. "Let go of me, I tell you!"

"Let her go, Depledge." Laura surprised herself with her tone of calm authority. Depledge straightened, looking embarrassed. "Leave her here and go about your duties."

He looked at Anna, who nodded. "Lizzie will sit quietly here, won't you, Lizzie?" she said.

"Yes," the girl said grudgingly, "'long as I'm not treated as a criminal. It's not fair. Mr. Williams hasn't dismissed Frank. It's a man's world, that's a fact."

Laura had not known Charles Lazenby was behind them until he spoke. "Fair or not, Lizzie, we wish you luck. We all wish you well."

"That's as maybe," she said grimly. "All the same, you're probably same as the rest of 'em, taking advantage of a girl if you get the chance. I should watch out for him if I was you, miss. Them quiet ones are usually the most dangerous, I've found."

Depledge returned. "The cab is at the door. Come, I'll help you in, Lizzie. What address shall I give the cabbie?"

"Tell him Piccadilly, Empire Theater," Lizzie said proudly as she rose and made for the front door. "I'll not go short, I won't. I got friends."

There was something plaintive in her defiant pride. Impulsively Laura touched her arm. "Good luck, Lizzie. I hope you'll prosper."

The fiery look in her eyes gave way to a softer expression. "And you, miss. You want to watch out for yerself in this house."

Laura squeezed her arm and watched her go. Emily led them away. "Come on now, or the porridge will be stone cold," she said. Lizzie was gone and forgotten already.

Anger on Lizzie's behalf and frustration that she could not help her stayed with Laura throughout breakfast. Anna had been wrong about her father. He did discriminate against women after all, it seemed.

At the conclusion of the meal Miss Oliphant reminded Laura of the summons to appear before her uncle.

"You will find him in his study by now, I expect," the housekeeper said. Anna watched with wide eyes as Laura rose to go. Defiantly she walked to the study and knocked. When no answer came, she went in. The strong sunlight illuminated the room, catching and displaying in its rays the dust specks hovering in the still air redolent with the mingled scent of tobacco and beeswax.

A sheet of lavender-scented paper lay on the desk covered with delicate, spidery handwriting. Recalling her uncle's annoyance when it arrived, Laura picked it up curiously.

My Dear Reginald,

Forgive me that I write to you at your home but in the circumstances I feel I must.

You know, my dear, that I always have your interests at heart, but now there comes a time when I must give thought to my own circumstances. It would be wiser, I feel, if your visits to me were to cease.

Not that I do not welcome your company, do not misunderstand me, but a lady in my position would be foolish to continue a liaison such as ours when matrimony would be a happier state of affairs. I would not wish to compromise either myself or you in your position of eminence in the community.

Forgive me, dear Reginald, but I know you value honesty and would prefer to know what is truly on my mind. In any event I wish you well.

Laura replaced the letter on the desk just as heavy footsteps announced Uncle Reginald's approach. But in the stormy scene that followed when he lectured her on the necessity of obedience to his commands, Laura was barely listening. She could feel no respect for this man, stern and unbending and all the while dallying with a woman friend. What a hypocrite he was! It was incongruous. In the face of his strict exhortations now, it was difficult not to laugh aloud at her portly, pompous uncle.

In her mind's eye Laura could see a mental picture of Uncle Reginald and this woman Dolly, and the meaning of the letter was clear. Uncle Reginald and she had been behaving like Frank and Lizzie in the basement yard last night.

Chapter Five

Anna and Laura sat demurely embroidering in the parlor one afternoon while Braithwaite rang the bell for tea to be brought in. Lazenby stood by the window, awaiting the invitation to be seated.

Braithwaite paced impatiently, waiting for the maid to answer his summons. He glanced at Lazenby. "Time you went on a reconnaissance trip, is it not, Lazenby? I've read your draft proposals, which I approve, and am anxious for a start to be made on the project."

"You shall have the first report tomorrow, sir. I plan to start this evening."

Laura noted the firmness of Lazenby's tone. He had evidently not been deterred by the nature of the work his employer proposed. Anna sewed on, blissfully unaware of the significance of the conversation.

Braithwaite grunted, glanced at his daughter, and decided to say no more. The door opened and the maid entered, not with the tea tray but a silver salver on which lay two small cards.

"There is a lady in her carriage outside, sir. She wishes to know if Miss Braithwaite is at home."

Braithwaite snatched up the cards eagerly. "The Honorable Gertrude Travers. She has kept her promise! Anna, the Honorable Gertrude is paying a call on us. Now do be bright and welcoming, there's a good girl!"

Laura's eagerness faded when she saw the upturned white face of Anna. She dropped her needle and stared speechlessly at her father. Braithwaite turned to the maid.

"Go tell the lady that Miss Braithwaite is at home and will be pleased to receive her," he said excitedly. "Come now, Anna, sit up and smile."

"No, Papa, oh, please, no!"

The maid halted on hearing her. Miss Oliphant appeared in the doorway, her shrewd eyes showing she had noticed the tension. Braithwaite advanced on her.

"The Honorable Gertrude Travers is calling on Anna, Emily. Tell her to pull herself together, for God's sake."

Emily's eyes turned on the girl, who rose and held out her hands beseechingly. "Emily, no, please stop her. I can't, I truly can't. Oh, I feel faint."

Lazenby crossed quickly to the girl and caught her as she wavered. She leaned heavily against him, cradling to his chest and moaning. Then suddenly she jerked away and ran from the room, nearly knocking into the waiting parlor maid.

"Damn the girl!" Braithwaite exploded. "She's weak and useless, just like her mother."

Miss Oliphant gave her employer a scathing look and hastened out after Anna. Braithwaite was pacing up and down, slapping a fist into his palm and muttering to himself.

"She'll damn well do as she's told, the stupid child. Can't she appreciate I'm doing it for her sake, not mine? If she wants a decent husband, she'll have to make herself meet people, like it or not. We can't any of us do just as we like."

Laura felt sorry for her cousin. She had leaned on Lazenby like a trembling, terrified little bird, and Laura guessed that his protective instincts were aroused.

"Perhaps it were best not to rush her, sir," said Lazenby. "Give her time. I'm sure Gertrude will call again."

"Yes, Uncle," Laura cut in. "Don't rush her."

Braithwaite ignored her. "Gertrude?" Braithwaite's

eyes were popping with indignation. "I take it you refer to the Honorable Gertrude, daughter of Lord Travers?"

"We were good friends, sir. She calls me Charles."

"No matter. We shall have the proprieties observed in this house." Braithwaite turned to the still-hovering maid. "Go tell the lady that Miss Braithwaite is unfortunately indisposed, but looks forward to make her acquaintance very soon."

The maid bobbed a curtsy and left. Braithwaite slumped into a chair. Lazenby seated himself in the chair recently vacated by Anna.

"You don't think I'm hard on the girl, do you, Lazenby? She needs ginering up or she'd mope indoors forever. I only want the best for her."

"And I'm sure she appreciates that, sir. But give her time, and she will come to it of her own accord, I feel sure."

But Laura was not at all sure. From all she had seen of Anna, she had not enough personality even to speak to a maidservant with confidence.

It was much later, after a silent dinner with Lazenby and her uncle at which neither Anna nor Emily Oliphant appeared, that Laura and Lazenby went upstairs. In the corridor of the bedroom floor they met Miss Oliphant just leaving Anna's room.

"How is she now, Miss Oliphant?" Laura asked.

"Quieter, but she's strange. She almost talks like one in a delirium, but she has no fever. I think perhaps she'll sleep now."

"What has she been saying?"

Miss Oliphant looked down to the floor and up again, and her reply was hesitant. "I hardly like to repeat it. She kept crying that men make use of women, that her papa is using her to advance his own purposes, and that you are his ally, Mr. Lazenby. She cries that you touched her."

"Touched her? I most certainly did not, that is, of course, except when she seemed about to faint."

Miss Oliphant nodded. "That was it. She felt the warmth and hardness of your body—her words, Mr. Lazenby, not mine—and felt you were a figure of menace."

"What utter nonsense! I hope you reassured her."

"To the best of my ability." Was it Laura's imagination that Miss Oliphant's gaze ran over him in an appreciative, caressing manner? True, she was about his age, but somehow there was something distinctly old-maidish about the lady, aseptic and asexual. Lazenby turned to go.

"Excuse me, Miss Oliphant, I have work to do." He could feel eyes boring into his back as he descended the stairs again.

Emily turned to Laura. "I've been thinking, Miss Laura. Would you mind very much if I asked you to sleep in another bedroom tonight? I would so like Miss Anna to sleep undisturbed."

"Not at all, Miss Oliphant."

"Then I'll have a maid prepare the room next door to hers for you. It won't take long."

"I'll go down and read for a while then before bed," Laura said. Miss Oliphant bustled away to arrange matters.

Without knocking this time, Laura went into the study. Lazenby was standing by the desk arranging a sheaf of papers.

"Oh, I'm sorry. I thought you had gone out," Laura apologized.

"I would have done so if my papers had not been disarranged. I found some of them on the floor."

There was a sharp note of accusation in his voice, which stung Laura.

"Are you suggesting that someone has tampered with them, Mr. Lazenby?" she demanded with some asperity.

"It is possible and, in view of the fact that they were left in a neat pile, indeed probable."

"Then I hope you do not look to *me* for a culprit. That would be unforgivable."

"But understandable."

"How do you mean, sir?"

"It would not be the first time I have found you here alone and near to private papers."

"How dare you! May I remind you that I am Mr. Braithwaite's niece and not to be interrogated by a mere servant." Laura flung the insult at him hotly, but Lazenby remained infuriatingly cool.

"Employee maybe, Miss Laura, but no servant. And I am loyal to Mr. Braithwaite. Obedience to one's benefactors is expected of one, and may I remind you that you already have had cause to be reprimanded for your remiss behavior."

Speechless with rage, Laura flung herself angrily from the room. The man's impudence and cold hauteur were exasperating in the extreme.

As she stormed through the vestibule, Laura caught sight of her jacket, reticule, and gloves still on the hall stand. Impulsively she snatched them up and went out into the square. Outside, she could walk and allow her temper to cool before returning. On her second circuit of the square she saw Lazenby emerge from the house and hail a cab. Laura watched him go.

On an impulse she ran to the curbside and raised a hand to signal another hansom.

"Follow that cab," she ordered a startled cabbie, and climbed inside. Obediently the cabbie whipped up and clattered off down the street.

It was one of those sultry summer evenings when all the world seemed to consider that staying indoors was a sinful waste of superb weather. The late June sun was still hovering above the western skyline of chimney tops. The streets were crowded with people strolling in the last glow of sunlight, stopping to chat and smile at the passing carriages. Laura leaned out to watch the cab in front. At nine o'clock in Piccadilly, a part of London renowned for its prostitutes and easy pickups, near the infamous Burlington Arcade she saw his cab stop.

Lazenby stood on the pavement and paid the cabby off. Laura's cab pulled up behind his and she sat watching. When he turned into the arcade, Laura quickly paid off her cab and followed him. The arcade was lined with shops, now closed for their usual trade but their doorways filled with groups of young women. Laura was aware of their speculative eyes upon Lazenby as he passed. Passing a shop window, he straightened his shoulders, losing his slouch—the silent testimony to years spent poring over books, she thought wryly. A young woman, vivid in silk and paint, detached herself from a cluster and came toward him with a smile. Immediately Laura turned away her back toward them, pretending to be engrossed in the contents of a haberdasher's window.

"Evening, sir," she heard her say. "Looking for a bit of fun, are yer?"

Laura caught her breath, waiting for his answer.

"Perhaps."

"I could give you a good time, sir. Just say the word." In the shop window Laura could see the woman's reflection as she moved toward a shop, indicating its interior with a jerk of her dark head. "In here. It'll cost yer seven and six."

Laura felt her curiosity melting into compassion. She could not be more than sixteen, painted and powdered as she was, and in her gay red silk dress with a green jacket she was dressed as fashionably as any lady.

"How long have you been at this work?" Lazenby asked her.

"Nearly a year. But why do you want to know? I'm clean, if that's what's bothering you, sir. Clean and able. I'll see you satisfied."

"What did you do before?"

"Worked in a laundry, but it was hard work and rotten wages. What's this all about, sir?" Her voice showed puzzlement. Suddenly a wary tone leaped into it. "Here, you aren't police, are yer?"

"No, I'm not."

"Or a do-gooder, then? We get sick to death of them. You coming or not, sir?" The girl stood poised, half-turned toward the shop.

"Not tonight, my dear."

She shrugged. "Please yerself, then. We get queer ones like you now and again."

She went to rejoin her companions, her head held high. Within seconds Laura heard her laugh as she joked with her friends. Undoubtedly they were laughing at him. A shrill voice pursued him.

"Here, we could do you a special reduction, sir. Three and six for five minutes with Maggie, how's that then?"

Gales of laughter followed him as he sauntered along up the arcade, Laura following at a discreet distance. Many more female eyes darted his way, some covertly but most brazenly and inviting. He chose to talk with no more.

For half an hour Lazenby strolled through Burlington Arcade, along Piccadilly, and up Regent Street. Several times he was invited either by a demure smile or by a lively remark to accompany one of the ladies of the demimonde, but he declined to accept. The usual invitation, Laura overheard, was the question, "Are you good-natured, dear?"

Turning along Regent Street he crossed Piccadilly Circus and headed for Trafalgar Square. At the Haymarket he stopped. In the Haymarket every theater's porticoed entrance sported its crowd of painted ladies in their vibrant satins, obviously awaiting hopefully an escort. Lazenby surveyed them with a look of curiosity. Fearful of losing sight of him in the crowd, Laura pressed close behind him.

"You seem at a loss, sir. Can I help you?" A voice as rich and mellow as a rare old port wine startled Laura. Lazenby turned in surprise to a fashionably dressed woman at his elbow. A half-smile curved her full lips, and eyes violet as midnight scanned him curiously. She puzzled Laura, for she did not look like the common crowd of streetwalkers. Abundant dark hair framed a face no longer young—perhaps thirty—but still fresh and attractive. Keeping her face averted, Laura listened intently.

"I beg your pardon, madam?"

"You appeared a trifle lost. Forgive my lack of ceremony, but I wondered if I could help."

Her speech showed her to be a lady, and Lazenby doffed his hat.

"It is very kind of you, madam, but I was simply enjoying the evening air and inspecting a part of London with which I am little acquainted. A tour of curiosity, you might say."

She turned and fell in step beside him.

"I was expecting an escort to take me to the theater, but he hasn't come," she confided in that smooth voice that gave pleasure to the ear.

"Then allow me to conduct you, madam, wherever you wish to go. It is the least I can do since your escort has failed you."

"Thank you. You may take me home."

"Shall I call a cab? Is it far?" he asked.

"Only a few steps."

Laura followed them to the corner of a side street and saw them stop outside the premises of an auctioneer. Producing a key from her handbag, the lady unlocked a door.

"I have apartments here. Please come in and take a cup of coffee with me," she said. Laura's surprise at the impropriety of her suggestion changed to disappointment when Lazenby followed her inside. Laura was about to turn away, dispirited, when a thought struck her. She hastened to the door where Lazenby and the woman had disappeared, and listened. Then, trying the handle of the door, she found it was unlocked. Cautiously she opened the door.

Inside, a flight of steps led upstairs and distantly she could hear subdued voices. Laura forgot caution. In her anxiety to know what was happening she crept silently up the stairs and stopped outside a door where she could hear the woman's laugh.

"Do come in and sit down. My name is Sybil. That is all you need to know. May I ask your first name?"

"Charles," she heard Lazenby reply.

"Then have no fear, Charles. I shall not importune you, though it is my trade to do so. Yes, I am a woman of the night, a *fille de joie* as the French say."

Laura trembled with excitement. It was the first time she had encountered a woman of this kind, and she was burning with curiosity to know what she would do and how Lazenby would handle the situation.

"I invited you in simply because I sense a *sympathie* about you, Charles," the woman's mellow voice went on, "not in search of an interlude. You probably feel it impertinent of me to feel an affinity with a gentleman."

"Not at all," Laura heard Lazenby reply gallantly. "I find it hard to believe that you are what you say. Your voice, your bearing, and your manner all belie you."

"Do not be deceived, Charles. All walks of life take to the streets if necessity compels."

"And necessity compelled you? Tell me about it," Lazenby replied.

"It's a common story," the musical voice went on. "Some girls turn to prostitution to escape poverty, some because they love sexual excitement, and some because they are misled or, as they say, 'betrayed.' I was one such."

"But you seem so intelligent, Sybil. How did it happen?" Lazenby asked.

Laura leaned closer to listen.

"I am intelligent. I earned my living as a governess until my charges went away to school and the family had no further need of me. Then I saw an advertisement in a newspaper for a governess's post to an English family in Cologne. As I had no family of my own, being an orphan by now, and since I spoke German, I decided to apply."

"That sounds a sensible idea. What went wrong?"

Sybil gave a short, bitter laugh. "I did not know then, as I do now, that many such advertisements are but a trap for the unwary. When I arrived in Cologne, alone and penniless, I discovered that no such English family existed, nor ever had. The gentleman who met me gradually disclosed to me that I had been lured there to join a house of ill repute."

"Did you not leave at once?" Lazenby asked sharply.

"How could I, without a penny to my name? It seems well-bred English girls are highly sought-after and high wages can be earned. I need to live and eat like anyone else. After the initial shock I became accustomed to it. After all, what else had I to sell but my body?"

Laura's amazement was matched only by her appreciation of the woman's candor. She made no effort to apologize for her shame and at best she had the pride to want to maintain herself. It seemed odd, though, that her way of life had not robbed her of her ladylike manner, not coarsened her and made her cynical. She felt herself warming to this proud, gracious woman of the night, as she styled herself. Not having made the acquaintance of a prostitute before, she had believed them all to be brash and mercenary. Sybil was giving her fresh insight.

Sybil was speaking again, ruefully now. "It was so cleverly done, so subtle and shrewd. I was made to feel that Erich was my protector, gallant and sincere, and I fell in love with him before I realized his intentions. I often wonder how many other innocents before me—and after—he captivated with his charm before delivering them to the brothel."

"I wonder you do not hate men as a result of your experience," Lazenby remarked.

"Hate them? Why should I? They are often the victims of circumstance just as I was. No, I came to despise Erich, but I am wise enough not to draw a generalization about men from the specific. Then I was incapable of assessing character, but now I have more experience. Your sincerity I do not doubt for a moment, though I hardly know you."

"You are kind, but you could be mistaken."

"I think not," Sybil replied, "but you interest me. You came to the Haymarket alone, and not to visit a theater, just like a gentleman in search of pleasure, and yet I feel it was not personal gratification you sought. Why were you there?"

Laura awaited Lazenby's reply with curiosity.

"You are perspicacious. I came to observe and report. I am doing a piece of private research."

"I thought so. I had you down in my mind as the intellectual rather than the hedonist. A thesis, perhaps, for a doctorate?"

Laura wondered how Lazenby would counter her question without betraying a confidence. She need not have worried.

"Something of that nature, though I am not at liberty to discuss it."

"I see," Sybil murmured, "and I respect your discretion. To tell the truth, I am enjoying your company, Charles, more than I can say. Stay awhile, Charles. Tonight I shall not work, for I am not destitute. A liaison with a wealthy gentleman just ended, has left me adequately provided for, for the time being."

Yes, of course, thought Laura, she was no common streetwalker who looked for quick, casual encounters. She was a prostitute of a higher class, who could always find a prosperous client who would set up his mistress in a comfortable establishment of her own.

There was a pause before Laura heard Sybil speak

again. "Tell me about your research, Charles. Will you write about all classes of prostitute? Will you investigate the dockland areas like Bluegate Fields? There you will find the sorriest of my sisters, sick and disease-ridden and living like rats in a sewer. Or will you write only of the well-set-up whores in Chelsea and Pimlico, and the introducing houses?"

Lazenby sighed. "The poorer prostitutes I am not to survey, for those are not my instructions."

"Then it will be a restricted view of London prostitutes. Is your report meant to better the lot of the whore?"

"I cannot say."

"Cannot, or will not?"

"I am unable to breach a confidence, but it is to be hoped that my work will be to their advantage, though I cannot ensure it."

"I see I must not press you further, but I too hope your work may better the lot of the poor. If only you could see them, Charles, I know you would pity them too, for I can see you are a compassionate man."

"You flatter me, Sybil. How can you know that?"

"Your manner is grave, but your eyes are gentle. And you bend your head as you listen—always the mark of the understanding man, I find."

Her next question startled Laura.

"Charles, have you ever slept with a woman?"

For several long seconds there was silence, then he spoke. "Yes, a long time ago." Laura was taken aback, but recognized that his directness matched Sybil's candor.

"When?"

"When I was a student at Oxford."

"But she was no whore."

"No. She was the daughter of the local bookseller. I loved her and planned to marry her one day."

"You speak in the past tense. You did not marry her then?"

"No. She died."

"I'm sorry. I should not have pried."

"It was a long time ago, and I know it was not just idle curiosity."

"No. There is an air of innocence about you, an untouched air that puzzled me. That is why I asked. And since you know so little of prostitutes, how will you find the kind you want to write about?"

"By hearsay."

Sybil laughed. "It would be far easier to let me direct you. Do you know the colony of French girls near Regent Street? Or the most popular introducing houses for gentlemen of your standing, like Mrs. Mott's and the Argyll Rooms?"

"No, but I shall be indebted to you for providing me with addresses. May I see you again?"

"You know where I live. Seek me out when you need me."

The rustle of Sybil's dress neared the door. Startled, Laura fled down the stairs, but on hearing Lazenby's voice behind her, she realized in alarm that it would be impossible to open and close the outer door undetected. She darted into a curtained archway near the door and found herself in a tiny cloakroom overlooking the street. Heart thumping, she crouched against the wall and listened to Lazenby bidding farewell.

"Then good night, Sybil, and many thanks. I am so glad we met."

"And I. Are you going to call a cab?"

"No, I prefer to walk."

Through the window Laura saw them standing on the doorstep. Sybil touched Lazenby's arm.

"You see the flower girl? How old is she?"

The dejected figure with a shawl about its thin shoulders and a basket of limp violets passed under the gaslamp. Laura saw her face, pallid and pockmarked and lined with care.

"It's hard to say. Thirty, perhaps."

"Alice is seventeen. She sells flowers in the Haymarket now because her days as a whore are over."

Lazenby was startled. "Seventeen? She had the raddled face of an old woman."

"That's what prostitution does for the poor, Charles. I know the girl. Her parents sold her to a brothel at the age of eleven, because they needed the money."

"Eleven? Scandalous!"

Sybil's smile was bitter. "There are those in your kind of circle, Charles, who believe they can cure themselves of a dose of the clap by sleeping with a young virgin, the younger the better. The poor do a fine trade selling their little girls for such a purpose. You can see what it's done to Alice."

"What will she do now?"

"Tonight? Probably she'll go back to her squalid hut and smoke a pipe of opium to forget. After, who knows?"

Lazenby was thunderstruck. "I thought I knew the iniquities of my fellow men," he murmured.

"Remember Alice. I doubt if she'll see next spring. Good night, Charles."

Sybil waited on the doorstep until Lazenby's tall figure had disappeared. When she had gone back upstairs and Laura heard the door close, she crept quietly out of the house and along to the end of the street. In order to get home to Hanbury Square before Lazenby, it was essential to get a hansom cab.

It was near the Haymarket that she caught sight of one. A bright cockney voice at her elbow surprised her as she made toward it.

"Here, miss, you ought not to be out alone at this time of night. Let me buy yer a glass of gin."

Brown eyes sparkled at her from under a cloth cap. He was a saucy-faced youth of seventeen or so, a tray of muffins in his hands. Laura smiled back at him.

"Not tonight, my friend."

He laughed impudently and winked as she climbed into the cab.

Depledge let her into the house, his sober frown displaying his disapproval, but he made no comment. Laura made ready for bed. Despite her anger with Lazenby and his insolence, she was bursting with curiosity to know more about what he was doing.

As she lay in bed, mentally going over what she had learned tonight, there was a sudden knocking at the door. A white-faced Emily hastened in, her usually confident and capable expression replaced by a look of utter fear.

"Oh, Miss Laura, have you seen Anna? Is she with you?"

"Why no, not since she went to bed. Is Anna ill?"

"Worse than that, Miss Laura. Oh, I don't know how I'm going to tell Mr. Braithwaite! He'll never forgive me for being so neglectful."

Laura felt her heart falter. "For pity's sake, Miss Oliphant, what is it? What's happened to her?"

"She's gone! I can't find her anywhere."

Laura's heart resumed its normal thump. "Nonsense, you know how timid she is. She'd never dare go out, and especially at night and alone. She's hiding somewhere to tease you."

"Oh, no, she's not." Emily Oliphant's voice was calm now, distant and almost resigned. "I've searched every inch of the house and cellars. She's taken too much lately, Miss Laura, and I fear she's gone out of her mind. She's run away, I'm sure of it. Oh, how on earth am I to tell Mr. Braithwaite?"

Chapter Six

Laura leaped out of bed and began to dress hastily. "I'll go and look for her. She can't have gone far."

"Go out? Alone? That you won't, Miss Laura," Miss Oliphant said in shocked tones.

"But someone must," Laura protested. "Otherwise we'll have to tell Uncle Reginald."

Miss Oliphant blanched. A footstep outside the door made her turn just as Lazenby passed.

"We'll tell Mr. Lazenby," Laura said firmly. "Call him back, Miss Oliphant. He'll know what to do."

Emily Oliphant grabbed at the straw, rushing after the secretary and gabbling something confused to him in a half-whisper. The secretary led her back toward Laura.

"Are you telling me Anna is missing, Miss Oliphant?" he asked.

"Gone, vanished, no message or anything," Emily said, gasping.

"Let's sit down and talk this over quietly," said Lazenby. Without invitation, to Laura's annoyance, he entered and seated himself in the only armchair in her room. Emily sat slowly on the ottoman opposite him. "Now, have you told anyone, the servants, for example, or sent a message to the police?"

Emily shook her head. "No, only Laura. I was too afraid to confess I had left Anna alone for so long. But I thought she was sleeping."

"Then Mr. Braithwaite will not hear of it from the

servants. If you go to bed now, there is no need for him
to know until the morning, and by then she may have
returned."

Blue eyes looked up, anxious for hope. "Do you really
think she will, Mr. Lazenby?"

He nodded confidently. "You go to bed, and in the
meantime I'll go out and look for her. She can't have
gone far."

"She was fully dressed. Her nightgown lay on the
floor."

"I'll search the nearby streets and the park. If I find
her, I'll wake you to tell you. Now go on to bed."

Emily rose reluctantly. "I hardly feel it to be right to
sleep at a time like this. As if I *could* sleep while that
poor child is out there in the dark alone . . ."

"I'll go at once." Lazenby rose and accompanied her
into the corridor. "Now remember, not a word to anyone. Good night, Miss Oliphant."

He watched her go to her room and then turned to
Laura. "Good night, Miss Sutcliffe," he said.

Laura pulled on her coat. "I'm coming with you."

"There is no need," he pointed out.

"But I shall come nonetheless. I insist," Laura replied
firmly.

Within minutes Lazenby and Laura were slipping quietly out of the door into the basement yard. A distant
clock chimed midnight as they walked under the
gaslamp outside the house and set off toward the park.

For over an hour they walked on through the streets,
anxious eyes probing every dark corner where a
frightened creature might hide from view. Every walk of
Regent's Park, every copse and thicket they searched by
moonlight, disturbing both sleeping birds and wakeful
lovers. Dawn was breaking, and still they had not
caught sight of the fair-headed girl who feared the
world at large and men in particular.

Exhausted and footsore, he decided it was time to return to Hanbury Square. "At worst we could call in the police," Lazenby remarked.

"If Anna were to come to harm, I could never forgive myself," Laura muttered.

They let themselves silently in by the basement door, relocked it, and climbed the stairs.

They crept quietly along the bedroom corridor, but evidently Miss Oliphant's keen ears were listening for their coming, for her door suddenly opened. Her plain face was rendered almost beautiful by her radiant smile, and she seemed oblivious of the fact that she was standing in front of a gentleman dressed only in her nightgown.

"Mr. Lazenby, she's come back!"

"Is she all right?" Laura could hear the concern in his voice.

"Perfectly, thank God. She's sleeping like a baby now."

Relief flooded Laura. She was safe and Braithwaite need never know what happened. But what *did* happen? She asked Emily.

"Did she tell you where she'd been?"

"No, she was too tired. She fell asleep almost at once. I'll find out in the morning. In the meantime I'm just happy that she's safe and well."

"And so am I. I'll look in before breakfast to see how she is."

"Good night, Miss Laura and Mr. Lazenby, and my deepest thanks," Miss Oliphant whispered, and then she disappeared within her room again.

In the morning Laura rose early, washed in the cold water on the washstand, and dressed, then went and tapped at Miss Oliphant's door. At seven-thirty she was surely up, preparing for prayers.

As she stood waiting for the housekeeper to answer her knock, Charles Lazenby came along the corridor, a sheaf of papers in his hand.

"Good morning." He smiled sleepily. "I was on my way to place my report on Mr. Braithwaite's desk. I wondered if Miss Anna was well."

"I too." Laura looked at his haggard face. He must have been writing ever since their return at dawn. A conscientious employee, whatever his other failings. "You look tired, Charles." Odd how the conspiracy between them last night had somehow conferred the right to address him by his first name. He did not seem to notice.

Miss Oliphant came to the door, her face pale and her sandy hair unusually straggly. Evidently it had not received the attention of the curling rags overnight.

"How is Anna today?" Laura whispered.

Miss Oliphant glanced back over her shoulder to the door connecting her room with Anna's.

"I'm not really sure," she replied in a whisper. "She slept soundly, but when I asked her this morning about where she was last night, she just stared at me in surprise. She says she went to bed at nine and never stirred out of bed."

Lazenby frowned. "Is this just teasing, do you think? Is she in the habit of playing make-believe?"

Emily shook her head firmly. "No, indeed. She's always been truthful and straightforward. I can't think what's come over her, but I'm certain she really doesn't remember about last night."

"I see. Then leave matters as they are for the time being."

"You still think we need not tell Mr. Braithwaite?" Emily's blue eyes were large with supplication.

"I think not. So long as no harm befell her . . ."

"Yes, precisely. All's well that ends well," Laura agreed.

Lazenby hesitated. "Perhaps I could offer to help, Emily, if you would permit."

Shrewd eyes questioned him. "Help? How?"

"Well, since Anna appears so timid and afraid to go

out and meet people, perhaps we could take her out to show her the sights of London. Riding in a cab would not oblige her to have to meet people. She could simply look around from the cab and perhaps later be persuaded to get out to inspect, the Tower, say? It is a pity to live in London and yet remain ignorant of all its treasures."

"Very true," said Laura emphatically.

Emily smiled. "You are very kind, Mr. Lazenby, and if Mr. Braithwaite approves, as I'm sure he will, I should be most obliged to you. I know you will understand if Anna finds it difficult to talk to you, however, on such an outing. By degrees she would come to know and trust you."

"May I come on the excursion too?" Laura asked Lazenby.

"By all means. I should be delighted."

"Then I'll ask Uncle Reginald after prayers," Laura said. "I'm sure he won't refuse me."

Lazenby smiled. "How could he refuse? Does everyone find it hard to win Anna's trust?"

"Most, but gentlemen particularly."

"Why is that?"

Emily shrugged. "Who knows? No one has ever given her cause to be so distrustful. I think myself it is her mother's nature asserting itself."

"Was Mrs. Braithwaite also timid?"

A veil of reserve dulled Emily's blue eyes, as though she considered she had said too much. "Ah, I hear Anna coming," she said, turning from Lazenby and reentering the bedroom.

Across her shoulder Laura could see Anna's fair head, hair neatly parted and swept back, and her calm face, pale but composed. She nodded as she caught sight of Lazenby.

"I trust you are not too tired this morning, Miss Braithwaite?" he inquired.

"Indeed, no, sir, why should I feel so? I slept well."

Her voice, though low, was as calm as her pretty face. Laura was amazed. She did not appear at all perturbed.

"You were out very late. Miss Oliphant was deeply concerned about you," Laura said.

Anna turned her deep blue gaze upon her cousin, and there was utter innocence in her eyes. "You and she are mistaken, I fear. I retired early and awoke this morning very refreshed. I cannot understand your mistaken notion, but I fear you and Emily are in error. I never left my bed."

Coolly she passed them toward the staircase. Lazenby and Laura exchanged a puzzled glance before following her. At the foot of the stairs the servants, marshaled by Depledge, were awaiting the master. As Laura reached the bottom step, the clock in the hall struck eight. Depledge struck the gong, and upstairs could be heard the sound of a door opening.

Braithwaite seemed a little abstracted this morning when he descended, preceded his family and flock into the parlor, and opened the Bible. He read in a monotone and omitted to give his customary exhortations when prayers were concluded. After the servants shuffled out again, he sat still at the table, twiddling his pince-nez and apparently unaware of his daughter and niece. The two girls hesitated, reluctant to disturb the master's reverie, then Anna and Emily went quietly out. Lazenby followed them, while Laura waited.

For some minutes she waited, then coughed in order to attract Braithwaite's attention.

"Uncle . . ."

"Yes, yes, what is it?" Braithwaite was evidently impatient at having his reverie interrupted. His attention was still only half-caught.

"Mr. Lazenby and I considered it might be a good idea to take Anna out in the carriage, show her the city."

"Good idea."

He was not listening. Laura tried again. "We thought it might help to combat her shyness, to take her out without forcing her to meet anyone. There is so much to be seen—Buckingham Palace, the Tower, the Houses of Parliament . . ."

"Yes, yes, of course. Off you go. Yes, a good idea. I shall be busy today and have no need of my secretary. You are free to do as you please."

"Thank you, Uncle."

Braithwaite rose, closed the Bible, and belched. He patted his ample stomach apologetically. "Touch of indigestion, I think. I'll forgo the kippers this morning."

More likely overindulgence with the port wine and brandy at the club after a heavy supper, thought Laura as she followed her uncle to the dining room. Emily and Anna were finishing breakfast as they entered, and Lazenby was still eating. Braithwaite now addressed his daughter for the first time.

"Leaving, Anna? Mr. Lazenby is to take you and Laura out in the carriage today, so if you would go and get yourself ready . . ."

Laura saw Emily flash Lazenby a quick look of gratitude, but Anna's expression she could not gauge. She had expected surprise, dismay, but Anna merely inclined her head.

"That is very kind of Mr. Lazenby. Come, Emily, let us go and prepare."

There was a distinct, if subtle, change in her cousin, reflected Laura as she ate breakfast. Braithwaite declined the kippers, but spooned the porridge into his mouth with absentminded speed. Laura decided not to intrude on his thoughts but mused instead about Anna. The girl was indefinably different somehow; cooler, a shade more poised, it seemed. Could it possibly have anything to do with her unexplained absence last night, if indeed she was absent? She only had Emily's word for it. But the housekeeper's agitation had not been feigned, so there was no reason to doubt her.

She studied Anna's face as she sat opposite in Braithwaite's pretentious dark-green carriage. She sat pale but composed alongside Lazenby, and though Laura remarked with interest at every building and church that Lazenby pointed out, Anna remained silent. But she was far from disinterested, for Laura could see her eyes darting from Lazenby to the building he indicated, interest alive in their blue depths. Different indeed from the apathetic creature Laura had believed her to be.

"Buckingham Palace," Laura said excitedly as they drove past the great iron gates. "Is Her Majesty in residence?"

Lazenby looked at the flagpole. "No, the flag is lowered. I believe she is at Osborne."

Outside the Houses of Parliament, Lazenby asked Anna if she would care to visit the Commons, where her papa worked such long hours.

"No, thank you," she replied. "I would prefer to remain in the carriage. It is so hot today."

Indeed it was, the heat of the sun bouncing in a hard white glare from the pavements. Laura too was relieved to stay in the cool of the carriage, fanning herself with a lace handkerchief from time to time.

In answer to Lazenby's question if there was any particular site she would care to inspect, Anna replied without hesitation. "The Tower," she said firmly. "I would like to see the Tower of London."

Laura's eyebrows rose in surprise at Anna's unaccustomed decisiveness. "Yes, that would be nice," she agreed.

At the Tower, Anna asked Lazenby to stop the carriage. "Let us inspect it closer," she said, and Lazenby helped her and Laura down. On their tour of the Tower, Anna revealed less interest in its history than Laura did. She remained impassive to the story of the little princes murdered in the Bloody Tower and to the story of Colonel Blood's daring theft of the crown jewels from the Martin Tower. Only at the site of the execution block on Tower Green did she reveal any emotion.

"It was here that Lady Jane Grey was beheaded?"

"That is correct." Lazenby inclined his head.

"And Anne Boleyn?"

"Yes. With a sword at her request, in place of the customary ax."

"Pawns. Poor things."

Lazenby arched his brows. "Pardon?"

"Pawns, both of them, to the ambition of men. They had to die through no fault of their own but only to pursue the ambitions of powerful men. Women are born to suffer for men."

There was a strength of feeling in her voice Laura had not heard before. Lazenby smiled at Anna.

"You are correct in your historical information, but do you really believe all women are the tools of men? It seems a cynical view of life for one so young."

Anna blushed and turned away. "Forgive me, Mr. Lazenby, I was thinking aloud. I am not usually given to making such outrageous statements. Please forget it."

Already she was moving away, back toward the carriage, and evidently anxious to eradicate the momentary lapse in her guard. Laura pondered over it for a second and then followed her. But she was to be reminded of it again later.

It was nearing noon and the heat was intense. Laura declared it was high time they returned home for lunch, though she was sincere in her thanks to Lazenby.

"My pleasure, Miss Laura, I assure you. We shall do it again if Miss Anna would like that."

"If you wish." Anna's voice had reverted to its normal lackluster tone, and she sat in the carriage as mute and expressionless as a statue. Laura was wondering about her, about the hidden depth of animosity toward men she had inadvertently revealed, when a glimpse of violet eyes under a silk parasol drove the thought from her mind. Lazenby leaned forward and it was evident he had seen her too, but if it was Sybil, the lady of the night, then they had lost sight of her in the crowd. With so many silk parasols lining the pavements, any one of them could be hers, or Laura could have been mistaken and it was not Sybil at all.

Throughout the afternoon as Laura and Anna sat sewing, thoughts of Sybil kept recurring. Laura was sure Lazenby would return to her house and seek her help in furthering his research. The prospect of her charming and intelligent company would surely draw him back very soon, and Laura felt a little piqued.

Over afternoon tea with Miss Oliphant and Anna in the hot, still closeness of the stuffy parlor, Lazenby excused himself from dinner. Laura fancied Miss Oliphant looked a little crestfallen at his announcement that he had work to do, but Anna seemed not to hear or care. During the fifteen minutes or so that he sipped tea from the rosebud-patterned china cup and nibbled a piece of lemon cake, she never spoke, nor did she seem aware of the presence of others. Gone altogether was her momentary animation of the morning, Laura reflected.

It was next day when Laura decided to tackle Anna about her alleged disappearance in the night. It was still difficult to visualize her timid cousin venturing out alone, even by day.

"Did you go out the other night, Anna?"

"I? Go out? I have only been out with you and Mr. Lazenby in the carriage, as well you know, Laura."

"But Miss Oliphant says you were missing from your bed for hours."

"She must have been dreaming. I told her next morning I had never moved." Anna's fair head was bent over her sampler. Laura leaned down and put a finger under her chin, obliging her to look up.

"Are you sure, Anna?"

There was a glint of annoyance in Anna's eyes, but there was no mistaking the sincerity in them. "Of course! I would not dream of going out alone."

Laura sighed, puzzled. How had Miss Oliphant been mistaken then? The occupants of Hanbury Square were a very strange assortment, to be sure, what with Miss

Oliphant, Charles Lazenby, who could be both arrogant and concerned, and an uncle who was a hypocritical but respected pillar of society.

And she was still curious about the relationship between Charles Lazenby and the attractive prostitute he must have gone to visit again last night. Suddenly it occurred to Laura that if he had been as prompt with his written report to his master as on the first occasion, his account of last night should be lying on Uncle Reginald's desk even now.

Impatiently she waited until her uncle went off after dinner to his club. Miss Oliphant suggested a game of bezique for herself and the girls, Mr. Lazenby being out also, but Laura excused herself. When at last the two women were engrossed with the cards, she slipped quietly into the study.

Yes, there it lay on the desk, the neat, precise handwriting of the secretary detailing the date and place.

Rosamund Street, off Piccadilly. An imposing residence . . . a high-class establishment that caters especially for gentlemen of means and position . . . run by a Madame de Sandrier, a French lady of taste and refinement.

My guide, a lady herself, brought into this way of life after having been betrayed, is recently appointed to the establishment to train the new girls . . . who must be refined and cultured, suitable companions to gentlemen . . . to train them in the arts of pleasing gentlemen of taste.

The villa is impressive and I could hear sounds of music and laughter . . . a soirée was in progress. The young ladies within were all attractive and decorous in behavior. I noted the discreet use of Christian names only, so as not to embarrass the clients. All the young ladies—Solange, Maisie, Grete, Marie, and others—were magnificently gowned and jeweled. Madame de Sandrier is a stately lady, welcoming and anxious to please.

Downstairs pastimes such as backgammon and piano-playing and singing were in progress. Clients were taken upstairs discreetly.

My visit was curtailed by my guide's being called away. I intend to return soon.

So that was where he went, Laura thought. But there was no hint of his relationship with Sybil. Laura was curiously anxious. Had Charles Lazenby left with her when she was called away? Had he gone to her room again? What had passed between them that Lazenby had not committed to his report?

Laura was still staring at the papers as if trying to extract more information than the written words divulged when Anna suddenly entered. She yawned.

"I was on my way to bed and saw the light and knew Papa was out. What are you doing, Laura?"

There was no point in trying to hide it. Laura held out the papers.

"I told you of Mr. Lazenby's mission to research vice for Uncle Reginald—well, I was just reading his report."

"Oh?" said Anna coolly, taking the papers. Then she started to read. Laura watched her. "Go on to bed, Laura. I'll be up soon."

"Do you plan to read it all?"

"I feel I ought to interest myself in Papa's work, as a dutiful daughter. Good night, Laura. I'll see you in the morning."

With a shrug Laura left her. If her innocent cousin was in for a shock, on her own head be it.

A rapid knocking at her bedroom door awakened Laura early. She sat up in bed. "Come in!" The door opened, and an agitated Miss Oliphant, already dressed and clutching a merino jacket in her hand, hurried in.

"Miss Laura, it's happened again. What are we do do?"

Still sleep-bemused, Laura stared at the housekeeper's figure in bewilderment. "What has happened, Miss Oliphant?"

Her sandy hair seemed to frizz in vexation. "Anna—she's been out in the night again. I'm so worried. Do you know anything about it?"

"No, indeed. Does she admit she went out this time?"

"Not she! And after all the years I trained her in the virtue of truthfulness. She says she never left her bed, but I know better."

"How do you know? Did you see her leave or come back?"

"No, but I found this on her bedroom chair."

She held up the jacket. "Feel it—it's damp, so she must have been out. It only rained once, in the night, and she must have been out in it. She's been lying to me, Miss Laura, so there must be something she wants to hide. What *are* we going to do about it?"

Miss Oliphant had bustled away with the damp jacket in the direction of the kitchen when Laura heard the laugh. It was coming from Anna's room, a low, amused laugh. She stood, puzzled. The laugh grew slowly until it became a crescendo of sound, and she could swear it was charged with mockery.

Chapter Seven

"Another glass of port, Lazenby?"

Braithwaite held out the decanter across the dinner table invitingly. Lazenby nodded and held out his glass.

"Thank you, sir."

"Research going well?"

"Pretty well, sir. A further report will be on your desk by morning."

Braithwaite nodded approvingly. The lad was a conscientious worker and discreet with it, just as Lord Travers had vouchsafed. Before long now his labor should bear fruit for his master. The time and expense Braithwaite had incurred on his behalf should bear dividends if today was anything to go by.

"Let's take our wine in the parlor." Braithwaite rose and led the way. In front of the great marble parlor fireplace he stood with legs astride and waved his wineglass toward one of the deep armchairs.

"Take the weight off thy feet, lad." He watched Lazenby seat himself and cross his long legs. Odd how some people seem to have the knack of making every movement seem elegant and rehearsed, he mused.

"I'll come straight to the point, Lazenby, for I'm not one for beating about the bush. And I think you're enough like me to appreciate directness."

"Indeed, sir." The younger man's voice was smooth and noncommittal.

Braithwaite hesitated. He did not want to offend the young fellow, but right was right for all that.

"Well, it's come to my notice that you've been hanging around my daughter's bedroom. No need to tell you how I know—let it suffice that my servants are loyal and I expect no less from you."

He paused, expecting a rush of denial, of apology, but the younger man sat silent, toying with his glass. Braithwaite felt a prick of irritation.

"Now let me make it clear, Lazenby, I want no hanky-panky in my house, and that's a fact. Even if it were a servant I would not condone it, but my own daughter . . ."

"Sir, you are mistaken." Lazenby's voice was cool and controlled, and Braithwaite felt the angrier for it. He should be blustering, apologetic, remorseful. Braithwaite's voice was sharper than he intended as he barked back.

"Nay, I'm not. Don't think to deceive me, lad, for I'm too worldly wise for that." Braithwaite flung himself into the chair opposite Lazenby, almost spilling the contents of his glass over his new breeches. He dabbed at the spot on his knee vexatiously. "Come to think on it, I've seen thee hanging around upstairs myself, but being a man who believes no evil of those he trusts, I've given no thought to it till now."

"Nor should you now, sir." The young fellow's tone was too calm by half and Braithwaite felt his cheeks reddening. A sudden suspicion came to him.

"It's not Laura you're after, then, is it? Do you fancy your chances with my niece, is that it?"

"Emphatically not, sir. You are completely mistaken. I told you once that I have no interest in young women."

"I'm glad to hear it. Dammit, man, you know what I stand for. An upholder of integrity and purity, I am, a staunch adherent of Church and the establishment. And what's more, you know better than most how I champion the purity of womanhood. Women are sacred, Lazenby, the pivot of our family life and the mothers of our children. You know how I labor to suppress the exploitation of the innocent by those who would profit from their innocence, and to protect the weak from the error of their ways. We must rescue them from the darkness of their ignorance."

"The girls who are betrayed into a life of sin being the innocents, I presume, sir?"

"Don't anger me, Lazenby. I meant the young and foolish men who fall into their clutches. And already my work is being noticed. Why, only today the prime minister himself paused in the lobby to inquire about my research and to commend my efforts."

Braithwaite could not resist a smile of satisfaction. Then he remembered what he'd been leading up to. He leaned forward to jab a finger at Lazenby's knee.

"So I'd have no nonsense here, lad. You just keep yourself away from Anna's room. Do I make myself clear?"

"Perfectly, sir, but I must explain. It was not your daughter I sought."

"Not Anna? Then whom, may I ask?"

"Miss Oliphant, sir."

Braithwaite's jaw dropped open in surprise. A presumptuous employee making an advance to the pretty daughter of the house or even a pretty penniless niece he could have understood, however reprehensible, but a man of Lazenby's background and education out to seduce a plain and aging housekeeper was beyond belief. He gulped a mouthful of port as he endeavored to digest the news.

"Miss Oliphant?" he repeated. "Is there summat afoot between you and her?" Again he wished he could suppress the Yorkshire turns of phrase he invariably let slip whenever he was caught off guard. He'd been doing so well while talking of upholding integrity and purity— he must remember that bit and rehearse it for his speech in the House.

"There is nothing at all between your housekeeper and myself, sir, beyond a loyal concern for your daugh-

ter's welfare. Miss Oliphant had expressed some misgivings about Miss Anna's recurrent headaches and I
was simply inquiring as to her progress."

"I see." Braithwaite savored the information slowly.
"Well, I'm indebted to you for that, but I assure you
there is no need to concern yourself with Anna. Emily
and I are quite able to supervise her needs."

"I'm sure, sir."

Braithwaite's antipathy toward the younger man lingered despite his words. After all, he could not be sure
that Lazenby spoke the truth. Like so many gentlemen,
he had the facility of speaking smooth words without
really revealing his feelings. Braithwaite was prepared
to believe Anna was not his quarry, for the girl had
nothing to offer a brilliant young academic beyond the
fortune she would one day inherit, and surely Lazenby
could not really find Laura of interest when she had
nothing at all to offer but her dark beauty. Lazenby was
too ambitious a man to settle for a poor relative of his
employer. And Emily Oliphant was a highly unlikely
prospect. Once, perhaps, eight or ten years ago, she
might have caught his eye—Braithwaite could still
remember her slim, lively figure and the russet curls now
turned sandy—but her attractions had long since faded
and atrophied. So he had no alternative but to accept
Lazenby's word. Anna's sick headaches had become too
much of a burden for Emily to carry alone and she had
confided in the young secretary. Nothing to fret about in
that. Still, it was as well to have a word about it; now
the air was cleared and Lazenby knew not to presume
too far.

Reassured, he returned to Lazenby's mission. "Whereabouts are you researching now, Lazenby? Still in the
West End?"

"Yes, sir." Lazenby leaned forward to place his empty
glass on the table. "But I understand the worst forms of
vice are to be found among the very poor, sir, in the

area of the docks. Do you not wish them to be included in my report?"

"No, Lazenby, I've told you. The middle and upper classes only, such as our sort might frequent. Now tell me which establishments you've visited."

Lazenby's fingers rested on the rim of the glass for a second before he leaned back in his chair. Braithwaite noted the momentary hesitation. "One to which I was introduced by the guide I mentioned in my report. In Duke Street."

"There is, of course, the noted one in Lupus Street, and I believe you've been to the one in Rosamund Street. Have you been there again?"

Braithwaite could not help blinking as he mentioned the latter house, calmly as he spoke. But it was essential to know if the secretary intended to go there again. A visit would be out of the question if he did, and Braithwaite was reluctant to forgo the prospect, having heard Lord Travers enthuse about it. A replacement for Dolly Winthrop was essential.

"No, sir," Lazenby replied coolly. "I felt it best not to visit too often establishments where I knew colleagues of yours in the House might well be present."

Braithwaite smiled in relief. "Very wise, my boy. It would help you not at all to embarrass them. I see I can trust to your discretion."

"I hope so, sir. Now if you will forgive me, I will go and prepare my report." Lazenby rose leisurely and left.

Braithwaite watched him go, envying the cool grace of his movements. Odd, how aristocratic a secretary could be. It must be the result of rubbing shoulders closely with the gentry, both at university and while working in Lord Travers' household.

Lord Travers. That reminded Braithwaite—it was high time the link between the Travers family and his own was strengthened. Since the Honorable Gertrude's call there had been no further move to make their acquaintance. What a silly foolish child Anna was! Despite

Lord Travers' promise it was beginning to look as if the family had no further time to spare on a nouveau-riche mill owner and his silly daughter. Braithwaite poured himself another glass of port and tossed it off irritably.

But as luck would have it, fortune favored him. Only a few days later he returned from an afternoon stroll in the sunlit square to find Anna and Laura in the parlor. His daughter's fair head was bent over an embroidery frame while Emily stood behind her shoulder. Braithwaite stood in the doorway, unobserved.

"No, no, Anna, have patience," Emily was saying. "Small, neat stitches are essential for needlepoint. Sulky moods don't help in the least. We want a sampler fine enough to frame and hang on the wall to display, don't we?"

"You may, but I don't," Anna replied crossly.

"Now don't be petulant, my dear. That is not like you," Emily chided.

"How do you know what is like me?" Anna demanded, stabbing the needle viciously into the canvas. "I don't want to sew. I want to sit in the sun and read."

"You want? Then want must be your master, Miss Sulks. We must learn that we cannot always have what we want."

Braithwaite saw the girl's face, flushed with anger as she turned to the housekeeper, but on catching sight of him, her color cooled. She put aside the sewing. "Good afternoon, Papa."

"Good afternoon, my dear. And why may not Anna walk in the sun, Emily? It seems to me that fresh air would help dispel these headaches that cause you so much concern."

Miss Oliphant blushed. "To be sure, sir, but I must convey to Miss Anna that petulant demands will not be met. It is not like her to behave thus, and I wonder what has come over her lately. A young lady of seventeen should not behave like a spoiled baby. Particularly as she never *was* spoiled and has never behaved like this before."

Emily folded her arms across her thin chest with a righteous air.

Braithwaite nodded. "I agree. Nevertheless, fetch Miss Anna's bonnet and let Miss Laura take her around the square for half an hour. The embroidery can wait."

With tight lips Miss Oliphant swept out of the room. Braithwaite looked at Anna. She was, if anything, a trifle paler than usual, despite her outburst. He patted the back of her chair, the nearest he could bring himself to touching her.

"How are you, my child? A little better today, I trust?"

"I am in excellent health, Papa. Emily fusses unduly."

He was about to say more when a maid entered with a tray on which lay two small white cards. "A lady is below and wishes to know if Miss Braithwaite is at home, sir," she addressed her master.

Braithwaite strode forward eagerly to snatch up the cards. "Anna, it is the Honorable Gertrude. She is gracious enough to call on you again." He turned to the waiting maid. "Wait outside for a moment. I'll give you orders in a moment."

When the girl had bobbed a curtsy and left, he turned to Anna. "Now listen to me, Anna. Opportunities such as this rarely come twice and you are indeed fortunate. For heaven's sake don't be so foolish as to throw this second chance away. It need only be for a few minutes and I'm sure you can bring yourself to face that. Are you listening to me, Anna? I *order* you to receive the Honorable Gertrude. It is my wish."

He drew his stocky figure erect, to present an impressive figure of authority that could not be disobeyed. Anna surveyed him calmly.

"I had no intention of refusing, Papa. I shall be pleased to receive the lady."

Braithwaite stared. "You will?" He could not understand her sudden change of heart, without even Emily here to exhort her. Perhaps he had underestimated the girl. "Why will you see her now if not the last time?"

"Because I am conscious of my duty to you, Papa. You must not be let down considering your relationship with Lord Travers."

"Very commendable," Braithwaite muttered. He opened the door and spoke to the maid outside before returning to his daughter. "Now don't be afraid, Anna. Take a leaf from Laura's book. Hold your head high and address the lady politely. Just remember that, after all, the aristocracy are only flesh and blood like ourselves."

The door opened. Braithwaite turned, all eager expectancy, but it was Emily Oliphant who entered, bonnet in hand. Irritably Braithwaite snapped at her. "The young ladies will not be going walking now, Emily. The Honorable Gertrude is here."

"Oh!" Miss Oliphant looked for somewhere to put down the bonnet, chose a corner chair, and busied herself pushing strands of sandy hair back into place and then folding her hands dutifully. Braithwaite watched his daughter, mentally noting Anna's pale calmness in contrast to Laura's vivid freshness. That's where Anna's breeding shows, he thought, the streak she inherited from her mother's side. If only she did not go the wavering, unbalanced way of her mother, she could do quite well for herself.

The maid reappeared. "The Honorable Miss Gertrude Travers," she announced, bobbed a curtsy, and waited for the lady to enter. Miss Gertrude dominated the room the moment she entered, the rose pink of her silk gown and hat giving the somber room a touch of color and vibrancy. Anna in gray silk and Laura in her pale blue looked decidedly dowdy by contrast, the thought flitted through Braithwaite's mind. He watched Anna rise to greet her.

"Miss Travers, how kind of you to call."

"And how kind of you to receive me, Miss Braithwaite. My father was most anxious for us to meet." Her voice was rich and kindly, with that note of patronizing that Braithwaite found immensely irritating in the well-born. Anna appeared not to notice it.

"Allow me to present my father," she said. Braithwaite moved forward and said "Good afternoon" gruffly. "And Laura, my cousin," Anna added. Laura bowed her head, and Miss Gertrude nodded graciously in acknowledgment. There was no need for Anna to ascribe a position to Emily—the severe black gown and little lace cap added to the bunch of keys at her waist made it clear.

"Do sit down," Anna invited her guest, indicating a chair and seating herself opposite. Braithwaite remained standing, unsure what to do. Laura was seated, but since Emily was standing, it seemed the best thing to do. After all, the Honorable Gertrude was Anna's guest.

He listened as the two ladies talked, small talk of feminine interest. He noted the ease with which Laura too joined in the conversation about the weather, about the latest fashions the Honorable Gertrude had seen at Ascot, about the difficulty of finding the parasol she held in the exact shade of pink to match her gown and hat. It was all of no interest at all to Braithwaite, but he stood amazed at the ease with which Anna held up her side of the conversation. He *had* underestimated the child. She was quite capable of entering society if she wished.

"Of course it is a little late in the season now," the lady was saying. "Derby Day and Ascot and the regatta are over, but there are still social events of a smaller kind. Dinners and parties and the like. I was thinking of planning a picnic along the river somewhere while this glorious weather continues. Perhaps you and your cousin would care to join us, Miss Braithwaite? Just a small group of family and friends."

"I should be honored, Miss Travers. Have you a day in mind?"

"Let us see. Today is Friday—let's say Tuesday afternoon. Will that suit you?"

"Admirably. I shall be charmed."

"Then that is settled. And now, if you will forgive me, I have some purchases to make before returning home. It has been a pleasure to meet you, Miss Braithwaite."

"A mutual pleasure, I assure you."

Before Braithwaite was aware of it, Miss Travers was gone, having arranged for Anna and Laura to drive to the Travers' household on Tuesday afternoon to join the party. Slowly Braithwaite recovered and began to feel pleased. Matters were turning out very well. Anna, once she was accepted by the Travers family, could do nothing but good both for him and herself. After all, young Lionel Travers, heir to a fortune and a title, could not help but be impressed by her pretty face and her expectations. This could turn out very well indeed. Braithwaite turned to Anna, beaming.

"There you are, my dear. It was not so terrible, was it? You handled that very well."

"Thank you, Papa. Miss Travers seems a very amiable lady."

"To be sure. Now you may go for your walk with Laura as you planned."

He watched from the window as the two figures left the house and walked slowly around the square, feeling very pleased. All it had needed was a touch of firmness combined with affection, and Anna could be as dutiful a daughter as one could wish. He had handled the matter rather well, he thought. Perhaps a glass of Madeira now before returning to the pile of papers on his desk . . .

Braithwaite's good humor began to dissipate as he reread his letters after dinner that night. The one from his mill manager, Fearnley, in a large, unformed hand, hinted that all was not going as well as it should be at Braithwaite mills. Orders were not being met on time, millhands were getting out of line, arriving late without good reason and complaining about the shortness of their dinner break. Braithwaite frowned. It was high time he paid another visit to Harrowfield to put his affairs in order. And if Fearnley could not control the men any better than that, a replacement must be found for him, and that right soon.

Lazenby's entrance into the lamplit study interrupted Braithwaite's train of thought. "Do you require my services, sir?" the younger man inquired.

"Ah, yes, Lazenby. Sit down. I have some letters to dictate."

Lazenby sat down opposite him, leaning across the desk to dip a quill into the inkstand. He was a handsome young fellow with his neat dark head and solemn face, Braithwaite reflected. How many of the maids had already fallen under the spell of his earnest brown eyes? Fortunately the secretary did not seem to find any such attentions distracting. He was an honest, industrious fellow.

Braithwaite began to dictate, rising after a time to pace the room. It was more conducive to concentration than to sit there with those piercing eyes upon him.

"Ah, no, change that last sentence. Make it 'as soon as circumstances permit.' What was that?"

Braithwaite broke off and glanced toward the door. In the corridor outside he could hear the sound of running footsteps followed by a knock at the door. Miss Oliphant entered, a look of surprise lifting her eyebrows on seeing her master.

"Oh, forgive me, sir. I thought Mr. Lazenby was here alone. I'm sorry if I have disturbed you."

Braithwaite clicked his tongue. "No matter. What do you want now you are here?"

"Oh, really, it can wait until later, sir. Please forgive me."

She was turning to go, but Lazenby put aside his pen and followed her. "Excuse me a moment, sir. I shall return directly."

Outside, Braithwaite could hear their voices low in conversation, and he felt piqued. What impudence, for an employee to put the needs of another employee be-

fore his own. He was mentally framing words of repri-
mand when Lazenby reappeared, sat down again, and
picked up the quill.

"If you would be so good as to continue, sir—"

"What did Emily want that was so important?" Braithwaite demanded angrily. The dark eyes met his levelly.

"She had mislaid something of importance. I promised
to help her search for it later."

"Indeed? Then it must be something of very great
value, to warrant such an intrusion."

"I believe it was, sir. Shall we continue?"

At last the pile of letters was complete. Braithwaite
signed them and pushed them back across the desk to
his secretary. Yawning, he glanced at the clock.

"I'm for bed. Will you take a nightcap with me?"

"Thank you, no, sir. I still have other tasks to
perform."

"Ah, yes. The chivalrous knight must go to aid the
lady in distress. Has she lost her trinket in the house,
for, if so, surely Laura could look for it or the maids will
find it for her?"

"It could have been lost out in the square, sir. I
propose to go out and search."

"Very noble of you. Then good night, Lazenby."

Braithwaite heard the front door closing a few
minutes later and crossed to the window. From up here
he could see Lazenby's slightly stooped figure as he
passed under the arc of light from the gaslamp and set
off around the square. Braithwaite returned to his desk.
There was one other letter still to be dealt with, one he
could not disclose to his secretary. The one from Dolly
Winthrop.

He retrieved the sheet of scented notepaper from the
drawer, where it lay concealed under other papers, and
reread it. "Such a pleasant acquaintanceship," she had
written. "Unfortunately it has to end. The major is a frequent caller these days. . . ." Braithwaite could see well
enough what she had in mind, for her last letter had

made it clear enough. It was matrimony or nothing, and she was not unduly concerned whether it was to himself or to this major.

Braithwaite was not in a mood to be blackmailed into a situation he had not planned. Nor would he visit her, as she probably hoped her letter would induce him to do. He snatched up the quill pen, rattled it in the inkstand, and began to write furiously.

"I shall always think well of you, and convey my best wishes for your future happiness," he wrote, cursing under his breath the waywardness of womenfolk. Why could she not have let the arrangement stand as it had done for the past few years? She had done quite well out of him, hadn't she? Never lacked for clothes or rent or fuel. Well, if she was going to try to force his hand, she would soon discover that a Yorkshire man was a harder nut to crack than her wretched major. She could have him, and good luck to her!

He signed the letter with a flourish, folded and sealed the letter, and placed it in his pocket. There, now it was done. That chapter of his life was concluded. Again irritation rippled the surface of his composure at the thought of Dolly's lack of consideration. He was beginning to feel the pinch of these recent celibate weeks, and his glimpse into the promised pleasures of Rosamund Street as recounted by Lord Travers had served only to reawaken old appetites. Damn Dolly!

He walked over to the window again, drawing back the curtain to look down on the now-deserted Hanbury Square. Young Lazenby must have given up his search by now, and the midnight silence lay like a blanket over the square. Few lights glowed in the surrounding windows. Most of his self-respecting neighbors had apparently gone to bed. The sense of loneliness heightened Braithwaite's need for human company and consolation.

Dash it all, for two pins he would call for his carriage and set off for Rosamund Street but for the fact that by now the coachman was probably snoring in his attic room. And if Braithwaite were to go there, it must be done with the utmost discretion, without the knowledge of any of the household. And discreet inquiries as to cost and the degree of privacy assured had satisfied him. It was certainly a tasteful establishment, one to bear in mind when the demands of the flesh became too urgent. After all, a man could not be expected to work at full capacity if all his needs were not satisfied. No one denied him the right to eat when he was hungry. . . .

Lord Travers' recent words reechoed in his mind. "Why don't you marry again, Braithwaite? A young wife, young enough to bear you a son to take over your business in time would seem the ideal solution for a man in your position," he had commented. Braithwaite rubbed his chin thoughtfully. Yes, but she might be demanding or, worse still, become sickly as Edith had done. A wife was for life like it or not. And she would have to be someone well-born to suit him, and few such women came his way, or at least, not young and single ones. No, for the time being Rosamund Street would suffice. And now that he was assured that Lazenby would not discover him there, he could begin to make plans accordingly.

Saturday morning Braithwaite rose early and was ready to go downstairs well before Depledge rang the bell at eight to signify to the household that morning prayers were about to begin. Footsteps scurried along the corridor outside. The family and servants were assembling to await his descent promptly on the bell. Braithwaite adjusted his stock before the mirror and thought for the thousandth time how well he looked his part—the prosperous mill owner with a position of prestige both locally in Harrowfield and in the government. He had reason to be proud of himself and how far he had come over the last thirty years.

The bell reechoed throughout the house. Braithwaite walked quickly but with the right amount of dignity to the staircase and made his way down the two flights to the vestibule. They were all there, waiting. Depledge stood slightly apart from his line of regimented servants. Lazenby and Miss Oliphant stood side by side. But one was missing. Anna was not there.

Braithwaite raised his eyebrows. "Is Miss Anna not down yet?" he addressed Emily. It was not like Anna to be late.

"Sir, she is unwell this morning. I have left her sleeping."

He saw the quick exchange of glances between the housekeeper and his secretary, which reminded him. "Did your trinket turn up, Emily?"

He could have sworn she blushed. "Thank you, sir, I found it this morning."

"Very well. Let us begin prayers." He led the way into the parlor. Once the shuffling and coughing had ceased, he opened the great Bible, which lay ready on the table, and put on his pince-nez.

"'Though I speak with the tongues of men and of angels, and have not charity, I am become as sounding brass or a tinkling cymbal,'" he read from Corinthians. "'Charity suffereth long and is kind. . . . Charity never faileth.'"

An elusive thought niggled at the back of his mind as he read on. "'And now abideth faith, hope, charity, these three; but the greatest of these is Charity.'"

As he replaced the bookmark and closed the Bible, he suddenly recaptured the fugitive thought that had been eluding him. Charity—yes, the donation he had intended to give the vicar toward the roof-restoration fund. He had meant to see to it for some weeks now, but somehow it had been overlooked. A sizeable gift, but not too pretentious, just enough to ensure that the vicar's gratitude would provoke a grateful acknowledgment from the pulpit. He would have a word with the vicar about it tomorrow, after the morning service.

Prayers over, he dismissed the staff but kept Emily and Lazenby back.

"About Anna," he began to the housekeeper, and again the woman blushed. "I've been thinking. Her gowns are not so fashionable as the Honorable Miss Gertrude's and she must not appear in company looking like some rustic girl. See to it that new gowns are ordered for her, will you, Emily? Nothing too ornate or expensive, but something that will do our position justice."

"Yes, sir. How many?"

"How many does she need? Two or three perhaps. I leave it to you. You've never been one to waste money."

"And Miss Laura, sir? Am I to order new gowns for her too?"

"Oh, yes, Laura. I suppose you'd better order the same for her," Braithwaite replied irritably.

"Very well, sir." She bobbed a curtsy, glanced at Lazenby, and left. For a fleeting second Braithwaite wondered again about her. All those blushes and secret looks—did the woman still fancy her chances with the secretary? He dismissed the thought as unimportant and addressed Lazenby.

"Make a note, will you, in case I forget again. I must discuss with the vicar of St. John's the matter of a donation to his roof fund."

"Very good, sir."

"And on your way out, tell Depledge to serve my breakfast now."

Braithwaite consumed all that was laid before him with relish—porridge, kipper, braised kidneys, scrambled eggs, and a heap of toasted brown bread with marmalade. After all, it was Saturday and he was free from having to go to the House today and so could afford to spend time over his breakfast. After that he could read *The Times* leisurely and perhaps go for a stroll in the park. Monday he was to catch the train home to Harrowfield to deal with Fearnley's problems at the mill. Braithwaite remembered he had forgotten to tell Emily he was going away. She would have to pack his bag in readiness, and relay the news to Anna.

Anna. Braithwaite felt a touch of paternal pride as he recalled her composed and ladylike meeting with the Honorable Gertrude. Well, perhaps as a gesture, to show his pleasure, he would take the trouble to go up to the girl and tell her himself of his visit to Yorkshire. He only hoped she would not take it into her head that she would like to come with him.

But of course. Emily had said the girl was off-color and in bed again with one of those migraines of hers, so she would not be likely to ask such a favor. These attacks often lasted for some days. Yes, he'd forgotten—that was why she wasn't down for prayers.

Oh, well, in that case there was no point in his climbing two flights of stairs to tell her about his trip. He'd ask Emily to tell her about it later.

Miss Oliphant spread out the samples of material on the drawing-room table. "There, what do you think of this blue for a new gown, Anna?"

"Charming."

"And this cherry red?"

Anna frowned. "A little brash, don't you think, Laura?"

"Not at all, my dear. You should be more adventurous. Miss Travers wears gowns brighter than that."

Anna shrugged. "Very well then, the red if you wish, Emily."

"And this black-and-white stripe is very attractive. I saw a fashionplate in the *Gentlewoman's Magazine* in just such a stripe as this," said Laura.

Anna shuddered. "No, not that. I hate stripes."

"Now, Anna, don't be unreasonable," Miss Oliphant cajoled. "It is just what you need to appear fashionable."

Anna's voice was low but firm. "I mean what I say, Miss Oliphant. I hate stripes. I have always hated stripes, and that is an end to it."

Miss Oliphant sighed and picked up the pieces of material again. Laura was puzzled. Anna was being

most irrational, but her set, white face indicated that she
was not in a tractable mood today. There was a sudden,
cold hardness about her, just as there had been when at
the Tower she had stared at Anne Boleyn's execution
site.

Chapter Eight

Something had to be done, of that there was no doubt, Laura resolved. There was now no doubt that Anna was sneaking out at nights. Once more she tried to get Anna to confess.

"Really, Laura! I have told you before and I tell you again now finally—I have *not* been out. I think Miss Oliphant must be ill to have such silly delusions." Anna's voice was so firm and her blue eyes clear and unwavering, and Laura was bewildered. Either Anna was speaking the truth, or she honestly was unaware of her nocturnal excursions. In the latter event, it was Anna who was ill and not the housekeeper.

A secret assignation with an admirer seemed unlikely, for Anna was incapable of duplicity. From now on someone must keep a vigilant eye on Anna. Charles Lazenby was evidently thinking the same, for when he came across Laura alone in the conservatory, he asked her politely to grant him a few moments' conversation.

"Anna must be watched closely from now on, for her own sake," he confided. "The streets of London are far from safe for a young girl alone."

"I know," Laura replied. "And I agree with you entirely."

"Could you not sleep with her again as you did? I myself would keep watch outside her door, but Mr. Braithwaite has forbidden me to linger there. It must therefore be your responsibility, Miss Laura, to ensure she does not escape again unseen."

"I cannot sleep in her room, for I have already asked and she has declined. But I shall listen carefully. I promise you she will not escape without my hearing."

"Good. Then if you hear her move, fetch me at once. I shall follow and see where she goes and what she does, and I shall see no harm befalls her. Thank you, Miss Laura. You have set my mind at rest."

Laura sat thinking about him after he had left the conservatory. A curious man. Despite his cold anger with her that time he thought, unwarrantably, that she was snooping, she could not help admiring him. She smiled to herself. Since then she had snooped on his papers and he had not noticed. In her own mind Laura was still not certain that silence about Anna was the best course. Emily, she knew, wanted to avoid the master's anger and also to protect him. After all, a police search for a member of Parliament's daughter would blacken Braithwaite's career, and hypocrite though he was, Laura had no wish to ruin him.

No, it was Anna they must think of. The girl was evidently sick, whether she stole out knowingly or not. It was curious that during her father's absence she seemed perfectly well and confident. Braithwaite's presence had an oppressive effect on everyone, but on his daughter's sensitive soul it evidently had a more damaging effect than most. Poor Anna. And poor Uncle Reginald, Laura could not help adding to herself, that he unwittingly destroyed his child's peace of mind. It was a measure of the man's brutish, unfeeling ways. Marriage was Anna's only hope of escape.

Unless she was married off to a man of no greater humanity than Braithwaite, which could happen. For her sake Laura hoped she would be lucky enough to find a sensitive, kindly man who would understand and protect her. She deserved no less. Someone like Lazenby, perhaps. But, no, she thought angrily, Lazenby would not suit Anna at all. She went upstairs in search of her cousin.

Summer sunlight streamed through the bedroom window, falling on the slight figure seated at the dressing table. Emily watched speculatively as Anna's slim arm rose and fell smoothly, brushing the gleaming curtain of blond hair.

"Let me do it for you," said Laura, taking the brush.

"Oh, Anna, by the way," Emily ventured to say. "I was tidying your drawer yesterday and you remember the little blue reticule, the one you hardly ever use nowadays?"

"Yes, Emily." Laura continued to brush rhythmically.

"Well, I found some money in it. Some sovereigns and a guinea."

"Indeed. I must have forgotten I had them."

"And a tie pin and a garnet ring."

Laura stopped brushing as Anna turned on her stool. "A ring and a tie pin? Show me."

Obediently Emily took the reticule from the drawer and spilled out its contents on the dressing table. Anna's pale face registered complete surprise.

"Now wherever did they come from?"

"Don't you know?" Laura asked.

"I haven't ever seen them before." There was no doubting the innocent bewilderment in her eyes.

"What shall I do with them?" Emily inquired.

Anna spread her hands. "Do with them as you think best, Emily. Take them to Papa if you wish. Perhaps he will find their true owner."

Sighing, Emily replaced the coins and jewelry in the reticule. Laura knew she had put hereslf in an awkward position, for to tell the master was the last thing she wanted to do.

"No, we'll leave them for a while. Perhaps one of the servants put them away in the wrong place. Leave it to me, Anna."

Laura was pinning up Anna's hair and the housekeeper busied herself tidying away Anna's nightgown and dressing robe. As she finished and was heading for the door to go downstairs, she turned. Laura, with her back toward the housekeeper, was looking into the mirror, pinning the last curl of Anna's hair into position.

Laura's eyes met Anna's in the mirror, and she stared at the girl's reflection. Her blue eyes were hard and cold, her lip curled back to show white teeth gleaming. It was a cruel, mocking sneer. But Laura was not prepared for the low words that came from Anna's lips.

"Stupid, interfering bitch!"

Laura gasped. In the doorway, Emily gasped in startled horror.

"What did you say?"

Anna swung around on her stool. "I? I said nothing." Her expression was calm and innocent, her eyes wide and blue as a baby's. "I did not say a word, Emily. Come, Laura, shall we go downstairs now? It's almost time for lunch."

Later, the housekeeper drew Laura aside.

"Miss Laura, a word with you if you please. I've been waiting for you."

She drew Laura by the arm to the end of the vestibule, near the baize door to the servants' quarters.

"What is it, Emily?"

"As I said, I was tidying Anna's things away in a drawer where she keeps her gloves and reticules, and I found money, two sovereigns, a guinea, and also a pearl tie pin and a garnet ring. Now how could they have come to be there?"

"I've no idea. Nor, apparently, has Anna. What do your surmise?"

"Well, as you know, she only disappeared when she had one of those nasty migraine attacks. It's my belief, knowing how blank and unlike herself she is at those times, that she went out and stole those things. What on earth am I to do?"

"You cannot be sure she stole them. Could they not be gifts, from her father, perhaps?"

"Not without my knowledge. And why should anyone make her a gift of a man's tie pin?"

Laura was thoughtful. "You think perhaps she was picking pockets?"

"Perhaps. And the police might come here and then what will Mr. Braithwaite say?"

"It is unlikely the police will come unless she was seen. The best thing to do is to ensure she does not go out again."

"But how may we do that?"

"You and I will both listen, and if she moves, call Mr. Lazenby."

"Yes. I'll sleep with the connecting door open. She won't elude us."

The housekeeper nodded in satisfaction and turned to go through the baize-covered door. As Laura moved away, she could swear she could hear the rustle of silk skirts on the landing above. Had Anna overheard their conversation? And if so, how would she react to it?

Miss Oliphant suddenly reappeared from the kitchens. "By the way, Miss Laura, I wanted to ask a favor of you . . ."

"Which I shall endeavor to grant if I may," Laura replied.

The housekeeper went pink. "It's just that the master commented before he went away that he wished Miss Anna was going on the picnic with the Honorable Gertrude alone. But since you were invited too . . ."

"I see. Then she may go alone if he wishes it," said Laura, not without disappointment, for outings were so rare and this one had held out a promise of pleasure. "I daresay Uncle Reginald has his reasons."

"Oh, thank you. It's today, you know. I'll help Miss Anna to prepare."

Anna left without question as to her cousin's refusal to accompany her. Laura sat in the garden on a rustic bench and read.

Lazenby appeared suddenly, his tall figure blotting

out the sunlight as he stood before her. In his hand he held a book.

"I thought you might care to read this, Miss Laura. You said you were fond of poetry."

She took the volume with interest. "How kind of you to remember! I am very fond of Lord Tennyson in particular."

"Well, this is Mr. Browning, and I think you will find him very different. But enjoyable nonetheless, I hope."

He turned quickly and strode away. Laura watched him go and then leaned back to bask in the sunlight.

It was a pleasant time of the year, Laura reflected as she gazed across the lawns. Ash and elm trees interlaced their branches across an azure sky and even the birds seemed to fly indolently in the summer sunlight. Everywhere breathed peace and contentment. Perhaps it was so idyllic because Uncle Reginald was still far away.

That was it. The very house seemed to breathe more easily in the absence of the self-important master and his ubiquitous presence. Even the clocks seemed to tick more leisurely, the maids to answer the summons of the bell less apprehensively, and even Depledge seemed less aloof and patronizing. Almost as though he deigned to acknowledge Laura as a lady in the absence of the master. Laura smiled. Yes, with her uncle far away in Yorkshire even little pallid Anna had seemed like a stone statue breathed into life at last. As a rule, she avoided conversation with her father's secretary, but now she seemed to have found the courage to speak. Freedom from her papa's overbearing presence was the only reason that could account for it.

"How did your picnic with Gertrude go?" Laura asked when Anna returned, pink and smiling as she cast her bonnet aside.

"It was delightful by the river, thank you."

"Did you meet any others of the family?"

"I believe I was to have been introduced to Mr.

Lionel, Gertrude's brother. He was unable to come, unfortunately."

Had found reasons not to come, Laura thought secretly, for like many young men he probably had little time for feminine chit-chat. Lazenby, who was listening to the conversation, cut in.

"Pity, he's a charming fellow. But no doubt you will meet him soon."

"I'm sure I shall. Of course, you know him well, having worked for his father for some time," Anna remarked.

"I knew him before that. We were friends at Oxford. He and I and another student named Robert Dalrymple—the three of us were always together. It was through Lionel that I secured the post of secretary to his father when I came down from Oxford." Suddenly he leaned across to Anna. "Are you sleeping well, Miss Braithwaite? I know Miss Oliphant is still concerned about you."

"And with reason, it seems. I believed I slept well, but it appears I must have been sleepwalking of late."

Swiftly Laura picked her up. "Sleepwalking? How do you know?"

Anna shrugged as if it were of little consequence. "Emily tells me I have left my bed at night, more than once, and since I have no recollection of rising, it must have been in my sleep." With a sudden flash she added, "But I pray you, do not tell Papa. There is no need to alarm him unduly when he is preoccupied with business matters. I'm sure it signifies little."

"I shall not tell him," Lazenby reassured her. "But I, too, am concerned that you should be so restless. If I may be of assistance in any way . . ."

"It is very kind of you, Mr. Lazenby, but truly there is nothing on my mind to cause me to sleep badly. A dream, perhaps. Nothing of consequence."

Laura was convinced of her sincerity, so innocently she looked up at Lazenby, her eyes large with trust. So there could have been no ulterior reason for her creeping from the house at night, she was sure of it. Sleepwalking as a result of one of those nightmares—yes, that was possible.

It was strange that, just a week after he had mentioned Robert Dalrymple's name for the first time, Lazenby should come into breakfast waving a letter from Robert. Lazenby broke the seal. "Odd," he said, "we lost contact after Oxford when Dalrymple went abroad to continue his work in Germany. He's a doctor," he told Laura. "Will you permit me to read it?"

Laura could see the large, lazy scrawl and was curious. Lazenby laughed aloud. "Listen to this. 'It's taken me a devil of a time to track you down, but I finally secured your address by dint of going down to Kent to visit your father. As I am now back home in London I fancied it would be a capital idea if we were to meet and dine together for old time's sake and discover how the world has treated us since we went our separate ways.'"

"How nice," Laura remarked.

"That is just like carefree, easygoing Robert, to take up an old acquaintanceship as casually as if it had never been interrupted. Perhaps one can never go back and recapture youthful anticipation and idealism, but it would be pleasant to taste just a fleeting moment of the old comraderie before Dalrymple moves on."

"Of course you must meet him," Laura urged. "Write to him at once."

"I'll write to the London hotel where Dalrymple is staying. Do you think Mr. Braithwaite would object if I invited him to Hanbury Square?"

"Of course not. After all, in his absence it would do no harm, and Miss Oliphant at least would be delighted to entertain a young doctor to lunch."

But they were to dine without the ladies. "That is the day I am to take Miss Anna and Miss Laura to the dressmaker's for fitting, and we planned to stay and lunch in town," Emily said, a trifle stiffly, Laura fancied, when Lazenby announced the doctor's visit.

"Then I would not derange your plans, Miss Oliphant. Dr. Dalrymple and I will take lunch alone, if you are agreeable."

"I shall give Cook orders to prepare lunch for you," she replied, and Laura could see she was torn between loyalty to her master and expenditure from his pocket, and curiosity about the visitor. Laura, too, was burning with curiosity. In the event she and the girls had left the house half an hour before Dalrymple arrived.

It really was too bad. The first time a visitor of real interest came to the house they had to be out and miss him, and Laura felt sure that if he was an old friend of Charles Lazenby's, then this Dr. Dalrymple was probably very interesting indeed. After the laborious business at the dressmaker's of fitting and pinning and tucking was concluded, Laura announced that she was not at all hungry and would prefer to walk in the sun.

"But it's half-past twelve already and we have a table booked for one o'clock," Emily protested.

"Then you and Anna go and eat and I'll take a leisurely walk back to Hanbury Square," Laura replied, and evading Miss Oliphant's further protests, she fled.

It was not far to the square and Laura walked quickly. Depledge let her in, eyebrows raised, and told her the gentlemen had lunched and were in the parlor.

"I'll join them later," Laura said, making as if for the stairs. Loitering until Depledge had disappeared, she moved nearer the parlor door. Deep male voices were clearly discernible.

"So you haven't married yet, Charles?"

"No. Nor you?"

The stranger laughed, a deep, infectious laugh. "I haven't yet found a girl tolerant enough to put up with me. I shall marry, one of these days, but I'm in no hurry. My work is my bride, I fear."

"You evidently enjoy medicine then, I'm glad."

"I hear your employer has not only a vast fortune but a pretty daughter too."

Laura caught her breath. Was that what the stranger was after?

"Who told you so?" Lazenby demanded.

"Lionel's sister. I dined with them last night."

"Miss Braithwaite is pretty, in a pallid way, but quite nondescript. Not for you, my friend."

"I was thinking of you, Charles. Your father seems to think it high time you were wed." Laura felt anger rising in her throat.

Lazenby laughed. "My father married my mother because he loved her and knew he would always be poor, as a vicar. I am poor, but I love no one. Ergo, I shall not marry."

"There was a time, long ago in Oxford, when you would have married, pauper as you were. But I will not open up old wounds. Still, it seems Miss Braithwaite would be a convenient way of disposing of one problem—your poverty—and surely she is not completely undesirable?"

"She is my employer's daughter."

"And therefore beyond your reach?"

"I don't much care for her. She's a mouse. But let us talk of you. Tell me about your work."

Laura could hear the enthusiasm glowing in Dalrymple's voice.

"There is a great deal of work being done on the Continent, particularly in Germany, about illnesses due, not just to the malfunction of the body, but to the influence of the mind over the body. Mental conditions such as stress and anxiety can cause physical disability. Eminent doctors there are making their name by researching in this field."

"So you left the hospitals to work on this new theory too?"

"Inside and out of hospital. It's fascinating work, believe me, Charles, and I hope to continue it here. I have theories of my own I wish to pursue."

Lazenby's reply was warm. "I am glad you pursue a way of life that gives you pleasure and fulfillment. Not everyone is so fortunate."

"It's like detective work, in a way," Dalrymple went on. "One sees the victim and his disability first, and then has to work back to find out the cause. And if the cause is in the mind, then analyzing the reasons, the motivation—this is where the fascination lies. Human nature is a strange thing, Charles."

"Do you find many such patients—whose illness stems from the mind?"

"More than you would credit. Hospitals are full of them, but many more are walking the streets, for the mind's illness does not always betray itself in physical illness. Many whom we call mad and clap into lunatic asylums are in truth only ill and need to find a cure. That is where the challenge lies for us, Charles, in finding and supplying that remedy."

Laura began to like the sound of this man, forgetting his suggestion that Charles Lazenby should pursue his employer's daughter, until he mentioned Braithwaite again.

"What kind of man is he, this Reginald Braithwaite, Charles? Born into his wealth, or has he acquired it himself?"

Lazenby laughed dryly. "He is very much the self-made man, and proud of it. Self-help is the secret of success, he always says. No doubt he will say so again when he comes to make his maiden speech in the House."

"And how does he make use of his success? Is he a liberal man, given to helping humanity?"

"Liberal in his politics, less so in outlook. Oh, he donates funds to the church and professes to labor for the underprivileged, but were I lucky enough to be in his shoes . . ."

"Ah, so you would fancy the life of a member of Parliament, full of reforming zeal, would you?" Dalrymple cut in. "Then why not? We should all do what we really want to do, and there are seats to be had in the House for a bright young man."

"One would need position and influence. I have neither. I must content myself with what I do for Braithwaite," Lazenby replied.

"And just what does he aim to do, politically?"

"To stamp out vice."

"What? All the vices?"

"Prostitution, mainly. My work is to research into London prostitution for him."

"Fascinating! May I accompany you on your research trips?" Dalrymple's voice rippled with amusement.

"Be serious, Robert. He is as dedicated to his cause as you to yours. To him the chief virtues are hard work, thrift, and temperance. Their opposite counterparts—laziness, gambling, and drunkenness—are the cause of the world's ills. We can hardly disagree with that."

"Yet it seems from what you say that Mr. Braithwaite has an end in view—promotion in the party, perhaps? He seems hardly the man to undertake work without return."

Lazenby laughed. "One would think you had met him, so shrewdly you comment."

"He seems a powerful man, overbearing, perhaps?"

Lazenby made no answer.

"And there is no Mrs. Braithwaite?" Dalrymple went on.

"She died when Anna was a child."

"Then that could account for your nondescript Miss Braithwaite. Subdued into silence by a dominating father?"

"Perhaps. But he treats her kindly. Do you quiz all your friends about their acquaintances?"

Dalrymple laughed that throaty laugh again. "Often, I'm afraid. Motivation for people's behavior obsesses me.

I'm sorry, my friend, let us talk of other things. Do you see Lionel often nowadays?"

"Rarely. He moves in circles where I cannot."

"A pity. But I hope the three of us will be able to meet, just like old times. I shall arrange for you both to dine with me."

"Make it soon, Robert, I've so enjoyed seeing you again."

Laura hastened away, for their words indicated that Dalrymple was about to leave. In the privacy of her room she thought over what she had heard. Charles Lazenby had seemed truly content in his friend's company, more relaxed and at ease than she had ever known him to be. It must be because Uncle Reginald was away. The ease one felt at Braithwaite's absence was like relief from a nagging toothache when it had gone. She wondered if Dalrymple was right and Anna felt the same, or whether filial concern made her miss her father despite his austere manner.

Anna certainly did not seem to miss him. In the succeeding days Laura heard her often singing or humming a tune or playing the piano. Sometimes she caught a glimpse of her playing backgammon in the parlor with Miss Oliphant or seated on the bench in the back garden, sunning herself and reading. She rarely dined in the dining room, preferring to eat in the privacy of her room, but on the occasions when she did dine downstairs, she seemed pleasantly lighthearted. Her palely pretty face gained enormously by losing its usual immobility, Laura decided. She could be a very attractive woman in a year or two if she put her mind to it.

All day the same thought kept recurring to Laura. If, as he had implied, Dr. Dalrymple was an expert in diagnosing people's motives for their behavior, why should he not be introduced to Anna? With what he had already learned of her cousin from Lazenby, added to his observation of her, he might be able to arrive at a solution as to the reason for her unaccountable behavior. It could be that her sleepwalking was simply the result of recurrent nightmares, but the doctor might be able to go further and discover the reason for the nightmares. And then there was the pickpocketing.

She resolved to put the idea to Lazenby, even if it meant confessing that she had eavesdropped on his conversation with Dalrymple. After all, she thought defiantly, she had nothing to lose and Anna could profit from it. And what better opportunity than now while Uncle Reginald was still away?

But the chance to put her proposal to the secretary did not arise that day. He was closeted in the study, busy writing, Miss Oliphant said, and Laura was obliged to go to bed that night with her scheme still an unfulfilled idea.

Outside the bedroom door Laura saw the housekeeper with a small wooden chest. She put it down on a side table and unlocked it with a key from the bunch she wore at her waist.

"What are you doing?" Laura asked.

"Taking some laudanum up to one of the maids. She's got dreadful toothache and I told her I had something to cure it. A dab of this on the tooth and she'll be able to sleep all right."

Miss Oliphant selected a small bottle from the contents, closed and relocked the box, and hurried away upstairs to the attic rooms where the maids slept. Laura yawned and went into her own room. Anna had gone to bed an hour ago.

It was just as Laura was about to peel off her gown that she heard a sound and stopped to listen. It was the sound of a door being cautiously opened and then closed, and she knew by the direction that it was Anna's room. Emily was up on the attic floor and Lazenby was at work in the study and neither would hear her. Laura listened and heard soft footsteps pass her door toward the servants' stairs.

She reached for her bonnet and jacket and went out

into the corridor. There was no time to fetch Lazenby—
the sound of the basement door closing showed that
Anna had already gone out. There was nothing for it but
to follow her, and tell Lazenby later.

Chapter Nine

It was not easy at first to catch sight of Anna's slim figure in the darkness once Laura had climbed out of the
basement yard, but then she glimpsed her passing under
a gaslamp toward the end of the square. Laura followed,
pulling on her jacket and trying to fix her bonnet as she
went.

It was necessary to stay some distance behind her
cousin so that her footsteps might not be heard. As Anna
walked resolutely on, Laura found the answer. By
matching her footsteps to her cousin's pace, their steps
synchronized and gradually she made her way closer to
Anna.

For ten minutes or so she walked, in the direction of
Piccadilly but avoiding that thoroughfare by means of
back streets. At last she turned into a street where a row
of imposing villas stood, and rang the bell of a house
from which the strains of a waltz were coming. Laura
drew back into the shadows to see what would happen
next, and to watch unseen. As Anna went up the steps of
the house, the front door opened, as if she had been
awaited, and Anna went in.

Outside, Laura hesitated, debating what to do. Should
she try and follow Anna in? From the sounds of music
and laughter that were coming from the house some sort
of ball seemed to be going on, and Anna had been
clearly expected. Laura felt a moment of blind panic
sweep over her, but she recovered her courage. Anna
was clearly unaware of what she was doing. She could

not just go home and leave her. She must somehow contrive to get into the house and discover what was going on.

With a feeling of great boldness, Laura stepped up to the door and rang the bell. To her surprise, the door was opened by a smartly dressed young woman wearing an evening gown who was clearly no maidservant.

"Good evening," Laura said smoothly. "I am with the young lady who just went in."

"Bella Marchant? Oh, and what connection have you with her?" she asked suspiciously.

Laura thought swiftly. Best not give her own name, since Anna evidently gave a false one. "I am her friend Lottie. She told me to come here as there might be a position for me."

For a moment she thought the girl was going to shut the door in her face. But then she seemed to have second thoughts.

"Well, I suppose you had better come in. Sit here," she said, indicating a bench in the vast vestibule. "I'll go and tell Madame."

When the girl turned and was gone, Laura sat down and waited. Through the hall, past the graceful balustraded staircase, Laura could see a large room through an archway. It was from this room that the music she had heard had been coming. She could hear, too, a woman's voice singing, and she could see the gliding shapes of elegantly dressed men and beautifully gowned women. There was, as well, the sound of laughter and the faint clink of wineglasses. But there was no sign of Anna.

Abruptly she was dragged from her contemplation of this sumptuous scene by the intrusion of a tall plump lady dressed in a black silk gown who seemed suddenly to loom into the hall. Laura stared at her openly, mesmerized by the red coiled hair, which was just a shade too red to be natural, the fleshy fingers literally emblazoned with rings, and the flashing emeralds, un-

doubtedly real, that enfolded her throat. Madame returned her stare but speculatively, looking her up and
down. Laura just wished she had been wearing a more
elegant dress. But Madame seemed to have made up her
mind.

"Come," she said, "this way."

Laura followed her through the archway into a room
ablaze with the light of a great chandelier. Laura stared
wide-eyed at the scene as they passed. Baize-topped
card tables, strewn with cards and wineglasses, gentlemen relaxing with glasses in their hands and girls on
their knees, the girls themselves were either fashionably
dressed or wearing a loose filmy garment resembling a
nightgown.

Madame caught her shocked expression and laughed.

"Well, my girl, do you not fancy a new sort of employ-
ment? We pride ourselves that our establishment can offer any man all that he can desire, whatever his
pleasure."

Madame raised her hand and beckoned a girl over to
them.

"Maisie! Come over here, my dear. This is Lottie. I
want you to show her around and introduce her to our
friends. She may be coming to join us."

"I'll have a talk with you later, Lottie," Madame said,
turning away to advance upon a new arrival, a portly,
bespectacled gentleman. "Ah, your Lordship! What a
pleasure to see you again so soon," she enthused. "Marie,
fetch a bottle of his Lordship's port, there's a good girl."

Laura saw the girl who had opened the door to her go
out.

Maisie smiled at Laura. "Won't you take off your
jacket? It's very warm in here."

"No, I won't, thank you."

"Then come and meet Grete."

She steered Laura toward a card table where a lanky
young man was leaning over a backgammon board, his

eyes intent on the blond young woman opposite him rather than on the pieces on the board.

"Grete, this is Lottie. This is her first visit to Madame de Sandrier's soirée."

The girl smiled, white even teeth sparkling and her blond curls gleaming, and glanced back at her companion. "Peter, come on, it's your turn to throw."

"And there's Marie at the piano," said Maisie, leading Laura away to a sofa in the corner. "She sings beautifully, doesn't she? To work for Madame a girl must be blessed with many attributes. Ah, there's Solange just leaving with her friend."

Laura saw the petite dark girl with her tall escort bidding good night to Madame. She was struck by the foreign names.

"Solange and Grete—are there many foreign girls here?" she inquired of Maisie.

She nodded. "Madame especially likes girls from the Continent because they are usually better versed in the arts of pleasing men. They attract the aristocrats here. Madame says the English girls still have much to learn. That's why Miss Sybil is here."

"Sybil?" Laura pricked up her ears.

Maisie nodded. "Yes. Her career began in Germany, and so she's able to teach us the refinements. Which reminds me—I must go and talk to Madame. Will you excuse me? Here, there's Madeira and a glass. Do have a drink while you're waiting."

As she rose to go, the blond girl Grete and her gawky young man rose also. Laura saw them go into the hallway and up the staircase. She poured herself a glass of wine and gulped it. It was all too clear now what kind of place she had come to—and Anna too.

His Lordship was sitting in an armchair, Marie perched on the arm beside him. He was puffing a fat cigar, the other arm encircling Marie's waist. Every now and again Marie bent over the wine table to refill his glass.

It was hot in here though the windows were open and the net curtains billowing in the gentle breeze. Laura began to feel uncomfortable. Somehow she must find Anna and get her out of this place. Just as she was about to rise to leave the room, she stopped with a shock. The violet-eyed Sybil entered with Madame and sat down on a sofa close by her. Above the chatter she could hear their voices.

"You say Mrs. Noyce found her, Madame?"

"That's right, and she brought her to me. She said she could see at once that the girl was too refined for the likes of her saloon. We agreed on a settlement, you see, for the girl is just what I needed."

"Bella has no experience, you think?"

Laura sat stunned. They were talking about Anna.

Madame shook her hennaed head firmly. "I'm sure of it. She had that bewildered look—one can tell. Lost her position, probably, and wandering the streets destitute. She will need careful handling, this one."

"Leave it to me," said Sybil.

"She needs breaking gently," Madame reiterated. "She has the right air of grace and breeding to be a great asset to us."

"Don't worry, Madame. By the way, what did you say her name was?"

Madame smiled, a light of amusement in her eyes. "Who knows? When I asked, she said Bella Marchant."

"Marchant? Why, that is—"

"Yes, the name over the wine merchant's across the road. I had my back to the window and she was facing me and could see out the window. But who can blame her for wanting to remain incognito?"

Sybil looked around the room, glowing with lamplight and polished brass. "Where is she now?"

"Upstairs with Maisie. Maisie knows to keep her from the others for the time being until you decide how to deal with her."

Upstairs, thought Laura. Then I must go up and find her.

"Does the girl know what kind of place this is? What did she say?" Sybil asked.

Madame spread her fingers expressively. "Only that she had come back to start work. I imagine she knew what kind of work was entailed, since she has been here once already."

"But she may not. We must handle her with care," Sybil murmured reflectively. "One move made too swiftly could frighten her away."

"Oh, you must not let that happen." Madame's eyes widened and the ringed fingers fluttered. "She is just what we need—cool, a trifle aloof, just what some of our clients adore in a woman. You know we cater only for the discriminating here, and she seems just the cultured kind we need."

"I shall do what I can, be assured of that, Madame." Sybil rose and then paused. "Maisie was a good choice of companion, Madame. She enjoys her work perhaps more than most, and her enthusiasm could be infectious. It would be a good idea to encourage their friendship if the girl is as you say."

Laura rose quickly to follow Sybil. Some excuse was necessary.

"Madame," she said to the red-haired woman, "I'm looking for Miss Bella. She's my mistress."

"Indeed?" The older woman's voice grew suddenly haughty. "Then I'm afraid I was mistaken. I took you for a new applicant."

"No, ma'am. I'm a lady's maid," Laura lied smoothly. "My mistress needs me, 'cos she can't button her dress nor do her hair without my help. That's why I'm here."

"Then you'd better follow this lady." Madame indicated Sybil, who was standing listening, a wry smile on her lips.

"Thank you, ma'am," said Laura.

Sybil led the way upstairs, the sound of distant laughter and conversation in the main parlor below indicating that the soirée was well under way. Maisie's bedroom, one of several along the gallery on the first floor, was a warm, inviting room, gay chintz on the bed and dressing table and subdued lamps burning in the corners. Two girls sat on the bed, one dark and the other fair. Laura recognized Anna. Dark-eyed Maisie leaped to her feet.

"Miss Sybil! I told Bella you wouldn't be long. I'm so glad you've come—I've an appointment in a few minutes."

"Then you go and see to your guest, Maisie, and I'll take Bella to her room if you'll tell me which is to be hers."

Sparrow-bright eyes smiled in answer. "This is Bella's room, miss. Madame says it has certain advantages for the new girl, and I'm to have another one along the corridor. I've already moved my things."

"And has Bella unpacked hers?"

"She brought none."

Sybil looked at Laura inquiringly. Anna simply turned her head away and made no reply.

"Go on then, Maisie, don't keep your guest waiting," Sybil said.

The girl nodded and left. Sybil took off her jacket leisurely. "Bella, here is your maid, Lottie." Anna's lips remained tightly compressed and her head averted. Laura could see Sybil was puzzled. She seated herself on a high-backed chair opposite Anna and leaned toward her.

"Bella?"

Blue eyes swiveled to meet Sybil's. "Yes?"

"You came back."

"Yes."

"Why?"

"To find work here. Madame promised me work."

"Do you know what kind of work?"

Slim shoulders shrugged carelessly. "It matters little."

Laura stood listening, reluctant to intervene. She too was anxious to know Anna's motives.

"You do not look as if you have worked for a living—not with your hands at least." Sybil took one of Anna's hands, which lay limp on her lap. At once the fingers stiffened and leaped from her touch.

Laura could guess that Sybil was assessing Anna shrewdly. Her posture was erect even as she sat, and her gray gown, though not in the height of fashion, was well-cut and of good material. Her figure, slight as it was, showed it owed none of its slenderness to constricting stays, however.

"Do you need money, Bella? Is that why you came here?"

"No." The girl's emphatic reply was startling.

"Then are you sure you have come to the right place?"

Laura took her cue. "I think that's it, miss. She's got the wrong house."

Anna's blue eyes lifted to stare at her. "This is what is known as a gay house, is it not?"

"It is," Sybil admitted.

"Then it is the right place. Tell me what I must do."

"I can do better. I can show you. Come."

Sybil rose and crossed to the wall. Next to a large oil painting of stags in a woodland glen there hung a chenille curtain behind which, Sybil revealed, were several knotholes in the paneling. Pulling the curtain aside, she pointed. "Look through there," she commanded. Anna did not move, but Laura looked. In the next room she could see clearly the vast double bed, the plump gentleman who lay sprawled on it, and the slumberous-eyed Solange, who was pouring wine at the side table.

"Come and see, Bella," Sybil invited. Anna rose slowly and came across the room. "Look through there and watch," Sybil commanded. The girl leaned to the hole next to Laura and stared through.

Laura stared, unable to believe what she saw: the loosening of the fat gentleman's stock, the unbuttoning of his shirt and later his breeches. She was fascinated by the writhing, the gradual slipping out of negligee and shift and the tormenting before the final action began.

Minutes passed, but Anna's face remained immobile. Sybil evidently was curious. "Most newcomers register some kind of reaction, Bella, but you show nothing. Has Solange decided to procrastinate, to tease?" Sybil rose quickly and peered through another knothole. No. Laura could see clearly that Solange lay on the bed, her legs entwined with his and his moans were clearly audible. Sybil glanced at Bella again.

"What are you thinking, Bella?"

The girl's expression was still impassive. Laura could not believe it. She herself was in a tumult. Either Anna was in a trance or she was remarkably self-controlled.

"Nothing. I am thinking of nothing. Just watching," Anna replied flatly. Odd, thought Laura. She spoke almost as though she was sleepwalking, aware of reality as though it were only a meaningless dream. Laura felt distinctly uneasy. Seating herself again, she watched Anna's face closely, but it remained as impassive and classically controlled as a statue. Anna, still watching through the hole, suddenly spoke.

"Oh, she's stopped. Is that all?"

Laura rose to look. Solange had indeed risen from the bed and the client was lying propped on his elbow, his plump face beaded with sweat. Solange was reaching for a short-handled whip on the wall. Sybil smiled.

"Watch again, Bella. The gentleman has unusual tastes."

Laura heard the crack of the whip and the client's squeal, his plump posterior striped by the whip and Solange's slim figure glowing in the lamplight. A few more cracks, a few more squeals, and it was over. She heard Anna's sharp intake of breath.

"Wonderful," she breathed.

Laura glanced at her sharply. Blue eyes gleamed in excitement and pink lips fell apart as she breathed more and more heavily. She was positively enjoying the scene. Suddenly Laura felt sickened.

Anna turned to face Sybil, her face aglow and her eyes dancing. "That was enjoyable, Miss Sybil. I have no doubts now."

Sybil demurred. "That is not typical of the work here, Bella, just the taste of one client, you understand. He enjoys suffering."

"And I should be glad to supply it."

Laura stared at her cousin, horrified.

Sybil regarded her quizzically. "You know the aim of a gay house is to please the gentlemen?"

"I do."

"And you are concerned to please them?"

"If *that* is what they want." Anna jerked a hand toward the wall separating them from Solange.

"Others prefer that the woman submits to them," Sybil remarked guardedly. "Do you think you could please all tastes?"

The girl's eyes flashed. "Did you see how the fat man lay at the end, gasping and weak? He was helpless as a kitten. Do they all end like that?"

"Yes," admitted Sybil.

"Then I'll take the work." Anna's voice was calm now but still emphatic. She held her fair head high, her face radiant. "I'll come back."

Sybil started. "Come back? You do not understand, Bella. Madame likes her girls to live here, permanently, not to come and go."

The girl shrugged. "But I cannot stay. If you wish me to return, I shall be glad to do so, but I cannot stay."

Thank goodness, thought Laura. Once we get out of here . . .

Sybil adopted a persuasive tone. "Tell me about it, Bella. Do you still have a position you wish to maintain? Would you prefer this work to remain discreetly unknown? Tell me, you can trust me."

Anna's eyes darkened and she turned away. "I do not know. I cannot tell you," she murmured.

"Where will you be, Bella. I must know, so I can contact you, even assuming Madame will agree. The usual arrangement is for a girl to have her own room here, her board free of charge, and her costume provided. What Madame calls a dress-lodger. And you have your own maid, Lottie here. Another arrangement may not be acceptable to Madame unless we know where to find you."

Anna remained resolutely with her back to Sybil. "I tell you I cannot stay. I only know I must be free to move as I please. If it does not suit you, let me go now."

"Let her go, miss," Laura whispered urgently. "She's not well."

Sybil regarded the averted back for a moment.

"I'll tell you what, Bella. I'll go down and talk to Madame de Sandrier. Wait here awhile. Perhaps we can arrive at some amicable arrangement to suit us both. Will you wait?"

Anna nodded and came to sit down again on the bed. Laura sat and watched Sybil go.

As soon as the door closed behind her, Laura leaped to her feet.

"Come on, Anna, it's time we went home," she said persuasively. "It's midnight already."

Anna stared at her, and there was irritation in her blue eyes. "Who are you, and why do you call me Anna? My name is Bella Marchant. You have evidently mistaken me for someone else."

Laura felt dismay. Anna genuinely did not recognize her. "Do you not know me? I am Lottie, your maid."

"I have never seen you before. Has Miss Sybil appointed you my maid?" Evidently she was not interested in the answer, for she rolled away on the bed and stared up at the ceiling. Laura felt helpless.

"Come on, let's leave this place," she urged.

"You go if you like. I'm staying," Anna replied dully.

Laura wondered how on earth she could persuade her to leave before Sybil returned.

Anna lay supine on the chintz-covered bed. She had removed her jacket and unfastened several of the tiny pearl buttons of the bodice of her gown.

She looked at her cousin, her blue eyes still lifted to the ceiling. "What are you thinking, Anna?"

"My name is Bella. I am watching the spider."

Laura's gaze followed Anna's. Above the bed, across one corner of the small bedchamber, a fat black spider sat motionless in the center of a silken web. Anna raised one arm to point.

"See? She has been busy spinning that web all the time you were away. Now she has done. I wonder what she will do now."

As Laura watched, a smaller spider appeared on the edge of the web, apparently from nowhere.

"She did not have to wait long," Laura remarked. "Here comes her mate, if I am not mistaken."

She looked at Anna's small, pointed face again and saw the glow of interest that gradually replaced her earlier air of apathy. For several minutes Laura studied the girl until she suddenly raised herself on one elbow, still staring upward.

"Curious," she said softly. "She let him approach her, but now she turns on him. What is she doing?"

Laura looked up again. The smaller spider sat motionless on the web, but the larger black one moved industriously about him, round and round his inert body. Then she stopped.

"She's bound him fast in a shroud of silk," Anna murmured in excitement. "Just as I have seen spiders trap flies."

She swung her legs over the side of the bed, still staring up in fascination. Laura could not move her gaze from the silent scene above. The she-spider moved close to the imprisoned spider and sat, apparently immobile.

Anna rose slowly from the bed, her hands clasped and her face aglow as she still stared upward.

"Magnificent," Anna said.

"Magnificent? What do you mean?" Laura said.

"Look what she has done." Anna was pointing at the web.

Laura followed her finger. The fat black she-spider sat now, possessive and satiated, in the center of the web while the trapped male spider dangled ignominiously from a thread, suspended at the lower edge of the web.

"What is magnificent about that?" Laura demanded.

"Can't you see? When she had him entangled, she sucked him dry, sucked every drop from his body, and then hung his empty carcass on a thread like a trophy. Look!"

Laura rose, disbelievingly, and peered closer at the web. It was true, incredible but true. The victim's transparent corpse swayed on the thread, lifeless and drained utterly. No wonder the she-spider sat so complacent in the center of her universe. Mating and a fine meal in one. Laura's disbelief changed to a feeling of nausea. Anna was smiling.

"Do you find that rather repellent episode pleasing?" Laura inquired curiously. "For myself I find it rather disgusting."

Anna turned swiftly. "Did you not find it disgusting to see the fat man next door equally drained and helpless? It seems to me the two situations have their similarities." Her blue eyes looked darkly angry in the lamplight. For a moment Laura was at a loss for words, surprised by the sudden fury in Anna's voice.

"Similarities?" she echoed. "I find none, Anna."

"My name is Bella," Anna asserted, but already the fire in her voice was dying. "It is beautiful, and poetic, in my eyes."

"What is?"

"The spider. I shall remember the spider."

There was a dreamy tone in her voice now, all anger

gone. Again Laura felt uneasy. Anna's sudden variations of mood could be a sign she was unwell, a little unstable, even. Sybil came back.

"Madame has agreed to your conditions, Bella. If you are to work here, I shall teach you how to dress and to apply cosmetics to your face. I grant you are pretty, but a touch of powder and paint and the exclusive perfumes Madame has sent from France can do much to improve a young lady's attractions."

"I shall do as you wish." Laura could hear the tiredness in Anna's voice.

"And there are other matters I shall teach you, but not tonight. I hear the tower striking midnight already and I have not eaten supper yet. Will you join me?"

Sybil rose to pull the bellpull, which would bring a maid to supply their wants, but Anna suddenly grew pale.

"Midnight already? Then I must be gone," she murmured, reaching for her jacket and pulling it on. Laura helped her.

"Where do you go, Bella?" Sybil asked.

"I cannot tell you."

"But I must know where I can reach you, mustn't I? Where will you be? Trust me, Bella, I can be discreet."

"I tell you I cannot say," the girl repeated angrily. "I shall be here when you want me."

"When will you come again?"

"What day is it?"

"Today is Sunday."

"Then I'll come on Friday. That's a promise—Friday night."

When the maid came in answer to the bell, Sybil asked her to see the young lady out. Anna left without another word, and Laura followed, relief flooding her that they had escaped at last.

Chapter Ten

Anna walked swiftly through London's dark streets and Laura hastened after her. Neither girl spoke. Anna's expression was strangely vacant, and Laura did not try to make her cousin talk. It was evident that Anna was seriously disturbed.

She followed Anna into the house by means of the basement door and breathed a sigh of relief that they reached the bedroom floor undetected. Anna went quickly into her own room and closed the door. Laura hesitated. At half-past midnight it was inadvisable to waken Lazenby. From the direction of Emily's room came the sound of deep, regular snoring.

Troubled though she was, Laura soon fell asleep, resolved to tell Lazenby all she had witnessed in the morning. Now there was an even stronger reason to beg the help of his friend the doctor. Only a man who could untangle the deep, inner, inexplicable workings of the mind could help to analyze Anna's strangely contradictory behavior. For a girl who by day shunned everything to do with men to become immeasurably excited and fascinated by the goings-on tonight, was completely incomprehensible. Anna must be very sick indeed, and somebody had to help her.

And there was the moral danger too, for her cousin was in jeopardy of losing her virginity as well as her sanity if she were to go to that place again. Charles Lazenby would know what to do. Comforted, Laura slept.

Lazenby's customary sanguinity soon changed to a look of alarm when Laura ran him to earth at last in the conservatory next day. "Anna went out, and you never told me!" he exclaimed. "Why did you not fetch me at once?"

"There was no time," Laura explained. "But, listen, there is more, much more to it than that. I beg you to listen and not interrupt me for a moment, for I must tell you all before Miss Oliphant comes looking for me."

"Go on, then," he replied. "I shall not interrupt."

Laura drew a deep breath and composed herself. This was not going to be easy. "As you are no doubt aware, Mr. Lazenby, my cousin Anna is far from well."

He nodded.

Encouraged, Laura went on. "Just how ill she is, however, I think none of us has guessed, until now, and now I have reason to believe she is acutely ill. She needs your help, Mr. Lazenby, or to be more precise, she needs the help of your friend Dr. Dalrymple."

Charles Lazenby's shrewd eyes narrowed, and Laura flushed. "Yes, I know of him, Mr. Lazenby, and have to confess that I listened to your conversation with him the other day. That is how I know he can help Anna, for she is sick in her mind and only a specialist like Dr. Dalrymple would know how to help her. I beg you to ask him to call again while my uncle is still away, and ask him to talk to Anna. Perhaps he can discover what the trouble is and help to cure her."

"I do not follow you, Miss Sutcliffe."

His cold, assessing stare irritated Laura. "My cousin is going out of her mind, Mr. Lazenby," she flared at him. "I want your friend to help her, for no one else can."

There was a flicker of light in his eyes that Laura interpreted as amusement. So let the fellow laugh at her, if he would, just so long as he believed her and fetched the specialist doctor to Anna.

"And what makes you so sure your cousin is mad, may I ask?" His tone was light, mocking, and provoking.

"I did not say mad, but she is unbalanced. There is another side to Anna that you do not know, but I have seen it and it is not a pleasant personality, Mr. Lazenby. There is something cold, evil even, in her."

"As there is in us all, my dear."

His patronizing tone infuriated Laura. She rose on tiptoe to glare up at him. "Not like this! Do you know that at night she turns into another creature, a woman of no emotion who goes out to a life of depravity?"

"Depravity? Where?" The amusement receded from his tone, but there was still an intonation of incredulity.

"She goes to a house of ill repute, Mr. Lazenby. I know for I myself have followed her there."

"That is where she went last night?"

Laura nodded. "And I too. But she has no recollection of me or of Anna Braithwaite while she was there. I was a stranger to her, and she thought herself a harlot."

Lazenby paled visibly. "Did she . . . Was she . . ."

Laura shook her head. "Not yet, but she promised to go back. But we must see to it that she never goes back, Mr. Lazenby, nor must we let her papa or Emily come to learn of it. That's why I want Dr. Dalrymple to come—to see if he can discover why she does this dreadful thing and perhaps find a way to stop her. Oh, please help me, Mr. Lazenby. I cannot protect her alone."

Lazenby gripped her shoulders, his firm grip making Laura wince. "You are right. If Anna is as ill as you say, something must be done. Leave this to me."

Turning quickly, Lazenby strode out of the conservatory. Somehow Laura felt a great weight had suddenly been lifted from her shoulders. The problem of Anna was still there, but at least now she had a partner in the secret and someone with whom she could share the burden of worry.

Over breakfast Miss Oliphant was decidedly quiet. She looked heavy-eyed and not at all her usual brisk self, Laura noted. Toward the end of the meal she actually yawned.

"Oh, do forgive me," the housekeeper said, pink with confusion. "I don't know what's come over me, but I feel so tired. It must be the weather, I think."

"It is rather close and heavy," Lazenby agreed.

Miss Oliphant dimpled gratefully. "Almost as though there was a storm brewing up, don't you think?"

"That would not surprise me at all."

"Still, I must not let it make me lazy," Miss Oliphant remarked as she rose from the table. "Miss Anna may be free to sleep late if she chooses, but I have work to do. I understand Mr. Braithwaite is to come home by the afternoon train the day after tomorrow, so there is much to prepare."

Laura looked up sharply. "Pray excuse me, Mr. Lazenby," the housekeeper said. "And Miss Laura, do you think you could find something to occupy Miss Anna usefully this afternoon? I shall be extremely busy."

"Of course," Laura replied. Now here was the perfect opportunity if only Lazenby would fetch Dalrymple. . . .

The moment the door had closed behind Miss Oliphant, Laura turned to Lazenby. "Can you get your doctor friend here today?" she asked directly. There was no time to be lost. To her disappointment, the secretary shook his head slowly.

"If my employer is to return on Wednesday I must have my reports ready," he replied. "But I have received a note from Dalrymple this morning. He invites me and a mutual friend, Lionel, to dinner at his hotel tonight. I shall discuss it with him then."

"Discuss?" Laura snapped. "There is no time for delay when Uncle Reginald is to return so soon. You know what my uncle is like. There will be no opportunity for Anna and the doctor to meet once he is here."

"Mr. Braithwaite will not be home until evening. There is still time if Dalrymple considers it advisable to see Anna," Lazenby pointed out.

"He will be paid, if it is his fee that you are thinking

of," Laura said impulsively, wondering how on earth she could find the money.

"If Dalrymple wishes to help, I think that will be ir-relevant," Lazenby said quietly. "Where is this place Anna goes to?"

"I do not know, but I could guide you there."

"And when does she plan to go again?"

"Friday."

"And today is Monday, so delay will do no harm. Leave it to me, Laura. I shall speak to Robert tonight."

It was only after the secretary had folded his napkin and left the dining room that Laura realized two things. First, she had forgotten to tell him that the woman in charge of the novice prostitutes in that house had been his friend Sybil. But maybe it was better not to reveal that, for in doing so Laura would have to admit having followed Lazenby that night and eavesdropping on him. He already had a low enough opinion of her, and she had confessed to eavesdropping on Dalrymple. To worsen her crimes in his eyes would lose his allegiance entirely. It would not be safe to risk that.

And the second realization was that Charles Lazenby had not called her Miss Laura or Miss Sutcliffe. He had called her Laura. She felt warm and secure now in the conspiracy with him to protect Anna. Somehow between them they would find the answer without Emily or Uncle Reginald coming to hear of it, she felt sure.

The day of Reginald Braithwaite's return to his Lon-don villa was cloudy and overcast, just as the house it-self. The maids flew hither and thither under Miss Oliphant and Depledge's critical eyes, rubbing and polishing till the furniture groaned in remonstrance. All must be perfection if the master was to keep an even temper. The general air of anxiety seemed to envelop Miss Anna too.

"Why don't you go and sit in the parlor and finish sewing your petit point?" Miss Oliphant suggested to

Anna. "Your papa will be pleased to see you have been industrious."

Laura sighed. Anna was wandering about the place abstractedly and needed occupying. All the signs of animation she had glimpsed in her cousin a week ago had completely vanished. That was the effect Braithwaite's imminent return had on everyone. Laura herself felt tired and dispirited. In answer to her inquiring gaze across the breakfast table, Lazenby had shaken his head. No Dr. Dalrymple, no hope for Anna. . . .

At the sound of the carriage bringing the master home, Depledge lined up the servants dutifully in the entrance hall. Laura stood a little apart, anticipating Braithwaite's brief words to Depledge would be followed by a curt command to his secretary to come to the study and render account of his activities. To the surprise of the household Braithwaite said little.

"Where is my daughter, Depledge?"

"In the parlor, sir."

"I'll see her and then have dinner."

"Very good, sir."

Unbidden, Laura followed her uncle to the parlor. Father kissed daughter briefly on the forehead and then nodded across her to Miss Oliphant.

"Has all gone well, Miss Oliphant?"

Pinkly, she bobbed a curtsy. "Very well, sir."

"Good."

He seemed moody and preoccupied, Laura thought. Best not to speak to him until spoken to. It was a relief when he suddenly strode out and went to his study.

At dinner the conversation between master and secretary, daughter, niece, and housekeeper was desultory. Each one around the table evidently found the occasion trying. Braithwaite ignored the women and addressed his secretary.

"I have been reading your reports, Lazenby," he said without preamble.

"I hope they are to your satisfaction, sir."

"Quite. Interesting reading, in fact."

"I'm glad you approve, sir."

"Approve? How could I approve of such scandalous goings-on? Dreadful, sir, that's what it is. Shocking and sadly to be deplored. Battening on human weakness and exploiting one's needs. Disgraceful!"

"Indeed, sir."

"What I want to know is, have you concluded your research at this particular house, Lazenby?"

Laura saw the pale tongue flick out nervously to wet the eager lips.

"I think so, sir. There are many establishments of other, less refined, nature I could investigate next, if you require more material."

"No. I think we have sufficient now for an attack on vice to be made in the House. I have other work you can be going on with in the meantime until I decide whether more material is necessary."

"As you wish, sir."

A lengthy silence followed. At last dinner was over and the ladies rose to leave, but in the doorway Laura heard her uncle clear his throat.

"Do you not agree it might be a wise move to inspect this place myself, Lazenby? It might add more force to my argument if I can claim to have witnessed this behavior firsthand, don't you think?"

Lazenby hesitated.

Braithwaite hastened on. "I only suggest it to strengthen my case, you understand. I know I said formerly that I should not be seen in such places, but on reflection. . ."

"You are the best judge, Mr. Braithwaite."

As she climbed the stairs, Laura smiled to herself grimly. The old hypocrite! London was full of hypocrites like him, preaching virtue and making worthy donations to the Church while secretly sinning as badly as the lower classes he abhorred.

Still, Laura reflected, who was she to pass judgment.

It was a measure of the man's success that he could present an air of such proud integrity and purity to the world while keeping the darker side of himself discreetly in the shadows.

Miss Oliphant stood on the landing, a puzzled look marring her face. "Miss Laura, do you remember the laudanum I took from the medical chest the other night? Do you recall seeing me replace it?"

"Why, no. I can't say that I did."

"Then I must have put it down somewhere. Never mind, I shall probably remember presently."

It was curiously quiet in the house that evening, Laura felt. Mr. Lazenby and Uncle Reginald both went out, separately, and Uncle Reginald left word that he would stay at the Reform Club overnight. Miss Oliphant and Anna both retired to their rooms early, and Anna was sleeping peacefully when Laura looked in on her at eleven o'clock. She was safe tonight. Friday would be the night to bring problems.

But despite the stillness, Laura felt uneasy. The quietness held that ominous air that threatened something dire to follow. It was too quiet, too still for comfort.

Reginald Braithwaite took a deep draft of his postprandial port and leaned confidentially across the table to address Lord Travers.

"So I put it to you, your Lordship, that such an alliance would be of distinct advantage to us both."

Lord Travers murmured in what could be taken for a sound of assent. Encouraged, Braithwaite went on.

"What I mean is, we both stand to benefit. I've been honest with you—I need someone to help me mind my factories. And as I'm a plain-speaking man, you'll forgive me for coming straight to the point. You need money, you've said so oft enough. Well, the answer's simple. Marry your son to my lass and we're both satisfied—I've a son-in-law to take over my mills, and you can dispose of Anna's dowry between you as you think fit."

His Lordship twirled his glass between his fingers and made no immediate reply. Braithwaite felt irritated by the man's slowness. Dammit, he was doing the man a favor, wasn't he? The offer of a pretty daughter-in-law and her money did not come his way every day.

Braithwaite signaled the waiter to refill the empty glasses. "Well, now, what's your answer? It's a business proposition that's fair and honest. I'll not let you down. The name Braithwaite is a byword for integrity in Harrowfield."

"I have no doubt of it, my dear fellow," Lord Travers replied coolly. "But since it is a proposition that involves others besides ourselves, there must be discussion. I must talk to Lionel, as I presume you have done with your daughter."

"Talk to her? Not I! Why should I? She'll be glad I looked after her welfare just as your son should be indebted to you."

"But the boy is of age, you know. I shall think the matter over and then discuss it with Lionel if I decide to accept. Will that suit you?"

Braithwaite was forced to agree, though secretly he despised Travers for his weakness. What need was there to consult a young wastrel, incapable of earning a brass farthing unaided? The lad should be delighted at the prospect of a seat on the board of Braithwaite Mills with a comfortable income, though Braithwaite would see to it the lad learned the trade the hard way. No man could run a business successfully unless he knew from experience every operation it entailed.

"When shall I have your answer, then?"

His Lordship shrugged. "Oh, give it a week, say. I'll let you know."

Braithwaite left the Reform Club still feeling irritated and frustrated. He would have liked his answer today, now, not a week away. It was no surprise to him that aristocrats were so rarely successful in business if they always adopted this tardy attitude toward decisions.

Braithwaite felt complacent. Now *he* had never put off a decision in his life. Quick to grasp a situation, he would assess its implications shrewdly and come to a conclusion on the instant. And he had never been proved wrong. That was what Travers needed—acumen, courage, and ambition—and if he had had those qualities, he would not be in need of cash as he was now.

Life could be very trying, Braithwaite reflected. It had taken a devil of a time to sort out the problems the mill manager, Fearnley, had allowed to accrue in Harrowfield, and now Lord Travers would not prove as eager and cooperative as he had hoped. A man must have respite from care and worry once in a while. He let his thoughts drift to the promised pleasures of Rosamund Street. Yes, he had denied himself long enough, putting duty before desire. Next week, when he had spent the requisite amount of time by his own fireside listening to the inconsequential chatter of Emily and Laura and the occasional word from Anna, then he could feel free. Dolly was probably wed to her major by now. Right, then, next week it would be Rosamund Street.

And he could rest easy about Travers. The fellow would make his son see the wisdom in Braithwaite's proposition. All would turn out well.

Chapter Eleven

Madame de Sandrier poured herself a cup of tea from the silver teapot, leaned back in her armchair, and put up her slippered feet on the tapestry footstool. It was a relief to slip away for a while to the seclusion of her private parlor, away from the reach of tiresome, petulant girls. Really, that Bella Marchant would try the patience of a saint.

Since Sunday the girl had not been near the house, and yet now on Thursday she had reappeared unexpectedly and without her maid as coolly as if she had been here only yesterday. Madame's inquiries as to her absence had not met with any explanation.

"You do not appreciate, my child, that several gentlemen have had to be disappointed."

"There were other girls."

Madame's irritation had bubbled to the surface. "What is wrong, Bella? Do you not like the idea of this work after all?"

The girl shrugged. "Well enough. But I do not like my room. I want another room."

"Impossible!"

"Then I will have it altered. I do not like the decor."

Madame was offended. "I have gone to a great deal of trouble to decorate all the rooms with taste. I have spared no expense. Yours is a beautiful room."

"But I do not like it. Nor do I like my clothes. I want new gowns and my room altered."

Madame was about to retort angrily that such demands were irrational and needlessly extravagant when she reflected it would be expedient to humor her a little. After all, the girl's future earnings would more than cover the outlay.

"Very well. Tell me what manner of gowns and decor you would prefer, and I will consider the matter."

Bella tilted her fair head to one side. "Well, for a start I want you to get rid of that dreadful wallpaper. All those vertical bars—it makes me feel like a prisoner in a cage. I want to feel free, unfettered. No tight stays either, but flowing gowns. Like an Eastern princess—yes, that's it! Queen of the East, that's what I want to be, mysterious and alluring, veiled like the women one sees in pictures of a harem. And the walls hung with silks, a sofa, and cushions on the floor. No bed, just a sofa."

Madame nodded thoughtfully as she penciled notes. Not a bad idea, and not too expensive to execute. Later, in discussing the idea with Sybil, Madame pursued the idea.

"There is no reason why Miss Bella should have the advantage over the others. We could hold an Oriental evening for all the girls and their clients—the main parlor could be designed as a harem with scents of musk and sandalwood. I rather think our gentlemen would appreciate a touch of the exotic."

Sybil was in complete agreement. Over tea they planned the girls' costumes and the details of the decor.

Upstairs Maisie Bull patted her dark curls, eyeing herself appreciatively in the mirror. Behind her she could see Solange's reflection as the French girl tied a red garter above her knee with precise, deft movements. Maisie laughed, a full-throated, infectious laugh that reflected her mood. She felt carefree and very happy. Life at Madame's made one feel contented.

"Your fellow likes a red garter, does he?" she asked. "I got that redheaded young fellow tonight, the one that fancies plenty of slap and tickle but seems to find it hard to get going. He'll be all right with me, though. I got the patience of a saint, Madame says."

"Mr. Henry?" Solange remarked. "Yes, you are well-suited for him, *mon ange*. You like the chase well enough to keep it going all night. Some of us like to get a little beauty sleep."

" 'S funny, isn't it? I love the men and their funny ways, more than most, it seems. But I ain't complaining, 'cos I like it."

"You had better mind your speech, Maisie. You know how Madame likes us all to be perpetually ladylike. She would not approve of your 'ain't' and 'cos,' so take care. *Faites attention.*"

Maisie chuckled. "Here, help me lace the back of my stays, will you? Funny. You don't talk proper English always, but Madame pays no heed to that. She says the men like your funny accent. It is rather nice. Me, though, I had no education to speak of, no fancy finishing schools and all like some of the girls. Can't think why Madame picked me, really."

"Can't you?" Solange smiled indulgently as she struggled with the laces. "Because of your love of the work, *chère*, that is why. Such enthusiasm! You are as tireless as a—how you say?—as a cat in the alleyway."

Maisie jerked free from Solange's fingers, turning to give her a playful slap. "I ain't no bleeding alley cat, damn you! I'm just a girl who likes the blokes, that's all. And why not? It pays a sight better than working in the factory. I can tell you."

Footsteps passed by the door. Maisie inclined her head to listen. A door in the distance closed. "Here," she demanded of Solange, "has that new girl come back?"

"Which girl?"

"That strange one I gave my room up for, the one who wouldn't talk. Madame said she was to come again on Friday. That's tomorrow."

"I do not concern myself, for I have my own work to do."

"Who you got tonight then?"

"Monsieur Michael."

Maisie's infectious laugh rang out again. "Oh, the one Madame calls her cousin. It'll be a bit of the French style tonight then, all them endearments in French and all, eh? Is it any different from the English style?"

Solange's dark eyes narrowed into a smile. "Making love is the same in any language, Maisie, as you no doubt will discover. The words may vary a little, but the choreography is the same."

"The what?" Maisie's blue eyes widened. "Here, what have I been missing? What's that?"

"Nothing. You have missed nothing, I am sure."

"Will the new girl learn it? That chore—whatever it was you said?"

Solange looked speculative. "I fancy Miss Sybil will see to it she learns all. She seems a very capable and conscientious teacher."

"Yes, she's a real lady. I wonder how she ever got into this game, don't you?" Maisie remarked.

Solange drew her petite figure upright. "So are we all, ladies, and do not forget it. Now you are laced, go back to your own room and dress. The gentlemen will be arriving shortly."

Dutifully Maisie returned to her own room along the corridor and pulled over her head the yellow silk gown that lay on the bed. Yellow was not the most becoming color for her, she thought as she surveyed herself in the mirror, but as one of Madame's favored dress lodgers she could not afford to sniff at the fine gowns Madame provided. Never, if she had remained with her family in the East End, could she have bought such a gown for herself. She was a lucky girl to have escaped poverty and drudgery, and the color of a gown was not going to make her forget that easily.

There was a light tap at the door and Miss Sybil came in without waiting for an invitation. "You look very pretty, my dear," she commented. "Now listen, Maisie.

The new girl, Bella, is in her room. I want you to go and talk to her until your gentleman comes. See what you can find out about her, for I find her most uncommunicative."

"She is quiet, miss, and that's a fact."

"But perhaps she will talk to you, someone of her own age. Be a dear and try."

"My age, miss? She's younger than me, surely. She only looks sixteen or so, and I'm twenty."

"She says she's nineteen, but no matter, she's well above the age of consent. What I really want to know is where she comes from and what she does. I fancy she's a governess or some such. See what you can discover."

"All right, I'll try. Maisie felt and sounded reluctant, but she could not refuse. When Miss Sybil had gone, she went along to her former room. There was no answer to her knock, so she went in. The new girl was already dressed for the evening in vivid blue silk edged with white lace, and was lying on the bed. There was no sign of her maid.

"Hello, Bella. I'm Maisie, remember?"

The girl did not answer. Maisie tried again.

"Nice dress you got. Madame give it you?"

The girl muttered something Maisie did not catch. She was staring at the ceiling intently. Maisie glanced up, but there was nothing of interest there.

"Warm night. Did you have far to walk here?"

"No."

"Live near, do you? Near the park perhaps?"

"Quite."

"Nice houses there."

"Yes."

"Your family's or your employer's?"

The girl's gaze came down to meet Maisie's. "I don't know what you mean."

"I mean, do you live or work at the house?"

"It's no business of yours. You ask too many questions."

"I was only trying to be friendly. I like to be friends. All the other girls and me get on well together."

"Then leave me alone. I want no friends."

"No friends? That's silly. Everyone needs friends."

"Why?" The question shot out like an arrow, direct and unequivocal. Maisie faltered.

"Well, we all need friends. Life's no fun without them, is it?"

"And life's no fun when we believe in people who then let us down. No trust means no one is hurt."

"You really think that?" Maisie was stunned at such a negative, pessimistic view in one so young and pretty.

"I know it. So leave me alone. I don't need your friendship."

Maisie thought for a moment. A rebuff such as this discouraged her, but she had promised Miss Sybil. She tried again.

"You working tonight?"

"Yes."

"Who you got?"

"They tell me his name is Mr. Cedric."

Maisie remembered him, the paunchy old, gray-haired man who used to come often but had been missing for some weeks. She shuddered at the thought of his trembling touch. Bella was welcome to him. For the first time Bella pursued the conversation.

"Do you know Mr. Celric? What's he like?"

Maisie hesitated. It was not for her to discourage a newcomer. "Oh, he's all right. Not young, you know, but quite pleasant. Many of our customers are middle-aged, successful men. Mr. Cedric's quite agreeable, and usually quite generous, I understand."

"How old?"

"Oh, fifties, I'd say."

The girl on the bed shuddered. Suddenly Maisie realized. She was afraid, apprehensive, and that was why she was so prickly. Sympathy flooded her.

"Here, you're nervous, aren't you? You're frightened

'cos it's your first time. That's why you was so surly—you're not really so bad-tempered, it's just that you're nervous. Well, cheer up, love, it's not that bad. We're all friends here, and we'll all vouch for that."

The girl leaped upright, her eyes brittle with flashing light. "I am not afraid, and I do not need your friendship, as I told you. Stay clear of me or I could lash out at you, I warn you, if you probe too far."

Maisie shrank back. "I did not mean to pry, not out of malice, that is. I meant you no harm."

"But I do! Take warning now—last time I was here I watched a spider up there." She flung one arm toward the ceiling. "Another spider approached too close, and within minutes he was a corpse, milked dry and hung like a trophy on her web. That is what will happen to those who try to come too close to me."

She sat on the bed, all fire gone. Maisie shivered, unable to speak or leave. Bella went on talking softly.

"I looked up insects in my books, but I could find no reference to that spider. But I did find the praying mantis. Do you know the mantis?"

Maisie shook her head nervously. If it was like the spider, she did not want to know.

"It's called the praying mantis because it sits up with its front legs together like this." Bella laid her palms together flat, like children in Sunday school, Maisie remembered. "It should really be called the preying mantis, with an *e*, for it is really lying in wait for its victim."

"Oh, like the spider waiting for a fly."

"Or for her mate, yes. And when a victim approaches, she leaps and bites. Her jaws are so strong that she often snaps off the head of her husband as he approaches."

"Ugh! How horrid!"

"But do you know, nature is so powerful that the poor decapitated male goes on to mate with her even so. How do you fancy a headless lover, Maisie?"

"Oh, Bella! How could you! It makes me feel quite sick!"

"Does it? I find it exciting that the male is so infatuated with the female that he even defies death for her. Rather romantic, I feel."

"It's disgusting! And you a lady, too!"

"Am I, Maisie? How can you tell?"

"I just know it. You are, aren't you?"

"I don't know. I don't know who I am."

Maisie had a sudden, unwelcome thought. This girl was so strange and unpredictable and spoke so oddly—could it be that she was mad? She'd better mention it to Miss Sybil, just in case.

As if summoned by the thought, Miss Sybil knocked at that moment and came in. She smiled at the girls.

"I hope you two are getting on well together, but I'm afraid for the moment I must separate you. Mr. Henry has just arrived, Maisie, and is waiting for you in the vestibule. A word with you before you go, however."

She drew Maisie out into the corridor and closed the door behind her. Not that Bella appeared to care, reflected Maisie, for she showed no flicker of interest when Miss Sybil entered.

Miss Sybil's fingers closed softly on Maisie's shoulder. "Now are you well prepared, my dear? Madame tells me you are often forgetful about taking precautions, and that we cannot have. I trust you remembered the sponge and vinegar?"

Maisie hung her head, but even so her watchful eye could glimpse Miss Sybil's sternly admonishing look. "Now, Maisie, you *must* be punctilious about these matters," the gentle voice reproved. "It is a safeguard both against infection and against conception. Return to your room at once and see to it."

"But, Miss Sybil, it is hardly necessary tonight. Mr. Henry usually can't manage to—"

"You mean he is impotent? Even so, my dear, the

stimulus of a pretty and lively girl like you could ensure that for once he is not. So see to it at once."

"Yes, ma'am."

The older woman's sharp gaze softened and she led Maisie farther from the bedroom door, lowering her voice. "How did you fare with Bella? Did you discover anything about her?"

"Very little," Maisie replied in a conspiratorial whisper. "She doesn't like questions. She got very cross with me."

"Did you learn nothing then?"

"Only that she seems to live in a big house near Regent's Park. Oh, and she has books. She's been reading about insects, spiders and things."

Miss Sybil nodded. "As I guessed. She's probably a governess. Well, that will suffice for now, but see what else you can discover when the opportunity occurs."

"I hardly like to, miss. She warned me she'd snap my head off if I interfered, like a praying mantle or something."

"Mantis. Did she now? Such aggression would seem to indicate vulnerability. I wonder what she fears."

"That's what I thought. She's frightened, but she wouldn't have it."

"Thank you, Maisie. Go down now to your gentleman. I must introduce Bella and Mr. Cedric."

It was as Miss Sybil turned to reenter the bedroom that Maisie realized Bella was standing at the door, leaning against the frame nonchalantly, a half-smile curving her lips. How much she had overheard it was impossible to tell. Miss Sybil at least did not show surprise, for Maisie heard her address the girl imperturbably before she moved away.

"Ah, Bella. A word with you now, my dear."

"Will you walk into my parlor?" Maisie heard the mocking reply, and shuddered as she remembered the nursery rhyme from her childhood. "Will you walk into my parlor, said a spider to a fly. 'Tis the prettiest little parlor that ever you did espy." Miss Bella's preoccupation with spiders was singularly unattractive, and Maisie felt relieved that Bella's disinclination to be friends would relieve her from further intimacy with her.

It was later, much later that night, toward dawn in fact, before Bella came to mind again. In the meantime Mr. Henry had kept Maisie well occupied, treating her to supper and champagne, and for once had had very nearly achieved his ambition. He was a pleasant enough young man, broad and ruddy as a country yokel but with an unfortunate stammer. Secretly Maisie believed both his stammer and his incapacity in the art of love were due to his domineering mother, of whom Mr. Henry often spoke. It must be difficult for him to maintain any degree of ardor when a stern mama's latest edicts filled his thoughts and conversation, even as he lay in Maisie's arms.

"I'm getting b-better, aren't I, Maisie? I nearly m-made it tonight, didn't I?" His anxious red face sought her approval as he dressed to go in the dawn light.

"You did, love. You soon will," she responded reassuringly from under the bedcovers. There was no need to rise and dress to see him out. Miss Sybil or Madame would be waiting below to ensure satisfaction had been achieved and the reckoning paid, before seeing each client out to a cab.

"I'll c-come again soon, then, Maisie. Good night, my dear." As he opened the door to leave, Maisie could hear low voices along the corridor. Evidently another client was almost making his departure.

"A lovely night, my dear," a voice like cracked china was saying. That was Mr. Cedric, his silvery old voice transmuted in an attempt to subdue itself to a discreet whisper. "I shall ask Madame to keep you solely for me."

Bella's answer, if any, Maisie did not hear. After the footsteps of the departing gentlemen had faded away down the stairs, she began to grow anxious. It had been Bella's first time, unfledged virgin as she was. How had she reacted to the shock of her first encounter with a man—and an old one at that? Quickly Maisie rose and pulled on the pink peignoir hanging on a hook behind the door. She loved the feel of its silky texture clinging to her naked skin.

Her tap at Bella's door evoked no answer. Curiously Maisie opened it and peeped in, unwilling to disturb the new girl if she was sleeping. But Bella lay supine, naked and wide awake, staring at the ceiling, her skin pale and lustrous in the light of the lamp on the bedside table.

"Bella?"

The girl neither moved nor spoke. But for her staring eyes she could have been asleep. Maisie came nearer the bed. "Bella. Are you all right?"

Blue eyes roved down from the ceiling to meet hers, but Maisie was aghast to see how vacant the eyes were, as if the girl were in a trance. Bella did not seem to see her at all. Had the ordeal been too much for her? Maisie laid a hand on Bella's limp, cold one.

"Bella, what is it? Don't you feel well?"

Bella stared but did not answer. Maisie, alarmed, was about to hurry downstairs in search of Miss Sybil when she heard Bella's voice, flat and expressionless.

"The routine of card leaving. A lady should bid her footman inquire if the mistress of the house is at home. If not, and it is her first call, she should bid him leave three cards, one of her own and two of her husband's or father's. Her card is for the mistress of the house, and her husband's or father's are for both master and mistress."

"Bella! What are you talking about?"

Maisie was quite at a loss to understand. The girl must be ill, rambling about etiquette at a time like this. She hurried downstairs. Miss Sybil, already dressed, was just emerging from Madame's parlor.

"Miss Sybil, I think Bella is ill. She does not speak except to talk about leaving cards. I wish you would come and see her."

"I'll come at once. I was coming to her in any event to ensure all was well. I'll follow you in a moment."

Maisie retraced her steps upstairs, stopping for a few minutes at the water closet. When she emerged, Miss Sybil reached the head of the stairs.

"Is she feverish, Maisie?"

"I don't think so. Her hands were cold."

Both women stopped at Bella's door, which stood ajar. A glance inside was enough to see the room was empty. A silk nightdress lay on the floor.

"She's gone. The back door at the foot of the servants' stairs is open."

Maisie followed her into Bella's room. True, Bella's clothes were gone and only her elegant gown lay across the chair. From the window Maisie could see a shadowy figure turn the corner of the street and disappear.

"There she is. Shall I go after her, miss?"

Miss Sybil shook her dark head. "It would be too late by the time you dress. Besides, we have no say over her comings and goings. I hope she comes back tomorrow for Mr. Cedric is so happy that he is prepared to pay very handsomely for her services. She has done well tonight. We have need of such as Bella Marchant."

"Then she'll be back—if only to claim her wages," said Maisie confidently. "Don't worry, Miss Sybil. Only she was talking funny. I do hope she isn't sick."

Miss Sybil was looking into the top drawer of the dressing chest. "She was talking about leaving cards, you say?"

"Yes. The routine of card leaving, she said."

"Then I wonder if we have been mistaken in our opinion about Miss Marchant, after all. Perhaps she is, in fact, a lady."

"What makes you say that, miss?"

"Because she brought a maid last time, and tonight she leaves her clothes and underwear scattered and the drawers untidy, as though she were accustomed to the services of a maid. And because she leaves these."

She held up a sovereign and a pearl pin.

"That looks like Mr. Cedric's tie pin," Maisie remarked.

"Exactly. A present to Bella, perhaps, and the sovereign too? If so, she evidently attaches little importance to either. If she does not take her sovereign, perhaps she will not return for her wages either. That young lady is a mystery, Maisie. There is more to her than meets the eye."

Maisie's curiosity leaped into life. "I'll dress and go look for her," she said with determination, and before Miss Sybil could protest, she was hastily dressed in day dress and a jacket. Leaving her hair down and unpinned, she hurried out by the servants' door.

The morning air was fresh and cool on Maisie's face as she walked quickly up the street and around the corner toward the park. Few souls were yet astir, except for the milkman, who doffed his cap and grunted a polite "good morning" as she hurried past. On any other occasion Maisie would have been tempted to stop and stroke the nose of the old gray horse pulling his milk cart, but not this morning. Past the park railings she scurried, oblivious of the sleepers on the benches who were beginning to emerge from their wrappings of newspaper, intent only on trying to catch up with the slim figure of Bella.

At the far end of the park she thought she caught a glimpse of her, slowly turning a corner into a square. But by the time Maisie reached the corner she found the square deserted. Only a maidservant stood at the top of a flight of steps of one of the villas, busy with her yellow duster polishing up the brass handle and door knocker. Hope faded. Slowly Maisie turned and retraced her steps to Rosamund Street.

Miss Sybil was drinking tea with Madame de Sandrier in Madame's parlor. She turned on Maisie's entrance.

"Did you find her?"

"No, miss. I thought I saw her near Hanbury Square, but if it was her, I lost her."

"Never mind," said Madame soothingly. "She will be back." She sounded very content. Mr. Henry must have been very pleased indeed for Madame to sound so equable. In her blue silk wrap and with her face as carefully made up as in the early evening, she looked as imposing and regal as she always did. Maisie yawned.

"I hope we can be sure of her return," Miss Sybil remarked as she sipped her tea. "Has she signed a contract with you yet, Madame?"

Madame shook her red curls. "No, and that was strange. I gave her the contract when she came last night, and she handed it back to me. She said she could not read, which struck me as very odd."

"Not read? I don't believe it!" The incredulity in Miss Sybil's voice was evident. "Moreover, did you not tell me, Maisie, that she told you she had been reading books at home?"

"Yes, miss, about insects."

"Then the girl is evidently a liar," Madame pronounced coolly. "But no harm. We have the measure of her and have dealt with harder girls in our time. She will learn to adapt to our ways."

I wonder, thought Maisie. Bella Marchant seemed a tougher proposition than her quiet manner would lead one to believe.

"And she is of use to us yet, as a virgin," Miss Sybil added. Maisie pricked up her ears.

"Not now, surely, not after last night. And anyway, I always meant to ask—why is a virgin so desirable? Why not a woman of more experience?"

She would not have liked to admit, even to herself, that her pride was hurt. Why should these two set so much store by a new girl rather than her, with her twelve months' experience of Madame's establishment? She noticed the quick look that passed between the two women, a look that was a mixture of conspiracy and amusement.

"Tell her the old wives' tale, Sybil."

Miss Sybil turned toward Maisie. "There is an old belief, held for centuries, that a man afflicted with what is commonly called a dose of the clap can be cured by having relations with a virgin. Mr. Cedric has been so afflicted and his doctor pronounces him cured, but Mr. Cedric wished to ensure the cure. Hence his desire for a virgin."

Maisie stared in horror. "The clap? But Madame is always so careful to see we don't catch it, with our own doctor and all! Why would she deliberately let a girl run the risk?"

"In this case there was little risk, Maisie."

Maisie's anger flared. "And the fee he offered was too high to ignore, I'll bet. So Bella, in her ignorance, had to be sacrificed. I think it's a crying shame, that's what it is. Her first time here and you cheat her like that. The poor girl was frightened enough as it was, and now she's gone and not knowing that she's probably got a dreadful disease. I'll find her and tell her, that's what I'll do!"

"Now calm yourself, Maisie. There is no cause for alarm." Miss Sybil's voice was calmly reassuring, and Maisie wanted to hear her say all was well. Miss Sybil seemed honest enough. "As I said, Mr. Cedric was cured before he came. Moreover, there is no possibility that he can have infected Bella."

"How can you possibly know that, after he's spent all night with her?" Maisie demanded.

Madame's smooth voice cut in. "Sybil is right, Maisie. He cannot have done any harm to the girl because he did not touch her. He told me so himself."

"Not touch her? Was she too frightened after all, then?"

"On the contrary, it seems she was anxious enough, but he could not bring himself to it."

Another impotent client, thought Maisie with grim

amusement. Madame's elegant establishment would soon earn itself a reputation as a house for incapables.

"He is an old man approaching senility, I fear," Madame went on. "It seems he was so touched by her youthful eagerness and her fair virginal appearance that he preferred to spend his time worshiping her as a deity rather than as a human being. Odd, but there is no understanding the ways of men, as we have learned. We must simply humor their whims."

Maisie grunted. "Sounds peculiar, if you ask me."

Madame sighed patiently. "I am not asking you, Maisie, but I hoped by now you would understand our function. We are here to cater for all men's sexual demands, whether we consider them quirks or not. By helping them to act out their fantasies we help them, so if Mr. Cedric wants to reserve Bella for his own use, to worship her as a goddess or not, that is for him to decide. He is paying."

"He who pays the piper calls the tune."

"Precisely, Maisie. Now go up to bed and have a good sleep. I shall see a good breakfast is ready for you at noon."

"Curious," Maisie heard Miss Sybil say as she turned to go, "that you should describe us as social do-gooders while in other times we would have either been branded as whores or burned as witches."

"And we still are reviled as criminals by many," Madame replied. Maisie heard no more. It was just a job of work, she reflected as she climbed the stairs, pleasanter than many jobs but just as tiring. Oh, how glad she would be to be between the sheets at last—alone, to sleep.

In Hanbury Square Laura rose slowly when the sound of the bell echoed through the villa. For some reason her head felt strangely heavy and throbbed with the effort of dressing. Laura steeled herself. She could not afford to become ill, for today was Friday and Anna must be watched with care.

Miss Oliphant was in the corridor outside when Laura left her room. She, too, looked weary, but made an effort to smile.

"Good morning, Miss Laura. Did you sleep well?"

"Very well, thank you. And you?"

"Thank you, yes, and I heard not a sound from Anna's room all night."

"Nor I."

At that moment Anna emerged from her room to join them in the procession to morning prayers. She must have slept well, thought Laura, for there was a contented smile playing about her lips. Across Anna's fair head she encountered Charles Lazenby's dark gaze, and he nodded. Conspiratorially Laura smiled. Between them they would see to it that Anna came to no harm.

The sultry heaviness of the day did not account for Laura's unusually heavy, aching head. Throughout the day she felt it increasingly difficult to concentrate whether on Emily's strictures on ladylike behavior or on Anna's lighthearted chat. Her cousin was unusually good-humored today, Laura noted, but it was annoying that Anna seemed so amiably communicative on a day when Laura felt completely unable to respond.

But it was Friday, she kept reminding herself, and no time to begin being ill. Whatever the feeling in her head betokened, Laura was resolved to keep it at bay. But the ache intensified when Charles Lazenby caught her arm and drew her aside.

"Robert cannot come, Laura, at least, not yet. He's promised to come next week."

Laura groaned. "That could be too late, Charles. If she goes out tonight . . ."

"We must see to it that she does not," Lazenby cut in forcibly. Then he cocked his head. "You look pale, Laura. Are you ill?"

Laura shook her head. "A headache, that is all. It will soon pass."

"Then don't forget—call me if Anna stirs tonight. I'll see to it she does not escape."

But Lazenby had not bargained for his employer's dedication to work. After dinner that night Laura heard her uncle bid his secretary attend him in the study.

"We'll compile all the reports together and prepare my speech," Uncle Reginald said as he rose from the table. "With luck we should have it done by midnight."

In dismay Laura watched the secretary's tall figure follow her uncle out of the dining room. Now it was up to her. If Anna made a move to go, it would be well before midnight.

For a time both girls sat reading, and at ten o'clock Anna yawned and stretched her arms. "Time for bed, Laura dear. You look tired. Come, I'll ring for our hot chocolate. Let's drink it upstairs, shall we?"

Anna rang the bell and waited until the maid had come and gone again. Laura rose to follow her upstairs, determined not to let Anna from her sight. Perhaps she could suggest sleeping with Anna.

"But why, my dear?" Anna asked, her eyebrows raised.

"In case you should dream again," Laura replied.

"Not I, for I do not feel upset at all."

Anna turned away, to pour out the hot chocolate the maid had placed on a side table. Laura heard the sound of the liquid pouring into the china cups.

"One spoon of sugar?" Anna inquired, her back turned toward Laura.

"Please." Over the side table, in the small mirror flanked by gilt cherubs, Laura could see Anna's face as she stirred. Instead of the calm smile of contentment, an excited look now colored Anna's pale face, her lips parted and her blue eyes gleaming. As Laura watched, the expression changed to a savage, sneering look. There was pure malice in those blue eyes, and at the same time she heard again the low, mocking laugh she had heard before.

"What is it, Anna? What amuses you?"

Anna turned and came toward her with the steaming cup of chocolate. "Amuses me? Why, nothing, my dear." The look and the laugh had completely disappeared and Anna's face wore its usual expression of sweet innocence. "Come, drink up your chocolate while it is hot, Laura, and then I'll tuck you into bed. You really do look dreadfully tired."

But I won't sleep, Laura vowed inwardly. Now I am convinced you plan mischief, Anna, and I intend to thwart you. Even if my head is throbbing and my eyes feel heavy. And as Laura rose to go to her room she discovered that her limbs, too, felt as though they were made of lead, stiff and cumbersome and barely able to walk. Anna watched her in concern.

"You are ill, Laura! I must call Emily," she cried, and before Laura could stop her, she had run and fetched the housekeeper. Miss Oliphant took Laura's arm and helped her walk unsteadily to her room.

"She is not well, Emily," Anna kept repeating. "She has not been well all day. It would be as well for you to stay by her tonight in case she needs you."

"To be sure I will," Emily responded soothingly as she helped Laura undress. "I'll stay right by her side all night. My goodness, you do feel rather hot, my dear. I do hope you aren't going to have a fever."

Laura tried to protest, to wave away the helping hands and undress herself, but it was no use. Her legs were unsteady now, almost too weak to support her, and her head was spinning dizzily.

She clutched Emily's arm as Anna left the room. "No, not me, Emily! Watch Anna—see to Anna—she needs you."

"Of course, my dear," Emily murmured, reaching for Laura's nightgown. "Just let's get you to bed first."

Laura swayed and fell on the bed. "Emily—Anna! Please! Don't let her go!"

A white face hovered like a crescent moon in the mist above her, and then Laura lost consciousness.

Chapter Twelve

Lionel Travers felt his apprehension beginning to lessen and fade away as he sipped the glass of Madeira the red-haired Madame had given him. When he had at first arrived at the establishment, he had felt a trifle dismayed at its elegance and tasteful furnishing, for it was not what he was accustomed to.

Not in a brothel, anyway. Not that he had visited many, for his passing amours up to now had usually been ladies of easy virtue one encountered in coffee houses or the public house, ladies who sat alone sipping a glass of port and lemon, casting covert glances from under lowered lashes. Lionel and his friends knew now how to recognize and respond to these glances, and how such encouragement led to a quick tumble in a rather drab apartment somewhere nearby.

Or there were the actresses, pert and pretty, who laughingly agreed to a candlelight supper and a furtive embrace in a back room. They, and their less fortunate sisters one could pick up on a street corner, Lionel knew well. But the street girls usually took one back to a rather dreary hotel with a greasy madame and a huge-limbed protector who eyed one speculatively. This house was very different.

He glanced about the room, evidently Madame's main parlor, where fresh-looking and well-dressed girls plied their male companions with wine while one played the piano softly. None of these girls had the wan, tired appearance of most of the whores he had come across. He wondered hopefully if his companion of the evening, this Bella, would be as attractive as the rest. So far she had not appeared. Madame had said she would be down soon.

A raven-haired beauty led her man friend toward the door. "Come with me, monsieur," she invited him in a deliciously soft and purring French accent. Lionel could feel his blood coursing more rapidly in his veins. Dammit, why was his girl taking so long? He was growing impatient.

At last the chenille curtains across the arched doorway swung back, and Madame, with the many rings and glittering jewels, reentered, followed by a fair girl. Madame advanced upon him, beaming.

"Mr. Lionel, may I present to you Miss Bella. I regret she has kept you waiting so long, but I am sure she will make amends for her tardiness, will you not, Bella?"

His gaze traveled on past Madame's plump figure to inspect the girl. Under the outlandish Oriental-style garb she was wearing, it was difficult to ascertain just what manner of girl she was. Blond, evidently, for a cloud of fair curls cascaded from under the veiled and jeweled headdress she wore, and her eyes were decidedly alluring, deep blue and smoky as they appraised him. But for her other features he could not judge, for she wore a veil across the lower half of her face.

"Good evening, Mr. Lionel."

Her voice was low and pleasant, and her fingers slim and smooth as she extended her hand to take his. Lionel gripped her hand and stared into the smoky depths of her eyes. "Good evening, Bella."

"I'll leave you two to get to know each other," Madame murmured, and glided away to greet her other guests.

"Will you sit and take more wine?" Bella asked.

"I have been sitting and taking wine," Lionel replied.

"Then shall we go up to my room?" The eyes lowered

gently, her translucent lids veiling them from his sight. He felt his blood pounding.

"Yes, yes." He could not hide the eagerness in his voice. After all, she had kept him waiting in order to whet his appetite, hadn't she? The room, Madame, the other girls and clients, all faded from his view. All he wanted now was to be alone with this mysterious creature, to wrench off the veil and discover her delights. Pray heaven he would not be disillusioned!

"Then come." She led the way, her movements slow and graceful, while Lionel followed, trying not to stumble and trip in his excitement. The half-subdued tumult within him reminded him of his seventh birthday. Mama had come to the nursery, kissed him, and bid him follow her to see his birthday present. The maddening frustration and excitement of the walk downstairs and out across the stable yard he could remember still. And the delight of discovering at last in the stable the wiry-haired pony that was to be his very own.

As this little blond filly preceding him now would soon be. As she mounted the stairs ahead of him, he watched the sinuous movement of her slender hips, the hand-span waist and her slim legs barely concealed beneath the voluminous gauze trousers she wore.

Along the corridor at the top of the stairs she went, throwing open a door at last.

"Enter," she said.

Lionel went in. It was a beautiful room, a paradise for lovers. Silk drapes hung across the walls, a rich red sofa was surrounded by scattered rugs and cushions. A low table held a bowl of fruit and two silver goblets, and the air was heady with a strange, exotic perfume. Bella sprawled lazily on the sofa and patted the seat beside her.

"Please be seated." As he sat, he could smell the sweetness of her flesh. His pulse began racing.

"Bella," he murmured. "Your name means beautiful

one. Let me remove your veil and see if in truth you are as lovely as your name."

As his hand rose to her face, her slim fingers covered his. "Why such haste, Mr. Lionel? Do you not like what you see?"

He breathed deeply. "Indeed I do. Your slender body and gleaming hair set me on fire." His hand moved to caress her hair, and she allowed him to stroke its softness. Like a cat she was, purring and sinuous and aloof. He let his caress run on down from her hair over her neck, her fine firm body. She stretched voluptuously. It was all he could do not to fling her down and throw himself upon her, so fierce a desire she stirred in him. But he must control himself. She was no ordinary woman of the streets. Those one could assail without wooing, use and discard without feeling, but here was a creature who, beautiful or not, would expect finesse as her due.

Lionel hesitated. Finesse was unknown to him, for he had not encountered a whore of her standing before. Conversation was probably expected of him, either before or as an accompaniment to action.

"Tell me about yourself, Bella," he murmured as he reached again for the tantalizing veil. This time her hand did not stay him.

"I am a witch," she replied in a whisper. The piece of gauze fell away to reveal an adorable face, small-featured and delicate with lips that held a promising pout. He yearned to kiss them—but, hold, not yet.

"A witch?" he repeated, barely aware of the words' significance. He was imagining the feel of those soft lips, yielding and vibrant, the weight of those slim arms about his neck, and the feel of that firm body under his.

"My mother was seventh daughter of a seventh daughter. That bestows upon me mystical powers. I can summon up strange powers to do my bidding."

"So you can cast spells and brew potions?" he

murmured teasingly as his hand caressed the curve of her young bosom.

"And more. Far more. I can curse those who cross me so that they never prosper. The powers of darkness are mine to command, to desecrate a life or to bestow untold riches and prosperity." She moved a little, curving her body against his own. Fire raged in Lionel's veins. He held her close against him.

"Long ago my forebears were rulers in the Orient. Madame laughs that I call myself Queen of the East, but it is not so far from the truth. In the East we knew marvels that the West has not yet learned. You shall see, Lionel. Come, hold me closer and kiss me."

Eagerly he obeyed, and the raging fire roared into an inferno. Fierce joy filled him when he felt demanding fingers loosening his clothing. He need wait and play the diplomat no longer.

"Come, my beautiful spider, I am waiting for you." Wild blue eyes stared up at him, and Lionel gave himself over to rapture. Ecstasy came too swiftly. Within moments he was lying, exhausted and panting in her arms.

Bella smiled and drew a wrap about her. "You are an ardent, even overzealous, lover. You will do better next time, I know it."

Next time? Tonight? Unusual. Whores usually threw one out rapidly after the event. Weary but content, Lionel began to doze. Within moments he was awakened by Bella's urgent hands.

"Come, my love, again, please."

Dutifully he mustered the energy to begin again, but it was some time before desire matched his effort. Violet-blue eyes searched him.

"Do I make you happy, Lionel?"

"Blissfully."

"Then make me happy." Seizing his hands she guided them to her will. For one so fragile-looking and ethereal, she had the energy and lascivity of an animal. Lionel felt delight rising again. This time it was longer and slower, ecstasy eddying relentlessly to an unhurried climax. He was in a wheeling vortex of delirium. And when it was finally over, Bella too lay panting and smiling radiantly.

"Wonderful, my lovely spider."

For a moment he lay, too exhausted and breathless to question her odd endearment. She was sitting up, looking down at his prostrate, half-naked figure.

"My first trophy," she murmured happily.

He lay there looking up at her and thinking what a wonderful woman she was. So lively, so accomplished, unlike those other women. She was beautiful too. Whatever charge Madame might make for her services, he would certainly visit this tantalizing girl again.

Bella leaned over toward the low table, the wrap slipping from her shoulders to reveal one small breast. "A goblet of wine, Lionel, to refresh you before we make love again?"

He sipped the wine, wondering. It was not yet midnight and he had booked to stay the whole night with this enchantress. After their third encounter Lionel began to feel embarrassed. He had never been put to the test like this before. Would he have the stamina to match up to Bella's desires? Embarrassment caused his stutter to recur.

"D-don't you think it time we had a little sleep, Bella?" he said at length.

She sighed. "Ten minutes then, and I'll wake you."

And she did. Three times he slept briefly and three times more she woke him. Finally, at dawn, she allowed him to sleep a whole hour together. When Lionel finally rose to leave, he wondered if his legs would carry him to the door. Even then he feared she might twine her arms about his neck and plead with him to begin again.

"G-good-bye, then, Bella. I'll see you again s-soon."

"Did you learn a few of the mysteries of the East, Lionel?" she teased.

"Indeed I did. And I shall return to learn more—soon."

"I am glad. Good-bye, Lionel."

Heavens, what a woman! She was insatiable. Never before had he realized that a woman's ardor could match and even surpass a man's.

"Did you find Miss Bella satisfactory?" Madame was waiting in the vestibule, already up and dressed. Lionel followed her sleepily into her private parlor to settle his dues.

"Entirely, Madame. A wonderful girl."

"Then you will wish to engage her services again?"

"Indeed. Next Friday perhaps?"

Madame flicked the pages of her ledger. "Ah, Friday she is engaged. Would Wednesday suit you?"

"Excellently." Wednesday he usually played cards, but this exciting new find superseded cards. By Wednesday he would have recouped his strength.

"How much do I owe you, Madame."

Mild eyes met his. "Ten guineas, sir."

"Ten guineas?" Lionel could not help the note of surprise in his voice. That was high, even for a high-class whore.

"Well, there was a room for the whole night, the wine, and of course, it always costs more for a virgin, as you know, sir."

"A virgin?" Again the words slipped out involuntarily. Bella had given no sign of being a newcomer to the game, so eager and demanding she had been. But then he remembered her words: "My first trophy." Dismissing the thought that Madame might be trying to dupe him, Lionel felt in his pockets.

"I fear I have only five guineas with me," he was forced to admit reluctantly. "Will you take my I.O.U. for the remaining five? I'll settle it next Wednesday."

Madame sighed. "We do not normally extend our services on credit, sir, but as I believe you are Lord Travers' son . . ."

Lionel admitted that he was.

"Then I'll accept your I.O.U., sir." Cheerfully Madame offered him pen and paper and watched him write, then with a charming smile she bid him *au revoir*.

On the homeward walk in the crisp dawn, Lionel's spirits rose. Dammit, it had been a night to remember. He would have something to brag about over the card game now—he had taken his first virgin, hadn't he? And he had made it six times in one night—or was it seven? He could not clearly remember anymore. Seven, that's what he'd say anyway.

The girl was indefatigable, there was no doubt about that. She would have gone on yet if he had not made his escape. Lionel was curious. Women were not supposed to be as insatiable as that, so far as he knew. He wondered if Dalrymple would find her eagerness unusual. He must tell Robert about her, suggest he visit her even. Or perhaps not. He'd like to keep the ravishing creature to himself, but he'd tell Robert about her anyway.

What a superb, fettlesome filly Bella was! He'd certainly nurse his energies to meet her again. There could not be a gentleman in London with a more beautiful, more accomplished or more alluring mistress than he had. He could forget the actresses and the street-corner wenches now. Then a fleeting thought dampened him. She was costly. And Papa was already bleating about his son's extravagance.

With sunny optimism Lionel pushed the unpleasant thought aside. He'd find the money somehow—and anyway, it couldn't cost ten guineas again for a girl who was no longer a virgin. He'd manage.

Lord Travers was sitting alone at the breakfast table reading *The Times* when Lionel came in. He would hardly have time to read it today as thoroughly as he liked, occupied as he would be with his mail and creditors even coming to the house. Distasteful as Braithwaite's proposition might appear, it would certainly allay a pressing need. He would have to broach the subject with Lionel.

Lord Travers could hear the butler's discreet voice in the hallway before Lionel came into the dining room. He made for the side table where the decanter and glasses stood.

"Good morning, my boy."

"Oh, Papa, I didn't see you there. Care for a glass of port?"

Lord Travers growled. "No, I'm eating breakfast."

How like his mother he was, fair and lean and fragile. The father could not help wishing the boy had a firmer jaw and less full lips. He looked far too effeminate to command respect.

"Help yourself to some porridge and sit with me, Lionel. I want to talk to you."

"Oh, not about my debts again, Papa. I'm so tired. I really have tried to cut down my expenditure. Has that wretch Dunn been here again about my gambling debts? I told him I'd straighten up with him at the end of the month."

"No, he hasn't. But I've had a business proposition put to me today that could solve our financial problems, if you are agreeable."

"I leave business affairs to you, Papa." Lionel sighed wearily. "You're so much shrewder and more practical than I. I'm sure whatever you decide will be right."

"But this concerns you, Lionel. Have you met Miss Anna Braithwaite?"

Sinking into a chair at the table, the young man shook his head. "Should have done—Gertrude arranged a picnic once—but I didn't fancy the sound of her. From what Gertrude says she's a bit of a bore. Why?"

"Because her father is a wealthy man and would like to see his daughter in line for a title one day. He offers his money in exchange for her marriage to you."

Lionel's jaw sagged open. "Marriage—to a Yorkshire

girl with no breeding and nothing to offer? What a ridiculous notion!"

"Not so ridiculous when you consider that he and we both gain what we want. His thousands will solve our present problems, and you will inherit his thriving mills."

"But I know nothing about running mills, or any other kind of business."

Lord Travers spread his hands. "That is no problem. A good manager will take all the work off your hands. Remember, a good income will be assured. Think it over, Lionel. I've promised Braithwaite a reply soon."

The young man stared moodily into his glass. "A drastic way to solve our problems, isn't it? Couldn't we raise a loan or mortgage one of the houses instead?"

"The girl is pretty, I believe, and no peasant like her father. Her mother was of good stock. A dutiful girl, too, I'm told, so she wouldn't try to interfere with your way of life, I'm sure."

Lionel grunted. His father rose and folded his napkin. "Well, my boy, think it over and let me know."

His son lay his head down on the table and began to snore.

Laura opened her eyes with difficulty and stirred feebly, her head pounding as if a thousand hammers were beating her brain to a pulp. Emily Oliphant's anxious face was still bending over her, and Laura fought desperately to try to remember what it was she must do. Something urgent, something vital . . .

"Anna! Emily, watch her! It's Friday, don't let her go out!"

"There, there, my dear. Rest and don't fret, for you are ill. Sleep, Laura, there's a good girl."

"I can't! Anna!" Laura gasped weakly.

"Anna is well, but you are not. The doctor says you have a fever and must rest and sleep."

"Let me see Anna!"

"No, I'm sorry. The doctor says it's too early to say what kind of a fever you have, but for safety's sake you must be isolated. You are burning hot, my dear, so let me give you a cool drink and then sleep."

"Doctor?" Laura repeated in a whisper. "I have seen no doctor. I only felt ill tonight."

"Last night, Laura. The doctor came today while you slept."

Laura's brain refused to acknowledge what Emily was saying. "It's Friday," she whispered.

"It's Saturday evening now. Now drink this and sleep," Emily said firmly, and placing a cup to Laura's lips, she forced the cold, sweet liquid down her throat. Laura coughed and pushed the cup weakly away.

"It can't be! No, it can't!"

And then the blackness closed in on her again.

As always on a Saturday night the house in Rosamund Street was busy. By now most of the activity had moved from the main parlor to the upstairs rooms, and Miss Sybil found a moment to talk to Madame de Sandrier.

"Is Bella here tonight? Has she a client?" Sybil asked.

"Yes. A newcomer, a Mr. Robert. He told me he sought Bella's services particularly, but his interest was in her mind rather than in her body, he said. Curious, but I agreed."

"Did Bella know what he wanted?"

Madame smiled. "Presumably she does by now. I do not pry. If he is prepared to pay the fee I ask, he may do as he wishes with her. He said he heard of her from Mr. Lionel. I think her fame must be spreading."

"Do you know who he is?"

"I am too discreet to inquire. Discretion, as you know, is our password to success."

"When does Mr. Lionel plan to come again?"

"On Wednesday. We must ensure that Bella returns without fail."

"Leave it to me, Madame. I shall see she is satisfied that all is as she requests."

Upstairs Sybil met Maisie on the landing, just closing the door of Solange's room.

"What are you doing there, Maisie? Where is your gentleman?"

Maisie flushed. "He's been asleep for ages. I was watching Bella through the peephole."

"Why?"

"'Cos I was curious. There's been voices talking all evening. All talk, no action. I wanted to see what she was up to."

"And what did you discover?"

"Just that. She's lying on the bed, alone, and he's sitting on a chair, writing. Been like that for hours. Must be daft, that man."

"Hush, Maisie, or he'll hear you. Back to your own room now—your gentleman may be awake and in need of refreshment or amusement."

"Daft," Maisie muttered, and went into her room.

Robert Dalrymple looked at the girl on the bed. It was difficult to learn anything from her facial expression, for she had insisted on keeping the lower half of her face veiled in heavy gauze. He'd have to take Lionel's word for it that she was pretty. All he could see was the high, intelligent forehead and the blue eyes, slightly dulled at the moment. She had responded well to hypnosis, still in a light state of trance, but even so she maintained a certain guard. It was like prizing open a stubborn oyster. More often than not she kept silent when others would have answered his questions responsively.

She kept staring at the ceiling, he noticed. Curiosity prodded him.

"What do you see on the ceiling, Bella?"

"Spiders."

He looked up. The white ceiling was unmarred.

"Do you like spiders?"

With closed eyes she nodded.

"And other insects?"

Her answer was low. "Predatory ones, like the praying mantis."

Odd. He made a note. "Look, Bella. See what I am drawing."

He came around the side of the bed. Bella opened her eyes but did not move. Robert sketched a housefly.

"Horrid. Pull its wings off," Bella said.

So her interest was not in all insects. She betrayed a streak of cruelty, and he wondered why. Another line of inquiry occurred to him. He sketched a picture of an open book. Bella watched with dull eyes.

"What is the book, Bella?"

"Mr. Browning's poems."

"Have you read them?"

"Yes." She leaned up on her elbow and stared into the distance. "I remember.

> I struck him. He grovelled, of course—
> For what was his force?
> I pinned him to earth with my weight
> and persistence of hate:
> And he lay, would not moan, would not curse,
> As his lot might be worse.

There, I remember that."

"What does it mean, Bella?"

She shrugged and lay down again, her momentary interest gone. "Men should be pinned down, trapped by hate. They force women to hate them."

He tried again to make her go on, but she would say no more. Robert scribbled notes. At least he had learned one thing—hatred of men was Bella's driving force. The reason for her intense hatred would have to be discovered at another session. It was high time he awoke her.

Dalrymple rose and made his way around the bed to waken her gently. Dull eyes followed his movement. As he passed close to a wall, his shoulder caught the flimsy drapery hung across it and lifted the drape to reveal a broad striped maroon-and-cream wallpaper beneath. Bella cried out and turned her face into the pillow. At once Dalrymple's curiosity was awakened.

"What is it, Bella? Don't you like the wallpaper?"

She moaned something into the pillow. Dalrymple grew eager. Inadvertently he could have stumbled upon something significant.

He took his notepad and drew a rectangle and filled in the rectangle with vertical lines. In her reaction he might discover the reason for her aversion to the striped wallpaper.

"Bella, what is that?"

Dull eyes swiveled up from the pillow to the paper. Instantly light leaped into the blue eyes.

"Bars. At the nursery window. Sunlight on the floor. Stripes everywhere. Oh, the beast! The animal! I'll kill him!"

Her eyes stared into space, full of hatred and venom while her fingers clutched at the bedcover and tore frantically at it. Robert leaped to his feet and came to her.

"Rest easy, Bella. Sleep and forget. Sleep, my dear, and when I count to five, you will awake. All will be forgotten, Bella. Sleep easy, Bella, deep and dreamless sleep."

She lay back, still, and closed her eyes. For several minutes he left her thus before waking her. In the meantime he wrote, thoughtfully and with a perplexed frown. There was great trouble in that fair little head sleeping on the pillow. This was going to be a more complicated case than he had anticipated.

Some time after Mr. Robert had paid his dues and left the house, Madame de Sandrier's peace was disturbed by the sound of shrieks from the upper floor. In haste she left her parlor and mounted the stairs, panting a little with the effort of moving her cumbersome body at high speed. It could be two of the girls squabbling again, or a client was maltreating one of her girls, and that would never do. Either way she would have to be firm.

Bella it was, standing by Maisie's door and shouting at her, tugging Maisie's hair as she did so.

"Telltale cat! Can't you keep your nose out of what's not your business? Can't you keep your blabbing mouth shut?"

"What's the matter, Bella?" Madame's voice was calmly authoritative.

Bella let go of Maisie and turned sullenly. "She was prying through the peephole at me, Solange told me. Then she went telling tales to Miss Sybil."

"Return to your room at once, and you, Maisie."

Maisie turned obediently to go, but Bella caught her arm, her eyes glittering viciously.

"Just you remember what I told you. I've got powers, I have, and my curse on you will put paid to your little game, just see if it doesn't."

She let go of Maisie and raised her arm, making a circular movement with her hand in the air and moaning strange words in a singsong chant. Maisie watched wide-eyed, fear distending her pupils.

"There," said Bella. "Now the curse cannot be lifted."

Maisie uttered a faint cry and ran into her room, slamming the door. Madame eyed Bella severely.

"What rubbish is this? Do not try to frighten the girl, Bella, just because she is ignorant."

Bella glared at her. "I do have powers, Madame, as you will see."

"Are you trying to frighten me, girl?" Though Madame's voice was icy with anger, she could feel a prickle on her spine.

"Would you put me to the test, Madame?" The girl's insolence was insufferable. Madame itched to slap her.

The taunting voice went on. "I do believe there are those who would destroy your house and your activities, Madame de Sandrier. A word in the right quarter . . ."

"*You* threaten *me!*" In a voice no more than a whisper Madame stared at her. "Get back to your room at once, my girl. Do you imagine for a moment that you can extort all you desire by threatening me? You have much to learn yet."

Bella watched her go back downstairs, a smile curving the corners of her lips.

Robert Dalrymple rang the doorbell in Hanbury Square. His blond head gleamed in the sunlight as he awaited an answer. At last the butler came.

"Is Mr. Lazenby at home?"

"He is."

"Then be so good as to inquire if he will see me, Robert Dalrymple."

"Come in, sir." Depledge stood back to allow him to enter. A few moments later Dalrymple was sitting in the study with Lazenby. As luck would have it, Mr. Braithwaite was out on business.

"Not come to take up your time, Charles, simply to tell you I met Lionel's Bella and a fascinating creature she seems to be. I shall certainly have to see more of her."

"Pretty, is she?" Lazenby inquired.

"Couldn't say. She was heavily veiled. But I meant that professionally I found her absorbing. A rare case, most stimulating."

"Really? What was unusual about her?" Dalrymple wondered whether he was imagining Lazenby's slightly disinterested tone.

"For one thing she hates men—and she in a job like that. Haven't found out why yet. And stripes upset her wildly. Some psychological significance is that, I'm certain, but it's far too early to tell. Some early-childhood incident with stripes connected—a barred nursery window she mentioned—must have had a marked effect on her."

"How did you find out?"

"Hypnosis, my friend. Inducing the patient into a light trance so that she becomes less defensive. She was still cautious, however; some blockage there that I will have to remove before I can learn more."

"What kind of girl is she?" Lazenby seemed genuinely interested now.

"Intelligent, well-educated. On seeing a picture of a book she began quoting poetry at me."

"She sounds a very interesting creature. Now why should a cultured girl hate men and yet work as a prostitute?"

"That is the mystery I hope to unravel in time. I shall see her again soon."

"And Lionel—how does he feel about her?"

Dalrymple laughed. "I believe he has an appointment to meet her again, but I don't imagine for one moment that his interest is as clinical and detached as mine. I shall see her again, and then your friend soon. Well, I must be on my way and leave you to work. Good of you to see me, Charles. One day next week suit you?"

"To see Anna, you mean? Yes, as soon as you can, Robert. Her cousin, Miss Sutcliffe, is convinced she is ill and that you can help, and I must confess I too am a little disturbed about her."

"Tuesday, then?"

"I'll let you know. At the moment Miss Sutcliffe is ill herself, but I know she'll be glad to hear you are coming. I'll send you a message to confirm."

It was just as Robert reached the door that he remembered. "Oh, yes, by the way, our little Bella is fascinated by insects, it seems. Particularly spiders. Now that's unusual, for most well-bred young ladies scream and faint at the sight of a spider. Cheerio, Charles. *A bientôt.*"

Chapter Thirteen

Lionel could barely wait with patience for Wednesday. By day he thought of Bella and by night he dreamed of her, and by the time Wednesday came, he could contain his impatience no longer. He arrived early at Madame's establishment and was delighted to find Bella was ready.

She held out her arms to him. "Come, my pet, I have been waiting for you."

As she reached up to entwine her arms about his neck, she suddenly paused, a look of revulsion marring her pretty face.

"What a horrible necktie! Take it off at once."

Baffled, Lionel removed it obediently, a trifle disappointed that she evidently found it distasteful. He had chosen it with care with his valet's assistance to enhance his embroidered shirt, a tie of fine silk in tasteful maroon-and-white stripes.

"Revolting," Bella said, taking it from him between finger and disdainful thumb and casting it as far away as she could. "I hate stripes."

The tie forgotten, she slid her arms around his neck. "Your tie pin is a pretty one, Lionel. What is it?"

"This?" He held it up. "Oh, it's a diamond. A gift from Mama once, long ago."

"Give it to me, Lionel. Make me a present of the pin, to show the depth of your love for me."

Her voice, silky smooth and seductive, held a promise of reward to follow such a gift. Lionel pressed it into her hand.

"It is yours, Bella, just as I am."

"Are you mine, Lionel? My servant, my slave?"

"Your abject slave. Yours to command as you will."

She purred contentedly and drew him down onto the sofa. Lionel lost the ability to count time and space, so intoxicating was this exotic woman of the East. All he knew was that by morning he felt satiated, supremely happy. What matter that his legs felt unsteady and he felt as drained as a wrung-out sponge?

"My beautiful spider," Bella murmured before he left, stroking his hair and obviously as contented as he was.

"Why do you call me your spider, Bella?"

"Because you are caught in my web. Are you not content to be enmeshed, Lionel."

"Completely." He sighed.

"And what gift will you bring me next time?"

"What would you like?"

She considered. "A little dog would be impractical. A horse, perhaps, or a carriage? That would be pleasant, to have a carriage of my own."

Lionel almost choked in surprise. He had expected her to ask for a scarf or a ring or some such trifle, but a carriage would set him back hundreds. Papa would not stand for that.

"Oh, surely not a carriage, Bella. I have seen a pretty garnet ring at the jeweler's—"

"No." Her voice was petulant now. "I have plenty of rings. I want a carriage. Do you not consider me worth a carriage, Lionel?"

"To be sure, you are, my love. It's just that—"

"Or better still, a necklace thick with emeralds such as Madame wears. Will you buy me an emerald necklace, Lionel?"

He gulped. She was adorable and worthy of all the riches in the world, but the size of bills she was implying would surely evoke Papa's wrath. A loan, perhaps, or a lucky night at the card table might solve the problem.

Bella grew impatient. "You take so long to answer. I think you do not really love me at all."

"I do, Bella, oh, I do!"

"Then my necklace?"

"You shall have it. Next week I shall bring it to you. Oh, Bella, kiss me again before I must leave you."

It was a foolhardy promise, he reflected as he made his way home. Morosely he kicked a pebble along the pavement before him. Suppose he could not win the money at cards, how then could he raise enough to buy a necklace such as Bella had requested? A loan from a friend was unlikely, since by now they all knew they were seldom repaid, or only very belatedly. And the moneylenders demanded some kind of security before advancing even a modest sum. He had no such security to offer.

It was Papa who gave him the idea. Over breakfast he put aside his newspaper.

"Have you thought over Braithwaite's proposition, Lionel?"

"I gave the matter some thought, sir."

"And what conclusion have you reached?"

Lionel hesitated. "I cannot say I fancy the sound of the milksop Braithwaite girl, Papa."

Lord Travers clicked his tongue impatiently. "That is neither here nor there. I fancy you are going to tell me next that you love another."

Ignoring the sneer, Lionel replied, "As a matter of fact, I do, sir."

His father's eyebrows rose fractionally. "You do? Good stock, is she? Prosperous background?"

This was difficult. Lionel tried again. "Not a girl one would marry, sir. Just a girl I love."

"Oh, I see." The disappointment was evident in Papa's tone. "One of your actresses, I suppose."

"Well, no, sir, not exactly."

"But of the same disreputable mold. Well, in that case she's likely to be expensive."

"Yes, sir." Papa could be remarkably astute at times.

"A mistress often wants to be set up in a place of her own. Well, then, marriage to Miss Braithwaite seems the obvious answer, my boy. Her money will keep both you and her and your mistress comfortably."

That was true. And if the Braithwaite girl was as dull as Gertrude had said, she'd probably never guess.

Then the flash of inspiration came. Any moneylender would cheerfully lend him the thousand pounds he desperately needed on hearing that he was affianced to the daughter of a wealthy mill owner. And with luck he might not actually have to marry the girl in the end. A protracted engagement could give time for anything to happen to change the course of events. . . .

"Then I'll follow your advice, sir, and marry Miss Braithwaite. After a sufficiently long engagement for us to get to know each other."

"Splendid, my boy. I'll let Braithwaite know at once."

Papa beamed in one of his rare expansive moods. He had cause to smile, Lionel reflected, for his financial problems . too would be solved by this advantageous marriage. He would never learn, of course, that his son planned no more than an engagement to the Braithwaite girl. . . .

It was late afternoon when one of the maids came down to the kitchen where Miss Oliphant was supervising the preserving of the plums she had had sent up from the market this morning.

"Miss Oliphant, the master bids me ask you to see him in the study at once," the girl said. Emily wiped her sticky fingers on a towel, took off her apron, and tidied back the wisps of hair that were escaping from under her cap. Mr. Braithwaite probably wanted her to fetch Anna to join him for afternoon tea.

The silver tea tray lay already on the side table when Emily entered and the master was standing with his back to her, looking out of the window.

"Shall I fetch Anna, sir?"

"No, pour the tea. I want to talk to you."

When the cups were filled, Braithwaite came to take his from her and sat down. He looked haggard, Emily thought, as though tired or frustrated. After a few moments' silence he spoke.

"Did you and Anna see anything of the Travers family while I was away in Yorkshire?" he demanded brusquely.

"Not after Miss Anna went on the picnic with the Honorable Gertrude, and I understand that Miss Travers then went to the seaside for a holiday, sir."

"I see. So Anna has not met Lionel Travers?"

"Miss Travers' brother? No, sir."

Mr. Braithwaite grunted and fell silent again, putting aside his cup and thrusting his hands into his trouser pockets as he sat back in the chair. Miss Oliphant wished he would not caress the coins in his pocket with that irritating jingle. Unfortunate habits like that revealed one's lack of breeding.

Mr. Braithwaite's next words made her jump; it was almost as though he had read her thoughts. "I may be no gentleman, Emily, but I'm determined that Anna shall be a lady. And her children, my grandchildren, will be gentlefolk too. To that end I have put myself to a great deal of trouble on her behalf."

"You are a good father to her, sir."

"Aye, and I hope as she'll remember it when I'm gone. Many a man in my position, with affairs of state to concern him as well as business problems, would not find the time, but I'm mindful of my duties. So, Emily, I've made plans for Anna."

"Plans, sir?"

"Aye, a husband, and a good one at that."

With effort, Emily kept the surprise from her voice. "You are very good to her, sir. A good husband who will cherish her is just what she needs, once she loses your parental concern."

Again he grunted. "Aye, well, as husbands go, he'll not be a bad one, I fancy. At least he'll be able to provide for her and give her a good name. I'm going to tell her directly, but first I wanted a word with you, to make sure she's ready."

"Ready for the news, sir?"

"Dammit, no. Ready to be a wife—knows all the responsibilities of running a house and servants and all that. And the responsibility of being a wife and mother."

Emily saw what he was driving at, and she colored. Within months she was twice being faced with those problems too delicate to face with ease. In case she was mistaken she taxed her employer.

"What exactly do you mean, sir?"

Braithwaite leaped up and paced back to the window. "You know what I mean, Emily," he said gruffly. "Though you've never married you must know what a wife has to do."

"About running a house, sir, yes."

"Dammit, don't be so deliberately obstinate, Emily. You know what I mean. Hang it all, you could have had a child, but you didn't. Now make sure Anna too knows how to protect herself. Do I make myself clear?"

Emily nodded, too engulfed with shame to answer. Why did he have to refer to that episode now, after all these years? An incident long-forgotten, pushed to a furthermost recess in her mind because it was too unpleasant to recall. How like a man, to trample ruthlessly on a delicate shred of memory.

Braithwaite spoke without turning from the window. "Now send her to me alone, and I'll break the good news to her."

She rose to go. "May I ask one question, sir?"

"What is it?"

"How long will it be—until the marriage?"

"The date is not settled yet. Lord Travers suggests a long engagement, a year at least, but I should like to see it take place before the end of the year."

"So soon, sir?"

"Time enough to arrange everything if we set our minds to it. Now fetch Anna."

She found Anna playing patience in her own little parlor. Told that her father wished to see her, the girl shuffled the cards together and rose. Emily watched her slender, graceful figure as she left the room. Would she look so cool and poised once she had heard the unexpected news? In a rush of maternal solicitude Emily decided she had better station herself near the study, to be on hand to console or congratulate.

Hovering in the corridor, she could hear muted voices, Braithwaite's deep and resonant and Anna's occasional faint reply. Lazenby came up the stairs toward her. Suddenly the study door opened and Anna emerged.

Emily saw the look of concern that crossed Lazenby's face when he saw the girl. She was leaning against the closed door, her head thrown back, and she was breathing deeply.

"Are you all right, Anna?" he asked.

She straightened and took a step forward, but it was evident she was unsteady. Lazenby stepped forward and put an arm about her.

"Come into the parlor and sit awhile." Emily led the way, opening the door so that the secretary could guide the girl. She was white-faced and her step uncertain as she walked. Sinking at last onto the sofa, she smiled wanly.

"You have no doubt heard the news." Her voice was faint and faltering. Emily was thinking of fetching the sal volatile when Lazenby snapped.

"News? What news?"

"Why, that I am to be married."

Lazenby's disbelieving eyes turned on Emily. "That is true, Mr. Lazenby; Miss Anna is soon to be wed to Mr. Lionel Travers."

"Lionel!" Lazenby's voice was an expression of anger

or disbelief, it was difficult to tell which. "Lionel Travers? Impossible!"

"Why so, sir? His Lordship and the master are good friends, and such a match seems highly desirable," Emily remonstrated mildly.

"Desirable for the fathers, but hardly for the children," Lazenby snapped. "Anna needs a strong man to protect her, and Lionel needs a strong woman to guide him in his weakness. It's a cruel notion to marry them to each other."

"If you feel so strongly about it, then perhaps you should register your objections to the master and not upset Anna when you can see she is in no fit state for further distress," Emily said firmly.

Lazenby glanced at the girl. "You are right. I am sorry. I let my tongue run away with me. Forgive me." He reached down and touched Anna's limp hand. "You must know, my dear, I wish you nothing but well. I hope you will be very happy."

"I know it," Anna whispered. Then she sighed and added, "But is it not strange, after my presentiment this morning, that it should come true?"

Emily and Lazenby exchanged glances. "Presentiment?" Lazenby echoed.

"Yes. Remember the poem:

"The mirror cracked from side to side.
A curse is come upon me, cried
The Lady of Shalott."

She foresaw her doom, just as I did."

"Rubbish," said Emily sharply. "You read too much poetry."

"Strange," Anna went on in a faraway voice, "but I knew there was something portentous about today as soon as I woke up, something threatening and evil. And then the letter I found in my reticule this afternoon proved it."

"Letter? What letter?" Emily demanded in surprise.

"Why, this." From her pocket Anna drew out slowly a folded sheet of white paper. "It had no envelope and I don't know how it came there, but it was obviously for me."

"Let me see." Emily snatched the letter, angered that it had eluded her jealous guard over the girl. What she read made her senses reel. Lazenby saw her reaction and took the note from her numb fingers.

> Do not think to escape me, Anna, for I am watching you and awaiting the moment. When it comes I shall strike, and then I shall come into my own again. You will be dispossessed, Anna, for you are for the moment only in possession of what is rightfully mine. Beware, Anna, for the time to strike is not far away. Bella.

Lazenby knelt before the girl. "What does it mean, Anna? Do you know?"

She shook her head feebly. "No. Nor does it seem to matter anymore. I am to marry a man I do not know, and that does not seem to matter either. What will be, will be, for I am cursed."

"Rubbish!" Anger born of frustration made Emily's voice brittle. "We'll find out who's at the bottom of this. Have no fear, Anna, we'll let no harm befall you, will we, Mr. Lazenby?"

She looked up at him hopefully and saw the anger smoldering in his eyes. "Not if I can help it," he muttered, and stormed out of the room.

"There now, we'll find out who dares to threaten you, my love," Emily said soothingly. "Would you like a cup of tea, my dear?"

As she went to pull the bellpull she could hear Anna singing softly:

"The mirror cracked from side to side.
A curse is come upon me, cried
The Lady of Shalott."

Bella reclined sulkily on her sofa. Robert Dalrymple sat on a cushion on the floor, since there was no other chair for him.

"Why do you just sit there and write?" Bella demanded angrily. "Mr. Lionel found no need to write. He found me of more interest."

"And I find you of interest, Bella, of very great interest. I have never met a woman like you before."

"Then why do you just sit there? Come, sit by me."

"My interest is more in your mind, Bella, than in your body, though I confess you are beautiful enough to captivate a king."

She glanced at him quickly. "You have seen me only when I am wearing a veil. How can you know?"

He could do nothing else but confess. "Because Mr. Lionel is a friend of mine. He told me you were beautiful beyond compare."

"Then why is *he* not here?"

"He is coming again soon. But tell me, Bella, why do you say you are Queen of the East?"

He watched her shrewdly. He knew he was less likely to learn the truth from her than when she was hypnotized, but he had decided to try it.

"Because I am. Or I should be, if I had not been dispossessed."

"Dispossessed?" He latched onto the word swiftly. It was a plea many of his patients had made in the past. He remembered the girl who felt displaced by the advent of a baby brother, the aging German *frau* deposed from her husband's affections by his new mistress. Dispossession was the starting point for many human ills.

Bella sighed wearily. "I cannot expect you to understand. You are a man."

"Try to explain to me, Bella."

"There is nothing much to tell. For centuries we ruled the Orient and all the powers known to man were ours. Then we were driven out. Gypsies, they called us."

"And that makes you sad?"

She sat up suddenly. "Sad? It makes me angry! Don't you see, I have no place of my own. I am a stranger in a foreign land, an alien alone and despised."

"You are not despised, Bella. From what I hear you are adored."

"Ah, Lionel. That is nothing. I want a place of my own, and one day I shall have it."

Dalrymple scribbled. "And where shall that place be, Bella?"

She draped herself slowly along the length of the sofa, resting her chin on her cupped hand. Although he could not see it, Dalrymple knew she was smiling beneath the veil.

"I know where it will be. I shall find my place—and soon now."

"Where, Bella?"

"In her body. Soon now I shall take over her body, not just now and again, but for good. And then she will be dead and I shall come into my own again."

Dalrymple's jaw dropped open. Whatever answer he had expected, it had not been this. But before he could speak again, Bella suddenly leaped to her feet.

"I am tired of talking. Will you lie with me or not? You will not? Then leave me, sir, for I will talk no more."

Dalrymple began to urge her. "Bella, my dear, I find you so stimulating—please tell me more."

"I will not, I tell you! What's the matter with you, you stupid dolt? Can't you understand plain English?" Her voice was shrill and hysterical now. Dalrymple rose to lay a hand on her arm. Instantly she mellowed.

"That is better. Touch me, feel how soft my skin is. Let me take off your jacket." Persuasive hands ran over him, and Dalrymple could feel his clinical objectivity melting into a far more basic emotion. With effort he removed her fingers.

"Then get out, you cold brute! You're no use to me or any woman," she screamed, her fingernails reaching for his face. Discretion was indicated, Dalrymple decided, and bidding her a hasty good night, he fled.

Charles Lazenby was on his way to the post office when he saw Robert Dalrymple's tall figure striding along on the far side of the road toward him. Dalrymple waved and crossed the cobbled street to join him.

"Ah, Lazenby! I was on my way to see you. Desperately wanted to have a talk with you about this Bella girl. Lionel is enraptured with her, but frankly, I find her disturbing," Dalrymple said pensively.

"Then walk with me as far as the post office on the corner, and then we'll sit in the park for a while," Lazenby replied. Dalrymple fell into step alongside him.

Lazenby smiled. "But she does not disturb you in the same way she does Lionel."

"Be serious, Charles. I am truly concerned about Bella. She is evidently suffering from some terrible experience in the past which has deranged her."

"Do you mean she is mad?"

"Not in the accepted sense. Ill, yes, extremely so. That is how it appears to me on only a cursory examination, mind you. One would need more clinical tests to be sure."

"But what do you surmise from what you have seen?"

"Well, whatever the experience was in her past, it has caused some kind of blockage in her mind. So much so that her personality is breaking down under the stress."

"How so?" Lazenby's questions were not simply polite interest. He was genuinely intrigued about this Bella, of whom he had heard so much and never met.

"The blockage seems to have caused her to disintegrate into two distinct personalities—a split personality, we call it. One or other of the two people within her will fight the other to predominate. I have only seen the one identity, of course, and very little of her. I wonder what kind of person she is in the other identity."

"Two people in one body?" Lazenby mused aloud. "To the rational mind that appears completely irrational, superstitious even. Are you sure?"

"Our researches in Germany have shown us that several such cases exist. To resolve the problem one identity has to supersede and drive out the other, or the patient will go mad. Superstitious, you say. Indeed, German folklore is full of the *doppelgänger*, the other self that haunts a man, his shadow that follows him everywhere and yet is not him, for it has an evil identity of its own. So it is with the split personality—the righteous, law-abiding person is dogged by his evil *alter ego*."

"And which of Bella's selves have you seen?"

Dalrymple shrugged. "I cannot tell. She was petulant and angry with me, but not vicious. Perhaps if I had hypnotized her again I could have learned more."

After he had concluded his business in the post office, Lazenby led Dalrymple to the park. There, seated on a park bench in the warm sunshine, he returned to the subject.

"Can she be cured?" Lazenby could not help feeling sorry for the poor, crazed whore.

"Perhaps. If the blockage, the event in her past that caused it, could be revealed and recognized, she might recover. But it is hard to tell. So many victims of this illness are not discovered until it is too late and they are already in a lunatic asylum."

Lazenby thought for a while. "Does Lionel know about this?"

"Not entirely. I tried to explain to him what I suspected, but he kept raving about her. He's quite besotted with the girl."

"Don't you think it would be as well to warn him?"

"That he's infatuated with a madwoman, you mean? But she's not mad, Charles, not yet. Though I confess she will be if the cause is not soon established and the problem somehow resolved."

"I see. I take it you are fairly certain of your diagnosis."

Dalrymple knitted his fingers together behind his head and stared up through the branches above. "As certain as one can be. She manifests certain symptoms I've come to find are habitual."

"What kind of symptoms?"

"Well, an obsession with spiders for one thing, according to Lionel. And she has that inexplicable aversion to stripes—she threw Lionel's striped necktie away as well as making Madame alter her room because of the striped wallpaper. Now that must have some connection with the experience I spoke of, possibly something that happened in her early childhood."

"Can you not get her to talk about it?"

"Under hypnosis possibly. Consciously, almost certainly not, for it is usual for the conscious mind to reject and forget an experience it prefers not to remember because it was too frightening."

"What puzzles me, Charles, is what the other Bella is like—presumably the better of the two, for I believe this one is the *doppelgänger*, freed from the constraints the better one clings to. I know nothing about her really. I have learned little from Madame because no one seems to know where she comes from."

"Can you not cure her then?"

Dalrymple shook his head slowly. "Not easily. I would have to learn much more."

"Then can you not put her in the hands of a good doctor who can?"

"She would probably not agree, and there are few doctors yet in this country who specialize in illnesses of the mind. A doctor could very easily certify her insane and commit her to an asylum."

For a few moments there was silence between the two men. Beyond the park railings a hansom cab clattered noisily by over the cobbles. When it had passed, Lazenby turned to Dalrymple.

"Robert, can I help in any way? I hate to think of that poor child, misunderstood and helpless to help herself. If there is any way I could help you to help her . . ."

Dalrymple smiled. "I always knew you were the tenderhearted one, rushing to the aid of a blind man or an injured animal. Lame dogs, and all that. I was hoping you would ask. Yes, I think perhaps your courteous, quiet manner, kind but firm, might help me get from Bella the answers I need. Would you visit her? See what you can learn for me?"

Lazenby smiled ruefully. "You do not know what you ask, Robert. My employer prefers me now to keep away from Rosamund Street, for perhaps I run the risk of embarrassing him with a chance meeting. But if it means so much to you, and that poor girl, I'll see to it that his path and mine do not cross. Can you arrange a meeting somewhere else?"

Dalrymple slapped him on the shoulder as he rose from the bench. "I knew I could rely on you. You know now what the problem is and what I need to learn, so I leave it to your good judgment to do the rest."

At the park gates they parted. Back at Hanbury Square Lazenby found Emily in the conservatory, watering the potted plants. He seated himself in one of the wicker chairs under a spreading palm and watched her. The housekeeper smiled and went on humming as she dipped the jug in the tank of water and continued her work.

"How is Miss Laura, Emily?"

"Better, I think. Less feverish and she seems to be sleeping well, I'm glad to say."

"And Miss Anna has not risen in the night again then, I take it?"

"Not a sound have I heard from her these past few nights. Slept like a baby, she has."

"I'm very glad to hear it."

"In fact, she seems quite sunny and contented. She's upstairs now, unpacking and trying on the new gowns I ordered to be made for her. I do hope Mr. Braithwaite will approve my choice."

"I'm sure he will."

Running footsteps pattered on the tessellated floor. Lazenby turned in his chair to see Anna standing there, white-faced and stiff.

"Emily."

The housekeeper turned, putting down the watering jug on seeing the tense face staring at her. "What is it, Anna? What's wrong, my dear?"

"Those gowns you ordered—you defied me."

"Defied you, Anna? What are you talking about?"

The girl held out a stiff arm. In her fingertips she was clenching a crumpled mass of black-and-white-striped material. "This one—I forbade you to order stripes, and yet you did."

"But I told you, Anna, it is the height of fashion this year. I believed you would come to like it once you saw it and I'm sure your papa would approve."

"You know how I hate stripes." Anna's voice was low and sibilant. "Take it away—burn it! I never want to see it again."

Dropping the offending gown on the conservatory floor, Anna turned and ran. The housekeeper stared at Lazenby in uncomprehending silence. Something twitched at the back of Lazenby's mind.

Lionel Travers leaped eagerly from the cab when it arrived at Rosamund Street; he paid off the cabbie and mounted the steps. He could feel his heart thudding with anticipation as he rang the bell. He was not expected tonight, but Bella would surely welcome him with ardent arms when she saw the contents of the parcel bulging in his pocket.

It was the petite dark French girl who answered the

door *"Entrez, monsieur,"* she said with a smile. "I will fetch Madame."

She left him to go to Madame's room. While he waited, Lionel became aware of a powerfully heady scent, such as Bella used in her room. Then he realized that the furnishings were different, the chenille curtains having given way to diaphanous chiffon and the girls wearing flimsy Oriental costumes such as Bella wore. Madame, gowned in sophisticated black velvet and sparkling with diamonds, came out to greet him.

"Why, Mr. Lionel! We were not expecting you tonight, but you are welcome nonetheless. As you can see, we are holding an Oriental evening and you are most welcome to join us."

"May I see Bella?" He could not help the eagerness in his face. To his dismay Madame frowned.

"I regret Miss Bella is engaged this evening, Mr. Lionel, to entertain another gentleman. But, never mind, if I consult my book I am sure I can find another young lady whom you will find equally charming."

"No, Madame. I must see Bella. I have brought something for her," Lionel protested. "I must see her, if only to give it to her."

Madame de Sandrier glanced at the clock. "Well, there is a little time yet before her gentleman is due to arrive. Perhaps she will see you for a few minutes."

"Please ask her," Lionel begged. Though he was forlorn at the thought of not having her to himself, a few minutes was better than nothing. . . .

It was Miss Sybil who came back with the news. "Bella will see you in her room. You know the way?"

Nodding, he hastened up the staircase. A pretty girl with saucy eyes was looking down over the balustrade and she gave him a wicked wink as he passed. At Bella's door he knocked, and heard her answer, "Come in."

She had her back to him, seated before a mirror and applying rouge to her cheeks and lips. Through the sheer fabric of her thin costume he could see the gleam of her flesh, and the blood pounded in his ears.

"I have brought you the necklace, Bella."

She turned on her stool, smiling approvingly like a teacher who has at last been brought a well-done piece of homework. "Let me see."

Clumsily he handed over the package, longing to see the delighted approbation he sought. Bella unwrapped the parcel and let the wrappings fall to the floor. Then she clicked open the box and lifted out the necklace. Emeralds cascaded from her fingers like brilliant green raindrops.

"Very pretty," she murmured. "Fasten it about my neck, Lionel." He did so, fumbling excitedly. She cocked her head to one side, surveying her reflection in the mirror.

"They become me well, don't you think?"

"No jewels could make you more beautiful than you are, Bella."

"Thank you, Lionel. And what shall you bring me next time as a mark of your appreciation?" She looked up at him under half-closed lids.

"Let me stay with you tonight, Bella. Tell Madame to arrange for someone else to entertain your gentleman and let me stay," Lionel said breathlessly.

"I cannot do that. You can come, say, Monday and bring me a diamond ring. A large single diamond, I think." She spread her slim fingers to consider them. "Yes, one large solitary stone in a platinum setting. Will you do that for me, Lionel?"

He caught his breath. Promises would be in vain, but he could not let her escape him. He caught her hand. "And if I do, Bella, will you do something for me?"

"That depends what it is," she replied archly.

"Keep yourself for me, only for me. I would take you away from all this if I could and keep you where only I could reach you. Would you like that, Bella?"

"With my own house and footman, my own carriage and all the money I wish?"

He gulped. "Yes, if that is what you want."

She laughed. "I want that and much more besides, much more than you can give me. I want men prostrate at my feet, worshiping and adoring me."

"I worship you, Bella."

"But you would hide me away where my beauty would be unappreciated by the rest of the world. I have no wish to be a rare curio in a display case where only you can come to admire. I want freedom."

"You shall have it, Bella. You shall have anything you want, if you will love me only."

He was kneeling now at her side, looking up at her imploringly. Bella pushed him away. "Go now, and remember my ring next visit. I have no more time for you now."

Before he could protest, there was a knock at the door and Miss Sybil entered. "Bella, it is almost time," she said.

"Lionel is just leaving," Bella replied coolly.

"You do not need to leave, Mr. Lionel," Sybil said with a smile, "for I am sure Madame will find you another partner for the evening. The festivities are yet to begin. Come with me and I shall see what can be arranged."

Lionel allowed himself to be led away. At the head of the stairs the pertly pretty girl was still standing watching over the balustrade. "Ah, Maisie," Miss Sybil said, "have you a partner for the evening?"

"Not tonight, miss. My gentleman sent word he could not come because he has influenza."

"Then perhaps you would entertain Mr. Lionel." She turned to indicate him, and Lionel did not know how to explain that if he did not have Bella, then he desired no one.

"It will be my pleasure, miss," the girl replied, coming up close to him and pressing her shoulder against his chest. "Would you care to join the party downstairs and have a glass of wine, sir?"

Lionel stepped back. She was pretty, there was no doubt of that, and in her thin robe she would excite an Eskimo to ardor, but in his mind and heart there was room only for Bella.

"Another time, perhaps, Maisie. I must . . ."

He was cut short when a small, slender figure thrust itself between him and Maisie. It was Bella, her eyes aflame with anger.

"Get out, you bitch," she snarled at Maisie. "He's mine, and you leave him alone."

"You've got a gentleman," Maisie protested. Miss Sybil made to intervene, but Bella thrust her aside, and then forcibly flung herself on Maisie. Lionel saw the two girls fall, rolling and writhing in a flurry of sea-green and mauve chiffon.

"Stop it at once!" Miss Sybil thundered. "Go back to your rooms, both of you!"

But she might as well have been crying to the wind, for Lionel saw the flashing nails that ripped down Maisie's cheek, leaving a reddened trail, and the handful of dark hair Bella wrenched from her head. Over and over the entwined figures rolled, pausing in a furious tangle on the very brink of the top step.

Miss Sybil leaped on them and pulled the flailing figures apart. Maisie staggered to her feet, fingering the scratches on her face. Bella, her blue eyes still flashing hatred and scorn, rose slowly.

"Now go," Miss Sybil snapped, "and I shall speak to you both later."

"I promised her a curse, and a curse she shall have," Bella's voice hissed venomously, and before anyone could move, she leaped toward Maisie again. Maisie teetered, lost her balance, and Lionel could see her dark eyes widen in disbelief. Before anyone could stop her, she fell down the staircase, rolling over and over till she reached the bottom. Not a soul moved; Lionel himself was frozen with horror. Miss Sybil was the first to recover her senses. She ran down the stairs and bent over the prostrate figure.

"Solange," she called crisply. "Go tell Madame to summon the doctor instantly. Mr. Lionel, be so good as to carry Maisie to her room."

Lionel hastened down to do as she bid. Miss Sybil looked up at Bella.

"I hope you realize what you have done, miss. Maisie is unconscious and may be badly injured."

Bella tossed her head. "And little I care. She meddled once too often for her own good. She can't say I didn't warn her."

Lionel carried the limp figure up the stairs. As he passed Bella, she looked at the unconscious girl.

"Serves her right," she said quietly. "I hope she dies."

Numb with shock, Lionel laid the girl on her bed and left her with Miss Sybil. On the landing Bella was waiting.

"Don't forget my ring, will you, Lionel?"

"I'll see. I can't promise," he stammered. It seemed unnatural, unholy, to think of jewels at a time like this.

"Then don't bother to come again. I do not wish to see you," she said, turning nonchalantly toward her room.

"No, Bella, wait! I only meant—I was somewhat distracted. I'll see what I can do."

"Then send it by a messenger. Don't come yourself." She yawned widely.

"But Bella, I must see you again."

She turned, her eyes icy with indifference. "No, you bore me. I want a man—one who can satisfy me."

His mouth gaped. "But surely I—"

She smiled. "Your masculinity leaves much to be desired, Lionel. You are too easily drained. No, I want a lover with stamina, and you will not do."

Coolly she turned and left him. Lionel felt the blood begin to pound in his ears again, but not this time with desire and passion. Horror and shame fought within him for supremacy, and he felt as if his head would burst. Down the stairs he leaped, two at a time, and out into the night, quite forgetting his cloak and cane.

Chapter Fourteen

Laura rolled over and opened her eyes. Sunlight streamed in across the bed, and despite its brightness, Laura realized, with relief, that she no longer had the headache that had dogged her for days.

Emily Oliphant came into the bedroom. She was still in her dressing gown and curlers and came to stand by the bed.

"How are you feeling today, Miss Laura?"

"Better, much better, thank you, Emily. My headache is gone."

"That's splendid. The doctor said that if the weather was fine and you felt up to it, you could go out into the garden today. Fresh air, that's what you need my dear, to blow the cobwebs away."

As Laura swung her legs out of bed and rose unsteadily, Emily poured out water into the washbasin. Laura held on tightly to the brass bedknob for a moment until the unsteady feeling faded. Emily watched her critically.

"Good," the housekeeper said. "Now I'll go and wake Anna."

At the mention of Anna, Laura grew agitated. For days now she had not been able to keep watch over her cousin. What had happened during the blank fever-ridden days of unconsciousness? Laura stumbled after Emily.

Emily went to stand by Anna's bed, looking down at the sleeping girl, Laura close behind her. Anna did not look well, Laura thought, for her cheeks were unusually rosy and there were dark circles under her eyelids.

"Anna." Emily shook the girl's shoulder gently. "Wake up, child, it's seven o'clock."

Blue eyes flickered open and slowly came to focus on Emily's face. "Not yet, it can't be."

"But it is. Look at the clock. Come now, get up and wash your face in cold water—that will waken you."

Anna's sleepy gaze fell on her cousin. "Laura, my dear, how nice to see you up again. I hope you're fully recovered." Laura smiled, but before she could answer, Emily Oliphant cut in.

"What is that perfume, Anna? I haven't smelled it before."

Anna turned a sleepy gaze on her. "Perfume? I have no perfume, Emily, except the lavender water you gave me at Christmas. It is the glycerine and rose water you can smell, probably."

Laura sniffed. Yes, she could detect it too. Odd, though. She had never guessed rose water could smell so heady.

"Rise and shine, Miss Anna," Emily said briskly. "We cannot be late for prayers or your papa will be angry. He'll be glad to see Miss Laura downstairs again."

Obediently Anna rose, slowly and with effort. Emily saw her splash her face with cold water before leaving.

After breakfast Laura was eager to go out into the fresh air, but Anna was reluctant. "I do not like cutting roses. I always get my fingers pricked by the thorns."

"Not if you wear gloves," Emily pointed out.

"I would prefer to stay indoors and read."

Laura heard Emily sigh, but she did not argue.

"Very well. You may read while I cut the roses. The dead heads must be pruned too if we are to encourage more blooms."

So it was that Emily, in sunbonnet and gloves, was busy among the rose beds and Laura was sitting reading in the little trellis arbor when she saw Mr. Lazenby appear. Emily reddened with pleasure, Laura noted with amusement, as he addressed her.

"A beautiful morning, Emily. Do you mind if I sit awhile and keep you and Miss Laura company?"

"Not at all, sir." She was about to put down the pruning scissors when Lazenby threw up his hands in mock horror.

"Pray, do not let me disturb you in your work. Please continue while, with your permission, I have a few words with Miss Laura."

Laura smiled. Emily had no choice but to nod her agreement and continue cutting the roses. Laura continued reading as he lowered himself to sit beside her. For a time there was silence, save for the sound of birds singing and the clip of Emily's shears. Evidently Emily considered it would not be indecorous to let the young couple out of her sight, for she moved along the rose beds and out of their view.

Still there was silence. Several minutes had elapsed before Laura heard Mr. Lazenby's deep voice break the silence.

"I am glad to see you recovered, Laura. I see you are still reading Mr. Browning. Are you enjoying it?"

Laura nodded. "I am, though at times I find it a little difficult to understand."

"What do you find hard?"

"Why, 'A Grammarian's Funeral' I have just read. I do not truly understand what Mr. Browning meant by it."

"Only that the grammarian was a product of his age, the age of the revival of learning. A high-seeking man of the mind must be buried in a high place, on a mountaintop."

"It appears he was an admirable man, or at least Mr. Browning admired him. He says of him:

"We would not discount life, as fools do here,
   Paid by instalment.

> He ventured neck or nothing—heaven's success
> Found, or earth's failure."

I do so admire those who tackle life wholeheartedly, don't you? Believing in one's path must be so satisfying."

Lazenby murmured agreement. "And what is your destined path in life, Laura?" His voice was gentle, and Laura responded to it.

"Oh, to marry and be a good wife, I suppose." She was aware of the detachment in her reply. Lazenby pursued his point.

"I did not mean what you are destined by your uncle to do, but what you yourself would like to do, given the opportunity. Do you know what would give you satisfaction, Laura?"

"I should like to do something useful in the world, but I am not sure what. To help Anna, first of all. Has Dr. Dalrymple seen her yet?"

"Not yet. We were waiting for you to recover. He's coming soon. What kind of useful work? Teaching, perhaps, or nursing?"

"No, not quite." Laura's voice was slow, deliberate. "Work among the poor or deprived in some way, I think. In the missionary field, perhaps. It always grieves me deeply to see others worse off than I. The millworkers in my uncle's mills, for example, with their thin, pinched faces and their children running around barefoot in the snow. I should like to be able to help them. I do not feel that gifts of money alone are enough. I should dearly like to *do* something, but I cannot tell what. But tell me about your aims, Charles. What would you like to do, or are you content in your present work?"

Lazenby's laugh was rich and deep. "I should like to be in your uncle's shoes—rich and influential and with a seat in the House. Then I too could carry out the reforming work you too could undertake alongside me. Would that not be wonderful, Laura?"

The two of them were laughing now. Suddenly the

sunlight faded, obscured by a bank of cloud. Laura glanced up. It looked as if it would rain soon.

"The sun's gone in," she remarked. "It makes me shiver, like that poem of Lord Tennyson's which Anna is always quoting."

"Which one, Laura," Lazenby inquired.

"The Lady of Shalott, who knows that a curse is upon her.

> "She knows not what the curse may be,
> And so she weaveth steadily,
> And little other care hath she,
>   The Lady of Shalott.
> And moving through a mirror clear
> That hangs before her all the year,
> Shadows of the world appear."

Anna says she sometimes feels like that when she looks in a mirror."

"Really? I wonder why?"

"I do not know. But she says she has this strange presentiment that something terrible will happen. She is afraid to look in the mirror."

"I wonder what it is she fears. Do you know?" Lazenby's voice was softly persuasive.

"I truly do not know. I only wish I could help her be rid of this silly fear, but it haunts her."

"Are you still shivering?" Lazenby's voice was concerned.

"Yes, I think I had better go in. It does not look as if the sun will reappear today."

"No, Laura, please let us not break off just yet. Your company pleases me greatly. I will go and get your shawl so that we can stay here a little longer."

He rose and left the arbor, and Laura watched him go with a feeling of pride. What a fine figure of a man he was, tall, elegant, and so understanding. His concern for her made her feel quite excited.

He was not gone long and returned carrying her bright blue shawl. She stood up to take it, and as he reached toward her to place the shawl over her shoulders, she felt the warmth and comfort of his strong arms. She trembled at his touch. For a moment, they stood in silence, each transfixed by the other's presence. Then Charles took her hand in his.

"Laura," he began. And then stopped. For he saw the small figure of Emily come into view. At that minute, Laura wished her a thousand miles away.

"I think I have cut all the roses now, see? And as the sun has gone, I think we had better go inside." She sighed, looking up at the sky. "A pity. I had meant to go to the circulating library again this morning. Miss Anna wants yet more books on spiders."

"Spiders?" Laura heard Lazenby repeat as Emily's thin figure retreated toward the house. "Spiders? Stripes? It sounds so like . . . and yet it cannot be." He was murmuring softly, as if to himself. Suddenly he turned to Laura.

"Tell me—where did Anna go that night you followed her? It was not to Rosamund Street, was it?"

Laura paled. His challenging gaze was so cold and unfriendly, so unlike a moment ago. "I don't know. I told you I never saw the street name. Somewhere near Piccadilly, but I could show you the place. Why?"

He groaned. "God forgive me if I am wrong, but I think it is possible we are too late. If only I knew . . ."

A sickening feeling gripped Laura. "Too late? What do you mean? You did see to it that Anna did not leave the house while I was ill?"

"I thought not, for Emily assured me she did not stir. And yet I begin to suspect . . ."

"Suspect what? Oh, tell me, Charles." Laura rose, but somehow the unsteadiness seemed to have returned. As she swayed, Lazenby gripped her arm firmly and began to lead her toward the house. His calm strength was reassuring, but the sick despair in his voice filled Laura with fear.

"Go to your room and rest, Laura. I'll talk to you later." Lazenby's firmness left Laura no choice.

Once upstairs, Laura decided to look in on her cousin. She saw Anna sitting at the dressing table and brushing her hair. As Laura moved across to her, she heard Anna singing softly as she brushed in rhythm.

"They say I killed a man, killed a man, killed a man,
They say I killed a man, killed a man;
I hit him on the head with a bloody lump of lead,
And now the fellow's dead,
Damn his eyes, blast his soul,
And now the fellow's dead, damn his eyes."

Laura stood dumbstruck. It was an old song, one she had heard long ago in her childhood when one of the servants had come home drunk from the music halls, but one Anna could not possibly have heard. She stared at the girl, incredulous.

"What is that you are singing, Anna? Where did you hear it?"

Anna turned around, brush poised in midair. "What song, Laura? Oh, I was singing 'Early One Morning' before you came in—is that the one you mean? Why, Nanny taught it to me as a child."

"Not that—the one about killing a man."

"Killing a man!" Anna's voice was shocked. "Why, really, Laura, do you think I would sing a song about such a dreadful thing? You must have misheard me."

But Laura knew she had not misheard. Equally she was convinced that Anna seemed unaware of what she was singing. What was one to believe? She drove from her mind the unpleasant thought that kept trying to insinuate itself. Anna was as sane as herself, not so strong, perhaps, but surely sane.

As Laura left, she could hear Anna's clear young voice

singing softly: "Early one morning, just as the sun was rising . . ."

Lazenby was outside the master's study with Emily as Laura came out. He nodded when he saw her before turning to Emily.

"Miss Oliphant, are you going to the library now? I wonder if you would be good enough to leave a message at Winterton's Hotel—you'll pass it on your way."

"But, of course, Mr. Lazenby."

He handed her a sealed letter. "It's a note to Dr. Dalrymple, asking him to see me at once. It is most urgent."

Emily tucked the letter between the books she was carrying. "I shall deliver it at once."

He cocked his head to one side, to scan the titles of the books. "What kind of book interests Miss Anna, I wonder?"

Emily stiffened with pride. "She has taken a profound interest lately in the wonders of the natural sciences, sir, much to my pleasure. Previously she was not deeply concerned. A sign of maturity, I've no doubt." She held out a book for his inspection. "*Lesser Known Customs of the Insect World,*" Laura heard him say.

"All four books are about insects. Why, she even asked if I would allow her to build a spider's nest colony in a box in her bedroom so that she might study it. Of course, I had to refuse. But I had better be on my way, Mr. Lazenby. Have no fear for your letter; I shall deliver it swiftly."

Emily must have carried out her promise with alacrity, for when Laura came downstairs again for lunch, she could hear male voices deep in conversation in the parlor. She was puzzled. Uncle Reginald was to be out for lunch, Emily had said. Curiosity filling her, Laura lingered outside the door to listen.

"It's this business of the mirror that perplexes me, Robert," Lazenby was saying. Robert? That must be Dr. Dalrymple, here already after the summons.

"It has a significance," she heard the doctor's deep

voice agree. "What do you know of its philosophical implications?"

"Philosophically, only what Plato said. He recommended the use of the mirror to young people to observe the development of virtue or vice, visible in their own faces."

"Exactly."

"And that is what you think Anna is doing?"

"In view of what you believe of her, yes."

"But I cannot be sure that my suspicions are correct. I told you my grounds. What Laura told me seems to confirm it."

"The stripes and the spiders. It seems too much of a coincidence to be other than the truth."

Laura heard footsteps behind her and a discreet cough. It was Depledge.

"Forgive me, Miss Sutcliffe, but lunch is served."

"Thank you, Depledge." Laura had no choice but to move on to the dining room, but her curiosity raged as to what the two men in the study were saying about Anna. Possessiveness engulfed Laura. Anna was *her* cousin, and they had no business to keep secrets from her about her cousin. She longed to go back to the study, to go in and demand to know, but etiquette prevented her. Perhaps later, after Dr. Dalrymple had gone, she could tax Mr. Lazenby about it.

But the secretary did not appear in the dining room for lunch. Laura guessed he must still be closeted with Dr. Dalrymple. She looked across the table to where Anna sat eating in silence. What were the two men saying about the girl? Anna's flushed look of the morning had gone now, leaving the customary pallor on her face. Laura had to admit she was nonplussed by her behavior, for Anna did not appear to be ill, and yet her strange behavior of late did not indicate a healthy, well-balanced girl. Once again she thought of Anna's mother, the ethereally beautiful Aunt Edith, whose gentle mind had given way under the stress of life. It was heartily to be hoped that her daughter was not treading the same dangerous path to madness, and Laura felt angered that fate could overcome her own fierce opposition. She would not allow Anna to go mad, not if she could help it.

Lazenby came in just as the girls were finishing dessert and ordered Depledge to bring tea for Dr. Dalrymple. Anna excused herself and left. Laura turned hopefully to the secretary.

"I believe you have talked with Dr. Dalrymple," she prompted.

"I have, but as yet we have reached no conclusions. I will inform you when we have discovered more," Lazenby replied. Laura was disappointed, for he evidently planned to reveal no more.

Offended by his cold, uncommunicative manner, Laura left the room. But she was not going to be cheated. She waited until Lazenby left and watched unobserved as he returned to the parlor, where Dalrymple was evidently still waiting. Then she crept up close again to the parlor door. Lazenby's voice was earnest.

"There can be little doubt now, Robert, I am sure of it. The aversion to stripes, the obsession with spiders, and your description of the girl at Rosamund Street. It all ties up. And yet . . ."

"You still entertain some doubt?"

"Well, it's curious, but recently Anna received a threatening letter from Bella. She found it in her reticule and has no idea how it came there."

Laura started. A threatening letter from Bella to Anna? But why should her cousin threaten herself? Lazenby's next words startled Laura even more.

"And then she learned she was to marry Lionel—"

"Lionel? But he's crazy about Bella!" Dalrymple replied.

Laura's brain was slow to react. Anna to marry a man she had not yet met? And a man, moreover, who had evidently met her in her other life? Realization dawned slowly. What would happen when Lionel met his future wife and recognized her?

"I know," Lazenby murmured. "And Anna nearly fainted with shock and horror at the thought of marrying a man she'd never met. She spoke of being cursed and started spouting Tennyson as though she were deranged. Honestly, Robert, on the surface of it, it is clear she is going mad."

"Not mad, Charles. She's very ill. Her mind is breaking down, but she's not mad. There is time yet."

"But what can we do? Robert, for God's sake, tell me how to handle this, for no one else can."

Laura could bear it no longer. It was *her* cousin they were discussing. Grasping the doorknob, she turned it and burst in.

"Charles! That's not quite true. Anna is my relation. I can help her and I will. After all, it is my prior right."

Lazenby rose swiftly. "Laura!" he cried. He seemed furious at her intrusion. But it was an icy anger. "Robert," he said coldly polite, "allow me to introduce Anna's cousin, Miss Laura Sutcliffe. Miss Sutcliffe, Dr. Robert Dalrymple."

For the first time, Laura saw Robert Dalrymple face to face. He was taller than Lazenby and very blond, with a tanned smiling face. He stretched out his hand and gripped hers firmly. Laura felt her agitation disappear, calmed by the reassuring confidence of his smile. Surely this man could help Anna.

"I am delighted to meet you, Miss Sutcliffe. Charles has told me many good things about you. Please sit down and join our talk," he said calmly, as if unaware of her gross breach of manners. Laura sat down next to Lazenby, whose anger seemed to have abated and who even contrived a stumbling apology.

Dalrymple ignored this interchange, leaned forward in his chair, and addressed them both.

"In the first place you must understand Anna's illness. The breakdown in personality is a form of hysteria brought about by some cause which we do not know. Its effect is to separate her personality into two distinct identities, each of which appears alternately."

"What causes this change?" Lazenby asked.

Dalrymple shrugged. "Who can say? Perhaps something associated with the unknown incident, or possibly the mirror, or both. It is a well-known fact that the mirror can represent the *alter ego* or other self I spoke of the other day."

"Emily says Anna uses unladylike words and sings bawdy songs when she looks in the mirror," Laura remarked. "And I too have heard her."

"Then that is the other personality asserting itself. And so is the threatening letter."

"But *why* does it happen?" Lazenby persisted.

"Because the hysterical character needs to appear, in her own eyes, as well as in others', more than she actually is. She needs to experience more than she is capable of, a theatrical and spurious experience. Not consciously so, you understand, for Anna knows nothing of what she undergoes in that other existence, but it arises from the need to live a life of her own, which she cannot as Anna. For the moment she identifies herself entirely with that theatrical character."

Lazenby rubbed his chin. "Is there any warning sign one can detect, to show when it might occur?"

"Symptoms can be anesthesia of some part of the body, paralysis or tremors or even fits. But the commonest sign is some form of bodily pain and possibly a blackout."

"That's it. She has had bad attacks of migraine and sleeps for hours," Laura cried.

"Then it is a true case of hysteria, for there is always dissociation—a flight from consciousness."

There was a harrowed look in Lazenby's eyes. "Robert, we know what is wrong with her, but how do we help her? What can we do?"

Dalrymple sighed and ran a perplexed hand through

his fair hair. "The cure is not so easy, my friend. Somehow we have to uncover the cause of her illness, get her to come to terms with it, and then the unhealthy *alter ego* will disappear."

"And if we cannot?"

"Then she will go mad."

Laura leaped to her feet. "No! For heaven's sake, don't say it so calmly. Can't you do something? Hypnotize her, perhaps? We can't go on doing nothing and let the poor girl go out of her mind."

Dalrymple thought. "Hypnotizing Anna might conceivably unearth the incident in the past. Then facing her with it would be up to you."

"And it could go wrong, you mean?" Laura demanded. "I'm willing to take the risk."

"Without her papa's knowledge, I take it."

Lazenby grunted in annoyance. "He would have no truck with the idea. Come with us now, Robert. Anna is at home and Mr. Braithwaite is out. We have so little time, for delay could be fatal."

Dalrymple eyed him wryly. "Fatal indeed, Charles, for in the battle between the two identities it is not unknown for the weaker to commit suicide."

Laura snorted. "What could be worse than marrying a man she does not know?"

"You do not consider Lionel a good husband for her?" Dalrymple inquired.

"I do not know the man," Laura had to admit.

"I do not consider him suitable," Lazenby said firmly, rising from his seat. "He is too weak to take care of himself, let alone another."

He led the way down to the conservatory. Anna was sitting writing something on her lap, but at the sight of her cousin and the men, Laura saw her push the paper under a book and look up with a welcoming smile.

"Miss Braithwaite, may I introduce to you my friend, Dr. Robert Dalrymple."

She extended her hand graciously, and as Dalrymple

took it, Lazenby met his gaze over the girl's head. From Dalrymple's barely perceptible nod Laura knew that the doctor recognized her.

"I hope you are not here for a second opinion, sir"—Anna laughed—"to try to cure me of my migraine."

"No," Dalrymple assured her. "But I know a capital method of relaxing the muscles so as to ward off an attack."

"Do you indeed? Then do tell me." She motioned the gentlemen to sit, and as Dalrymple sat down facing her, Lazenby pulled a chair half to the side of her for Laura to sit.

"You simply close your eyes and think beautiful thoughts," Dalrymple said pleasantly. "Think of a hot summer's day and you're lying in a field, listening to the song of the birds and watching the butterflies hovering."

"Beautiful," said Anna, closing her eyes and smiling. "I can see it all, can't you, Laura? Do go on."

Laura listened, watching Anna's face as Dalrymple went on, talking softly of puffy white clouds and zephyr breezes. In a little while, Anna's smile drooped and faded, but her eyes remained closed.

"I think she's asleep," Dalrymple whispered. "Don't speak." Then aloud he said commandingly, "Anna, can you hear me?"

"I can hear you." Her voice was barely a whisper.

"What are you thinking, Anna?"

"I am thinking how beautiful it is, to be free of pain and free of responsibility. It is wonderful, to be free."

"What were you writing, Anna?"

For a moment, there was silence. Dalrymple repeated the question. Laura saw Anna's lips set hard.

"Why do you call me Anna? I am not Anna."

"Then who are you?"

"Annabella."

Laura saw Robert's puzzled glance and remembered. Emily had said Annabella was her dead aunt's pet name for Anna, but she could not interrupt now to explain.

"And what were you writing, Annabella?" Dalrymple repeated.

The girl threw back her head and laughed, a hard, unpleasant laugh. Laura recognized it, the harsh, mocking laughter of the night.

"I was writing to Anna, for I am sick of waiting. I want to take over her body, but she won't get out. So I must *make* her get out, for there is not room for the two of us. She must die so that I can live."

Laura felt fear mingled with sick horror flood her veins. She cast an anxious look at Dalrymple, silently imploring him to get rid of this creature. Dalrymple sat silent.

Anna moved in her chair, extending her body in the leisurely manner of a cat. A half-smile played on her lips.

"A half a crown will lay me down," she sang in a full music-hall voice. "Won't one of you gentlemen take me on? What about you, Mr. Robert, instead of your eternal scribbling?"

In her half-closed eyes, her teasing smile, and her lascivious movements there was a kind of primitive, greedy sensuality that both repelled and fascinated Laura. She caught hold of Dalrymple's arm.

"Listen to me, Bella," Dalrymple said calmly. "Anna has done you no harm. Let her be."

"No harm? She usurps my body," the girl shrieked. "But only for a little longer," she added in a maliciously soft tone. "Only a few days more, and then . . ." She threw back her head and laughed the most evil laugh Laura had ever heard.

When the laugh died, Dalrymple spoke again. "Bella, it is time to sleep now. Do you hear me, Bella? When I count to five you will be asleep."

Laura listened as Dalrymple repeated the instructions. The girl's head nodded forward on her chest, and as Dalrymple counted, she fell still. On the count of five she was deeply asleep.

Dalrymple leaned forward. "Anna," he said softly to the sleeping girl. "Anna, are you there?"

A faint voice answered him. "I am here."

"Talk to me, Anna. Bella is gone and you may speak safely now. Tell me, Anna, why do you fear stripes so much? Go back in time, back to when the stripes frightened you, Anna." He paused a moment while the girl raised her head and opened her eyes.

"Yes," she said dully.

"Are you there, Anna? Can you see the stripes?"

For a moment she did not speak, but Laura could see she was reliving the moment, for her eyes looked surprised, then bewildered.

"The bars. The iron bars," she whispered.

"Yes," said Dalrymple. "What is happening, Anna?"

The bewildered expression melted into fear, her eyes dilated and staring. "He is attacking her, pushing her over and beating her. He's hurting her. Nanny is crying. Oh, help her, somebody!" Anna covered her face with her hands as if to wipe out the picture. Dalrymple leaned closer.

"Iron bars. Where are you, Anna? In the park? Looking through the railings?"

"No, no," she moaned. "Oh, please stop the cruel beast. He is hurting her." Sobs shook her bent body and Laura could bear it no longer. She touched Dalrymple's arm.

"No more, for pity's sake! Not now. She cannot take it."

Dalrymple leaned back and dimly Laura heard him tell Anna that he would count to five, by which time she would awake, refreshed and unmindful of all that had happened.

On the count of five Anna awoke.

"Why, Dr. Dalrymple." She smiled. "I do believe your method would work very well, I feel so relaxed. I shall certainly bear it in mind when I feel an attack coming on again."

227

"Glad to have been of service, Miss Braithwaite," Dalrymple replied. "It is a trick many of my patients have found useful."

"If you will forgive me, I will leave you gentlemen with Laura, for I have matters to attend to," Anna said, rising and smiling at them. It was after she had gone that Laura saw she had left her book on the chair. She retrieved the sheet of paper that lay between its leaves and read it, then handed it to Charles.

"Only a few more days, Anna, and then you must DIE."

Chapter Fifteen

"Tear it up!" Dalrymple advised, "otherwise Miss Oliphant or one of the servants could discover it and raise the alarm. Mr. Braithwaite would no doubt call in the police."

"He would indeed, if he believed anyone was threatening his daughter's life," Lazenby agreed. "His whole future depends on her and her marriage," Lazenby replied with bitterness.

"I fancy you do not hold your employer in very high esteem," Dalrymple commented.

"Nor would you if you knew how ambitious and scheming he is," Laura cut in. "He will sacrifice all, even his child, to pursue his ambition."

"Then we cannot reveal Anna's trouble to him?"

Lazenby shook his head. "Emphatically not. Out of shame he would commit her to an asylum at once, as I believe he did his wife. We must save Anna without him."

"You must," Dalrymple corrected him. "It is up to you two now."

Lazenby looked earnest. "What can we do?"

"Well, we now know Annabella is one and the same person. We know Anna, as the weaker personality, will submit to Bella's power—unless she can be brought to face herself."

"How?"

"The problem stems from an attack the child witnessed on her nurse and has since discarded from her conscious memory. She must remember it. Perhaps Miss Oliphant will recall the nurse and the incident in question."

"I think she was the nurse," Laura said.

"Better still. She can give you a true account. Perhaps it was a footpad, a burglar, a vagrant in the streets. Find out what happened and face Anna with it. No doubt her childish imagination magnified it into far worse an event than it really was. Then once the blockage to Anna's personality is removed, Bella can be banished."

"And Anna will recover? Dr. Dalrymple, tell me she *will* recover." Laura's voice was pleading.

"If all goes well, which is why I leave the matter in your sensitive hands. Now I must go." Dalrymple rose from his chair. "I have other patients awaiting me. Keep me informed, won't you?"

In the vestibule another thought seized Lazenby. He smiled grimly. "At least Lionel will be content to find he is to marry the woman he idolizes," he remarked.

Dalrymple nodded. "Only, if you succeed, it will not be the Bella he knows. By the way, do you know he has got himself deeply in debt over her? He tells me he got an advance of a thousand pounds from a moneylender on the strength of his impending marriage to the Braithwaite heiress. At twenty-percent interest. All because his lady love desires emeralds. He'll get himself into serious trouble if he goes on."

"All the more reason to hurry," Lazenby replied. "We shall see you again soon."

Emily was in Anna's bedroom doorway when Laura went back upstairs. "Just look at this, Miss Laura," she said with a sigh. "I sometimes believe Anna is still only a child, to behave so stupidly."

"What is it?" Laura asked, looking at what she held. In one hand was a doll dressed as a bride, and in the other what looked like a handful of rags and woolen stuffing.

"It *was* a pair of dolls, a bride and groom, but she's

ripped one doll to pieces. I found it just now while I was tidying. Why she did it I cannot imagine, for she's had no temper tantrums that I know of."

"Are you sure Anna did it?"

"Who else, when it was back in the cupboard? I *might* have blamed the kitten I had brought for her this morning, only the creature committed a rather unfortunate error on the floor and I had it removed to the kitchen. It must have been Anna, but why?"

"Where is she now?"

"In the kitchen. I felt it would be useful to her to learn something of pastry making, so I gave her into Cook's hands. I shall speak to her about this."

"I'll go down to her," Laura said.

Beyond the baize door dividing the main part of the house from the kitchen area Laura could hear voices raised. As she entered the kitchen she could see Anna, in a checked apron and with a smudge of flour on her cheek, standing demurely by the table. A kitchenmaid with a snub nose and an adenoidal voice was glaring at her.

"You shouldn't have done that, miss. It was cruel!"

"Done what? What did I do wrong, Cook?"

All three faces turned to Laura. She could smell a curious aroma, of something pungent, something burning.

"What is wrong, Anna?" she asked.

"Cook and Edna here accuse me of hurting that poor little kitten, but I did not touch her."

"Edna? Cook?" Laura's tone was crisp. Servants had no business to accuse their betters.

"It's nothing to do with me, miss, what the young lady does," Cook muttered, disappearing into the pantry.

"Well, I think she's cruel," the little kitchenmaid wailed. "She stuck its tail in the fire and burned it, and the poor little thing screamed. It's run outside now. It didn't do her no harm."

Cook reappeared to tweak the girl's ear. "You mind

your own business, girl, and come and help me," she said sharply, and dragged the maid into the pantry with her. Laura turned to Anna.

"It's not true, Laura. I wouldn't dream of hurting a little creature." There were tears in Anna's eyes as she spoke, and Laura knew she spoke the truth. It was that other, vicious girl who had perpetrated the cruel act. Not Anna. She led her cousin from the kitchen.

Upstairs in the parlor she suggested Anna take off her apron and sit down. Then she told her about the mutilated doll. Anna listened.

"I shall be blamed for that," she said as Laura finished. "I am blamed so often for what I have not done. I think *she* is doing all these things, to discredit me. Why else should she send me threatening letters?"

Laura scrutinized her expression, surprised at her calm tones. It was as though she accepted Bella's domination, and she felt fearful for her cousin.

"Who is she, Anna?"

"Bella, of course. But I don't know who she is or why she hates me so. Oh, Laura! I feel so frightened when I go to bed at night. I fear the darkness. What may she do to me?"

Rising quickly from her chair, she came to sit close beside Laura on the sofa, as though to gain comfort from her proximity. Laura put a protective arm about her.

"She will not harm you, Anna, I promise you that." The firmness and resolution in her voice were not conscious. Anna laid a grateful hand on hers.

"Save me from her, Laura, I beg you. There is no one else I can turn to."

Laura withdrew her arm quickly and rose. "Be sure I shall get to the bottom of this, Anna. You may rely upon me."

It was a rash promise, but somehow she must fulfill it, for Anna's sake. With Dalrymple's advice in mind Laura

went in search of **Emily** Oliphant. She surely must hold
the key to Anna's illness.

Emily was in the vestibule, scolding the parlormaid
for wearing a grubby apron.

"Suppose a guest were to call and see you in that
filthy state," she was expostulating. "The master would
be furious, and rightly so."

The girl went off, muttering. Laura asked Emily if she
could spare five minutes to speak to her. Emily glanced
at the grandfather clock.

"Five minutes only then, for the master will be home
soon." She led the way into the parlor and sat down.
Laura went to stand by the window, looking out over
the rain-soaked square.

"Emily," she said hesitantly. "I am right in believing
you were Anna's nurse when she was a child?"

"From the time she was seven," Emily replied
proudly.

"Forgive me if I touch upon a painful memory, Emily,
but I fear I must for Anna's sake."

"Do so if you must. You refer to Mrs. Braithwaite's
death, I take it."

"No. I believe Anna witnessed an attack upon you."

She saw Emily's face grow pale and her hands clasp
more tightly in her lap. "Did she tell you that? I thought
she had forgotten."

"In a manner of speaking, she has. But it troubles her
yet; in fact, it could be the reason for her odd behavior.
Will you tell me about it, Emily?"

The housekeeper's pointed chin rose high. "I will not,
and it is unseemly of you to inquire. Now was there
anything else?"

Laura turned quickly. "Emily, I would not pursue an
unpleasant memory if I did not think it necessary. Please
trust me. Was it a tramp in the streets, a molester in the
park? I must know."

"I cannot tell you."

"Emily, please."

"I do not know what she thinks she remembers. Forgive me, but you know how she is, full of imagination and not always truthful. She could have made it all up."

"But you said you thought she had forgotten. You yourself remember such an attack. There were iron bars there, were there not?" Laura was being ruthless, but to a purpose. Emily's face crumpled and grew red.

"Yes, I was attacked. Molested, rather."

"Where?"

"In Aspley Hall. But it was all a long time ago and best forgotten now. Let me go, for I must see to the dinner before Mr. Braithwaite comes." She rose to go, but Laura was not to be thwarted.

"Who was he, Emily, and how did Anna come to see it?"

Emily looked desperate. "She was playing under the table, unobserved, as children do. Playing house with her dolls."

"In her nursery?"

"Yes. There were iron bars at the window, for safety. But, really, it was nothing, I was not hurt."

Laura remembered Anna's words, that the nurse was weeping. A glimmer of understanding glowed. "Who was he, Emily? A manservant, footman? The butler?"

Emily's pale eyes looked distraught. "Miss Laura, why does it matter? You say the incident disturbed Anna, and that is all you need to understand. She was in a strained state at the time, for her mother was dying. In memory she probably magnifies the whole thing. Now I must go."

She turned to go to the door, and in the doorway she paused. Without turning she drew her thin figure erect and spoke to Laura. "You know all you need to know about the matter now. I pray you will not refer to it again."

"Nor will I, Emily, I assure you, unless it is absolutely necessary."

"And as to Anna, I think perhaps the time has come

for us both to admit that she is not normal. Destroying toys, tormenting a cat, sleepwalking, and apparently stealing too. Perhaps it would be best after all to tell Mr. Braithwaite of our suspicions and let him decide what is to be done."

"What suspicions?"

Emily turned slowly. "Why, what we would not admit before. That she is, unfortunately, as unbalanced as her mother. It is only right that I should tell her father of what has been going on."

Laura stepped forward a pace. "You cannot do that. To admit that she eluded you at night would mean your instant dismissal."

"I must risk that, for her sake."

"For her sake you would be wiser to remain silent."

Emily's sandy eyebrows rose. "How can silence help her? I think you argue only to protect yourself, Laura, for we have both been remiss in this matter. Mr. Braithwaite should be told at once."

"No, Emily." In her anxiety Laura caught hold of Emily's arm and Emily drew back in alarm. "Anna is ill, very ill, but there is a chance she can be cured. But only if you hold your tongue and give me time. Will you do that? Will you trust me?"

Emily stood, perplexed. "An illness that can be cured? How so?"

"I cannot explain, but give me time. My uncle will not thank you for the ignominy of discovering his daughter is mad, so wait a few days at least. Please."

The housekeeper spread her hands in bewilderment. "I do not understand what you say, but there can be no harm in waiting a little longer, I suppose. Very well."

Laura sank into a chair after she had gone, relieved that she had gained a little time. But the problem still remained—what were they to do?

Dinner was a tense affair. Uncle Reginald talked quite affably to his secretary while Laura ate in silence, watching every movement that Anna made. Her cousin seemed subdued, Laura thought.

"Tonight I am going out to supper with friends and shall not be home until late," Braithwaite informed Emily. "Depledge need not wait up for me. I'll let myself in."

"Very good, sir."

"Which reminds me. It is time we entertained, so next week I propose to invite Lord Travers and his son and daughter to dine with us. You'll get to know your be-trothed then, eh, Anna?"

"Yes, Papa."

"And I hope you'll put yourself out a bit to impress the boy, eh?"

"Yes, Papa."

Laura could see that though she answered dutifully, Anna's teeth were clenched tightly and her fingers gripped the dessert spoon and fork with such an inten-sity that one almost expected her to use them as weapons.

"Right then," Braithwaite said genially. "That's settled. Now I'll go to the study for an hour and read those papers of yours, Lazenby. The House reconvenes again shortly and I want to make certain all my case is ready."

"The papers are ready on your desk." It seemed to Laura that Lazenby could barely bring himself to be civil to the man. All the drama and anxiety taking place under his roof could not be communicated to this self-centered creature. If only circumstances were different and Laura could tell him how heartily she despised him . . . But Anna's plight was more pressing than any other consideration on earth. Laura looked across the table at the girl's tense face and felt her heart swell with compassion for her. If only she could get her away, out of this repressive house with its unfeeling master.

Braithwaite wiped his greasy mouth on his napkin and rose from the table, patting his ample stomach. "Good dinner that, Emily. I always enjoy boiled mutton. Perhaps we'll have something a little fancier for the dinner party next week, however."

Emily flushed at the unexpected compliment. "Thank you, sir. I was thinking about next week—some game, I thought. Grouse, perhaps?"

"Aye, if that's what you think best for gentry. Mustn't let them think I can't afford the best."

"I'll see your table does you justice, sir," Emily assured him, "and that Depledge selects the best wines from your cellar."

Braithwaite nodded and left. Almost at once the parlormaid came in and Anna rose from the table.

Laura saw her cousin go to look out the window, her hands clasped tightly together. Emily rose and instructed the parlormaid to clear the dishes and bring port for Mr. Lazenby. The secretary waved his hand.

"Not for me, thank you."

As Laura made to leave, a small clear voice came across the room. "I could kill him, the beast."

Emily turned a shocked face to Anna. "What are you saying, child?"

"He will ruin my life. I hate him."

"Anna!" The housekeeper turned to the maid. "Leave the dishes till later. Go and leave us."

"I am going too," Anna said firmly, turning from the window. "I am going to bed."

Emily cast a helpless glance at Laura. "Do that, my dear, and Miss Laura shall join you shortly." Anna nodded and left, with a calm "Good night" to Lazenby.

When she was out of their hearing, Emily turned to the secretary. "Do not worry, I too shall be close by her. She will not walk in her sleep tonight."

Laura watched the sprightly figure of the housekeeper sweep out of the dining room. She would watch over her charge with especially possessive concern tonight. Laura could not help admiring the woman and her devotion, however misguided her influence over her charge might have been. If only she had married and mothered children of her own . . . Laura felt irritated with herself. She was indulging in too many speculative "if only's" tonight. Unfortunate circumstances called for positive action, not wishful thinking.

Lazenby, still seated at the dinner table, was watching Laura thoughtfully. "I must apologize, Laura. I had no business to try and conceal anything from you about Anna. She is, after all, your cousin and no relative of mine. Please forgive me."

"Don't fret about it, Charles. I too was remiss in forgetting to tell you that she called herself Bella in the other life. We might have discovered sooner."

"That she is a liar, a cheat, a thief? Who exploits men for her own gain? That is no pleasant discovery for anyone. I was reluctant to believe what I was beginning to suspect and wanted only to spare you unnecessary anxiety."

"I know it, and am grateful. But how on earth did Anna manage to keep eluding us, that's what I cannot understand."

Lazenby shrugged. "The means hardly matter. We need now to discover the reason for Anna's disturbance."

"Ah, yes, I taxed Emily about it. She told me she was molested in the nursery by a man, and Anna was playing under the table and witnessed the event."

"I see," Lazenby said slowly. "Did she tell you who the man was?"

"A servant, I guessed. She would not say."

"Then I will ask her. It is important to know if, as Robert suggests, we are to try and make Anna face up to the fact. It is late now. I'll see what I can discover in the morning. Then we'll plan what to do next, Laura."

Charles' smile was thin, but Laura knew he was as anxious as herself. Once again she sensed the warm bond of conspiracy between them, and thought how she would have enjoyed closeness with this man were it not for Anna's plight.

"There is not much time, Charles," Laura murmured.

"I can feel it. After what she has just said about hating him. And today she destroyed a man doll too, and then she tortured the kitchen cat, and when we were alone, she told me she was afraid of Bella."

Lazenby looked startled. "You mean she knows about Bella?"

"She seems to think its another woman who is threatening her, not a creature inside her own head. Charles, I'm afraid of her. If we don't do something soon, I fear she'll go completely mad."

Lazenby crossed to Laura and put his hand on her shoulder. "No, we must see she does not, Laura. Together we can save her, I'm certain. Sleep on it and tomorrow we will decide what to do."

The hansom cab clattered to a halt on the greasy cobblestones and Reginald Braithwaite stepped out into the arc of dull yellow light from the gaslamp. He paid the cabbie and added an extra sixpence to the fare. Tonight he was feeling in an expansive mood.

"Thank you kindly, guv." The cabbie grinned, doffing his cloth cap before flicking the reins and driving off.

Pleasure warmed Braithwaite. It was good to extend generosity to less-fortunate mortals, for the deed gave contentment to both recipient and donor. He congratulated himself. Many Christians could preach the virtues, but few put them into practice.

Madame de Sandrier's russet head with its lace cap shone in a red halo from the light behind her as she welcomed him at the door.

"Mr. Reginald, do come in." She beamed. "Let Solange take your coat and hat and come and join us in the salon. Tonight is a special event."

He followed her through the chiffon drapes into the main room, his senses excited by the perfume and the sound of a harp gently plucked by a lissome girl who appeared to be ready for bed in a diaphanous nightgown of some kind. Wordlessly he took the goblet of

wine Madame poured from a jug, his eyes darting from
one girl to another. They were all scantily dressed in
similar gauzy robes, and he could feel his heart pounding as he stared at the flesh he could see gleaming
beneath the gowns. Which one had Madame reserved
for him, he wondered? He had specified someone young
and fairly raw, for the idea of much-used shop-soiled
goods was distasteful. Madame had assured him she
could supply what he sought—a new girl, barely fledged,
but one who could offer the enthusiasm and excitement
fit for a king.

"Reserved only for our very special clients," she had
murmured discreetly with an understanding smile, and
Braithwaite was flattered. Only for the highbrow or very
wealthy, she had implied, and she had obviously recognized him for one or the other.

"Sit on the sofa here, Mr. Reginald. Your companion
will not be long," Madame said, ushering him to be
seated. Braithwaite fought down his impatience. No
need to hurry matters, he scolded himself. Having
waited so long and denied the needs of the flesh, he
could wait a little longer and savor the pleasure of the
moment. These lush-limbed girls were a delight to behold, so juicy-looking and full of promise. The silver
goblet between his fingers trembled.

Madame beckoned to a young woman of large-boned
blond beauty clad in flimsy blue. "Grete, please see Mr.
Reginald has all he requires until Bella comes down,"
she purred. The statuesque blond looked down on him
haughtily, and Braithwaite could not help hoping his
companion for the evening would not be as powerfully
built and imposing. Someone pretty and feminine, he
wanted, someone fragile and yet accustomed to endur-
ance, for his need was great. . . .

"Would you like some Eastern sweetmeats, sir?" the
tall blond said, but her tone seemed to indicate that she
was asking more out of duty than concern. Braithwaite

felt irritated that her manner made him feel of no consequence.

"Thank you, no."

She shrugged and moved away. Braithwaite sipped his wine nervously. It was pleasant stuff, whatever it was, with a strange, exotic taste that vied with the perfume filling the air. All around him he could hear subdued laughter and contented chatter.

"Come, Solange, dance for us," a gentleman reclining in a deep armchair called out. The dark-eyed girl cast him a slumberous glance and smiled. The girl at the harp broke off the melody she was playing and began another slow tune in a minor key. Solange put down her goblet and, picking up a sea-green length of chiffon, began to move slowly and rhythmically to the music.

Braithwaite watched appreciatively. The slender figure moved, sinuous and graceful as a cat, drawing the veil across her face and down her body as she moved. Her young skin gleamed through the fabric of her robe, and as the music quickened, so did her movements, voluptuous and inviting. Braithwaite's temples throbbed. Solange wove dexterously between the guests, flicking her veil across the face of a gentleman here and grazing her body against that of another gentleman there. Braithwaite saw that they all stood motionless and entranced, and he licked his lips as the music grew to a climax.

It ended abruptly as Solange flung herself on her knees before him and bent her head to her knees, like a captive slave before a sultan. It was all Braithwaite could do not to reach forward and touch that provocative body, abased at his feet. The emotions churning within him at that moment were far fiercer than anything Dolly Winthrop had ever aroused in him, and Braithwaite was almost afraid of their intensity. Solange threw up her head with a mocking smile, rose, and walked away.

Dammit, would Madame never return with his escort

for the night? He felt annoyed. After all, he was paying a handsome fee for tonight and time was slipping by. He drew out his gold watch, and as he did so, Madame reentered the room.

"Mr. Reginald, Bella is just coming," she assured him. "I'm sorry for the delay, but minor mishaps will disturb even the best-managed ménage, you know. Nothing of consequence. All is well now and Bella will be here directly."

He grunted and looked toward the door. Madame sat down beside him. "Do tell me, Mr. Reginald, have you any special preferences Bella should know? We like to please our guests in every possible way." She smiled archly. Braithwaite looked at her, puzzled.

"How do you mean?"

Madame laughed and flicked back a wayward red curl. "Well, every gentleman has his own tastes, his idiosyncrasies, one might say. Some like a slave girl to master, others like to be mastered by a powerful woman."

"Be mastered?" repeated Braithwaite in disbelief.

"Indeed." Madame nodded. "Some find that being oppressed, even bullied, awakens their appetite. Now tell me, would a touch of pain perhaps give you pleasure? Our girls are well-trained to submit to all a gentleman's desires. A taste of the whip is not unknown here if it gives pleasure. Pray tell me what you would desire, sir."

Braithwaite ran his tongue over his dry lips. Cautiously he gave way to the mounting enthusiasm he could feel deep in his insides. "I am not averse to the idea of the whip, Madame, if you permit it. In the past I've only beaten my horse, but the idea of beating a woman has its appeal."

Madame's gaze slid away, but she made no comment. Braithwaite was musing over this new prospect offered to him, and he found it exciting. A woman should be beaten into submission, and then taking her was final proof of his mastery. What a sensible, understanding woman Madame was.

"Ah, here she is now." Madame rose as a girl entered and came toward them. Braithwaite rose too, eager eyes scanning the slim figure totally veiled in lavender. He could see she was shapely, small, high breasts rising above a tiny waist that curved out again to swaying hips. She was long-legged and graceful, and Madame beamed on her approvingly. Her face Braithwaite could not see except for deep blue eyes that surveyed him languorously over the veil that obscured the lower half of her face.

"Mr. Reginald, may I present to you Bella, Queen of the East," Madame said softly. "You have already met the courtiers of the harem, and now the queen herself comes to serve you. All the beauty and excitement of the Orient is yours, Mr. Reginald. Bella will obey your commands."

Braithwaite smiled sheepishly at the girl, and she lowered her lashes demurely. Madame made her excuses and withdrew. The big blond girl, Grete, was laughing and tugging her escort's sleeve, motioning toward the door. Braithwaite looked at Bella, waiting for her to make the first move. After all, she was accustomed to the game, and he was but a novice. He did not want to reveal himself as such by rushing matters.

"Come," said Bella huskily, moving toward the door. Eagerly Braithwaite leaped to follow her. Good. She was a no-nonsense type, anxious to get down to business, and that was how he liked it.

He watched her hips snaking from side to side as he mounted the stairs behind her. Soon would come his reward for patience, he thought happily. The anticipation of the moment recalled to mind the day he went up on the platform at Sunday school when he was eleven, to receive a prize for an unblemished record of attendance.

"Virtue," the Sunday-school teacher used to say, "is its own reward." If she could only see him now.

Along the corridor Bella opened a door and beckoned him to enter, then stood aside to let him pass. She watched him silently as he took in the draped room with its candles and sofa at a glance and then turned back to her.

"Bella," he murmured anxiously.

"Yes?" The voice was soft and sweet as honey. "No need to talk. Take off your jacket."

Slim fingers rose to help him, and Braithwaite trembled at their touch. His jacket fell unheeled to the floor. The fingers slid down his shirtfront, unfastening the pearl buttons and caressing his skin. Braithwaite tingled from head to toe. His hands reached up eagerly to touch her, but she slid from his reach and bent to pick up the fallen jacket.

"Pretty," she murmured, and in her hand he saw the little carved silver match case he carried in his fob pocket.

"A present last Christmas," he replied with pride, stopping himself in time from saying that it was from his daughter. There was no need to point the difference in age between himself and this tantalizing girl before him. She could be no more than twenty, possibly less.

"May I keep it?" the husky voice inquired.

Braithwaite was about to refuse, then thought better of it. "Perhaps. We'll see." Rewards have to be won, he thought privately. Let's see what you can do for me first, my lass.

She gave a little chuckle and moved to a dressing chest in the corner, opened the drawer, and put the match case inside. "A memento," she said.

Irritation found no time to play in Braithwaite's mind, for his eyes rested on the curve of her breast and his fingers itched to touch her. He remembered Madame's promise of a willing slave, and thought how mistaken she was in this girl. So far she had shown little sign of submissive abasement. He was reminding himself to retrieve the silver case from the drawer before he left when Bella came toward him, throwing back her flimsy robe to reveal her shapely form. Braithwaite stood entranced. Veiled as she was but with her glowing flesh completely revealed, she was intoxicating, the summit of any man's desires.

"Bella," he croaked, and lunged forward.

"Come," she said, avoiding his clutch and reclining herself on the sofa. Torment throbbed in his temples and his loins, and dimly Braithwaite remembered Madame's words.

"The whip," he suggested in a voice so hoarse he could barely recognize it as his own.

"Not now, later, perhaps. Come, my luscious spider, I want you now."

She reached up slim arms and Braithwaite wrenched at his trouser buttons with feverish haste. The anguish that had tormented him so long was about to be fulfilled at last.

The door crashed open. Braithwaite could scarcely believe it. On the brink of his ecstasy that abominable red-haired Madame stood in the doorway, her eyes registering horror. Bella did not move, but Braithwaite rebuttoned himself quickly and turned on the woman. Before he could speak she stepped past him.

"Bella, come quickly. I think Maisie is dying."

Braithwaite checked the angry words, born of frustrated misery, that sprang to his lips. Bella half-rose indolently.

"What of it? It does not concern me."

"But it does, Bella. Come at once and I'll explain," the woman insisted. Bella drew her robe together and got up from the sofa without haste. Braithwaite resolved to put his frantic disappointment aside for the moment and be chivalrous.

"A lady in danger, Madame? Can I help?"

"Thank you, no, sir. The doctor is with her, but I need Bella for the moment. If you would care to rejoin the others downstairs, I shall endeavor to atone later. I am most sorry, sir."

She hustled Bella out, leaving him to dress again alone. He hesitated, undecided whether to face the strangers downstairs or wait, then made up his mind to do as Madame suggested. Perhaps the evening might not be lost, only delayed, and he and Bella could renew their encounter soon. At the door he paused, hearing voices outside.

"I don't care," Bella's voice said sulkily. "You interrupted me. I had what I waited for for so long."

"What are you talking about?" Madame's voice snapped. "The man can wait."

"He was what I sought, a fat and greedy specimen, ready and ripe. Maisie can wait."

Braithwaite drew back from the door and saw the handle turn. Fat and greedy indeed! He would teach this insolent girl a lesson.

"You do not understand, Bella," Madame went on. "It seems Maisie must have become pregnant."

"The more fool she. She was always careless."

"But the fall the other night has brought on a miscarriage. She is bleeding heavily, such torrents of blood you never saw. The doctor fears for her life."

"Then remove her somewhere."

"We cannot while she is in this state. But you must go, Bella, for if the story comes out and Maisie dies, there could be trouble for you. You must go."

"I'm not leaving. You can do as you like with Maisie. I'm staying, for a man awaits me."

Madame's voice grew shrill. "Let me make it plain, Bella, since you will not listen. You are nothing but trouble and I have had enough of you. You will leave my establishment and never return. Do you understand now?"

There was a sound of scuffling and muffled cries of protest and then silence. Braithwaite could only guess that Madame had dragged the girl away. Soberly he reflected that his evening's fun now seemed to have receded similarly, for even if Madame later offered him another girl she could not be as intoxicating as Bella. Furtively he opened the door and peeped out. The corridor was deserted.

Braithwaite hurried down the stairs. Solange was at the foot of the stairs, playfully tugging her escort's mustache. She looked up in surprise as Braithwaite descended.

"Leaving so soon, Mr. Reginald?"

"I must. Matters to see to, you understand. Would you be so kind as to find my coat and hat for me?"

She smiled mischievously, no doubt supposing Bella had either failed to please or had dispatched her business with him swiftly. Braithwaite no longer cared what they thought. His dignity was battered, and he wanted only to leave this place, and quickly.

When Solange reappeared with his belongings, he thanked her and strode out into the street. There was not a cab in sight, so Braithwaite began walking. Thank God it was no longer raining.

Turning the corner of Rosamund Street Braithwaite found a hansom cab standing at the curbside. Gratefully he opened the door and called up to the cabbie.

"Hanbury Square, my man."

The cabbie doffed his cap. "Sorry, sir, I'm waiting for a customer."

"And I am your customer. Dammit, take me to Hanbury Square," Braithwaite snapped back, and made to climb in. The cabbie jumped down from the box.

"I'm sorry, sir, but I'm ordered to wait, for a lady. She'll be here any minute."

"While you're arguing, you could drive me to the square and be back. It's not far," Braithwaite argued, but he was beginning to feel that this night was not his luckiest. At the moment a lady appeared from out of the darkness. She was quite young and very handsome, Braithwaite thought as she approached and raised inquiring eyes to him and the cabbie.

"Forgive me, madam," he began awkwardly. "I want to go to Hanbury Square."

She smiled and made no answer as she climbed into the cab. Braithwaite began to walk away. "Excuse me, sir," he heard a pleasant voice call.

He turned back. She was leaning out and smiling at him. "It's a dirty night for walking. I am going home near the Haymarket after nursing a sick friend, and the square is not far from there. Would you care to share my cab?"

"You are very kind." Braithwaite climbed in eagerly and the cab set off. Such a charming lady, he must make an effort at polite conversation.

"I hope your friend is not very ill, madam."

She sighed. "Very poorly, I'm afraid, but there is still hope."

He grunted. "If I may say so, you are a very Christian lady to go out alone at night to tend a sick friend. Your husband must be proud of such a wife."

She laughed softly, a pleasant, musical sound. "I am not married, sir. I live alone."

That surprised him. A woman so attractive and refined and tastefully dressed deserved to be wed. Must have a private income, he reflected.

In a small street off the Haymarket the cab drew up and the lady rose. With alacrity Braithwaite opened the door and helped her alight, and was rewarded with a gracious smile. He felt a degree of reluctance to let her go without at least learning who she was. Directness was the best method.

"Good night, sir," she said, holding out to him a shilling. "My share of the cab fare."

"Allow me the pleasure," Braithwaite replied chivalrously, pushing her hand away. "And may I know the name of the angel of mercy who shared by cab?"

"Miss Barrington. Sybil Barrington," she answered with equal directness.

"Barrington? Of Barrington's Chocolate Company?"

She smiled and turned. "Distant relatives," he heard her say. He watched her mount the steps.

"May I call on you, Miss Barrington?" It was not in his nature to be so impulsive, but if he did not speak now, he might never see this gracious woman again, and that would be a pity. Barrington's Chocolate Company was a thriving concern whose shares rose daily.

She turned on the top step and looked back at him curiously. Braithwaite fished in his waistcoat pocket for a visiting card. "My intentions are honorable, madam, I assure you, for I am no mere stage-door Johnny, as you see."

She screwed up her eyes to peer at the card. "Mr. Reginald Braithwaite, M.P.," she read aloud, and then laughed that musical laugh again. "Then I think I need not fear you, Mr. Braithwaite, if you are a member of the august House of Commons. You will be welcome to call. Tuesday afternoon, perhaps, about three?"

Braithwaite drove off again, contented. At least the whole night had not been wasted and could, with careful ingenuity, be put to good use. This Barrington woman was a delight, charming and refined enough to grace any man's table as hostess. Miles superior to the Bella girl he might now have been with but for fate. Fate plays funny tricks sometimes. Barrington's. It might be worthwhile to look into the price of their shares to-morrow with a view to buying some. It could be a good move.

It was only when he reached Hanbury Square and let himself quietly into the house that he remembered the lucifer case. That damned girl had stolen his silver case. It was too much. She had humiliated him and, true, he had not offered to pay Madame for a disastrous night, but the case was of far more value than the wine he had drunk. In the morning he must set about getting it back, for he was damned if that little whore was going to get away with it.

Chapter Sixteen

Morning prayers were mercifully short. The master read only a brief lesson from the Holy Book, and Laura noted how hollow-eyed and weary he looked. Anna, too, was dreamy and uncommunicative over breakfast, and Laura began to wonder if they, too, were sickening for something. All this recent hot weather and flies and city dirt often gave rise to some kind of outbreak. Nowhere near so healthy as country life, she reflected, and longed for a breath of clear Yorkshire air.

After breakfast Laura returned to her bedroom. Through her cousin's doorway she could see Anna sitting at her dressing table and staring at her reflection.

She felt uneasy seeing the girl at the mirror. After all, it was through the mirror she had seen her act and speak strangely. "Come on now, you know what they say about staring in a mirror, don't you," she said briskly.

Anna did not move. "No. What do they say?"

"Why, that if you look in a mirror long enough you will see the devil's face."

Anna's reflection looked startled, and then regained its composure again. She cocked her head to one side. "Am I pretty, Laura? Would a man find me attractive?"

Laura was surprised. "What a question, Anna! A wise man cares less for looks than for intelligence. It is pure vanity to admire yourself."

"I was not admiring, Laura, I was wondering. Do you think Dr. Dalrymple finds me pretty?"

"Why do you ask?"

Anna shrugged. "Oh, because I think he is handsome, and clever. And he is kind, too. Do you think he will marry, Laura? She will be a fortunate woman indeed if he does."

"I have no time for idle speculation of that kind, Anna. Will you come down?"

Anna sighed and rose. "I'll go in the garden for a while and join you downstairs later."

"Very well." Laura left her and went out. In the corridor she saw Emily accosting one of the chambermaids emerging from Mr. Lazenby's room. "Ah, Janet, don't forget I want you to change Miss Anna's bedding today. And don't forget to turn the mattress."

"No, miss. I'm just about to do it," the girl replied.

Mr. Lazenby, hearing voices, came out of his room. "Miss Oliphant, could I have a word with you in private?"

"Of course. Perhaps you'd like to come to my room downstairs."

Laura guessed Charles' intention and followed discreetly when the housekeeper led the way and Lazenby followed in silence. After Emily had unlocked the door and entered, Laura listened unashamedly outside.

"Emily," she heard Charles say, "I'm very anxious. I wanted to tell Mr. Braithwaite last night, but though I waited up till two, he did not come home. I've made up my mind that pleasant or not, both he and you should know."

"Know what, Mr. Lazenby?" The housekeeper's voice was puzzled.

"It's Anna. You know she is ill."

"Well, she has always been delicate. This sleepwalking of late seems to have ceased—"

"It has not," Charles said firmly. "And it is not sleepwalking. Anna has been evading us deliberately—I don't know how—and going out to . . . What I am trying to tell you is that in her illness, she does not know she is doing it. Nor is she accountable for how she behaves."

"Now, come, Mr. Lazenby," Emily said smoothly. "I think you have taken this too much to heart and let it upset you. Anna cannot have been evading us or I should know."

"She still evades us," Lazenby burst out. "Oh, Emily! I would break it gently if I could but however the words are spoken, they are cruel. Anna changes her personality, becomes another person, and behaves in a manner you and her father would find shocking."

Emily hesitated, and Laura guessed she was remembering Anna's words at the mirror. "But why, Mr. Lazenby? What makes her do it, if she does?"

"I am not sure. Certain things seem to trigger off the change, like seeing stripes. Now we have discovered their significance—the nursery window bars and that incident when you were attacked. But why the incident should have such a long-lasting effect on her, I cannot tell. I fancy there is more yet. But I had to tell you, Emily, that you will not like what you learn of Anna's other self, Bella."

"Bella?"

"That is the name she calls herself by in the other life. And as Bella, she is the exact opposite of Anna. She is untruthful, dishonest, unscrupulous, and completely without morals."

Emily flared. "Do you expect me to believe that of Anna?"

"Not of Anna, but of Bella. It is hard to understand, Emily, but the two personalities are entirely distinct, and Anna is not responsible for Bella's actions."

"I remember," Emily said slowly. "The letter in Anna's reticule—that was from Bella . . ."

"Threatening to get rid of Anna. Don't you see the danger, Emily? The more powerful personality could drive Anna out and take over."

The conviction in his voice evidently worried Emily.

"That's rubbish, Mr. Lazenby. You make it sound as if Anna is possessed."

"So she is, in a way."

"Then surely the problem is one for a priest and not for a layman. Exorcism is the answer, if you are right." Emily conveyed by her tone that she did not believe him to be right.

Charles sounded weary. "Unfortunately I know I am right, Emily. Dr. Dalrymple has diagnosed Anna's illness. But she could be cured, if only we knew the way."

"Cured? How?"

"Tell me what you omitted to tell Miss Laura about your attack, Emily. There is something you wanted to hide. What is it?"

There was a long pause before Laura heard Emily's reply. "Of what possible interest is that to you? I told Miss Laura I prefer to forget what I found so—distasteful." Another pause. "In any event, I am not sure I can believe what you tell me about Anna acting as a wicked girl. It all seems too fanciful. No, I cannot bring myself to believe it."

Laura had to move away quickly as Janet came along the corridor and knocked at the door. In answer to Emily's call, the chambermaid went in. Laura crept back.

"Excuse me, Miss Oliphant. I found this under Miss Anna's mattress. It's your laudanum bottle, nearly empty, but I know you keep it locked up."

Emily remained calm. "Thank you, Janet. You did right."

Laura pretended to be returning as the maid came out and went upstairs. Then Laura returned to the housekeeper's door.

"Will you believe me now?" Charles said, his voice gentler now. "You were raped, weren't you, Emily? Tell me who the man was."

Emily replied slowly. "Do you really think this has anything to do with Anna's illness?"

"Only you can tell me that, Emily. Who was he?"

A faint whisper, and yet it sound to Laura like a judgment of doom. "Mr. Braithwaite."

Laura gasped.

"Reginald Braithwaite?" Charles echoed. "No wonder it became a nightmare to the child, not understanding but only seeing the violence of such an act. Her own father." The shock in Lazenby's voice echoed Laura's own.

Emily sounded near to tears. "You understand why I had to keep silent, Mr. Lazenby? I would have lost my position if I had complained. And I felt sorry for him."

"Sorry for Braithwaite?"

"You don't understand. He was very lonely and worried, for young Mrs. Braithwaite was in the sanatorium. She was dying."

Charles' reply was low. "And the child saw her father go berserk, like an animal, while her mother was dying. God help her, the poor child!"

Laura, her fingers to her lips, nodded fiercely. She had always known Uncle Reginald was a hypocrite, but this . . .

"Mr. Lazenby, it is not for you to pronounce judgment," Emily was saying tearfully. "I entrusted a confidence to you because you needed to know, for Anna."

"You are right. Thank you, Miss Oliphant." Laura, realizing he might be leaving, moved away just as Cook came along. She put her head around the door. "You want me to send up the market for some turbot for tonight's dinner, Miss Oliphant?"

As Laura hurried away, she heard Emily reply, "I'll come, Cook."

After Mr. Lazenby had gone, Emily pored over the figures in her ledger, but she found it hard to concentrate. Thoughts kept coming, unbidden, to get in the way. Anna, daydreaming before the mirror and mouthing obscenities, Anna with the bottle of laudanum. And fleeting memories of the schoolmistress in Harrowfield and her warning.

"A Gemini child," Miss Pargeter had said, "the twin sign of the stars. She has a dual nature." Little had Emily dreamed then how true the prophecy would become.

"A dark, disturbing stranger in the cards," Miss Pargeter had also predicted. Emily sighed. Mr. Lazenby had come into their life, and for a time she had allowed her romantic mind to be disturbed by him, but that was before her natural common sense had prevailed. Now it was Anna who was far more disturbing. The outwardly guileless child had evidently been drugging her with all the cunning of a criminal. No wonder she had felt unable to get up in the mornings, Emily mused, remembering the heavy-headed feeling. Reluctant or not, Emily could no longer disbelieve Mr. Lazenby's strange story of the child being possessed, though he had denied the word. What was Emily to think?

She thought of writing to Miss Pargeter for advice, but on second thoughts discarded the idea. It would entail revealing the incident she had long ago pushed out of her mind but for Miss Laura and Mr. Lazenby's persistence. She colored even now at the memory of it, swift and brutal and loveless. And the little white face of the child under the table, screened by the overhanging cloth. Mr. Braithwaite had never known she was there, and Anna made no sound. Emily could remember it still. No words were spoken, no sound but swift breaths and her own faint cries of protest, quickly silenced.

There had been no warning. The long rays of the late-afternoon sun glowed in through the nursery window, casting long barred shadows across the parquet floor. Emily had just finished starching and ironing some of Anna's little white smocks, and the warm air was full of the scent of hot starched linen. Emily hummed as she hung the garments over the clothes maiden to air, and Anna was playing house contentedly with her doll under the table.

Suddenly the door opened and Mr. Braithwaite stood there, his eyes dark with worry. Knowing he had just visited the hospital, Emily looked at him in concern.

"How is the mistress, sir?"

He just stood there, shaking his head, and then suddenly he strode forward and caught hold of her. Before Emily could say a word, he had ripped the buttoned front of her gown and pushed her down on the nursery sofa. Then suddenly her skirt was over her head. Emily cried out, but his mouth came down hard on hers. She felt his hands and knew what he was about, but she dared not fight with him. A glimpse of a little terrified face, and then his reddened, savage face obscured the other. Emily took the line of least resistance.

It was not pleasant, but it was not as agonizing as she had heard tell. When he had done, he got up and left without a word. Emily had straightened her dress and, for the child's sake, tried to act as though nothing untoward had occurred. As it was, the terrible news had to be broken to Anna a few days later that her mama had gone to join the angels. Mr. Braithwaite never referred to the incident again, and as time passed and Emily discovered that no child had been conceived from their sordid little encounter, with typical practicality she had put the matter from her mind. After all, she could profit from it, she reasoned. And it seemed she did, for from a nursery maid she had been promoted to nanny and ultimately to housekeeper. Not a bad exchange for a brief humoring of a man's need, she reckoned.

And if the affair had strengthened her belief that men were animals, greedy and oblivious of women's needs, what of it? Mr. Braithwaite had acted just as selfishly as her father toward her mother, but at least he made sure Emily did not suffer for it. He was not a bad man as masters went, and he had never sought to take advantage of her again. It had only been the once, in his moment of despair.

No, she could not tell Miss Pargeter. This time Emily was glad to leave the solution of this particular problem to Mr. Lazenby. He was educated and clever, he and his friend Dr. Dalrymple. So if Mr. Braithwaite discovered about Anna, as he undoubtedly would, his anger would be directed against them, and not against her. After all, she had her future to protect. . . .

Janet knocked at the door and came in. "Miss Oliphant, there's a gentleman at the back door for you."

"For me? Who is he, Janet?"

"Mr . Bedford, the draper. He says he has some material for you, miss. Can't think why he didn't send the boy with it."

Emily rose quickly, her problems forgotten. "Bid him come in, Janet. Bring him in here. And make us a pot of tea, will you?"

She put away her ledger and patted her hair into place under her cap, pleased that her instincts had proved correct. That Mr. Bedford should call in person could only mean that he wanted to improve their acquaintanceship. A pang of remorse over Anna's problem receded as Janet returned, followed by a plump, broad gentleman with a genial smile.

"Mr. Bedford, miss."

The next half-hour was the pleasantest she had experienced for a long time, Emily thought as she made her way to the dining room to check that all was ready for lunch. Miss Laura was already there and Mr. Lazenby was gazing moodily out of the window. He turned as Emily entered.

"Is Mr. Braithwaite back yet?" he asked.

"I was not aware he had gone out," Emily replied.

"He received a message that the prime minister's secretary wanted to see him at once. He's been gone for nearly two hours. I still haven't had chance to tell him about Anna."

"I'm sure he'll be here soon. By the way, did you take the bottle of laudanum from my room? I could not find it." He nodded. "I have a toothache, and took it with me. I meant to tell you."

"Then be sure to return it to me personally when you have finished with it," Emily replied, satisfied.

"I will."

Depledge entered. "Excuse me, there is a gentleman to see Mr. Lazenby. Dr. Dalrymple would like a word with you, sir."

Laura leaped to her feet. "I'll come too, Charles," she said.

Emily glanced at the mantel clock. "It's almost one o'clock and time for lunch."

"It must be urgent, Emily. Forgive me." Mr. Lazenby strode quickly from the room and Laura hastened after him. Emily was curious. Mr. Lazenby and Dr. Dalrymple were probably discussing Anna, and it was Emily's right to know what was being said just as much as Miss Laura's. Opening the door quietly and going out in the corridor, she could hear their voices in the vestibule.

"How do you know?" the secretary was asking.

"Sybil came to my hotel to tell me. She said Madame had ordered them all to leave the house at once until the outbreak was past, if indeed the rumor is true." Dr. Dalrymple's tone was serious.

"Is Sybil not leaving town then?"

"No. She thinks it is an exaggeration and not to be feared. But she asked me to tell you that Bella was dismissed by Madame before the alarm."

"Does she know?"

"Who Bella Marchant really is? No, but she had to get rid of Bella because she caused nothing but trouble." Emily was perplexed by all this talk of strangers. But Bella's name she did know.

"For stealing?" Laura inquired.

"And worse. She pushed Maisie downstairs and caused her miscarriage. The girl nearly bled to death, but fortunately she is recovering now in a nursing home. Recovering, that is, if she has not caught the infection. But it could be only a false alarm. Then there was Lionel, of course."

Lionel, thought Emily. That must be Anna's betrothed they spoke of.

"What of him?" Emily could hear the concern in Mr. Lazenby's voice.

"He's nearly out of his mind over Bella's treatment of him. They say he almost tried to drown himself. Anyway, Madame had had enough. She sent Bella packing and has not seen her since. I thought you should know."

"Thank you, Robert." Lazenby's voice was strangled and Emily listened, stunned. This vile creature Bella they were talking about—was it really Anna?

"I must go now," Dr. Dalrymple was saying. "Oh, by the way, Sybil told me that she saw Mr. Reginald at the house last night."

"My uncle?" Laura said in alarm. Emily wondered what house they referred to.

"Well, she said she knew him as Mr. Reginald, but later, from his card, that he's a gentleman of some eminence. He was there last night, but left before the alarm. Perhaps, if you see him, you could warn him that he may be in danger. Cholera is no joke, but you know how soon young women can panic. It may not have been cholera the young fellow had after all. I'm sure one of them would have developed symptoms by now if it was, but Madame was taking no chances. She evacuated the house first thing this morning. Now I'll be off and let you get to your lunch before it goes cold."

"One thing more before you go, Robert," Emily heard Lazenby intervene. "Tell me—which girl was Mr. Reginald with last night?" Emily could barely make out Lazenby's whisper.

"Why, Bella," replied Dr. Dalrymple.

The strange moan she heard from Laura made Emily retreat to the dining room. In a few seconds she heard Miss Laura come running upstairs, past the dining room, and on up to her own room.

Chapter Seventeen

Disappointment, resentment, and anger bubbled within Reginald Braithwaite as he left the office of the prime minister's secretary and came out into the street. He raised his cane to hail a cab, hesitated, and lowered it again. No, he was in no mood to go home yet. Perhaps his simmering emotions would have better chance to cool to equanimity if he had a drink first. The club was not far away.

He marched along the street and crossed, jabbing his cane angrily on the cobblestones and recalling the interview. That young secretary, Philpotts, was an insolent fellow. He sat behind his desk, smiling urbanely and omitting to invite Braithwaite to be seated. His high-domed head, with its dark red hair plastered with Macassar oil till it shone, reminded Braithwaite of highly polished mahogany. He had been very suave and polite, using all the correct phrases.

"The prime minister regrets . . ." he had intoned coolly. "He is well aware of your industrious efforts on the party's behalf . . . deeply conscious of your zeal and energy, but . . ."

If Braithwaite had been wondering what he was leading up to, he was soon enlightened. What it boiled down to was that his master wanted the matter of criminal law reform to be dealt with in the coming session of Parliament, but not introduced by Reginald Braithwaite.

"A matter of such weighty importance calls for the shrewd handling of an experienced member," Philpotts had said, and Braithwaite could see what they were up to. An eminent figure must introduce the bill, not a lowly merchant from the northern wilds, a party zealot who would reap the rewards Braithwaite had so earnestly hoped and worked for. Dimly he could hear Philpott's voice.

"Your work and research need not be wasted, for you could back the motion with all the weight of your findings," he was saying smoothly. "Every particle of evidence is invaluable. The prime minister, as you know, is anxious that reform measures are taken, and he is arranging to that end the best possible person to introduce the bill."

Again there was assurance of the prime minister's regret that Braithwaite should be disappointed, and murmured words about the master hoping to see Braithwaite at some not-far-distant occasion with a view to possible palliative measures. Braithwaite did not understand the words, but it did not matter. He was conscious only of a sense of failure, of rejection by his political masters, and the sting was painful to his pride.

Damn them for their ingratitude! For them he had neglected his own business with the result that there was still trouble in his mills. Had he been a more selfish man, less concerned with the welfare of society, he'd have spent the time ironing out his own problems instead of concentrating on this vice problem. Why, he'd even demeaned himself to visit one of these dens of iniquity himself, had he not, to verify his secretary's reports? A man of integrity sacrificing himself in a cause, only, it seemed, to have his altruism flung back in his face. Inwardly he fumed.

Palliative. What had Philpotts meant by that? He was not sure, but it sounded like some kind of sweetening offer to atone for the disappointment of not being allowed to father the new bill. He wondered what kind of offer it could be. Another contract perhaps, a larger order for his woolen cloth for army uniforms? Well, that would be better than nothing, and a good excuse to get back up to Yorkshire to reorganize his mills.

His effort would not have been in vain if the contract was a good one. And there was Anna's marriage in the offing. Between the two events he could do himself a great deal of good. And, he reminded himself, he must look into the Barrington shares. The thought of the violet-eyed Miss Barrington began to dissipate Braithwaite's vexation. He turned into the Reform Club and greeted the porter cheerfully.

"Is his Lordship here by any chance, Lord Travers?"

"He is, sir, in the library."

"Then I'll join him. Tell the waiter to bring us brandy there."

There were very few members in the library at this hour of the day, and Braithwaite could see Lord Travers slumped in an armchair at the far end, half-hidden behind a potted palm. Braithwaite sat down in the armchair next to him.

"Good day, your Lordship. I've taken the liberty of ordering brandy for us both."

"Good of you, Braithwaite," Travers murmured. "Actually, I've had several already. Fact of the matter is, I've some rather disappointing news to tell you. Was deliberating whether to write you a note or call to see you about it."

"If it's about the Criminal Law Amendment Bill, I've already heard. The prime minister sent for me this morning."

His Lordship's eyebrows rose with mild interest. "The bill? What of it? I've heard nothing about that. No, it was a personal matter I find rather difficult to talk about. Embarrassing, you understand."

"If I can help in any way, you know you can trust me," Braithwaite replied gravely. "Personal matters of a delicate nature can be confided in me with complete confidence." He leaned forward eagerly, curious to know what his Lordship was about to reveal.

"I'm afraid this matter concerns us both, Braithwaite. It's my son, Lionel. I fear he is no longer in a position to marry your daughter."

Braithwaite sat bolt upright. "No longer in a position? Do you mean he's married already?"

"Not exactly. I'm afraid the young fool became infatuated with some young woman of the lower orders and has let himself be milked by her. He is hopelessly in debt and nearly out of his mind."

"What kind of young woman? Has he compromised her? Is he forced to marry her?" Braithwaite could not help the curt, demanding tone in his voice. He could see his prize of a title for Anna slipping from his reach.

"No, no, nothing like that. She is not the sort one marries, you understand, an actress or some such. But because of her he has borrowed huge sums of money to satisfy her demands and I cannot hope to help him repay. Knowing this, the boy even attempted suicide. I beg you keep this matter to yourself, Braithwaite, for the details are embarrassingly sordid."

"That's what comes of letting oneself become entangled with a wanton," Braithwaite declared angrily. "Such women are evil, and young men are easy meat to them. It's the likes of her that I hope the bill will rob of their power. But Lionel—he's still free to marry, isn't he?"

He could not let the title go easily, even if it meant paying off heavy debts first. It would only mean that Anna would begin married life in a less ostentatious house and perhaps a reduced dowry. Lord Travers shook his head.

"It's not that simple, Braithwaite. As I said, Lionel's experiences have unbalanced him and I have found it necessary to send him away. He's recuperating in a private nursing home in the country. Later, perhaps, when he is fully recovered, we can discuss the wedding again." Lord Travers' eyes at last met his, and Braithwaite could read the hope that still lingered there. The frustrations and resentment of his day boiled up in him and Braithwaite stood up angrily.

"That we'll not! From what you tell me it seems perfectly clear that your son is no fit husband for my daughter. Private nursing home, indeed. You've committed him to an insane asylum, and do you think I'll marry my lass to a lunatic, a weak fool who can't handle women! We'll forget the whole business, your Lordship, and I'll look elsewhere for a son-in-law. Good day to you."

Fury bubbled in his veins as he strode out of the club, forgetting the brandy he had ordered, and hailed a cab. Not only was the lad not a fit husband, he was not a fit mill manager for Braithwaite's either. Nor was a weak-minded, dissolute aristocrat going to inherit the wealth accrued from all Braithwaite's years of hard toil. Inherit it, only to squander it on a succession of actresses and whores? Not likely! Unless, negative folk like the Travers family could look elsewhere for a gold mine to finance their feckless way of life, for they were not going to gain Braithwaite's money. He had been prepared to buy a title for Anna, at his price, but not sell his birthright for it. The lass could use her own resources now if she wanted to get on in the world, for he had had enough of trying to be the beneficent father. A man's patience could be tried too far. . . .

The cab set him down at Hanbury Square and Depledge opened the door in answer to his ring.

"Beg pardon, sir, but I believe Miss Oliphant has not kept lunch hot for you, not knowing when you would return. There is cold chicken, however."

"Then bring some chicken sandwiches and a bottle of dry white wine to the study."

"Very good, sir."

"And tell Miss Anna I want to see her." He might as well get the business over of breaking the news to her. No doubt she would be disappointed that she was not to marry into the aristocracy after all, but that was life and she would have to learn to accept it. He looked up at her knock and noted how weary she looked as she entered. Perhaps it was time to send her home for a dose of good Yorkshire air. Good idea that. If he accompanied her, then there would be no need to parry the inevitable inquiries about her broken betrothal.

"You wanted to see me, Papa?" What a pretty child she was, fair as an English rose and as meek and obedient as any man could wish.

"I'll come straight to the point, lass. No point in beating about the bush. You and Lionel Travers are not to be wed after all."

To his surprise her cheeks flushed pinkly and her eyes glowed. "Truly, Papa? Oh, thank you! I feared I was going to have to disobey you and refuse him."

"Disobey? Refuse? What is the world coming to? No, I have decided he is not good enough for you, my girl, and we must look elsewhere for a husband. But where? We know so few gentlemen in London."

"We know some, Papa."

"Oh, who?"

"Well, there's Mr. Lazenby. And Dr. Dalrymple. He's a very clever and refined gentleman. A woman could respect him."

"Dalrymple? Who's he? Never met the man."

The girl's chin thrust out in a defiant gesture Braithwaite found hard to credit. "He is the kind of gentleman I admire, Papa. He's kind and considerate, and he cares about people."

"Cares about people?" Braithwaite almost exploded. "What kind of credential is that for a prospective husband, I'd like to know? Has he money or influence? Does he own land or shares? Is he of a good family? These are the advantages you should be seeking, lass, not a soft tongue or a glib manner. But be off with you, for I've had a trying day and I've a lot to think over. Tell Miss Oliphant the wedding is off, and we'll think about going to Harrowfield for a week or two. Off with you now."

Silly child, he thought irritably when she was gone. Just like her mother, easily won over by a smoothly spoken manner. She'd be easy prey for any unscrupulous adventurer if she had not a shrewd father to watch over her interests.

He pushed the pile of Lazenby's neatly written sheets of paper to one side of his desk to make space for the tray Depledge brought, and sat chewing his sandwiches in annoyance. In the past twenty-four hours nothing had gone right for him, from the fiasco at Madame de Sandrier's last night to the prime minister's and then Lord Travers' announcements today. He could almost believe, if he was given to such nonsense, that someone had laid a curse on him.

He reached the bell to summon Depledge, but before he could touch it, there was an urgent knock at the door.

"Come in," Braithwaite called.

It was Lazenby, his earnest face tense and white. "Mr. Braithwaite, I have been wanting to talk to you. I could not find you last night and you were out all morning."

"Sit down." Braithwaite waved his sandwich toward a chair. Whatever Lazenby wanted to say could wait. "Now, about this research you've been doing—"

"Mr. Braithwaite, please listen to me. It's a matter of vital importance—" Lazenby interrupted.

"Dammit, man, who's the master here, you or I? Have the goodness to wait till I've finished what I'm saying."

Lazenby sprang to his feet, his eyes glittering. "This cannot wait. I should have told you long ago what I feared, but mistakenly I tried to spare you."

"Spare me?" What kind of patronizing was this, from servant to master? Braithwaite grew icy cold with righteous rage. "Sit down, Lazenby. Do you hear me? Sit!"

Lazenby sat and leaned forward. "Despite your anger I must speak. No, hear me out and then judge me. Anna is seriously ill and I fear for her life. She suffers from a mental illness that has broken her personality and she has become two distinct people. The evil half is threatening Anna's better half."

Braithwaite stared at him. "Are you trying to tell me my daughter is mad? Is that what you are saying?"

"She could become so, but—"

Braithwaite leaped to his feet. "Have you been talking to Emily of this?" The younger man nodded. "I thought so. She has blabbed to you about Anna's mother. Well, she was not mad, nervous debility the doctors said, and she went into a decline. If you are implying that there is some kind of hereditary taint in Anna, then you are lying, both of you, and I'll have you for slander."

"For God's sake, Braithwaite, I am not concerned with your whitewashing," Lazenby flashed. "Anna in her other life is an evil, unscrupulous woman."

"Do you expect me to believe that? My gentle, dutiful Anna a wicked woman? It is evil of you to speak such vile words of a virtuous girl. You have met evil women—I have too. In fact, I am about to call in the police to investigate the theft of my silver match case by such a woman. Would you have me believe my child is so wicked as to steal?"

"And worse. By night she has crept from this house to steal, lie, and cheat. She has almost caused the death of another girl and driven a friend of mine to near suicide. But Anna does not know she does these things."

"And yet you know, and Miss Oliphant?" Could it be possible there was truth in Lazenby's wild story?

"And Miss Laura too. We knew she went out. Only later did we begin to suspect the rest."

"So you, Laura, and Emily were in a conspiracy together to keep Anna's disappearances from me, is that it?"

"To save you worry. Now matters have gone too far, and I confess I should have spoken to you earlier. I am to blame, not the ladies."

"You and Miss Oliphant shall both leave my employ without references, if your story is true. Emily shows neglect by letting Anna disappear, and you confess your failure."

"And what of your own?" Lazenby's voice was cold. Braithwaite had expected him to crumble under the threat of dismissal. He stared. "Do you not think you have failed your daughter?" Lazenby went on. "You, who profess to work for the benefit of others, could you not have spared a little time and thought for her?"

"What are you saying, man? I threaten you with shameful dismissal, and yet you try to lay blame on me? I, who have done more than most fathers would for a child? I, who took in my fatherless niece? Is there no limit to your insolence?"

"Just as there is no limit to your hypocrisy," Lazenby replied icily, standing to glare back at him.

"What?" Braithwaite thundered.

"Hypocrite, that's what I call you. You campaign in the House against evil women, yet you make use of them yourself. You dismissed Lizzie for giving in to a man. You want to call in the police to harness a whore who took your match case, and yet you call yourself a virtuous man. Yes, you use women, those you malign and those you profess to love. Even Anna was to be used, to marry off to your advantage. Hypocrite! You, with your public purity and your private shame. Hypocrite!"

Braithwaite felt the blood thundering in his ears as he advanced on Lazenby, his hand raised to strike him. But reason prevailed and he lowered his clenched fist. "How dare you! Leave my house this instant. I will have no ungrateful, puffed-up servant speak to me like that. Get out, tonight!"

Lazenby sank back on his chair and buried his face in his hands. "Willingly I would go," Braithwaite heard him mutter, "but for Anna."

"Anna? What have you and she been up to?" Braithwaite demanded, suspicion dawning. "Have you been putting ideas into the girl's head? Do you fancy your chance as a prospective husband for her, for if so, you can put that crazy scheme right out of your mind. You'll not have her or my money either. I'd see her dead first."

Lazenby's tense face rose from his hands. "I do believe you mean that. I care nothing for your money, Braithwaite, only for that poor girl. The child you caused almost to lose her mind with your brutality."

"Brutality? What lies are these? I warn you, Lazenby, that if you don't get out now, you'll answer for this in court. I, brutal to my beloved child."

"Yes, when you raped Emily in her presence."

Braithwaite's jaw sagged and all power of thought left him. For a moment he stood, dumbstruck. At last he found his voice. "Did Emily tell you this?"

Lazenby nodded. "And I have confirmation from Anna. That sordid incident was the start of Anna's illness, an illness that has resulted in her becoming an evil, scheming whore."

"Now you go too far! A thief and a liar I can accept, but a whore! Quite impossible! You know my revulsion for such women, and nothing you say could convince me that my dear child could have learned the vice you speak of." But despite the vehemence of his words, Braithwaite felt a sneaking despair. If all the rest were true, about her mind breaking up and stealing and lying, it was not beyond the realms of possibility that in her crazed state she had stooped to folly. Lazenby would not be saying it without proof.

Lazenby rose slowly and went to look out of the window. For a moment he stood, silent. "Where were you last night?" he asked quietly.

"What business is it of yours? I told you, I was dining with friends."

"Was it at Madame de Sandrier's, in Rosamund Street?"

Braithwaite, caught out, blustered. "And what if I was? I had to verify your information."

"And who was your partner for the evening?"

"Now really, Lazenby, you go too far. Perhaps we should rather discuss what is to be done for Anna. A holiday, eh? Or a spell in a nursing home, would you suggest?"

"Was it Bella Marchant?"

Braithwaite sat down abruptly at his desk and, taking out a large handkerchief, mopped his brow. "I did spend some little time with the young woman you mention, and in fact, it was she who took my match case. But what has this to do with Anna?"

Lazenby turned from the window to face him. "You took Bella in your arms? You lay with her, perhaps? She is an intoxicating woman, they tell me."

Braithwaite felt the droplets of sweat beginning to trickle down his forehead again. "I've had enough of this interrogation. Go now, Lazenby, and we'll talk more about this tomorrow. I've had a dreadful day and I don't think I can take any more today."

Lazenby came forward and leaned his hands on the desk, his face barely inches away from Braithwaite's. "You were consumed with passion for a lovely young girl and did not even recognize she was your own daughter? My God, it passes human belief."

The room swam to Braithwaite's dimmed vision. He felt suddenly very sick. "Anna?" he croaked.

"Anna, or Bella in her other life."

Braithwaite felt very ill, dizzy and too weak to hold his head upright. He lay his head on his folded arms on the desk. Before his inner eye swam a vision of a painted, exotic creature clad only in diaphanous gauze, a creature whose sensuality had torn his guts out with desire for her. Anna? He almost retched.

After a few minutes he managed to steady the reeling sensation in his head and sat up slowly. "There is no doubt, then, that the poor child is going the way of her mother. Insane, poor thing. It would be kindest to put her in some quiet place where her poor little mind will not be troubled unduly."

"Into an asylum?" Lazenby demanded. "Hiding your failure, just as you did your wife? That will do Anna no good at all."

"Then what does she need?"

"Love and security and peace. What you never gave her, though I admit in your misguided way you did what you thought best. You failed. But you cannot bury her in an asylum, that would be too cruel."

"What do you propose, then, may I ask?"

"Leave her to Dr. Dalrymple. Let me take her to him."

"To marry her, do you mean?"

"Not necessarily, but if she survives, he will take care of her."

Braithwaite thought for a moment. Anna, mad, would be a distinct disadvantage. To let some fellow have the responsibility of her would be preferable.

"What kind of man is this Dr. Dalrymple?" he inquired of Lazenby. "A reputable doctor?"

"Of the highest order, eminent in his field. He is a psychiatrist and he knows of Anna's problem. He is deeply concerned for her and I know he would care for her well."

Braithwaite thought it over for a moment. Lazenby's judgment could be relied upon and it did seem a good solution. "Very well, make the necessary arrangements with the doctor." Then he suddenly remembered something. "What do you mean, if she survives?"

Lazenby's expression was grave. "I fear the inner torment could kill her. She could even take her own life."

"Perhaps death would be preferable to dishonor," Braithwaite murmured. He was desolate. His whole world was crumbling and there seemed no rhyme or reason in what was happening anymore. The world had suddenly gone crazy.

"You will leave Anna to Dalrymple then?" Lazenby asked.

Braithwaite rose, feeling very old and very weary. "If

you think he can do something for her. We'll talk more tomorrow." A sudden afterthought struck him. "She won't try to go back to Rosamund Street, will she?"

Lazenby shook his head slowly. "Madame dismissed Bella and closed the establishment. There was a rumor that one of the clients had cholera."

"Cholera? And I was there last night!" Braithwaite rushed from the room, unable to take any more.

"Hypocrite," he heard Lazenby mutter as he left.

For the next couple of hours Braithwaite sat alone in his bedroom, unwilling to face anyone. He needed time to think and reorientate himself in the wildly changing circumstances of his life. He did not spend long in bemoaning his misfortunes, for if there was anything he despised it was the weakling who wailed. Better by far to mold something positive out of the chaos that threatened to engulf him.

So he sat and planned. Having once checked with Emily that Lazenby's story about Anna was true, though there was little reason to doubt it, he would give up the London villa and take apartments. There was no point in running two establishments if Anna was to retire from society, and Aspley Hall was expensive enough to maintain. He would continue in the House, of course, for his career there was still intact, though undoubtedly he had now lost Lord Travers' friendship and he was known to have the ear of the prime minister. Still, Travers could find nothing to say that would damn his career. Braithwaite congratulated himself at having kept his counsel. That only left Laura to dispose of. Well, she could always go home to her mother.

Just before the dinner bell he left his room and found Emily about to enter Anna's room.

"A word with you, Emily." He followed her into the bedroom. Fortunately Anna was not there. He came straight to the point. "Is it true what Lazenby tells me, about Anna going out at nights?"

She hung her head. "Yes, sir. I wanted to tell you long ago."

"How did she manage it? Didn't you or Laura hear her?"

"She must have drugged the bedtime hot chocolate. The laudanum bottle was found under her mattress."

Dear Lord, he thought, the child was capable of far more cunning than he could have believed possible. "And is it true that she cheated and stole?"

Emily nodded. "She did steal, sir. There are things here in the drawer." She turned to open a drawer in the dressing chest and lifted out several objects. "You see, sir? A ring, a tie clip, several coins, and a match case. I don't remember seeing that before."

She held it up curiously, and it was all Braithwaite could do not to snatch it. It was his, and he knew now with sickening certainty that the voluptuous Bella was none other than his own child. Momentarily he felt nauseous at the thought of the hideous sin he had so nearly committed, but for the timely intervention of a divine Providence. Sternly he addressed Emily.

"I must inform you, Miss Oliphant, that the wedding between Anna and the Honorable Lionel Travers will not now take place."

Emily looked as if she were near to tears. "I'm sorry, Mr. Braithwaite. I feel partly to blame. I wish I could do something to make amends."

He patted her arm. "Do not fret. I think Anna was not overhappy at the prospect anyway. Perhaps she would be happier with another man. Ah, well, we cannot always have what we desire, Emily. In view of her feelings, I think it would be kindest to put aside my ambition for her."

"You are a very kind man, Mr. Braithwaite. I trust Anna appreciates how indulgent a papa she has."

Braithwaite patted his stomach contentedly. "It's almost time for dinner. Shall we go down?"

There, he thought as he followed Emily downstairs,

now all that remained was to break the news that he was going to close the Hanbury Square house. Emily would be free to go her own way if she chose, or to return to Aspley Hall. After all, she was a capable and conscientious servant and she knew the value of a discreet tongue. Laura presented no problem. Lazenby was another matter. He ought to be in some obscure country place, far from London's wagging tongues. A village schoolmaster, perhaps. Braithwaite must give the matter some thought so that all was settled before he broke the news.

Dinner was a dismal affair. Laura was unusually quiet and Lazenby sat silent, as if turned to stone, and ate little. Braithwaite noted that the young man never took his eyes off Anna, while Emily looked as if she wished she was not there, picking at her food nervously and never uttering a word. Braithwaite himself felt reluctant to talk, but Anna chatted on in unconcern, unaware of the tension around her. As she talked, quietly but with animation, Braithwaite reflected that it was difficult to realize that the girl was mad. She seemed completely rational and at ease, charming in her simplicity. Could this child truly be the same creature who laid men low with her exciting sensuality, the creature of cunning and evil who robbed and killed? Only one who was totally amoral could wear the look of innocence so convincingly. Insane, completely mad. He shook his head sorrowfully.

Depledge poured the wine. Braithwaite raised his glass. "Let's drink a toast," he said in an effort to alleviate the air of gloom. "What shall we drink to?"

Lazenby picked up his glass and stared across the table at his employer. "May I make a suggestion?"

"Of course."

"Death before dishonor."

Braithwaite lifted his glass and drank, unsure what Lazenby implied but suspecting that it was a taunt. Either way it was best to remain silent.

"Death," repeated Emily, "that's an unpleasant thought."

"But a noble sentiment, nonetheless," Anna said. "It seems to me that death is far more preferable than dishonor. Don't you agree, Papa?"

Braithwaite grunted. "Lazenby, I'd like a word with you alone when we've finished dinner."

The ladies recognized their cue and rose to go. Lazenby stood until they had gone and then sat down again.

"I've decided not to stand in the way of Anna's welfare," Braithwaite said. "You may arrange for her to be placed in the doctor's care as soon as you like. I can see you two are fond of each other, for I'm not blind, you know. Anna's happiness is important to me, despite what you think, so you have my blessing." He smiled in an effort at geniality, but Lazenby still stared back dispassionately.

"Very good of you, sir. Since she's no longer of any use to you, you cast her off. But you are mistaken in one thing. I care for Anna's welfare, but it is Laura I love. I would welcome your approval of my paying court to her. If she agrees, I would do my best to make her happy, you can be sure of that."

Braithwaite swallowed his amazement. "Then go to her, my boy. Tip the wink to Emily to leave you two alone. She's a shrewd and discreet woman."

"Discreet indeed," Lazenby murmured, and pushing his chair back, he rose and left. Half an hour later Braithwaite peeped into the main parlor and saw Lazenby's dark head close to Laura's on the sofa. Feeling more at ease than he had done all day, Braithwaite went upstairs. The first hurdle was overcome. Now, step by step he could begin to rebuild his life. Today had been perhaps the most trying and critical day of his life, but he had handled it well. Troubles never came singly, it was said, and sure enough they came in threes today. The lost bill, the broken wedding, and

then the discovery of Anna's madness. What a heap of
calamities! And the nerve of young Lazenby, trying to
blame Anna's madness on her father. As if a child of
eight or so could possibly understand the significance of
what she had chanced to observe, if indeed she had. A
man in despair needs succor, and that brief moment
with Emily in the nursery had been but a moment of
weakness, quickly over and never repeated.

No, the blame did not lie at his door but with her
mother's tainted blood. Heredity would not be cheated.
Still, he would see the girl was well cared for. Dr. Dalrymple would be well paid for his services. Never let it
be said he cast off a child of his. Thank God he was a
man not to lose his head in a crisis. Thanks to his
acumen, all would turn out well after all. He made
ready for bed, pulled on his nightcap, and was about to
climb into bed.

As an afterthought, he knelt by the bedside and
thanked God for His mercy, then climbed into bed
contented that the Good Lord would take care of His
own.

Laura sat listening while Charles Lazenby spoke
softly and encouragingly to her cousin. "So you see,
Anna, your father has agreed to my suggestion, and if
you, too, are agreeable, I am sure Robert will try to help
you forget the troubles of the past."

Laura willed her to agree, for perhaps contentment
could drive away the threatening specter of Bella. She
watched her face closely to see her reaction. Anna lowered her lashes and would not meet Lazenby's gaze.

"I am happy, Mr. Lazenby, for I am no longer
threatened with marriage to a stranger. That thought
frightened and repelled me. I like Dr. Dalrymple, but I
do not want to run away."

So she did not entertain any feeling of love for Dalrymple, thought Laura, only gratitude that he offered to

rescue her. Still, out of liking, love could grow if he nurtured it.

He was waiting outside now in the vestibule, anxious to take over the care of her sick cousin if she would agree. Signaling to Charles, Laura rose.

"Dr. Dalrymple is here, Anna," she said softly.

Anna simply smiled when Robert Dalrymple followed her cousin back into the room. "Good evening," she said pleasantly.

Dalrymple sat down beside her in the seat Lazenby had just vacated. For a moment there was silence between them, a close, companionable intimacy. Then Dalrymple leaned close to Anna and whispered.

"Anna," he murmured, "will you come with me?"

She drew her hand away from his. "I am sorry. I cannot."

"Cannot, or will not."

"I cannot. Oh, I can't explain, Dr. Dalrymple—"

"Robert. We are friends, are we not?"

"I do not truly understand, Robert, but I do not feel myself these days. Sometimes when I look in the mirror I seem to see a stranger there, and a feeling of panic overwhelms me. Perhaps I am ill, but whatever it is, I am not ready to go away. Forgive me, for I would not lose you as a friend, a very dear and trusted friend."

"Nor shall you, my dear. I shall always be here. I shall not leave you, I promise, until you feel strong enough to cope alone."

"Not ever then, my friend, for I want you close by me always."

"To the end," he promised in a whisper.

He leaned down and kissed her gently on her cheek, and she did not pull away. If only Robert could give her the comfort and reassurance she needed, Laura reasoned, the strength to fight and perhaps yet, the specter could be dispelled.

Laura rose from the sofa. "I did not realize it was so late. Good night, Charles. Good night, Robert, and bless you." She smiled and turned to go. Charles rose to accompany her to the door. Laura opened it and turned, to see Anna staring into the mirror over the mantelshelf, her face suddenly white and drawn.

"No," she murmured. "No, no!"

Two strides carried Charles to her side. "What is it, Anna? What do you see there?"

She moaned and turned away, but Robert grabbed her arm and forced her to look again in the mirror. "Look, Anna, look! What is it that frightens you?"

She stared, her eyes wide and her lips apart. Then slowly she composed herself. Her lips curved into a smile. "Why, nothing. Only a beautiful woman ready for love, and a gentleman she would gladly have supply her needs," she said, a hint of mocking laughter in her voice. She raised her arms and slid them about Robert's neck. Laura stood stock-still, barely able to believe the sudden transformation.

"Anna," Robert said.

"Bella," she corrected him, and then suddenly her eyes glazed over. Then, without warning, she snatched her arms away from him and a look of confusion came over her. "Robert, forgive me," she stammered. "I don't know what came over me. I could not help it, I am no longer in control of myself. Oh, Robert! I don't know what is happening to me. Help me! My head is beginning to throb again. Please help me upstairs."

One arm about her waist, Robert led her up the staircase to her room, followed by Laura. Emily was turning back the counterpane.

"Anna is not well," Laura explained briefly. "She has a headache."

"I'll see to her, doctor. Too much excitement for one day. A good night's sleep and all will be well," the housekeeper replied briskly. "Come, Anna, into your nightgown and I'll bathe your forehead with eau de cologne. Thank you, Dr. Dalrymple. Good night."

As Laura lay in bed she felt full of sorrow and pity for

Anna. It had been a forlorn hope to think Robert's protective concern could ward off the threat of Bella, for she had appeared under Laura's very nose to taunt her. But the evil creature could not be allowed to live, to usurp Anna's innocence and purity. Somehow she must be stamped out, eradicated completely. The only hazy plan that had occurred to Laura she hesitated to try, for Robert had been dubious.

"Very dangerous, my dear. You could kill Anna, and the rest of your life would be spent in an agony of remorse."

If even he could find no solution, what chance had Anna? She tossed about in bed, unable to find the comforting oblivion of sleep.

Somewhere in the night a dog howled at the moon. Laura sat up, hearing a sound in the house. Footsteps went pattering past the door and someone knocked urgently.

"Laura, wake up!" It was Emily's voice.

Throwing on her dressing gown, Laura opened the door. "What is it, Emily? Is it Anna?"

"Yes." Emily's face, distraught, looked years older. "She's gone again. What shall I do? I thought she would sleep deeply all night, but somehow she slipped out."

Charles appeared in his dressing gown. Emily turned to him. "I was not deeply asleep, sir, for you have the laudanum bottle."

"Go and tell Mr. Braithwaite. And tell him I have gone to look for her. I think I know where I shall find her."

"And I'm coming with you," said Laura.

Emily fled. As she dressed rapidly, Laura could hear the housekeeper's voice and the irritable replies from Braithwaite, but the master did not appear. Evidently he was content to leave his daughter's welfare in the hands of the man to whom he had consigned her.

"Are you coming?" she heard Charles call as she buttoned her boots. For a moment she hesitated then, going to the drawer she took out a little bottle. After all, she had thought it all out carefully in the light of day and her visit this afternoon to the apothecary was deliberate. In the event that it should become necessary she knew she would have to be prepared, and with cold resolution she put the bottle in her pocket.

Chapter Eighteen

Stopping only to take her cloak from the coat stand in the vestibule, Laura followed Charles out into the night and they walked briskly in the direction of the Haymarket.

"Where are you going, Charles?" Laura panted as she hurried after him. "Where do you think Anna will be?"

"Rosamund Street. That's where she always goes," he replied stiffly.

Of course, thought Laura. Anna did not know the occupants of the house had fled. Bella had been dismissed, but it would be in Bella's stubborn nature to defy Madame de Sandrier and return. After a few minutes Charles spotted a hansom cab at the curbside, its driver dozing on the box.

"Rosamund Street," he ordered the cabbie. "And we'll ride up top with you. We're looking for someone."

Without question the driver moved over and made room for them. Laura was glad of her cloak, for a stiff wind had blown up during the night. Crisp leaves fluttered down in their faces as they rode.

Lazenby peered eagerly into the darkness to either side of them as the horse's hooves clopped through the otherwise-silent London streets. Laura, too, sought a glimpse of a small figure with fair hair, but all the way to Rosamund Street they saw no one. The cab pulled up outside Madame de Sandrier's house. It was in complete darkness, and Laura began to have doubts. Anna was not outside in the street, and if the place was locked up and all its inhabitants fled, where else could she have gone?

"Wait here," Charles told the cabbie tersely, "until we return."

He rang the bell, and Laura heard its echo ring through the house. Then he walked along the street until he found a passage that led around to the back. Laura followed. Counting the houses they reached the rear of Madame's and its railed-in basement yard. Charles descended the steps and tried the back door. It yielded to his touch. Laura hastened down the steps after him.

Hope leaped in her. If Anna had found it open too, she could be here still. Finding their way through the kitchen quarters, they climbed the servants' stairs to the vestibule. Fumbling in the darkness Charles found a candlestick on the hall table, and striking a lucifer, he lit the tall candle. By its light Laura could see the signs of confusion that gave testimony to Madame's hasty flight. Even the chiffon drapes over the arched doorway hung awry. Not a sound disturbed the silence except for the wind outside. It would seem that the house was deserted.

"Anna!" Charles called out loudly, then listened. No answering sound came. "I must have been wrong, after all," he said sadly. "She has not come here." Opening all the doors on the ground floor, he looked in, the candle aloft, but found nothing. Disappointed, he returned to the vestibule and climbed the stairs, Laura following. At the top was the long corridor with many doors off. On an impulse, Lazenby shouted.

"Bella!"

A soft laugh answered him, somewhere along the corridor. Lazenby stepped forward eagerly, and a door on the left opened.

"Come in, sir. I have been waiting."

Signaling to Laura with his finger to his lips, he followed the sound of the disembodied voice and Laura paused in the open doorway. A heap of discarded clothing lay on a chair just inside, and she recognized Anna's dove-gray silk afternoon gown, but her gaze passed on to the girl sitting at the dressing table. An oil lamp glowing beside her revealed an exotic creature flimsily clad in a transparent sea-green robe with jewels in her flowing blond hair and her face heavily painted with carmine and kohl. Large, lustrous eyes watched Charles curiously through the mirror. It was Anna, but Anna as Laura had never seen her before. She turned on her stool and smiled.

"Welcome, stranger. You have not visited me before have you? And yet somehow you seem familiar. What is your name?"

"Charles."

Heavens, thought Laura, but she was beautiful! No wonder Lionel had lost his heart to this beauty. She could rob many a stronger man than he of his reason.

"Charles," Anna repeated thoughtfully. "No, I do not know you, and yet I feel we may have met some time, long ago and far away."

"Why are you here, Bella?" he asked. "The others have all gone away. There was a threat of cholera."

She shrugged. "They are all frightened fools, but I do not take flight easily. And as you see, my maid Lottie is still here. I came back for my jewels."

She opened a drawer and picked up a handful of baubles. Laura saw a trickle of emeralds run through her fingers. "They are mine," Anna said possessively. "I had to fetch them. Madame has forbidden me to come again."

"Why?"

She chuckled. "The others are jealous of me because the gentlemen like me and bring me gifts. But it makes no odds. I shall find my gentlemen to bleed in another place if not here."

"Why must you bleed them? What harm have they done you?" Charles asked softly.

"Because I hate men. They bleed women of everything—of their goods and of their self-respect. Why should we not retaliate?"

"So far as to drive a man to suicide?" Laura could hear the edge in Charles' tone.

Anna laughed harshly. "Ah, Lionel, you mean. He is a weak, stupid fool and deserves no better."

"So he must suffer for the sins of other men."

"What do you mean?" Anna's eyes challenged him sharply.

"Who is the man you really hate? Is it Reginald Braithwaite?"

Laura saw Anna's eyes glitter now with venom. "He is the worst of his kind. Pompous, hypocritical pig! He is a cruel, self-seeking animal, and if ever I get the chance, I shall bleed him dry, drain him, and hang up his carcass as a trophy. There is no justice in this world when hypocrites such as he prosper and flourish."

"Can you feel no pity for a man perhaps deluded and mistaken?" Charles asked quietly.

"Not when he sacrifices the happiness of others in order to satisfy his own vanity," the girl flashed back angrily. "It is time he was made to suffer as he has caused others to suffer. He deserves to die."

"Death is a harsh penance, Bella."

"Not too harsh for a man so wicked. He killed his wife and raped his maid."

"How do you know that, Bella?"

She flounced across the room and flung herself on the sofa. "I do not know, but I know it is true. And he drained his child of confidence, leaving her weak and stupid. What kind of man is that, to revere as a pillar of the Church and the state? Hypocrisy. That's what it is."

"Then have you no pity for poor Anna?"

Her laugh was ironic. "The only significance she has for me is that she gives me the chance to live. She must die too, so that I can reach her father." Laura stifled the gasp that escaped her.

"Anna is good and sincere and honest, all the things

that you are not. She has more reason to survive than you with all your malice and cynicsm," Charles pointed out.

"But she has no choice. She is weak and I am strong. Tomorrow she dies and I am born."

"Tomorrow? So soon?" The words escaped Laura unbidden. Anna gave her cousin an insolent look.

"I have waited long enough. Daily I have watched her grow weaker, and now the time is ripe. Tomorrow she will not awake, and I shall live forever."

Charles sat down beside her. "It will not be as easy as you think. Braithwaite will have you put away in a safe place where you can do him no harm. You will be powerless to harm him."

There was wine on the table and two goblets. Anna picked up the jug and poured herself a drink. "I am no fool. I shall threaten to reveal his shame and he will capitulate."

"Blackmail? Will you stop at nothing, Bella?"

She shook her head firmly, her jeweled earrings swinging vigorously. Then turning to Charles, she smiled. "But we waste time, Charles. Am I not beautiful? Do you not long to take me in your arms?"

She slid her fingertips up from his hand along his inner forearm and Charles shivered.

"You are very desirable, Bella," he murmured.

"Then hold me and kiss me."

For a moment he hesitated, and then he took her in his arms. She tilted her head back and closed her eyes, and he kissed her. Laura saw her ardor and vehemence and was angered. Such a woman could distract even the most levelheaded and resolute of men. Charles broke away.

"Do I alarm you, my friend?" Her voice was mockingly gentle. "Pour wine for us both and perhaps it will give you courage."

"I'll do it," said Laura.

Anna rose, returned to the dressing table, and began

titivating her long curls. Laura slipped the bottle from her pocket and poured half its contents into one goblet before filling them both with wine. For a second Charles' eyes met hers, then he nodded. In a moment Anna came back.

"Let us drink to your courage, Charles."

"Death before dishonor," he replied gravely, raising his goblet. She chuckled.

"A curious toast, and hardly appropriate, but let us drink nonetheless." She tilted back her head, her white throat moving as she drained the goblet. Laura watched, mesmerized. There, it was done now, and she could not revoke the action. Anna put down the empty goblet and made a grimace.

"Not one of Madame's best wines, I think. I note you speak of Anna with affection, Charles. Can you truly like the girl?"

"I am very fond of her."

"And when I take her place, as a wealthy heiress, will you come to me and love me too?"

He shook his head. "You are evil personified and therefore not worthy of love. But you will never take Anna's place now."

She laughed again. "I could almost envy her that she inspires such loyalty in you. But it is too late now to save her, my chivalrous friend. She is doomed."

"Not she, but you," Laura said quietly.

A look of curiosity veiled Anna's eyes. "What do you mean? You think you can stop me?" She glared at Laura.

"We must. We have no choice," Charles said gravely.

Anna cocked her head to one side. "You know, it's odd, but I believe you are the one person who could. From the moment I saw you tonight I sensed something different about you, Charles. I don't know what it is, but you are the only man I've met that I did not want to take captive, not the way I wanted to torture the others. Till now I thought I despised every man. I wonder what is different about you?"

Her blue eyes raked his face for a moment. Laura began to doubt the wisdom of what they had done. Perhaps the girl would have reacted to reason and persuasion after all. She felt apprehensive.

Anna looked at Charles curiously.

"You look pale, Charles. Do you think you have the cholera too?"

"Would you be sad?"

"I would not care. Do not think I have any fondness for you just because I say you are different. You are a man like all the rest and therefore not to be trusted."

He smiled weakly. "You speak more truth than you know. I have deceived you, Bella."

"I am growing tired of this conversation and my head is beginning to ache. Go away, Charles. See him out, Lottie. I am too tired to talk any longer."

"Then it is beginning to work," Laura said.

Light sprang into Anna's eyes. "What is beginning to work? What are you saying, girl?"

"The potion I put in your wine. I told you you were doomed. It is beginning to take effect already, but don't worry, Bella. It will not hurt. The apothecary promised me there would be no pain." It was surprising how detached and cool Laura's voice could sound in such a moment. Her strength surprised even her.

"No pain? What have you done to me?" Fear stared out of Anna's eyes. When Lazenby did not answer, she leaped from her seat and grabbed his arms. "What have you done to me, for God's sake? Have you drugged me?"

He shook his head. Laura saw the suspicion in her eyes give way to fear, and she pitied her. "Sit and rest, Bella, and let it take effect," Charles urged. "Don't fight it or it could be the worse for you." He tried to make her sit, but she clung to his arms.

"What was it, damn you? Tell me! No, I see what you are at. There was nothing in the wine; you and she are only trying to frighten me. Well, you fail, Charles. I do not believe you."

Laura stepped between them, obliging Anna to let go of Charles.

"Do you not begin to feel drowsy? Your limbs will start to grow heavy and then your eyelids. You will fall asleep, Bella, as easily as a child. The only difference is that you will not awaken."

Anna looked down at her arms disbelievingly and than held them up. "They do feel heavy," she whispered. "What have you done? What did you give me?"

"Poison, Bella. There is no escape," Charles replied.

She sagged onto the couch, her eyes wide in horror. "Poison? I thought the wine tasted odd. What was it?"

Charles' smile was bitter. "Belladonna. A curiously apt name for you. Otherwise known as deadly nightshade, and there again most appropriate, for what deadlier shadow of the night ever haunted London than you. You will see there is a kind of poetic justice in your death, Bella."

"I don't believe you," she cried. "You would not dare!"

Laura reached in her pocket. "Here is the bottle, Bella. See for yourself."

With effort Anna screwed up her eyes to read the label. There, clear enough, was printed the word *Belladonna.*

"You fools," she muttered, her voice already fainter, though loaded with venom. "Do you not see, if you kill me you kill her too! You lose your beloved Anna! You cannot kill me!"

"Too late, Bella. It is done." Charles' voice was incredibly cold even to Laura's ears. "Drastic situations call for drastic remedies. We weighed the consequences well, believe me. Better by far to lose Anna than to let a creature of evil usurp her body and destroy her. Either way Anna had to die. Her father himself chose, death before dishonor."

Anna laughed feebly. "Hence your toast, I see it now. But you cannot escape, Charles. You and Lottie will die for what you have done tonight. Before long you will swing from the gallows."

"No," Charles replied. "A painted whore found dead in a house where there was known to be cholera—who will question that? No one saw us come or go."

"And your conscience, Charles? It will not let you rest in peace. My murder will haunt you both for the rest of your lives." Her voice was growing feebler, but Laura resisted the impulse to stoop to comfort her.

"For ridding the world of evil? On the contrary, we shall feel righteous and content, regretting only that the world does not know of our noble action. Others besides ourselves will weep for Anna, but no one will mourn your passing."

Anna passed a feeble hand across her brow and lay back limply on the sofa. Charles moved aside the bowl of fruit on the low table before her and leaned over her.

"Does the mist close in about your eyes, Bella? It will not be long now, for it is the mist of death that closes in about you. Have you no remorse for all you have done?"

"No," she moaned. "I regret nothing. I am cheated!"

"Just as you cheated others. Do you feel death's clammy grip on your arms and legs? Soon he will enfold you in an eternal embrace."

Laura reeled with dizziness. It was far worse than she had anticipated.

Anna opened her eyes, savage hatred and fury burning fiercely in their depths. "Then if I die, you will go with me," she cried, and leaned over to the table, snatched the silver paring knife that lay in the fruit bowl, and flung herself upon Charles. He seized her upraised arm and held it in a vicious grip. Laura could see her eyes glittering with hate. "You bastard! You cunning bastard!" Anna hissed. "I was a fool to trust you!"

"One unguarded moment which cost you your life," he replied icily. The slender figure in his arms slumped, her eyes closed, and she uttered a long sigh. Charles lay her down on the sofa and she did not move.

For a second Laura stood, staring down at her; then, bending forward, she put an ear to Anna's lips. There was no sound of breathing. She lifted Anna's eyelid and could see her pupils contracted to a pinprick and almost disappeared from view. It was over. Instantly Laura's coolness fled. She fell to her knees beside the inert figure.

"God forgive me," she moaned.

Charles touched her shoulder. "Come, there is much to be done."

There was no time for brooding or remorse. They must act quickly. Charles wrapped his cloak about Anna's body and Laura blew out the lamp. Then they carried Anna's body carefully down the darkened staircase. Outside the front door, the cab was still waiting.

"Give me a hand," Charles called out to the dozing cabbie. "Help me lift her into the cab."

The cabbie obeyed, and then cast suspicious eyes at the girl's body. "Here, what's up with her? They tell me there's cholera hereabouts. She ain't got cholera, has she?"

"No. She's drunk, that's all," Laura reassured him.

Once inside the cab Laura sat with her cousin's motionless fair head on her knees. She could not bring herself to look at Anna, the painted face once so vital and full of allure now pale in death's clasp. Laura's mind was numb.

Charles, sitting silent, seemed as stricken as she was. The thing was done and there was no going back. As the horse's hooves clopped slowly over the cobblestones they seemed to ring out the same insistent message over and over again.

"Bella is dead. Bella is dead. Bella is dead."

The blustering winds of the night had abated by morning, lessened to a gentle breeze that brought only the occasional golden leaf fluttering down from the elms in Hanbury Square. It was almost as though the weather was in sympathy with the solemn air of constraint that pervaded the Braithwaite villa, holding its breath just as the household did. No one knew for sure quite what was wrong, only that for once the unchanging routine of the day was thrown topsy-turvy and that no one was permitted to go upstairs.

There had been no family prayers today. Mr. Braithwaite had not come down from his room and only Depledge had seen him when he took up a tray. The housekeeper had appeared briefly in the kitchen, her lips in a tighter line than usual and lines of care etching her white face.

"You will all carry on as usual," she said tersely, "except that no one shall go upstairs without my express order. There must be absolute quiet in the house, and no callers will be received."

She had offered no explanation, but Janet had been quick to supply one to the curious ears of Cook and the scullery maid. "It's Miss Anna, she's very ill, that's what I think. She's got two doctors up in her room now, came in the early hours of the morning. I think she must be very bad, 'cos Miss Oliphant's had the curtains drawn, and if she won't let us go up, even to make the beds, I reckon Miss Anna is in a very bad way."

"Cut the gossip and get on with your work, girl," said Cook, mindful of her duty and her position in the housekeeper's absence. But as the day wore on and the two doctors were seen to leave and then return to the house again, it began to appear that the young mistress's condition must indeed be grave. Cook saw to it that the maids crept silently about their business, though it was hard to keep them occupied now their routine was shattered. None of the gentry came down to the dining room to eat and ruefully Cook watched Mr. Depledge and the servants tuck into the boiled mutton and parsnips that should have gone upstairs.

Suddenly a bell rang. Looking up at the board, Cook saw it was the study. "Janet, quick! The master probably wants to eat now."

Janet was gone for some minutes. When she returned, her pretty face was flushed with importance. "It was Mr. Lazenby. He wants a tray for himself and Miss Laura and Dr. Dalrymple."

"I'll cut some of the cold mutton," said Cook briskly, and as she carved, Janet could scarcely contain herself.

"Mr. Lazenby was telling the doctor as Miss Anna was critical and it was because of Bella's death, whoever she is. The doctor said it could kill Miss Anna and the danger was not yet over. They'd only know if she came to. Seems she's in a coma or something."

"Dear heaven," muttered Cook. "What a tragedy, a girl young as her."

Janet sped away with the tray. When she returned, she looked pale.

"The other doctor came out of Miss Anna's room and into the study. He said something to Mr. Lazenby and Miss Laura started crying and then Dr. Dalrymple said they'd better cover all the mirrors. Then they all went back to Miss Anna's room." Janet's face crumpled. Cook looked at her, flabbergasted.

"Cover the mirrors? That can only mean—"

"Yes, Cook. She's gone!" Janet burst into tears and fled from the kitchen.

Cook felt disconcerted. The death of a young lady in the family was a new occurrence to her and she was unsure what to do. Miss Oliphant had told them to carry on as usual. In the absence of orders to the contrary she would get on with the suet pudding for dinner tonight. She weighed flour into the large earthenware mixing bowl, grated the suet, and plunged her arms into the mixture. Pounding the dough helped to dispel her irresolution. Poor girl, only seventeen years old. Still, she had always looked fragile, though lately Cook had thought she'd begun to look much rosier and livelier. Still, there was no understanding the quirks of fate. That young Mrs. Benbury up the road had always looked pink and plump but she had been snatched suddenly by consumption.

She rolled out the dough and covered it with raspberry jam, then rolled it up and wrapped it in a cloth to boil. More than likely no one would come down to eat tonight in the circumstances, but it was comforting to carry on as though nothing had happened.

The bell rang at the back door. Cook sighed, wiped the flour from her arms on her apron, and went to answer it. Mr. Bedford's plump, genial face beamed at her.

"Sorry to trouble you, ma'am," he said, doffing his cap politely, "but I wonder if I could have a word with Miss Oliphant."

"I'm sorry." Cook shook her head and saw his smile fade to a look of disappointment. "There's trouble in the house, Mr. Bedford, and this is not a fit time."

"Oh, I'm sorry to hear it. Please tell Miss Oliphant I hope as it'll all clear up soon, and I'll call on her again in a day or two. With luck all will be well again then."

"I doubt it, but I'll tell her." She watched his portly figure mount the basement steps and wondered whether she had said the right thing. After all, she had not yet been told officially. Yes, to say there was trouble was enough without revealing too much. . . .

Laura hesitated outside Anna's door and turned to Charles. "Charles, leave me, will you? I want to go in alone."

Charles pressed her hand. "I understand. I'll wait for you in the study. Come to me there when you are ready, and then Robert will go to her."

Laura watched him stride away, then took a deep breath and entered the darkened room. In the narrow bed with its chintz counterpane she could see the outline of Anna's slim body under the covers. Her fair head lay motionless on the pillow, her eyes closed.

Laura came close and knelt by her side, taking the limp hand in hers. Anna's golden beauty swam before her eyes, blurred with unshed tears. She leaned her face on the cold fingers.

"Laura, is that you?" A faint whisper made her start upright.

"Anna, my dearest Anna!"

Her cousin's fingers curled gently around Laura's. "I am so glad you are there. I need you, Laura."

"I shall always be here now, Anna, forever." Laura's voice was choking with emotion. So nearly she had lost Anna; happiness surged in her that she could make the promise.

"I dreamed in the night, Laura, the old dream that always used to frighten me. Nanny used to say it was the bogeyman come to punish me for my sins."

"What utter nonsense," Laura protested.

"But you came in my dream and chased him away. He will not come again." Anna was murmuring drowsily, but her tone was pure contentment.

"How do you feel, Anna?"

"Strangely light-headed, but content. I sought you earlier in my dream, but you were not here. Where were you, Laura?"

Laura hesitated before answering. "I had to go out during the night. An acquaintance of mine was very ill. I stayed by her until she died."

"Oh, Laura!" Blue eyes turned on her in compassion. "Were you very upset?"

"No. I barely knew her, and it was best for her to die, in the circumstances."

"It must have been a dreadful disease, and I am glad she is free from suffering. Poor lady. Who was she?"

Laura took a deep breath. "Her name was Bella."

"Bella." Anna repeated the name softly. "The name sounds familiar, and yet I did not know her, did I?"

"No," Laura replied emphatically. "You did not know her."

Anna stirred and half-raised herself on one elbow. "Open the curtains, Laura. It is dark and I cannot see you properly."

Laura let go of her hand and did as she asked. Anna stared in surprise at the sunlight that filtered in through the window. "What time is it?"

"Six o'clock."

"In the evening? Have I slept all day?"

Laura came back to sit on the chair beside the bed. "Yes, you were not well last night, and you needed a good night's sleep. I gave you a sleeping draft, but I fear I must have poured you too liberal a dose."

She looked puzzled. "I do not remember. What kind of a draft?"

"Laudanum." Laura retrieved the bottle from her pocket, relieved that she had remembered to remove the misleading label. Now no one would ever know of the deception, none but Charles and Robert Dalrymple. Thank God the deceit had fooled Bella at least. She looked earnestly at Anna's pale, innocent face and wondered. Had she truly deceived Bella, or did she still lurk in that beautiful blond head?

"You know," Anna said thoughtfully, "I think that long sleep did me good. Somehow I feel so refreshed and alive—I feel myself again, in a way I haven't felt for a long time." She smiled.

Laura leaned over and took her hand. "I am so happy to hear it, my dear."

"And I'll be happy to go away with Robert, as soon as Papa will permit."

Laura seized both her hands. "Are you sure? Will you not mind leaving your papa and going to live elsewhere?"

"No," Anna replied calmly. "I have a fancy he may decide to marry again himself before long."

Laura looked up in surprise that she could conceive such an odd notion.

"Just think of all the wonderful things we can do together, Robert and I, working for the sick. I shall work with him." She was smiling happily at the prospect, and Laura felt almost dizzy with happiness. No longer did she talk meekly as the old Anna would have done.

Anna lay back on the pillows, still clasping Laura's hands, as a peremptory knock came at the door. Reginald Braithwaite hurried in without waiting for an answer. His plump face was flushed and his double chin trembled as he held out a sheet of paper in his hand.

"Anna, my dear, are you better?" He crossed to the bedside and stood beaming down at her. "Anna, such news! I've just had a letter from the prime minister himself, in his own hand, and do you know what he offers me, as 'a reward for services,' he says?"

"No, Papa."

"A baronetcy, my dear. Just imagine that! Sir Reginald Braithwaite, Bart. The title could only pass to a son, so you would have no title, but think of the honor! All my work was not in vain after all."

"May I offer my congratulations, Uncle," Laura said quietly. She could afford to be generous even to a man she could not respect, in view of her own happiness.

"Ah, well, it's not official yet, of course. He says the matter will have to have the official seal of approval—Her Majesty's, of course—but it's only a question of due procedure. Think of it! I always knew there were men in the party who could recognize merit and integrity."

"I am very happy for you, Papa," Anna said with a smile. "I have news to impart to you too. I have decided to go away with Dr. Dalrymple."

"Ah, splendid! Excellent news. We must celebrate," Braithwaite said enthusiastically. "As soon as you are well enough, of course, Anna."

"I am perfectly well, Papa. I never felt better in my life. I think I shall get up now and dress."

As Braithwaite left and Laura rose to follow him, Anna suddenly frowned.

"Why is the wall mirror turned back to front? And my

dressing table draped with a sheet? What does it mean, Laura?"

Laura's mind raced. This would be the final test, the moment of truth. She went over to the dressing table, removed the dust sheet, and picked up a small, silver-backed hand mirror. Returning to the bedside, she handed it to Anna.

"Look in the mirror, Anna, and tell me what you see there." As she opened her mouth to answer Laura stopped her. "No, look long and hard. Stare into it for a moment or two, then tell me."

Anna's earnest little face peered at the mirror and Laura watched her expression. She saw Anna look puzzled at her request, and as the moments ticked by, the puzzlement softened to a gently confident smile.

"Well?" Laura demanded at last.

"I see a woman in love." She put the mirror down and smiled up at her. "A woman in love with life. I feel so well and happy, Laura."

Relief surged through Laura mingled with delight. She would have flung her arms about her cousin but for Emily's entrance.

"Are you all right now, Anna dear?" Concern filled the housekeeper's eyes.

"Perfectly, Emily, and I want to get up for dinner. Has Papa told you I am to go away with Dr. Dalrymple?"

Emily's face softened. "Yes, and I'm very happy for you." Emily's mind was already back on her housekeeping duties. "Well, there'll be six for dinner then, so I'd better tell Cook. And do you want me to order more insect books from the library tomorrow, Anna?"

Anna looked surprised. "Good gracious, no! Spiders are horrid creatures! I can't think what got into me to want to read those books. I think I'll wear that black-striped dress I've never worn yet—is it pressed and ready?"

Emily bustled over to the wardrobe. Laura rose to go.

"I'll leave you to dress then, Anna, and see you down at dinner."

She had reached the doorway when suddenly the door opened, almost knocking into her. Uncle Reginald stood there, excitement still burning his cheeks.

"Emily! Did you remember to tell Cook we have a guest for dinner? Tell her it must be a good meal, to impress an important lady."

"I'm just going down, sir," Emily replied patiently. "Your gown is ready, Anna. Can you dress alone?"

"A lady?" Anna repeated with a smile. "Who is she, Papa?"

"Her name is Miss Sybil Barrington, a young lady of great refinement and excellent family." He beamed at Laura, unaware of his niece's startled expression.

"Then I look forward to meeting her at dinner," Anna said. Emily hurried off to the kitchen and Braithwaite hastened after her. Laura stood in the doorway. She could not refrain from smiling to herself at the thought of Braithwaite being so impressed by Sybil, whose trade he could not know. There was poetic justice in the old hypocrite falling victim to the kind of woman he affected to despise. . . .

A knock came at the door and Laura opened it. Robert Dalrymple stood there.

"Ah, Robert, come here," said Anna, holding up her arms.

Laura saw him stride across to her and lean forward. Anna slid her arms about his neck and Laura remembered Bella's embrace last night. The same strange, exciting creature lingered in Anna yet. Her lips were close to his ear, and Laura knew now that though the evil of Bella was dead, the ardor she could arouse in men lingered still in Anna's vibrant body. In this woman were combined the trust and love of the one with the disturbing fire of the other. The best of both worlds.

"Annabella," Robert whispered.

Laura closed the door quietly behind her.

Along the corridor Charlés was waiting. He came forward to meet Laura, taking her hands in his.

"How is she, Laura? Is she conscious yet?" There was no mistaking the depth of his concern.

Laura smiled. "She is well, Charles, fully recovered and all sign of Bella is gone. In the mirror she saw only a woman in love with life."

Charles sighed deeply. "Thank God! Oh, Laura, I am so happy. I knew that if she died I would have lost you too. I was so afraid you would never trust me or speak to me again."

To break the tension Laura answered lightly. "Escape me? Never, beloved," she quoted with a smile. Recognizing the poem, Charles spoke the next lines.

"While I am I and you are you,
    So long as the world contains us both,
    Me and loving and you the loath . . ."

Laura interrupted him. "I was never loath, Charles, only afraid. Afraid that what we did could misfire and cause Anna to die, and then you and I could never . . ." Her voice trailed away as Charles took her hand and led her downstairs.

"Come to the conservatory and let us talk, Laura, for there is much to plan," he said softly. "Robert is with Anna, your uncle with Sybil . . ."

"And God's in His heaven, all's right with the world," said Laura contentedly.

Emily Oliphant opened the bedroom door and came in. Seeing Anna and Dr. Dalrymple holding hands, she clicked her tongue loudly in disapproval; then, remembering that they were doctor and patient, she went out again and closed the door. There was still time to write a note to Mr. Bedford before dinner, expressing regret at having missed his visit and with just the right note of encouragement.

CAMBERMERE

1

In the corner of the train compartment a young woman dozed, her fair head leaning against the window pane. Outside, trees and farmhouses sped by as the train rattled on, and now and again the solitary traveller sighed in her sleep.

All of a sudden the slim figure stiffened and cried out, and her green eyes opened wide in alarm. She stared anxiously about her in an effort to recall where she was, and then leaned back against the upholstery again. Three deep, slow breaths and she began to relax.

That nightmare again. Ever since her childhood the recurring dream of darkness — complete and utter blackness, where unseen terror stalked her steps — had haunted Philippa Korvak. She felt angry with herself for letting it happen again, after an interval of years, on a train of all places, where she might well have appeared an utter fool if anyone had chanced to be there when she cried out. She looked out and found comfort in the sight of sunlit Berkshire fields. Darkness and nightmare were quickly banished in the soothing view.

It was too silly for words, she thought as she took a mirror and lipstick from her handbag. Always it was the same dream: the slowly-thudding footsteps coming nearer and nearer while she cowered in some labyrinthine underground place where not a chink of light penetrated the oppressive blackness that threatened to choke her in its intensity. And always she awoke with a cry, bathed in sweat, at the very moment when the menacing footsteps at last reached her. Ridiculous that a childhood dream should recur now, when the reality was already far more catastrophic than any nightmare.

She was a fool; she must be, or she would have seen it
coming. But that night when Clive came to her Paris
apartment, poised and self-possessed like the man of the
world he was, she had been unaware of any difference in
him. She must have been blind. His averted cheek when
she reached up to kiss him should have warned her, but
even after she had poured out a pernod and water for him,
just as she had done for the past two years, she still sensed
nothing wrong. It was only when she went through to the
little kitchen to dish up the ragoût and he followed her,
leaning diffidently against the doorframe to watch her, that
she began to sense a subtle change in him. Normally Clive
left the mysteries of the kitchen severely alone, preferring
to wait with his drink until she carried in the evening meal.
His grey eyes were unusually sombre.

'There's something I must tell you, Philippa,' he had
said, and only then, at the sight of his eyes and the tone of
his voice, had her heart leapt in apprehension. As he went
on speaking she had watched the steam rise from the dish of
ragoût in her hands, the misty swirls vanishing swiftly before
her gaze as she felt her hopes shrivel and die.

'Believe me, my dear, it's better this way,' he had said at
last. 'Better for both of us,' he added, and the calmness in
his voice angered her, but she stayed silent. Diplomat
though he was, Clive had had to struggle to find the right
words.

'I was taken by surprise, Philippa. I did not expect this,
but now Joyce has decided to come and join me here, you
must realise it would be very difficult for us to go on as we
were . . . '

Difficult, but not impossible, she recalled thinking
fiercely. Her first impulse had been to fight, to re-attach to
herself that part of her which was about to be severed, but
the look in Clive's eyes told her he was already gone from
her, already in spirit with his wife. Instantly she made a
decision; if she could not have Clive, then amputation,
however painful, was the cleanest and most sensible solution. She could remember even now the involuntary expression of relief on his handsome face when she told him
that she would go home to London at once on a long-

overdue leave. But after he had gone, the meal still uneaten, she had been able to feel nothing but a vast, swamping sense of desolation.

So it was that Pippa was now speeding from London to Cambermere, far from the scent of garlic and Gauloises, of steaming French coffee and croissants, away from Paris and Clive. She was glad she was alone in the compartment as she fought to keep back the tears that brimmed behind her eyelids. A girl jilted in love usually fled home to mother, she supposed, but Pippa had neither mother nor home to run to. It was over twenty years ago that Mother had died, when Pippa was still only six, and now all she could recall of the legendary Carrie Hope, idol of millions, was a mass of Titian-red hair and warm arms and a haunting scent of perfume.

Pippa stared at her pale-faced reflection in the train window. The tawny hair and oval face bore little resemblance to the striking beauty whose face smiled seductively from the magazine and newspaper cuttings Pippa had stuck lovingly into a scrapbook all those years ago. In fact, thought Pippa ruefully, she was not really very pretty at all and she had often wondered what Clive had seen in her. Intelligent, yes, but no match for his debonair charm and complete self-assurance. He could have had his pick of all the women in Paris, but he claimed it was her mind which had attracted him.

'We are soul-mates, Philippa, you and I,' he had murmured. 'We share a common interest in art and music and all things beautiful. We aesthetes are rare creatures. A marriage of true minds, as Donne says. That is what we have, my dear, something unique and special.'

But marriage of the minds had not precluded his interest in her body, cultural attaché at the British Embassy or not, Pippa thought bitterly as the train sped on. Was it because she was the child of a mourned film idol and a world-renowned film producer that she had first evoked Clive's interest, or was she being savagely unfair to him now he had cast her off? She must try firmly to put it all out of her mind and think only of Cambermere and the future. Perhaps in time she could face going back to the Sorbonne and Professor Garnier, to pick up her secretarial work for him again, but right now all she wanted was a haven of peace to forget and try to regather her scattered mind.

Engrossed in her thoughts, Pippa barely noticed when the train pulled up at a small station and the door of the compartment opened. She looked up to see a young man climbing in, his hand on the steel harness of a large golden labrador dog. The dark spectacles confirmed that he was blind.

'Let me take your bag,' Pippa said shyly. She was conscious of not knowing how much help a blind person would accept without feeling patronised. He held out the bag with a mumured thanks, and she was aware of his free hand groping for a seat as she reached up to the rack. Once he was seated, the dog lay down at his feet and Pippa re-seated herself. To her relief the young man did not seem disposed to begin a conversation so she was able to revert to her own private thoughts.

How dreadful it must be to be blind, to be perpetually in the dark, she thought compassionately. His was a nightmare far worse than any of her dreaded dreams, and yet his expression was composed, even cheerful. He must be gifted with far greater courage than she was, running away from life because it had dealt her a blow. She should learn from his fortitude, put the past behind her and think positively.

She tried to visualise Cambermere and the house she had not known her father owned, until today. Alexis Korvak owned flats and villas all over the globe, many of which Pippa had visited, but Cambermere was a surprise to her. It was only when she landed from the Paris plane and headed for Father's luxury flat in fashionable West Kensington that she first learned of it.

'Sorry, miss, the flat has been stripped and closed for redecoration,' the elderly janitor had told her. 'I reckon Mrs Purvis wasn't expecting you. She's gone down to Mr Korvak's place in Buckinghamshire.'

True, the housekeeper had not expected her because Pippa had left Paris in such a hurry, but then she often used Father's flat since he so rarely came to England these days. After some little time turning over the papers and ledgers on the desk in his dusty little office, the janitor had finally

10

unearthed the address.

'Cambermere Hall, near Marlow,' he had announced. 'That'll mean a train from Paddington. Shall I ring Mrs Purvis to expect you?'

It would be a country gentleman's residence, Pippa decided, a house that befitted Father's standing as an international film-maker. Strange he had never mentioned the place, but then there was no reason why he should. He and Pippa were comparative strangers; since Mother died they had only met during Pippa's school and college vacations, and then only briefly because he was always flying off to some far location for a new film.

It was a sad admission to make, even if only to oneself, Pippa thought. At her age still to know her father only as a passing stranger somehow seemed an admission of failure. She was shy of him and his powerful presence, but he had always been generous and she could have made more effort to get to know him better, sought his company more often and made a friend of him.

'Are you going far, miss?'

She was jerked out of her reverie by the cheerful voice of the blind man opposite.

'Oh, Cambermere, near Marlow,' she replied.

'Then you must change at the next stop too,' he told her. 'We're nearly in Maidenhead.' In a few moments the train slowed and stopped. Pippa reached down his bag and her own suitcase.

'Platform five,' he told her as the labrador led him out. Pippa walked beside him as he moved confidently from platform four to five. He was evidently accustomed to the journey.

'How did you know I was a miss?' she asked him as they stood waiting for the next train.

He smiled. 'Deduction. Your voice is young, the skin of your hand is young and firm, and your perfume is youthful. It's nice, by the way. What is it?'

'Rive Gauche.'

'French? You have expensive tastes,' he laughed.

Pippa smiled. 'Not really. I work in France and perfume is not so expensive there.'

'You're going to Cambermere on holiday, then?'

11

'Yes. I've never been there before.'

'Pretty village. The big house is a curious place, though. Belongs to some film producer, I understand. Korval, or something.'

'Korvak. Alexis Korvak. He's my father,' Pippa said. 'Where are you going?'

'Bourne End. The stop before yours. We live in the village there.'

'We?'

'Shula and I.' He reached down to pat the golden labrador's head. 'Don't know what I'd do without Shula.' There was gentle affection in his voice and she liked the man for it.

'How do you cope?' she ventured shyly. She had always found it difficult to talk to anyone who was physically handicapped, but this man was different.

'We have a routine, Shula and I, and one learns to adapt. It wasn't easy at first, but I learnt to develop other senses to compensate. One can see a lot with one's ears, you know. And you learn to count steps, lamp posts — everything. But the hardest thing to accept is other people's attitudes.'

'What attitudes?' Pippa asked with curiosity.

He shrugged his broad shoulders. 'Some people often seem to think the blind — or any other handicapped people for that matter — are mentally defective in some way. They shout, or talk to us like children. Or they just feel ill-at-ease with us. You can hear the constraint in their voices. We are ordinary people who just can't see, that's all.'

Pippa felt guilty, for she recognised herself. But before she could answer, the Marlow train came in and they climbed aboard.

For a time there was silence and the man appeared to doze. Then he awoke and reached down again to pat the dog's head affectionately. 'Cambermere, eh?' he remarked. 'And you're Miss Korvak?'

'That's right.'

'Your father doesn't go to the Hall very much these days, I believe. At one time he was often there.'

'He's a very busy man. He's in America now.'

'Strange. I was in a pub in Marlow only last week and I heard someone mention his name. I gathered from the

12

conversation that Mr Korvak is not a very popular man thereabouts. But then, I don't suppose that troubles you. Famous people are no doubt used to being either admired or disliked.'

Pippa's eyebrows rose. 'Why should he be unpopular? Father is a very charming, agreeable person.' She felt irritated with him now.

'I'm sorry. I was only repeating what I overheard. You know him best, Miss Korvak. I did not mean to offend. Ah, the fourth stop,' he went on as the train began to slow. 'This is Bourne End, and yours is the next stop. Good day to you, Miss Korvak. It was nice meeting you. I hope you have a pleasant stay at Cambermere.'

She watched him follow the dog down the steps and stride away along the little platform, wishing belatedly that she had asked him what he meant about Cambermere Hall being a curious place and just what these people in the pub had said about Father. He's got it all wrong, of course. Or if unkind words had been spoken it was probably only out of envy.

Very soon the train began to slow down again and Pippa gathered her suitcase and handbag. So far as she knew no one would be awaiting her at the station in Marlow since only Mrs Purvis, the housekeeper, now remained in Alexis Korvak's employ. So it was with surprise that she heard a man's voice address her.

'Miss Korvak? I have the car waiting for you outside.'

Sure enough there was a large gleaming Daimler standing in the evening sun. She looked at the man's grey head and bland face curiously, as he took her suitcase.

'I'm Carson, the jobbing gardener,' he explained. 'Mrs Purvis sent me to meet you.'

'It's very kind of you but there was no need to bring the Daimler,' Pippa murmured as she climbed in beside him.

'Mrs Purvis says Mr Korvak would have wanted it,' he replied briefly, and drove away out of the village and along darkening country lanes. Pippa knew her father would have insisted on all the signs of status, but she and her father were very different people. On the rare occasions they met he seemed to be surrounded by gay, exciting people, laughing and drinking and living life at a furious

13

pace. Pippa preferred peace and a gentler more ordered way of living. At Cambermere, with luck, she would find quiet solace where she could forget the scar of Clive.

'Here we are,' said Carson, turning the car off a tree-lined lane and up a long gravel drive. Through the avenue of trees bordering the drive Pippa caught sight of the house in the dusk and drew a deep breath of pleasure. It was beautiful. Its marble colonnaded terrace was reflected in the purpling waters of the lake before it, as it lay, tranquil and splendid, a magnificent Georgian house, its beauty enhanced by its elegant simplicity. Here was a building after her own heart, and she congratulated her Father's good taste. Usually he was given to opulence and exaggerated magnificence, but Cambermere showed he had an eye for genuine beauty too. Pippa felt reassured. Here was the perfect place to lie low and lick one's wounds.

She ascended the marble steps of the great double doors while Carson drove the car round the back to garage it. Mrs Purvis's familiar thin figure opened the door and her angular face permitted itself only the thinnest glimmer of a smile.

'So you found us. Come on in, Philippa. There's a nice hot cup of tea ready in the kitchen.'

Mrs Purvis was one of the few people apart from Clive who called her by her full name. It was as though she was prepared to admit a certain degree of intimacy with her but not presume too far. Philippa she had been in the nursery all those years ago, and Philippa she was to remain. Not that she wanted Mrs Purvis to be too friendly with her, for the housekeeper's thin features and pursed lips indicated a cold nature, and in any event Pippa wanted no close acquaintance to pry into her reasons for being there. All she wanted was to be left alone.

She watched Mrs Purvis's figure as she moved about the kitchen, fetching cups and pouring tea. She must be nearing sixty now, Pippa thought, despite her jet-black hair and sharp gaze. And she still wore the same kind of dress, Pippa noted, dark and high-necked like a Victorian governess. Her neat, deft movements and reserved manner completed the picture. In a modern kitchen that gleamed with stainless steel and futuristic equipment she looked oddly out of place.

'A lovely house,' Pippa commented as she took a cup of tea.

'Nice enough,' Mrs Purvis replied crisply.

'Funny I did not know of it before, though.'

'Not really,' the housekeeper said firmly. 'Your father kept this place as his private hideaway. Few people know of it.'

Not even his daughter, Pippa thought. Still, even he had need of retreat from the world on occasions, so why should he not indulge himself in such a country paradise? He had a villa or apartment in every European capital as well as in California and he could well afford to have a rural hide-away.

'Do you think Father will mind my being here?' she asked.

The housekeeper shrugged her thin shoulders. 'Your father sent word he would not be using the place this summer. He's not well again.'

'Is he back in hospital?'

'Yes. For several weeks, I understand.'

The news did not shock Pippa, for it was common knowledge that Alexis Korvak drank far more than his constitution could cope with, and periodically he was taken into hospital for a lengthy stay to be 'dried out'. He always intended to keep off alcohol thereafter, but the habits of a lifetime die hard. Pippa was not unduly alarmed to hear he was having the cure once again.

After a simple meal of cold chicken and salad in the kitchen with Mrs Purvis, the housekeeper offered to show Pippa up to her room. As they passed through the great marble-floored entrance hall with its graceful pillars and climbed the wide staircase Mrs Purvis questioned Pippa.

'How long will you be staying, Philippa?'

'I have two months' leave,' Pippa replied.

'Two months?' Her thin eyebrows arched. 'You've not stayed in England so long before.'

Pippa sought an excuse. 'Paris in the summer is very hot and very dull. All the inhabitants leave for the country, and my boss at the university was going abroad. And I had two months due to me, so I've no need to go back until the university reopens.'

Without comment, Mrs Purvis opened a tall white door to a bedroom and stood back as Pippa entered. It was enchanting: deep-piled pink carpet and lush rose-pink velvet drapes, a huge rose-canopied bed and draped dressing table. The whole room was in muted shades of pink and cream, and it was just what Pippa might have chosen for herself.

'It must be hard work for you, running such a huge house after the London flat,' she commented.

The housekeeper shook her neat dark head. 'We only keep part of Cambermere open. The wings are closed off, and I have help in from the village, Carson and a cleaning woman. It's many a year now since the whole house was in use, when your father held house parties here and the place was thronged with people. Those were the old days . . .'

Pippa frowned. So she was wrong to think he came to Cambermere to hide and rest. It had been, after all, just another venue for his countless banquets and revels.

'Your mother hated it,' Mrs Purvis went on. Pippa could see her lips pursed in a thin, hard line. 'She must have had some kind of presentiment about the place, for it was here she died.'

The housekeeper had closed the door and left before Pippa could answer. She stood motionless, taken aback. She had always understood that her mother had died in a nursing home. She could remember, child of six though she was, that Mother had gone away, and then the day came when they told her she would not be coming back to their home in Kent.

That was when life changed dramatically for Pippa. Suddenly there was no longer a home with a bright, gay father and ethereal mother who came and went, but a boarding school and the unaccountably guilty feeling that one had done something wrong in losing one's mother when all the other girls still had theirs. Pippa went through her schooldays feeling inadequate. When she went to university and later to Paris, she had learnt to live and cope alone. But why had she never known until now that her mother had died at Cambermere?

Having unpacked her case. Pippa put her things away in the drawers and looked about for a wardrobe. There was none in the bedroom. She opened a door in the corner of the room and found it led into a smaller room, a dressing-room evidently, for it was lined with sliding doors. Beyond it lay a bathroom, and she smiled. Father's restraint had given way to his customary ostentation here, for the sunken bath was of white marble with glistening gold taps and so were the washbasin and shower cubicle. Over a vast white dressing table, triple gilt mirrors surmounted by cherubs gleamed in the subdued lighting. Pippa became aware that she was not alone; Mrs Purvis was standing in the doorway watching.

'I see you have found your bathroom. Is there anything else you need, Philippa?'

Her expression was so severe that Pippa felt obliged to make an agreeable comment in an effort to please her.

'Thank you, no. This is a beautiful suite, Mrs Purvis. My father is to be complimented on his taste.'

Mrs Purvis's expression did not soften as she answered. 'Your father? This suite was designed and decorated to your mother's taste, Philippa. She always had excellent taste.'

Pippa turned to her. 'My mother — yes. You told me she died here at Cambermere. I did not know that. Was it here?'

Pippa indicated the bedroom. The housekeeper turned away sharply. 'No, not here. You can sleep in peace. My room is along at the far end of the corridor if you need anything. Goodnight then, Philippa.'

Pippa refused to allow herself to cry as she switched off the light and settled down to sleep. After all, she had two months in England ahead of her in which to forget Clive. She was 26 years old and she had an excellent job as a secretary to return to at the university. She could travel — she was fluent in French and German and Italian and could surely find a similar post far from Paris if she chose. And Clive had done her morale a power of good; he had proved to Pippa that a man could find her attractive even if she had not inherited her mother's incredible beauty. And he had taught her depths of passion she had never known before.

17

She rolled over, thinking sleepily of Mother and Mrs Purvis's words. Had Mother really died here at Cambermere and not in the nursing home? If so, why had they always told her otherwise? Pippa shuddered. Out in the darkness an owl hooted.

She did not know whether it was the thought of Mother's death here, or the death of the affair with Clive that gave her a sudden sense of chill. Perhaps it had something to do with the blind stranger on the train telling her of Father's unpopularity in the area too. Whatever the reason, she had a distinct feeling that however beautiful Cambermere was, it held a quietly ominous air. Ridiculous, she told herself sternly. It was remote and tranquil, that was all, and a place so lovely could not possess the sinister air she was attributing to it. By September she would have regained her peace of mind and be in a better position to plan the future. Just now, so soon after leaving Paris, she was still upset and vulnerable, but she must not let her vivid imagination spoil the peace of Cambermere . . .

Pippa must have slept, for the hands of her wrist watch were nearing four o'clock when she awoke, clammy with sweat. Something had roused her for she could vaguely remember a pounding sound. Probably her own heartbeat, she reassured herself, for she recalled the childhood nightmares which often woke her in tears, terrified by the sound of her own heartbeat throbbing in her ears. Recent events must be causing a return of the old childhood terror.

But as she turned over to settle down to sleep she heard the sound again. It was a footstep, heavy and resolute, followed by another. Pippa sat upright, reaching for the light switch. Once the room was flooded with soft light and no further sound came, she began to relax. The housekeeper was sleeping not far away, just along the corridor, but there was no need to disturb her just because she felt uneasy in her new surroundings. A cigarette, perhaps, and then she would go back to sleep.

But as Pippa reached for the cigarette packet she heard the sound again, clear and echoing, and she stiffened. It was hard to tell where it was: either in the room, outside or overhead. A quick glance outside in the corridor revealed no one there. Who could it be? Mrs Purvis was asleep, and there was no one else in the Hall.

Pippa trembled, remembering her mother. Whose were the restless steps disturbing the peace of Cambermere on the night she came to it for the first time?

2

Cambermere Hall lay like a pale jewel amid the deep green fields of high summer, early morning sunshine bathing it and its surroundings in crystal-clear light. The air was heavy with the rich sweet scent of elder flowers. It was a perfect English summer morning.

Pippa awoke, not to the sound of Parisian sparrows chattering excitedly to each other on the eaves, but to the mellow cooing of English wood-pigeons in the nearby trees. For a moment she lay wondering, until reality asserted itself.

She was here, in England and far from Paris. Sternly she reproached herself for thinking of the past as soon as she awoke when she had promised herself not to think of it at all. Activity — that was the best way to banish thought.

Sunlight streamed in upon her when she swished back the heavy drapes at the window, and instantly she felt glad to be alive. The sky was Wedgewood blue with cloud-puffs trailing gently across it, a beautiful morning, as delicate and soul-refreshing as she could wish. Pippa's tremors and fears of the night melted like morning mist over the soft green fields, and she determined anew to begin life again positively. No nostalgia, no regrets, no haunting memories were going to mar the future.

The scene below took her breath away. Somehow she had expected a stately terraced garden, in keeping with the impressive façade of the mansion, but she was wrong. Between the two projecting wings at the back of the hall lay a vast marble terrace with an irregularly-shaped swimming pool, and around the pool white tubs containing leafy palms. Gaily-coloured tables and sunlounging chairs were scattered between the foliage and the whole scene looked far more like a Riviera hotel than a rural English retreat. Or like a Hollywood film set, Pippa thought. That was it. The palm trees were surely plastic imitations. This was undoubtedly another of Father's extravagant notions, like the push-button panel in the bedroom of his London flat where a touch could draw the curtains, turn on the lights or the television, or bring forth a concealed cocktail cabinet.

Instead of her customary shower Pippa decided she would have a dip in that beckoning pool below. It was more than time she broke her old habits. She put on a swimsuit and a towelling robe over it, then hurried downstairs and unlocked the glass door leading from the back of the vestibule to the terrace. No one else seemed to be up yet.

Flinging her robe over one of the sunchairs Pippa stepped gingerly down into the pool. The water was invigoratingly cool but not too cold, and in seconds she was swimming leisurely, enjoying the caress of the water on her skin. How beautiful it was, she thought contentedly. As she climbed out and pulled on her robe again she felt positively glad to be alive. Just at that moment she caught sight of a movement at an upstairs window, and stopped to peer against the sunlight. Something moved suddenly behind the curtain in an upper room in the east wing, but she could not be sure what it was. Maybe it was a trick of the morning sunlight, but it had appeared to be a lightning glimpse of a blond head. Carson was greying and the housekeeper decidedly dark, and so far as Pippa knew there was no one else at Cambermere. Suddenly she recalled the footsteps in the night, and wondered. But the steps had been in the main wing, not in the closed down east wing. No, the blond head must have been a trick of the light, after all, she decided. She hurried back up to her room to rub herself down and dress for breakfast.

The succulent smell of frying bacon reached her nostrils as she came down again to the kitchen and found Mrs

20

Purvis busy at the cooker.

'Lovely morning, Mrs Purvis,' she said cheerfully. 'I've been for a swim.'

'I saw you,' Mrs Purvis replied without looking round.

'Were you up in the east wing?' Pippa asked as she sat down at the table. 'I thought I saw someone up there.'

The housekeeper still did not turn round. 'In the east wing? No. I told you that's not open. Now, do you want boiled eggs?'

Pippa was about to reply that she was used to only a light breakfast, coffee and buttered rolls, when she remembered her decision not to stick to outworn routine. 'I'd love eggs, or bacon, or whatever you have, Mrs Purvis. That swim gave me quite an appetite.'

Mrs Purvis placed two boiled eggs in front of her. 'I remember, you see. Always, right from your nursery days, you liked two boiled eggs, soft and with a pat of butter on. You can have bacon too if you like.' The words were kind, but the housekeeper's voice remained cool and distant.

'No, that's fine, thanks,' Pippa replied, wondering. Mrs Purvis was right: Pippa had forgotten she used to ask for eggs but was usually given porridge. Eggs were only for holidays and birthdays or when she behaved well. Fancy Mrs Purvis remembering that! The thought warmed Pippa, but the tight, uninviting expression on her thin face did not encourage Pippa to talk about the past. She remembered in silence as she ate. Pippa recalled that Mrs Purvis, looked exactly the same as she did now when Pippa was small. She had seemed a very stern, forbidding character then, yet Pippa could recall how she fussed over her mother.

'Hush now, Philippa! Go out and play in the garden quietly. You're mother has a headache and wants to rest,' she would admonish Pippa. Or, 'No, Mother can't come and read a story to you tonight. Go to sleep and perhaps she'll come tomorrow if you're a good girl.'

But Mother rarely came. Pippa had a misty vision of an angel with creamy skin and russet hair that fell in tumbling curls on her shoulders, a delicate creature who languished often in her room on the rare occasions she was at home, and the flurry and scurry of packing trunks when she and

Father were off on their travels again. And for a time there had been Irma too, a young woman she had seemed, although they said she was Pippa's sister, but she had gone away to marry and never came back. Pippa remembered little of her, only that she was always cross with her, and Pippa had not missed her angry scowl when she vanished from her life.

And then Mother had gone away for ever too, and Pippa had only Gwen for company. Mrs Purvis had been most vexed. 'You must not talk to imaginary friends, Philippa, or people will think you are mad,' she had scolded, but Gwen was dear to Pippa and Pippa needed her. Now, looking back with the wisdom of years, she could see what a lonely, frightened child she must have been to need a friend who existed only inside her head. Loneliness is an inexplicable terror to a small child, and she could not understand why her father was always away on business, her mother dead, and her sister presumably dead too. No one troubled to explain to a child of nearly six.

'Coffee?' asked Mrs Purvis, holding out the steaming coffee pot.

'Please,' Pippa said, pushing her cup forward. The aroma of coffee reminded her instantly of Paris. 'With milk,' she added quickly. Pippa always drank her coffee black, but habit must be broken and tamed. Concentrating on altering all the minutiae of her life would give her less time to look back, she reasoned.

Mrs Purvis fetched hot milk from the stove. 'Nice pool, isn't it?' she commented. 'Your father had it built years ago. The back of the hall faces south and he said the terrace was a natural sun-trap and the perfect place for a pool.'

'I thought perhaps it was his idea,' Pippa replied. 'And the plastic trees too. Did he make many other alterations?'

The housekeeper shrugged. 'Some, but then he wasn't here often. Not like the London flat. Now, what would you like to do this morning?'

'Oh, nothing special,' Pippa answered. 'Just laze about, inspect the hall and the grounds perhaps.'

'It's too fine to stay indoors,' the housekeeper replied promptly. 'I'd go down to the village if I were you. Or go for a ride — you used to like horses, as I remember.'

22

Pippa pricked up her ears. If there was one sport Pippa loved it was horse-riding. 'Does father have horses here then?'

'Two. He keeps them at Walters' livery stables down the road, just before you reach the village. Mr Walters will saddle up for you — he'll be glad of someone to help exercise them.'

Having no jodhpurs with her, Pippa dressed after breakfast in grey jeans and a pale blue shirt she had bought at the Galerie Maréchal in Paris specially to have dinner with Clive . . . Fiercely Pippa banished the thought of the dinner that never came about, put on a pair of strong walking shoes and set off down the gravel drive and out along the country lane towards Marlow. It was a magnificent morning, the birds singing and the hedgerows scented with wild columbine and honeysuckle as she walked along under the interlaced branches of the old oaks. Pippa was young and healthy and free and she was going riding over the rural peace of this lovely countryside.

As she neared the cluster of cottages which evidently marked the outskirts of the village, Pippa saw a white five-barred gate to her right, and alongside it a painted sign. *Cambermere Riding Stables. Proprietor, Geoffrey Walters,* it read. Pippa pushed open the gate and walked up the lane towards the low outline of stable roofs. A dark-haired man, probably in his thirties, was mucking out one of the stalls.

'Mr Walters?'

He turned at the sound of her voice and straightened. He was darkly good-looking but there was no trace of a friendly smile as he answered, 'Geoff Walters, that's me. What can I do for you?'

He leaned his tall frame against the rake and surveyed her curiously. At that moment a young boy of about nine or ten came out of a nearby stall with a leading rein in his hands and stood watching.

'I'm told there are some horses belonging to Mr Korvak at livery here,' Pippa said to Walters, 'and Mrs Purvis thought you'd be glad of someone to exercise one of them. Could I see them, please?'

23

He did not move, but the boy sidled round Pippa. 'The big chestnut is probably too big for you,' Walters commented slowly, 'but the grey gelding might be about your size.' He was surveying Pippa's five-foot-five critically, too intently for her liking.

'I'm used to a big horse,' she told him. 'Show me them both.'

He straightened slowly and walked towards another stall. Pippa followed him.

'You're staying up at the Hall, I presume,' he remarked as he unlatched the door. 'Friend of Mr Korvak's perhaps? Get on well with him, do you?'

'I can't say. I hardly know him,' Pippa replied as she peered past him into the gloom. A grey horse raised gentle eyes to inspect the intruders. He was beautiful and Pippa would have been glad to ride him but the man irritated her with his casual questioning. Pippa wanted to see the other horse before making her own choice.

'That's Alouette, and Copper is over here,' he said, crossing the cobbled yard to unlatch another stall door. 'Fetch him out, Robin, will you?'

The boy went inside and emerged in a few moments leading a magnificent chestnut. The horse snorted at the sight of Pippa.

'Not keen on strangers, our Copper, is he, Robin?' the dark man smiled. The boy shook his fair head vigorously. 'Alouette seems much more your style, miss,' he added with a patronising smile which irritated Pippa. She was about to retort defiantly that she would ride the chestnut when the beast bared its teeth at her, and she decided that discretion was the better part of valour. She nodded. Walters strode back across the yard to Alouette's stall and Pippa watched as he saddled the grey.

'Copper is a bit sharp, you know,' he remarked. 'An ex-racehorse and rather temperamental. Not like Alouette here — he's a real schoolmaster, as gentle and wise a cob as anyone could wish.' While Walters adjusted the girth Pippa watched the boy. He grinned at her sheepishly and led the big chestnut back into its stall. Then Pippa heard the sound of regular brushing. Robin was evidently grooming him.

Walters watched her as she climbed into the saddle and

rode off down the lane, and Pippa guessed he must be appreciating her style, for the one thing she knew she could do well was to ride. The grey was a pleasure, docile and quick to respond, and he and Pippa cantered along the lane, away from the village and up towards the woods. Below her the Thames snaked lazily through the trees.

For half an hour or so Pippa rode, revelling in the beauty of the morning and feeling the contentment that the serenity of the Thames Valley could bring to a tired soul. Then she turned the grey gelding towards the woods on the upper slopes of the valley, sensing that Alouette too was content. Pippa and the horse would soon become friends.

A breeze rustled through the branches of the bushes and trees when they reached the woods, and Pippa saw Alouette's ears twitch. A horse disliked wind, she knew, for it disturbed his perception, relying as he did more upon hearing than sight. But the gentle horse trotted on along the moss-grown path at Pippa's bidding.

Suddenly, and without any warning, Alouette uttered a strange shriek and reared up on his hind legs. For a split second panic seized Pippa as she caught sight of a pair of blue jeans flashing down from the low branches of a tree in front of her, and then Alouette turned and bolted. Alarmed, Pippa crouched in the saddle, giving the horse rein and as her brain began to function again murmuring words of reassurance. Within a hundred yards Alouette recovered, slowed and stopped.

Pippa turned in the saddle. A tall figure in blue jeans, broad-shouldered and with blond hair was running away across the fields.

'You! Come here!' Pippa called out after him. 'Come back here! You could have killed me!'

But the fair-haired man vanished among the trees, either deaf or too alarmed to listen. What on earth was he doing up a tree over the path she was riding, she wondered. And whatever it was, why on earth should he decide to drop down right in front of Alouette, startling the poor gelding out of its wits and putting Pippa's life in danger?

The idiot. He evidently knew nothing about horses. It was a pity she had not caught sight of his face so that she could give him a piece of her mind if she chanced to see and

25

recognise him again. He was young and of a fine athletic build and he was blond. There could not be many men answering to that description in the area. Unless he was a holidaymaker and only passing through Marlow, of course.

Alouette and Pippa had both fully recovered their good spirits when they turned back at last for the stables. At the sound of hoofbeats on the cobbled yard Walters emerged from the tack room. He watched Pippa critically as she dismounted.

'Alouette is a beauty,' Pippa remarked as she handed over the reins. 'I look forward to riding Copper next.'

'At your own risk,' Walters said, his good looks marred by a scowl. 'Copper is very choosy.'

'And so am I,' Pippa retorted levelly. 'I shall come again soon to ride him.'

She was turning to leave when Walters spoke. 'I've been thinking. You must be the writer they've been talking about.'

'Writer?' Pippa echoed as she turned to face him.

'Well, journalist or whatever. Someone told me a writer was coming to Cambermere. I'm not surprised. There's plenty to tell that even the gossip-columns didn't get to know about. Funny, though, I didn't think it would be a woman.'

Pippa was about to deny it when she stopped, her curiosity aroused. What was it that Walters considered of such interest, she wondered. Suddenly she recollected the blind man's remarks about her father.

'Do you mean gossip about Korvak?' she asked casually.

'To be sure. Who else but the renowned Alexis, jet-setting multi-millionaire.' Walters replied coldly. Pippa's curiosity was aroused further. Her father's activities often reached the newspapers, but why should Walters speak so scornfully of him?

'What is there about Alexis Korvak to interest the press?' Pippa asked coolly but Walters was quick to note the interest she tried to conceal.

'Ah, you scent new material, do you? Well, there's a lot I *could* tell you if I wanted, but why should I? Would your newspaper pay well? Is it to be an exposé in one of the Sunday papers?' he demanded.

Pippa hesitated, reluctant to admit she was no journalist but Korvak's daughter. Walters would probably tell her nothing then. For the time being she would have to curb her impatience to know more.

She turned away. 'I'll come again soon,' she called back over her shoulder. After all, if he was going to be mysterious she could play the game too. Keep him guessing, that was the trick. She did not like Geoffrey Walters.

Skirting the lake, Pippa reached the top of the drive and caught sight of Carson, bucket in hand, disappearing round the side of the house. She followed him and saw him leathering the Daimler, which was parked outside what was evidently once the stables and coach house.

'Morning,' he grunted as she approached, and went on rubbing energetically. He was a strange little man, with a grey fringe surrounding his glistening bald pate and a silvery moustache on his pudgy top lip. He was small, plump and insignificant, but industrious. The Daimler shone almost as brightly as the less ostentatious green saloon parked nearby.

'How many cars are there?' Pippa enquired.

'Three. And all neat as a new pin, the way Mr Korvak likes them kept.' Carson replied proudly. 'The little Fiat's in the mews.'

'Is Mrs Purvis in?' Pippa asked, starting towards the kitchen door.

'Gone down to the village. She'll be back any minute,' Carson replied, bending to inspect the gloss on the paint-work. Pippa went into the kitchen.

Mrs Purvis had evidently been busy too since Pippa left, for the floor gleamed and not a pan was out of place. It looked like a model kitchen in an exhibition ideal home. Curiously Pippa opened the refrigerator and the deep freeze and the pantry. Mrs Purvis was a good housekeeper, for there was an abundance of provisions — there must be at least five dozen eggs in the larder and six pounds of butter. Ample provision for such a small ménage.

Anxious for a cup of coffee, Pippa found the percolator and some coffee and switched on. As she sat down the door

27

opened and Mrs Purvis came in, her thin features aglow from the walk.

'Oh, Philippa, back already? I've just been down to the farm. We needed eggs and I fancied you might care for a fresh chicken — free range, none of your battery or deep frozen birds. You'll have forgotten the taste of fresh chicken, I'll be bound.'

She took the chicken and eggs from her basket and left them on the table while she saw to the coffee, which was now beginning to bubble. Momentarily the thought flitted through Pippa's mind that an extra dozen eggs was hardly necessary when there was already a huge tray of eggs in the larder, but the thought was quickly driven from her mind when the housekeeper asked about Walters.

'How did you find Mr Walters then, Philippa?'

'Curt, not very friendly,' Pippa replied.

Mrs Purvis sighed. 'Ah well, that's a reaction I'm afraid you'll have to expect hereabouts. Your father is not very popular locally and you are your father's daughter. In time perhaps, they'll come to know you better.'

Pippa eyed her curiously. 'Why should Father be unpopular here? What did he do?'

Mrs Purvis raised her thin shoulders in a shrug. 'Oh, you know film people. He used to bring many of his film friends down here at different times, and I suppose their noisy parties scandalised the local worthies.'

'Is that all?' Pippa queried. 'From what Mr Walters hinted I suspected there was more than that.'

'Walters?' the housekeeper said sharply. 'What did he tell you?'

Pippa put down her cup of coffee. 'He didn't actually tell me anything, just hinted darkly that there was a lot he could say if he had a mind to. Actually, he thought I was a journalist or something, and wasn't prepared to talk until he knew how much my newspaper would pay.' Pippa chuckled, but Mrs Purvis's face remained set.

'I'm not in the habit of warning folk about others,' she said quietly, 'but I'd advise you not to get too friendly with that man. He can be malicious if he's a mind to it. Pay no heed to what he says.'

'I shall not. I promise you. I don't care for Mr Walters.

Actually, I'm going to ride Copper because he told me not to. He's not going to dictate to me.'

A hint of a smile curved the housekeeper's thin lips. 'You haven't changed much, Philippa. Still as defiant as ever, I see.'

'I? Defiant?' Pippa echoed in surprise. She thought she had always been a meek, submissive child.

'Oh yes,' Mrs Purvis said firmly. 'You were always a handful, as I remember. Whenever you did anything and I found out about it you used to flare up angrily and say she did it, not you — you know, that imaginary little friend you used to have. I forget what you called her.'

'Gwen,' Pippa said absently. She could picture her still, blonde and fragile, and with the innocent expression of an angel.

'That's right. You used to rage with injured innocence, I remember. Stubborn as a mule, you were.'

Carson interrupted her at this point, pushing open the back door and trudging in across the kitchen. Mrs Purvis stared in horror at the trail of muddy footmarks he left behind him on the sparkling floor.

'Carson!' she cried, putting down her cup with a clatter and pursuing him out of the kitchen. 'Where do you think you are going?'

Pippa smiled. Poor little man. She put down her empty cup and strolled out into the sunlit stable yard. The Daimler was now as brilliant and immaculate as a show-room car. Pippa walked on round the coach house and behind it, half-screened by a clump of laurel bushes, she saw the Fiat. It was yellow, or should be, but beneath its coating of mud and grime it was more grey than yellow.

Pippa walked closer to it. It was hardly in the condition Carson had claimed, she mused. He must be slipping. And on its seats Pippa could see various oddments scattered about — an old trench coat, a heap of untidy papers, a cigarette packet and a half-eaten bar of chocolate. And the keys were in the ignition. Curiously, Pippa opened the door and slid in behind the wheel. She could go for a short spin in this car and not feel guilty that she was spoiling Carson's hard work.

But before she had reached for the keys her gaze alighted

on the blue cardboard folder lying on the passenger seat beside her. She might have taken no notice of it but for the bold capital letters inked on it: ALEXIS KORVAK.

Her curiosity was aroused. Why should Carson have any papers belonging to her father? She lifted the folder and opened the flap. Inside were a bunch of photographs, newspaper cuttings and a sheet of handwritten notes.

The photographs she barely glanced at. Some she had seen before in gossip magazines, pictures of Father in his younger days looking extraordinarily handsome and with that devastating smile of his which could out-rival the most debonair of his leading men.

The newspaper cuttings bore such lurid headlines as SCANDAL AT MALIBU BEACH or FILM PRODUCER CITED and these Pippa dropped on her lap. She had no time for the lies that always surrounded a person of world repute. It was the sheet of paper that interested her. She scanned the closely-written words and felt a sense of disappointment. Though she received letters from Father only very rarely, she knew this was not his handwriting.

'Hungarian Jew — early life in obscurity — exiled because of oppression. Industrious, opportunist, made good use of looks and charm — weakness — obsession with women. Disastrous marriage. Hints of blackmail, corruption, even murder.'

Pippa could read no more. Her blood was thundering in her ears. Whoever had written this libellous pack of lies ought to be punished! However indifferent he might be as a father, Alexis Korvak was none of the things someone had written down here. Pippa tore up the sheet of paper, fury boiling in her veins.

But who could it be? Mrs Purvis had worked for Father for years — she would never betray him. But how could papers belonging to someone else have come to be in Father's car at Cambermere? Pippa threw the torn notes on the car floor, stuffed the rest of the papers back in the folder and got out of the car. As she marched back into the kitchen Mrs Purvis was alone.

'Whose is this file?' Pippa demanded loudly, tossing it on the table. Mrs Purvis stared at it for a second. 'Tell me,' Pippa thundered. 'Who wrote those scandalous lies about my father? You must know, Mrs Purvis, and I demand to be told.'

The housekeeper drew herself up to her full height, a clear two inches taller than Pippa. Without taking the file from Pippa she scanned it for a moment. 'Where did you find that?' she asked quietly.

'Does that matter? In the Fiat, as it happens.'

'What colour was the car?'

Pippa felt riled. 'What does the colour matter, for heaven's sake? Yellow, or rather it would be yellow if it were clean.'

'I see,' Mrs Purvis turned calmly towards the cupboard. 'Then it is none of your business, Philippa.'

'What do you mean?' Pippa demanded. 'Someone wrote this vicious calumny, and I want to know who it is.'

The housekeeper eyed her coolly. 'Jumping to conclusions again, Philippa? It could be an outline, a synopsis of a film, for all you know. Why should you demand to know what is none of your business?' she asked quietly.

Her manner infuriated Pippa. 'Because you, of all people, should be loyal to him and not allow anyone to do this!' she said firmly. 'He has been a good employer to you, hasn't he?'

'He pays well,' Mrs Purvis agreed calmly. 'And I obey his orders.'

'Then why do you condone this? Did you know about this file?'

'I did.'

At that moment an elusive thought came back to Pippa. Walters had spoken of a journalist coming to Cambermere.

'It's the journalist, isn't it?' Pippa said in excitement. 'That's it, you've agreed to his coming here, haven't you? Well, I'm not going to let him, and that's that. You can forget the whole thing, Mrs Purvis,' Pippa said emphatically. 'No writer is coming here to make up lies about my father. As his daughter I have a duty to protect him.'

The housekeeper smiled thinly and turned away again. 'Orders are all very well, Philippa, but I already have my orders,' Pippa heard her say. 'You are too late. He is already here. That is his car.'

'Here? In Marlow? In Cambermere?' Pippa exclaimed.

Then she remembered the footsteps in the night and the face at the window. 'Are you telling me that the man who wants to blacken my father's name is here — in this house?' The housekeeper inclined her head. Her coolness infuriated Pippa. 'Then please get him out of here, Mrs Purvis. If you don't, then I will.'

Pippa turned to march to the door, but the housekeeper's quiet voice stopped her. 'You can do that if you wish, Philippa, but I fear you'll make a fool of yourself. He has every right to be here — more so, in fact, than you have.'

'What?' Pippa turned incredulously.

The housekeeper smiled that infuriating humourless smile again. 'That's right, Philippa. He is here with your father's consent. Mr Korvak does not know, however, that you are here. So you see, it is you who are the intruder at Cambermere Hall, not he.'

3

The girl stared at the older woman in disbelief. How could she be an intruder in her father's house? And more than that, she did not care for the tone of pleasure in the housekeeper's voice. Pippa glared at her.

'How can you say that, Mrs Purvis?' she demanded icily. 'To imply that a stranger has more right to be here than a daughter in her father's home is sheer nonsense. So the journalist has Father's permission, but are you saying my father would not have allowed me here if he knew?'

Mrs Purvis gathered up the empty cups and clattered them into the sink. 'He would probably not be very pleased with me for allowing you here. The London flat he didn't mind you using for a week or two, but Cambermere is

32

different. As I told you, this was his private retreat.' She turned and met Pippa's gaze directly. 'But I had little choice. I must confess I did not think it would be for two months. I was stripping the flat for six months, so where else could you go?' Her sharp eyes narrowed. 'It's not like you to arrive so unexpectedly, Philippa. Were you in trouble, a disagreement with the professor, perhaps?'

'Indeed I was not,' Pippa retorted sharply. 'I just felt in need of a holiday. But I did not expect to share my holiday with a snooping journalist.'

Her acid tone was due, she knew to the fact that Mrs Purvis was too shrewd for her comfort. She wanted no further questioning.

'No need for you to see him,' Mrs Purvis replied smoothly as she turned on the tap to fill the sink with suds. 'Just keep out of his way and let him get on with his job. The Hall is large enough for you to avoid each other.'

'A good idea,' Pippa muttered in agreement. 'I have no wish to meet a man who has come here muck-raking. Keep him well out of my sight, Mrs Purvis, for his own sake.'

Mrs Purvis lifted a finger. 'Listen! Isn't that a lorry I hear? That must be the rest of the staff arriving from the flat. I must go and see to the unloading.'

She dried her hands quickly and hurried out. Pippa followed her into the vestibule. Two men in overalls were carrying in a packing case. The housekeeper watched for a moment, her thin arms folded.

'I want these crates stored in the east wing,' she said finally, and Pippa saw her go to the far side of the vestibule beyond the marble pillars and unlock a great double door. As she opened it Pippa could see a vista of long, dusty corridor, arched and vaulted. Not having any interest in the storing of crates she turned away and went up the wide staircase to her room.

Having changed out of trousers into a crisp linen dress, she loitered in her room, undecided. If she went downstairs to lunch, she reflected as she brushed her hair before the dressing-table mirror, she might be obliged to come face-to-face with that journalist fellow before Mrs Purvis had time to tell him to leave. He might even be brash enough to think he could elicit some material about Father from her, and the last thing she wanted was an unholy row with the man. Once he had gone she could forget he existed. She looked at her reflection in the mirror. Judging by her appearance he probably would never guess she was the daughter of the illustrious Alexis Korvak and the beautiful Carrie Hope. With her roundish, snub-nosed face inclining to freckles and her reddish-gold hair she was like neither parent. She had inherited neither Father's dark, flashing-eyed vitality and charm, nor her mother's russet fragility.

Mousy, that's what I am, Pippa thought sadly, fingering her shoulder-length hair. It was soft and with a tendency to curl, and Clive had once described it as leonine; tawny as a mountain lion, he had said. Abruptly Pippa rose from the dressing table and went downstairs.

Carson was alone in the kitchen, munching sandwiches at the table. He wiped the back of a horny hand across his mouth and indicated the plate of sandwiches, some fruit and a bottle of cider on the table before him. 'Mrs Purvis says to help yourself. She's busy unpacking the stuff.'

Pippa sat down opposite him. 'Has the writer-fellow had lunch?' she asked.

Carson shook his grey head. 'He eats out, not with us. Down in the village, I reckon.'

That was a relief. Carson tossed off the glass of cider and rose, trying to muffle a belch. 'Got to get back and clip the hedges,' he muttered by way of an excuse, and trudged out. Pippa ate leisurely and then debated what to do with a whole sunny afternoon before her. Explore, yes that was it. She would investigate the gardens and the Hall.

She caught sight of Carson in the garden in dungarees clipping hedges as she strolled round the lake with its lily pads and darting fish, but on the far side of the Hall, in the shady walks between the lawns she saw no one. It was a stately garden of formal flower beds and terraced lawns, with a delightful herb garden and an orchard where young damsons and apples ripened in the sunshine. For a time Pippa sat in a latticed arbour far from the house and listened to the birdsong, but she found the peace and stillness too nostalgic to bear. It recalled all too vividly the secret moments alone with Clive in the Bois, and the memory was painful to her wounded soul. Pippa left the arbour and retraced her steps quickly towards the Hall.

The great entrance hall was deserted as she entered. From the direction of the kitchen came the sound of men's voices laughing and the clink of cups. Mrs Purvis was evidently entertaining the workmen. As Pippa crossed the hall she noticed that the double doors to the east wing were open, and she could see that one packing case stood in the dusty corridor, its lid off and a heap of what looked like papers lying beside it on the floor.

Curiosity prodded her to go and have a look. She picked up some of the papers and found that they were a collection of old movie magazines, yellowing with age. Through an open doorway leading into a room, Pippa could see more opened packing cases, more papers and folders. She went in and idly picked up more magazines. Flicking over the pages, she was amused by the quaint swimsuits the pin-up girls of yesteryear were obliged to wear, and then suddenly she stopped.

The luscious redhead in the white swimsuit on the centre pages was Pippa's mother. *'Carrie Hope, the sweetheart of the nation,'* the caption read, and Pippa stared at the pouting lips and half-closed eyes. It was her mother as she had never seen her, a siren's face half-veiled by the russet mass of wavy hair. Pippa turned to the next magazine and flicked the pages. Betty Grable, Dorothy Lamour, Esther Williams — and Carrie Hope, this time in a slinky black satin evening gown beaded with diamanté and her head thrown back in a seductive laugh.

Then Pippa realised what all this collection of magazines and papers was. It was a storehouse of photographs and newspaper cuttings from the late 1940s, about the legendary Carrie Hope. Her father's treasured collection of memories, she thought guiltily, his personal mementoes of an adored wife. Pippa was replacing the papers as she had found them when she caught sight of a newspaper cutting dated the year before Mother died.

'WILL CARRIE HOPE MAKE A COMEBACK?' the headline demanded. The paragraphs below hinted that it was unlikely:

'After five years in almost total seclusion Carrie still sees few visitors. It has been rumoured that she has been

35

suffering from a nervous illness ever since the birth of her child, the daughter of Alexis Korvak. Once the glamour queen the nation adored, Carrie will find it increasingly difficult to make a comeback unless she yields soon to her husband's persuasions. Now in her mid-thirties, Carrie's virginal charms will elude her unless she steps back into the studio lights very soon . . .'

Voices in the hallway interrupted Pippa's reading. She pushed the magazines back as they were when she heard Mrs Purvis showing the workmen out. Then she stood quietly, unwilling to be found prying in Father's papers, as the front door closed.

'Now listen, Carson,' she heard the housekeeper say, 'I've got to go out again, and then I'll finish the unpacking. But you must make certain that Miss Korvak is kept in ignorance of what is going on. Do I make myself clear?'

Carson grunted some reply about having to cut the hedges and Pippa heard their footsteps fade away. She stood there, curious. What was she to be kept in ignorance of, she wondered? About Father's papers? No, that was unlikely, for Mrs Purvis had said she was not to know 'what was going on'. What *was* going on? The journalist's activities, perhaps?

Then she had an idea. Could it be Mrs Purvis's activities she was not to know? After all, she was going out again, and she had made a flimsily transparent excuse for going out this morning. What was her errand? To meet the journalist who always ate down in the village? To supply him with information about Father that she knew would make Pippa angry?

Well, she decided, if Mrs Purvis proposed to give him access to this collection of Father's memorabilia she would be disappointed. After all, Pippa was custodian of his welfare in his absence, and mistress of Cambermere. Pippa returned to the double doors to the vestibule, closed them after her and locked them with the key which was still in the lock. Then purposefully she put the key in her pocket and went out into the grounds. Now no one else could gain entrance to the east wing but herself, unless there was another key. She looked across the smooth, serene expanse

36

of the lake with a feeling of satisfaction.

Far away beyond the lake, where the gravel drive skirted it towards the stone-pillared entrance of the Hall, Pippa caught sight of a diminutive navy-coated figure in the distance hurrying along. It was Mrs Purvis. On an impulse Pippa hastened after her, anxious to know her destination. But by the time she rounded the lake and reached the foot of the drive, there was no sign of the housekeeper in the leafy lane.

To the left there was only a mile of dense woodland, so she must have turned right towards the village, Pippa decided, although she could not see her brisk little figure on the long lane ahead. Pippa walked rapidly, almost running, but by the time she reached Walters' riding stables she still had not seen her. She must have cut off the road and across the fields.

Pippa loitered by the gate, undecided what to do. Suddenly she heard the sound of an engine and saw the Land Rover coming towards her. Behind the wheel Pippa could see Geoffrey Walters' dark head. He drew up at the gate when he saw her, and Pippa could see the horse-box behind him.

'Any luck so far with your story?' he called out. 'Can I give you a lift?'

'Thanks,' she said. 'Going far?'

'Only up to Lane End to collect a horse for livery,' he replied. 'Like to come along for the ride?'

She was mildly surprised at his hospitable tone, far less provocative than his unfriendly tone that morning. Perhaps, he regretted his churlish behaviour. Pippa settled back to enjoy the ride. Country lanes on a hot summer afternoon were undeniably peaceful.

'Haven't you brought your little boy along?' she enquired.

'Robin? He's mending the chicken run. Very clever with his hands. And he's not my son but my nephew.'

'Oh, I'm sorry.'

'Understandable mistake,' Walters said smoothly. 'He's my sister's boy, but as he's an orphan now he lives with me. Bright lad.'

'I'm very sorry,' Pippa said quietly. 'Your sister must

37

have been young.'

'She was.' Walters' voice was quiet now and she thought she detected an edge of bitterness. 'But that's in the past. Robin's crazy about animals so I guess I now have someone to inherit my stables. I can't grumble. It's only fair the lad has something to inherit. By the way, I hear you have competition.'

'Competition?'

'Well, they tell me there's another journalist fellow in the village who's asking about old Alexis. I'm not surprised, mind you. He was a real swine and no mistake. He caused more trouble than any other ten men I've ever known. About time someone blew the lid on him.'

'What do you mean?' Pippa asked sharply.

'Well, everyone hereabouts knows what a bastard Alexis Korvak is, and I bet many others do too, here and in America. But he's too rich and powerful to challenge. So far no one has ever dared to tell the truth about him for fear of litigation, or worse. Now if you and this other fellow spill everything . . . '

Pippa was about to interrupt, to retort acidly that she had no such intention, that he'd got it all wrong, when Walters suddenly pulled up.

'Here we are,' he said. 'Do you want to get out or wait here?'

They were outside the neatly-painted five-barred gates of a farm. As she made no answer, fuming as she was, Walters strode away, unlatched the gate and went in. After some moments he returned, followed by a greying man in dungarees who was leading a roan. Pippa heard the clatter of the horse-box being unlocked and the coaxing words of the older man to the horse. Within a few more moments she heard the men saying their farewells, and Walters climbed back into the Land Rover. By this time she had managed to control the anger bubbling inside her.

Sunlight flickered through the archway of trees, dappling the lane ahead of them as Walters put the vehicle into gear and set off on the homeward journey. He drove more slowly this time, so as not to jolt the roan she guessed. She sat without speaking, pondering over Walters' words. At length she broke the silence.

38

'It seems to me that Alexis Korvak is a misunderstood man,' she remarked quietly.

Walters looked at her in sharp surprise. 'Misunderstood? Whatever gives you that idea?'

'Well, he lost his beloved wife at a very early age. Doesn't it occur to you that a man grieving as deeply as he must have done may act rather oddly at times? Perhaps he was not really accountable for his actions, if he really behaved as badly as you say.'

'Behaved oddly?' Walters repeated in a tone of disbelief. 'He behaved outrageously, in a way that would have put a poorer man in prison, but Korvak appeared to be beyond the law. And grieving? You must be mad to believe that! Korvak never felt a prick of emotion for anyone in his whole life except himself. He must be the most selfish, egocentric man that ever existed.'

'You can't say that!' Pippa exploded. 'Did you ever meet him and get to know him?'

'I did, to my sorrow. To my dying day I shall regret holding out the hand of friendship to that fiend. He betrayed me, and my sister's life was the forfeit for my mistake. I hate the man and so, you will find, does everyone else around here.'

'Hate? That is a very strong word.'

'Not too strong for Alexis Korvak. The only excuse I can find for his cruelty is that he must be crazed. Only a lunatic could take all from life and give nothing the way he does. It would be a mercy for everyone if he were dead.' There was no doubting Walters' sincerity, for the hatred in his voice was as sharp and cold as ice. Pippa was shocked by the intensity of his feelings.

The Land Rover drew to a halt and Pippa realised they were back at Cambermere. Walters pulled on the handbrake and grinned at her. 'So you see, you have a lot to uncover about Korvak if you plan to write the whole truth about him, and even I don't know it all. I'll bet there's a whole heap more crimes he's committed in the States.'

'You don't know him,' Pippa argued. 'You're prejudiced by what you've experienced.'

'And another thing you'll have to learn, it seems to me,' Walters went on, 'is objectivity. You appear to be determined not to believe what I say. If you are going to write truthfully about Korvak, you will have to learn to be more dispassionate, more objective.'

Pippa made no answer as she climbed down. Walters leaned out and called after her. 'By the way, you haven't told me your name, young lady. Do tell me your name, or at least your pen-name.'

Pippa paused. Sooner or later he was sure to discover his mistake anyway. She turned to face him. 'Philippa Korvak.'

The teasing smile on his handsome face fled and an angry look of suspicion filled his eyes. 'Korvak? His daughter?' She nodded. 'Why the hell didn't you tell me?' he snapped.

'You didn't ask. You shouldn't jump to conclusions. I'm no writer but a secretary,' she replied levelly. It gave her satisfaction that this arrogant young man's confidence should be deflated. 'Thank you for the ride,' she added, turning to go.

'Miss Korvak,' Walters' voice cracked like a whip. She hesitated, then turned.

'Yes?'

'I made a mistake once in befriending a Korvak. I shall not do the same again. I just want to make it clear that I hope our paths do not cross again.' The scorn on his face chilled her, for he was evidently transferring his hatred from Father to herself.

'Have no fear, Mr Walters, I shall not seek you out,' Pippa replied calmly. 'But whether you like it or not I shall come to the stables to ride Copper as I promised.'

'Don't bother,' he snarled.

'But I shall. Have someone else saddle up if you prefer to avoid me, but I shall be there. Don't forget, those are Korvak horses and I shall ride them whenever I choose. Good day, Mr Walters.'

Pippa could feel his eyes boring into her back, penetrating her thin linen frock like daggers as she marched up the drive to the Hall. But he could feel no more fury than she did. Who was he, this arrogant Walters, to set himself up as judge on her father and on her?

For a time she sat on the terrace, unwilling to go indoors while she still felt so angry. When she finally did get up to go in, she realised that for a whole four hours together she hadn't once thought of Clive.

From the hallway she could hear Mrs Purvis's agitated voice in the kitchen. 'Are you *sure* you haven't got it in your pocket, Carson? You must have locked the door because it was open when I left, and you know how absent-minded you can be. Look again.'

'I haven't been in the house all afternoon, I tell you,' Pippa heard Carson grumble. 'I've been cutting hedges. That damn maze goes on for ever and ever. I haven't finished it yet.'

'Well the key's not in the door so you must have it,' Mrs Purvis snapped. It was unusual, thought Pippa, for the usually calm housekeeper to sound so agitated.

Pippa smiled to herself as she went towards the stairs, fingering the key in her pocket. 'For heaven's sake, Carson, you *must* remember,' the housekeeper cried angrily. 'You know there's no other key and the master would be furious if Philippa discovered what's in there. Here, let me turn your pockets out.'

Pippa's curiosity rippled. Whatever Mrs Purvis was trying to hide from her, she would discover it the very next time the housekeeper was out of the way.

4

Pippa declined Mrs Purvis's rather distant invitation to play cards after dinner. The housekeeper was seated at the table with a pack of cards before her.

'Cribbage is quite a good game, Philippa. I'll teach you, if you like,' Mrs Purvis offered.

'Not tonight, thanks. I'm no good at cards anyway,' Pippa replied.

But the night was far too close and sultry to sleep yet, and in any case Pippa felt restless. She was not welcome here, she knew. Mrs Purvis was polite and efficient but hardly welcoming. She had never been warm towards her in the past and now it appeared she was being even more distant. Secretive was the word, and Pippa did not like the feeling of being deceived. Whatever it was she was trying to keep from Pippa, out of defiance she now wanted to know what it was.

Pippa fingered the key in her pocket again. It was no use trying to evade the housekeeper's keen eye and get into the east wing unobserved right now. It would have to be later, when she had gone to bed.

Pippa fidgetted about her room, opening the casement window wide to try to cool the stifling closeness. Outside, the garden lay still and ethereal in the twilight of evening. Something caught her eyes. For a second she thought she glimpsed a movement under the trees beyond the lake, no more than a fleeting shadow. Then it was gone. She must have been mistaken. A cat, perhaps, or a rabbit.

But still Pippa felt edgy. The encounter with Walters had made her irritable, she thought as she undressed. She could not help being her father's daughter and Walters had no right to dislike her so intensely for her accidental parentage. And more than that, she felt he had accused Father unjustly, implying he was a villain of the worst kind. Father was not like that; he was charming and gay and carefree, casting a sunny radiance all about him, a little forgetful and possibly even inconsiderate at times, but no more than that, Pippa was sure. It was true they were comparative strangers, she and he, but from their few encounters and from his TV appearances Pippa knew how vital and glowing he was. Walters must have some personal axe to grind against him, but for what reason, Pippa wondered?

A cool shower, that was what was needed to calm and freshen her. This thick heat had made her sticky and uncomfortable. Pippa walked naked through to the dressing room, switched on the light and opened the shower cubicle. It was a larger shower than she was used to, with many gleaming steel pipes running up the walls. She turned on the water, and watched with pleasure the myriad tiny jets of water that played through countless outlets. Stepping into the cubicle was like standing under a fast-flowing waterfall, caressing and stimulating every inch of her body at once. Trust Father to have such a superb shower. It was just a fraction too warm for her, however, so she adjusted the control to her taste. Evidently it had not been altered for some time for the knob was dusty and stiff to turn.

Having towelled herself down with one of the luxuriously thick bath sheets on the rail, Pippa put on a crisp cotton nightdress and felt infinitely cool and comfortable. She lay on the bed and listened to the owl in the elms outside, trying to keep her mind clear of thoughts of Walters and Clive. She would think of nothing that would disturb her. But the question kept returning to her mind — what was in the east wing that Mrs Purvis did not want her to discover?

At last Pippa heard the sound of footsteps and a closing door. Mrs Purvis was going to bed. Pippa picked up her wristwatch. Ten past eleven. She would wait until midnight to make sure she was asleep. To pass the time she brushed her hair with slow, methodical strokes, just as she had been taught as a child by Mrs Purvis. By midnight her hair was a glossy mane and her right arm ached.

Pippa put on a cotton housecoat and transferred the key to her pocket, together with a tiny torch from her handbag, then opened her door quietly and crept barefoot along the dark corridor to the main staircase. Not a sound stirred the silence. The marble of the stairs was cold to her feet as she went quickly down and crossed the vestibule. There she switched on her torch momentarily to find the lock.

Unlocking the great doors Pippa pushed one of them open with caution. Fortunately the hinges were well-oiled and it made no sound. She pushed it to behind her and switched on her torch again, for the corridor was pitch dark, but when she opened the door of the room where the packing cases were, moonlight streamed in across the floor from the high windows. Outside the owl began its dismal hooting again.

Switching off her torch Pippa deliberated. It would surely be safe to switch on the lights even with the curtains undrawn, for no light here would be seen from the main wing. It would be safe so long as she did not switch on lights in the rooms across the corridor, where the east wing overlooked the terrace and the swimming pool. Here, on the outer side, she would remain undetected. She switched on.

In the light she could appreciate for the first time how elegant and handsomely-furnished the room was: a long, graceful chamber in Regency style with a plush red velvet couch and drapes to match. But Pippa was eager to investigate further the contents of the cases on the floor by the table. She knelt beside them, pulling out a wad of glossy photographs. There were many film stills of her mother: Carrie Hope in all kinds of costume from period fashion to the slick, sophisticated styles of the 'fifties. Only one was not a promotion photograph, but evidently a snap from a family album. It showed the young Carrie Hope smiling shyly at the camera, while beside her Mrs Purvis, looking exactly the same as she did today, held a dark-haired infant in her arms.

A dark child? Pippa frowned, puzzled. At that moment an unexpected sound alarmed her, and without thinking she thrust the snap into her pocket. She froze, listening, but no further sound came to her ears.

After a moment Pippa rose, crossed the room and switched off the light. She opened the door cautiously but in the corridor all was silence. She moved along, away from the vestibule, in the direction whence the bump had come. Outside the next door Pippa paused and listened intently. Only the owl's distant howl broke the stillness. She opened the door and went in, reaching up the wall for the light switch and finding it, she pulled it down.

A gentle glow of light suffused the room and Pippa saw, to her surprise, not the elegant Regency style of all the other rooms she had seen in Cambermere, but a replica of a mid-Victorian parlour complete with horsehair sofa, chenille-covered table and draped mantelshelf over an iron grate. Staid, upright furniture, heavy and cumbersome, filled the room. A rocking chair stood beside the hearth with its dog-irons and countless miniature pictures in frames arrayed along the shelf. Pippa fingered the leaves of the aspidistra in a brass pot and found it to be imitation. The solitary lamp above the table appeared to be a gas lamp, though she knew it was really electric. It was a strange, stifling room, completely out of character with the spacious elegance of the rest of Cambermere Hall. She was puzzled.

Then she caught sight of the dull sepia portrait, larger than the others, on the mantelshelf and went closer to inspect it. The prim woman with demurely clasped hands and hair neatly piled into a bun on top of her head was Pippa's mother. And then she realised it was Mother in one of the roles she had made famous, the heroine of the Victorian film whose title Pippa could not recall, and this room was a replica of the one where the terrified heroine had listened to the menacing footsteps above and watched the lamp dim.

It came to Pippa in a flash that Father had had this room designed in memory of Mother and her triumph. A shrine, in a way, to commemorate her skill and beauty, that's what this room was. A sad and beautiful gesture. Pippa went out and closed the door, feeling like an intruder on Father's private grief.

If that was what Mrs Purvis had not wanted Pippa to discover, then she need not have feared, Pippa thought. There was no reason to keep the room a secret unless Mrs Purvis thought Pippa might consider Father over-sentimental, but Mrs Purvis should have known Pippa would be the first to respect his privacy. Actually, Pippa was rather touched that a man could feel such sentiment. It made her Father seem somehow more human and real to her. She went on along the corridor and opened the door to the next room.

A touch on the light switch revealed a totally different scene this time, one belonging neither to Cambermere nor to England even. It was at first glance a gambling casino, complete with shaded lights and baize-covered tables and roulette wheels and deep-piled Turkey carpet. Then Pippa noted the false walls with circular windows – portholes – and the sepia photographs on the walls. Each one displayed a bare-shouldered lady in evening dress and Edwardian coiffure. None of the beauties appeared to be Carrie Hope, but Pippa recognised that this was the set of a Deep South gambling-boat, probably the scene of yet another of

45

Mother's triumphs. Idly she rolled the roulette wheel and watched the ball rattle into one of the dust-filled niches. Black three. She felt a shiver touch her spine. Whether it was because the summer night was chillier than she had thought, or because she felt an intruder here in a dusty shrine, or because three was her unlucky number, she refused to ponder.

For a moment she stood in the doorway, then switched off the light and went out again into the corridor, closing the door behind her. Then suddenly she had the strangest feeling, the certain sensation that she was not alone. She leaned against the door and held her breath.

The torch in her pocket — she closed her fingers on it but could not for the life of her force herself to take it out. Whoever was there in the dense blackness of the corridor was close to her, for she heard an indrawn breath. She felt the back of her neck begin to prickle with fear.

'Who's there?' she demanded sharply, in a voice so thin it sounded like a child's. No one answered, but she felt the movement of air as someone moved quickly past her towards the vestibule. She heard the soft pad of footsteps and then the door open and close, but no light relieved the gloom, not even a silhouette as the figure went through the open door. She took several deep breaths in an attempt to recover her composure.

Why should she be frightened? she asked herself. She was in her father's house, and therefore unnecessarily afraid of being caught down here in the middle of the night. Her actions could be construed as snooping, but why should that disturb her? It was only natural curiosity about her Father and his way of life, since he was a comparative stranger to her. And curiosity about her long-dead mother too. In over twenty years facts became magnified myths and it was hard to know what kind of woman she was. A six-year-old child's hazy memories were hardly to be trusted. Was Carrie the ethereal fairy-princess she remembered, and Father the handsome prince on a dashing charger who came to rescue her from poverty and sadness? Pippa wished she knew more about her parents, apart from the lurid tales the press presented to the world.

And who could it be who surprised her in the dark and yet was unwilling to be recognised? Without warning the lights snapped on and the corridor was flooded with light. By the double doors stood a tight-lipped Mrs Purvis in a woollen dressing gown and with her hair no longer coiled but falling to her shoulders.

'May I ask what you are doing, Philippa?' she asked coldly.

'Just having a look around. I was curious.' Mrs Purvis still managed to make her feel like some miscreant school-girl even after all these years.

'Then if you don't mind, I'll lock up again now and we can all get some sleep,' she said, standing back to allow Pippa to pass. She did so sheepishly. Mrs Purvis re-locked the doors, put on the hall light and pocketed the key. Pippa felt resentful at being made to feel guilty, and turned to the housekeeper.

'Was that you who passed me in the corridor just now, in the dark?'

Mrs Purvis's eyes narrowed. 'Indeed it was not. I've just come downstairs because I thought I heard sounds. Can't be too careful, you know. There's been a lot of burglaries in these parts, and Cambermere is very remote.'

'Then who was it?'

The housekeeper shrugged. 'How should I know? Not Carson, that's for sure, because he's snoring in his own bed in the village by now, where anyone in his right mind should be. Come now, Philippa, upstairs with you.'

Pippa stood her ground. 'And what is there worth steal-ing in any case? So far as I could see everything in that wing is false − wax fruit, plastic plants − even the Victorian bric-a-brac is probably only copies. They're film-sets in those rooms, aren't they?'

Mrs Purvis nodded as she headed towards the staircase and Pippa was obliged to follow her. 'Some of the rooms are film-sets, yes. Some are copied and some Mr Korvak had flown from Hollywood. But other rooms contain real objets d'art and are worth a lot of money, so you see vigilance is essential.'

In silence Pippa followed her upstairs and along the bedroom corridor. 'Are the film-sets in memory of my mother, Mrs Purvis?' she added as she paused at her own doorway. She saw the hard light in the housekeeper's eyes soften.

'Some of them are, like the Victorian one. She was magnificent in that. And in *Salome*. Your father worshipped her then.'

'And kept the sets in memory?' Pippa asked.

Opening her door Mrs Purvis turned away. 'You could say that. Those sets were the scenes of his great triumphs more than hers. Now goodnight to you, Philippa, and no more wandering about in the middle of the night, if you please.'

'I'm sorry if I alarmed you,' she said contritely, then added, 'but I should like to have the key again tomorrow and investigate the rest of the wing. Goodnight, Mrs Purvis.'

Pippa walked quietly away towards her room before the housekeeper could argue. After all, it was Pippa's home and she was going to have the freedom of it, and the sooner the housekeeper realised, the better.

Father's triumphs she had said, Pippa mused as she got into bed. As a producer, she guessed. He had kept the sets of the films he had produced which had been box-office successes. Perhaps not all of them were ones in which Mother had starred. That would account for no picture of her being in the gambling saloon. She must ask Mrs Purvis about that tomorrow.

A thought crossed Pippa's mind as she settled down to sleep. The unseen person who brushed by her in the darkness — of course, it might have been the journalist. He could have broken in and been snooping, but at least the thought that it was a real live person removed the chilly feeling she had had. Not that she was foolish enough to believe in the supernatural, but that wing of Cambermere did hold a haunting strangeness that was not quite of this world.

Carson was unbolting the front door as Pippa crossed the vestibule next morning. He grunted an acknowledgement of Pippa's cheerful 'Good morning.' Mrs Purvis was already in the kitchen, beating eggs.

The housekeeper paused in her brisk beating and glanced at Pippa curiously. 'You're up early, Philippa, considering your late night. Breakfast isn't ready yet.'

'No matter. I'll go down to the stables to ride Copper and eat when I get back,' Pippa told her, then added, 'By the way, could it have been that journalist fellow in the east wing last night?'

The housekeeper shook her head firmly. 'It could not. He moved out to the village inn when I told him how you felt. He said he'd come back in a few days when you were settled. I haven't seen him since.'

'Could he have broken in?' Pippa asked.

'Not he. He's a straightforward young man. I told you, he'll come back to ask you if he can carry on. What wild ideas you still have, Philippa.'

Pippa frowned, puzzled. Then who could have been in the house last night? And who else but an inquisitive journalist could be interested in the east wing? The packing cases, that was what he was after, she felt sure, and the stories they could reveal. Perhaps he had had a tantalising glimpse of the contents before he was obliged to leave, and somehow had contrived to get back into the house just at an opportune moment when the wing chanced to be unlocked. Pippa asked Mrs Purvis if he had already had access to the cuttings and photographs.

The housekeeper's keen eyes regarded her penetratingly. 'So you've seen what's in the cases. Well yes, he's seen some of them, not all. Those relating to Mr Alexis.'

'That reminds me,' said Pippa. 'Do you remember this?'

She took the snap from her pocket and handed it to the housekeeper, who laid aside her whisk and inspected it closely. Pippa saw her thin lips soften into a hint of a smile.

'Why, yes. That's my Miss Carrie before she became ill. That's the real Miss Carrie, shy and kind and not all seductive like the films made her look.'

'And the baby? It isn't me, is it? The baby is dark,' Pippa commented. Mrs Purvis's lips snapped into a straight line again.

'Red, not dark. Irma's hair was as red as her mother's, natural Titian. Miss Carrie didn't need dye like the others. All the blondes used bleach and even Rita Hayworth

49

wasn't really a redhead. She was black, you know, Spanish. Had to have electrolysis to give her a higher brow line, and her hair bleached out and then dyed. But not Miss Carrie. She was a natural born beauty.'

There was no doubting the love in her tone as she spoke of her dead mistress. Pippa turned to leave. 'I see. Well, I'll be back by nine.' A ride over the fields in the cool morning air was just what she needed to clear her brain.

She was setting off down the drive to skirt around the lake when the scent of woodsmoke caught her nostrils. Over to the left she could see Carson's stocky figure leaning on a rake beside a tall hedge. And he was not alone; a young man in blue jeans stood chatting to him, tall and broad-shouldered and with fair hair that gleamed in the morning sunlight. Carson caught sight of her and nodded. Pippa set off across the lawns towards them.

'Morning, miss,' said Carson gruffly. 'I were collecting all these hedge-clippings to burn and Mr Lorant here were kind enough to offer to help.'

Pippa looked up at the stranger. His keen eyes were regarding her with an air of interest. 'Good morning. I'm Pippa Korvak.' She held out her hand and felt him take it firmly. 'Haven't we met somewhere?'

He smiled, and his tanned face became decidedly good-looking. 'A pleasure to meet you, Miss Korvak. My name is Stephen Lorant, and so far I don't think I've had the pleasure.'

Blond. And blue jeans. For a moment she had taken him for the stranger in the woods nearby who almost caused Alouette to throw her. But this man's accent was slightly American; no doubt he was a tourist passing through Marlow.

'I'm sorry. I just felt you were somehow familiar,' she murmured in embarrassment. He was smiling still, a hint of amusement in his hazel eyes.

'No matter, we've met now,' he remarked. 'And may I compliment you on the very fine grounds you have here, Miss Korvak. The lawns are beautifully kept, the roses magnificent and, if I'm not mistaken, this is a maze here, isn't it?'

Carson's normally expressionless face lit up. Pippa

50

smiled. 'I take no credit, Mr Lorant. Mr Carson here is responsible and as you say, he has reason to be proud of his handiwork. Is this indeed a maze, Carson?'

He nodded. 'A copy of the one at Hampton Court they say, Miss. Trouble is, it makes a lot of work clipping and burning the clippings.'

The stranger turned away from Pippa to look at the maze. 'But well worth the effort, Mr Carson. I'd like to have a go at finding my way to the centre one day.'

Carson was positively beaming. Pippa admired the easy way this young man could talk to him and draw him out. Perhaps he seemed familiar because he gave people a feeling of being relaxed and made them seem old friends. But as he stood there, his broad back towards her and his hands on his hips she suddenly started. She *did* know that back! It *was* the man who had dropped from the tree and then raced off across the fields, she was sure of it. He was talking about the trees and that gave her an opening.

'Have you been in the wood up alongside the north wall of Cambermere?' she asked quietly. He turned to face her. 'Were you by any chance up there yesterday?'

'As a matter of fact . . . ' he began hesitantly.

'I thought so!' Pippa broke in. 'Mr Lorant, I have a bone to pick with you.'

'Ah, excuse me, miss,' Carson muttered, 'but I'd best get back to my bonfire. Not safe to leave it for long.'

Picking up his rake he left them. Pippa turned to the stranger. 'It was you up in the tree, wasn't it? It was you who jumped down and frightened my horse.'

He cocked his head to one side and shrugged apologetically. 'I'm sorry. It wasn't on purpose, I assure you. I fell, and that's the truth. After all my misspent years as a boy climbing trees there's no excuse for such clumsiness, but I lost my hold and fell. On my feet, fortunately, but I'm sorry I scared your horse.'

'And you didn't even wait to see if I was hurt!' Pippa exclaimed. 'You just ran off like a boy caught stealing apples! Not only clumsy, but thoughtless, Mr Lorant!'

'Unforgivable,' he murmured, and his contrite tone added to the faint American drawl made him sound as appealing as a small boy caught red-handed. 'Truth is, I was

51

scared stiff you'd discover me when I was trying to track you down.'

'Track me down?' Pippa echoed. 'Why?'

A slight flicker of a smile illuminated his rueful expression. 'Two reasons, really. One, curiosity to see the daughter of the famed Alexis Korvak, and two, to ask a favour of you. In the circumstances, however, I think I'm no longer in a position to do the latter. I admit I was in the wrong. I confess it unreservedly, and I won't object if you think fit to order me off your property. Shall I go, Miss Korvak?'

He stood there, towering a clear head above her with such a penitent expression that Pippa was tempted to laugh. Abject contrition looked so incongruous on the face of this tall, lithe man. At once she felt guilty.

'No, of course not. I've said my piece and you've explained and apologised, so now that's over. Please feel free to walk in the grounds whenever you like since you obviously admire Carson's handiwork — I'm sure he'll be delighted.'

'But you will not,' he murmured.

'No, please, don't misunderstand me,' Pippa hastened to assure him. She did not want to make this warm and likeable young man feel so uncomfortable. 'And you mentioned a favour — what was it you were going to ask?'

He smiled quizzically. 'You mean you would forgive me enough to consider it?'

'It depends what it is. Tell me.'

His hazel eyes challenged hers directly. 'Allow me access to your father's papers so that I may continue my work.' His tone was level, his gaze calm, but Pippa's heart leapt.

'Papers? You mean, you are the journalist?' Of course, she thought angrily, she should have guessed. Loitering near the Hall yesterday, hiding in the trees when he saw her — she ought to have realised. She held her chin high. 'No, I see no reason why you should pry into private documents. If you must write about Father, you can research in the normal way. I cannot help you.'

'You have not forgiven me or you would not refuse before asking me more,' Stephen Lorant remarked. 'Hearing about me has prejudiced you, and my clumsiness yesterday has steeled you against me. That is hardly rational.'

52

'Rational?' Pippa retorted. 'Your behaviour — snooping around the Hall and then hiding up that tree is hardly rational, or commendable for that matter!' She felt herself shaking with anger, and knew the extent of her anger was unreasonable. She was angry because she had allowed herself to warm to this young man before discovering what he was. She was tense, but he still stood, relaxed and completely at ease, a tolerant, undismayed expression on his handsome face.

'Miss Korvak, I have already apologised and I think I should add that I have your father's permission to look through his papers. It seems your housekeeper omitted to tell you that.'

Pippa blushed. She had completely forgotten, but now he reminded her she remembered Mrs Purvis's words — that he was invited, whereas she was an intruder at Cambermere. With difficulty she searched for words.

'I see,' she murmured, unwilling to admit she had forgotten. 'You have a letter of introduction, no doubt?'

'Which I gave to Mrs Purvis. You do not doubt my word, surely?' His face remained composed, not unfriendly despite his words.

'No. Then you'd better come up to the Hall. Would this afternoon suit you?' She could not help it. Anger still prevented warmth from entering her tone.

'Fine. I'll come up after lunch. So long, then, Miss Korvak. I look forward to seeing you.'

He strode away across the lawn towards the gates. Pippa watched his long, easy stride and his broad back until he was lost to view behind the rhododendron bushes. Then she sighed. No time to ride now — she would go in for breakfast.

Mrs Purvis barely glanced at Pippa as she came into the kitchen. 'There was a telephone call for you, Philippa. Mr Bainbridge asked if he might call to visit you.'

'Bainbridge?' repeated Pippa. 'I don't know him, do I? I don't recall the name.'

'He owns the estate adjoining Cambermere Hall. He used to visit your father sometimes, a long time ago. I expect he wants to welcome you, and one must accept such courtesy with grace.'

Pippa smiled to herself as she began eating. Mrs Purvis sounded like a governess as well as looking like one. Her tone was always equable and patient as though humouring a child.

'What is he like, this Mr Bainbridge?' Pippa enquired.

Mrs Purvis thought for a moment. 'Nearing fifty, I would say, very rich and a bachelor.'

That was the housekeeper's summary of him, concise but outlining only what she considered relevant.

'No, I meant what is he like as a person?' Pippa persisted. 'Pleasant? Argumentative? Generous? That kind of thing.'

'I hardly know the gentleman, Philippa. He's a north-country man, sometimes a little abrupt as I recall, but he's highly-respected in the area. A churchwarden, I believe, and perhaps a magistrate too.'

'I see. Then I suppose I'd better receive him, in the best English country lady tradition,' Pippa said with a smile. The housekeeper cast her a quick glance.

'I've already told him you will be at home this afternoon,' she announced calmly. 'He will be here at two-thirty. I suggest you receive him in the drawing room, and I will bring you tea at three.'

Pippa looked up at her in surprise but Mrs Purvis appeared unaware. Really, thought Pippa, this is taking matters too far, to decide for me and give me instructions as if I were incapable of deciding for myself. But then another thought struck her — Bainbridge's presence would probably prevent her from seeing Stephen Lorant when he came, and she wondered at the feeling of disappointment it caused her. Still, there would be other days . . .

At half-past two precisely there was a knock at the drawing room door and Mrs Purvis entered, followed by a thick-set man with greying hair and a moustache. His face remained expressionless as the housekeeper introduced him.

'Mr Bainbridge, Philippa,' she said, and then withdrew discreetly.

Pippa rose, her hand outstretched. 'How kind of you to call, Mr Bainbridge,' she said warmly. 'You are a near neighbour, I believe.'

'Next door,' he grunted as he touched her hand briefly. 'I only heard last night when I were down at the George and Dragon that you were here.'

'I came unexpectedly,' Pippa explained, wondering if he always spoke in that staccato way or whether he was uncomfortable in her presence. She made an effort to put him at ease. 'I believe you were a friend of my father's,' she commented, indicating a chair for him to be seated.

'Not really. More a business acquaintance.'

Pippa observed him unobtrusively. He was unprepossessing in appearance, inclining to corpulence, with a hard, uncompromising voice and little red veins in his eyes. 'I see, you did business together.'

'Tried to, but his mind was always on films, not interested in business. Never would give me a straight answer, and that's not my way. Where I come from we pride ourselves on forthrightness. Saves time in the long run, and time's a very valuable commodity.'

'I do so agree.' By now Stephen Lorant would be in the east wing, going through those packing cases. Pippa would dearly like to be down there too.

'Then I'll waste no more time but come straight to the point, Miss Korvak,' Bainbridge said leaning forward in his chair, his cheeks flushed. 'I've come here not for idle chat, but for serious talk. I've come to make a proposal.'

'Proposal?'

'Aye. A proposal of marriage. I want you to marry me, Miss Korvak.'

5

Pippa jerked upright in her chair, incredulous.

'I beg your pardon?' she stammered. Bainbridge spread

his thick fingers in an apologetic gesture.

'There, I've blurted it out and taken you by surprise, I can see. But I've always found that's the best way to do business — come straight to the point and no beating about the bush. I fancy it would be an advantage to both of us if we were wed. If you'll bear with me, I'll explain.'

Pippa cut in. 'There's no need, Mr Bainbridge, because however good your reasons, I'm afraid I'm not contemplating marriage at the moment, not to you nor to anyone else. Your bluntness does you credit, but I fear you are wasting your time.'

She rose to indicate she had done, but Bainbridge held up a restraining hand. 'Hold hard a moment, Miss Korvak. Hear me out, at least. I know we're total strangers — why, you don't know me from Adam any more than I know you from Eve, but at least let me explain.'

'If you insist,' Pippa said in a weary tone, 'but really it is a waste of time.'

'I've sprung it on you too sudden. You see, I'm a land-owner first and foremost — I've got land up north as well as here, land I inherited from my mother. Came south years ago. Splendid farming land here. I wanted more — I tried to buy some from your father.'

'And he would not sell?'

'He wouldn't discuss it much, but I wanted to extend my farm. Whenever I thought I'd get an answer at last, off he'd shoot to Istanbul or Fiji or somewhere for a new film.'

Pippa smiled, recognising the truth of what he said. 'That's my father, all right. As hard to pin down as a ball of mercury. Does he have a lot of land here then?'

'Several hundred acres — more than he needs. He could have let some of it go without missing it. Walters was after some too, at one time, to extend his stables, but he got nowhere.'

'I'm very sorry, Mr Bainbridge, but I'm afraid I can't help you there. My father is a law unto himself.'

'Too right he is,' Bainbridge muttered. 'But you could help me all the same.'

'I could? How?'

'Well, if you've come back here to settle down . . .'

'But I don't know that I have. I may only stay briefly,' she

56

corrected him.

'That's as maybe. But in any event, as Korvak's only living child, one day you'll inherit.'

'Ah well, perhaps. But I hope that day is a long way off. When it comes, then you can talk to me again.' She waved the matter aside with a smile, but Bainbridge was not to be deterred.

'I don't see as we need wait,' he said urgently, leaning forward again and fixing Pippa with his keen gaze. 'That day may not be so far off as you think, and in the meantime it seems to me as we could solve both your problems and mine by acting now. One neat and simple solution would solve the matter for once and for all.'

Pippa sat up, intrigued. What was the man talking about? What did he know of her problems? The only way to find out was to encourage him to continue in a subject she would really have preferred to drop.

'You mean our marriage, I take it. But I fail to see how that would help, Mr Bainbridge.'

'Arthur, please. Well, that way I'd be sure of the land once you inherit. And what's more it's high time I was wed if I'm going to have an heir to succeed to my land and my money, and looking at you I guess you must be thirty already . . . '

'Twenty-six,' she corrected him stiffly.

'Well, old enough to be classed as a spinster if you've not had a proposal yet. Seems to me you should be glad to get off the shelf.'

Pippa stared in amazement at his insolence, and he seemed to realise he had been hasty and abrupt. He spread his hands and grunted.

'I don't think I expressed myself too well, Philippa, but I'd no intention of being rude. Regard it as a business proposition, if you like. I need a wife and an heir — '

'And Korvak land,' she could not help interrupting.

'Aye, and the land too. But I'm not asking you to make a free gift of it. I'd see you had all you wanted — a fine house, cars, furs, jewels — whatever a woman wants. I'm not short of a pound or two.'

'I hear you're a wealthy man,' she commented.

'Wealthy enough to give you all you're accustomed to as

a rich man's daughter, I can promise you,' he agreed.

'Everything except what I want,' she murmured.

'What do you want that I can't give? Money can buy anything.'

'Except love. When I marry I want to feel secure in the love of a man,' Pippa said. Her tone was light, but the sentiment was sincere. Recent experience had taught her the hard way the difference between being loved and being used.

'Aye, well, it doesn't come easy to me to talk about feelings,' Bainbridge muttered. 'But I reckon as we'd come to like each other well enough.'

'That's not enough.'

'Enough for me. I won't ask you to feel what you can't.'

Pippa rose and crossed the room to ring the bell. Bainbridge watched her, his eyes betraying his anxiety for an answer, but she was in no mood to hasten to satisfy him. What a nerve he had, proposing marriage to a total stranger in the hope of acquiring Father's land, and under the pretext that he was doing her a favour!

'What are you doing?' Bainbridge asked. It amused her to think that perhaps he suspected she was going to have him thrown out.

'Ringing for Mrs Purvis to bring tea,' she replied coolly. 'Or would you prefer coffee?'

'Tea's fine,' he grunted.

Mrs Purvis's sharp eyes surveyed both Pippa and her visitor curiously as she came in, and Pippa guessed she was wondering what had been said. When she returned a few moments later with a tea tray Pippa could not resist a sudden impulse.

'Mr Bainbridge has proposed to me, Mrs Purvis,' Pippa said and saw his startled look, but the housekeeper remained placid.

'Indeed?'

'What do you think, Mrs Purvis?' Pippa asked her.

She shrugged. 'It's not for me to comment, I'm sure.'

'But I need your help and guidance,' Pippa teased. Arthur Bainbridge looked downright embarrassed.

'There's no need for an immediate answer, Philippa,' he said jerkily. 'Take your time and think it over.'

'Oh, I will. But I'd like to hear what Mrs Purvis thinks all the same.' It was wicked of her, she knew, but she felt his importunate behaviour warranted it. She was enjoying the game.

The housekeeper poured out the tea, and as she handed a cup to Bainbridge she said, 'Well, it's a bit sudden, when you've only just met, but it seems to me you could do worse, Philippa. Mr Bainbridge is a respected gentleman.'

'And wealthy,' Pippa added.

'So it's perhaps not an idea to be dismissed lightly,' the housekeeper concluded, and then she left them.

Decidedly she must be feeling better than she did a few days ago, Pippa thought, to be in such a wilful, capricious mood. Only a week ago, still sorrowing at the loss of Clive, she could not have undergone the ordeal of having a proposal of marriage from a man she did not even know, let alone like. Now she could face the situation with comparative equanimity.

Bainbridge drained his tea and put down the cup. 'Well, I'd best be off,' he said laconically, rising from his chair.

'So soon?' Pippa said. 'Then let me see you out.'

In the hallway he shook hands with her. 'Let me know your decision when you've had time to think it over,' he said gruffly.

'By the way,' she said on the doorstep, 'I'm curious about what you said. You said marriage would solve my problems as well as yours. Do I have any problems, apart from being an old maid left on the shelf?' she smiled at him, and he coloured slightly.

'Aye, well, you need looking after, don't you? You're not liked hereabouts as you probably know, but I doubt as anyone would dare to harm Mrs Bainbridge. You'll be safer with me.'

'Not liked? Harm me?' Pippa echoed in surprise. 'The people here hardly know me, and I've done no harm to anyone.'

'You're Korvak's daughter, aren't you? That's enough for them. And as you'd well find out, they'll stop at nothing.'

'I know no such thing. What are you talking about?'

He looked at her keenly for a moment and could see she

was genuinely mystified. 'You mean you don't know about your father? They haven't told you?'

'What should they tell me?'

'Nay, it's not for me to tell tales, but I'd have thought your housekeeper would have done well to warn you before letting you come here. Must be loyalty to her master that she's held her tongue. We must give her credit for that at least.'

Pippa felt hurt and angry. 'What are you hinting at, Mr Bainbridge? I do not care for your insinuations.'

'Like I said, I'll let them who have reason to hate Korvak for the way he's deceived them tell you for themselves. It's not for me to say.'

'No. So you should have held your tongue. My father has not deceived you, has he?'

A veiled look came into Bainbridge's bloodshot eyes. 'As a matter of fact – but then, it were a long time ago. I'll say good day to you, Philippa, and let me know when you make up your mind. My proposal stays open.'

He nodded and went out. Stunned, Pippa stood in the doorway and watched his stocky figure receding down the drive. What an overwhelming man, and how insolent! How dare he suggest Father was some kind of cheat or fraud – but then, she recollected sadly, it was not the first time there had been hints. First the blind man, then Walters, and now Bainbridge. There must be some kind of misunderstanding if several people believed ill of Father.

Across the green sward Pippa caught sight of the tall, rangy figure of Stephen Lorant. He was standing where she had met him this morning, by the maze. Pippa's spirits lifted as she walked across the lawns to him.

'Hello, Stephen.' The warmth in her voice added to her smile was meant to show him that she intended friendship with him, past misunderstandings forgotten.

His tanned face creased into a smile in response. 'Hi. That was Arthur Bainbridge I saw just now, wasn't it?'

'You've met him? A strange man,' Pippa remarked.

'Saw him in the pub, that's all, and heard people say he was a rich landowner.'

'Have you been to look at the papers?'

'Not yet. I wanted to have a go at this maze and put a theory to the test. If you've got an hour or so to spare, maybe you'd like to take a chance on getting completely lost in there with me?'

'Not just now, thanks. To tell the truth, mazes frighten me — I get so disorientated and confused at having lost my sense of direction that I begin to feel quite dizzy.'

'Pity,' he murmured. 'I wanted to try out my friend's theory. He tells me that if you chalk a line on the right-hand wall continuously, whatever corners you turn, you'll eventually arrive at the centre and then find your way out again. I wonder if it really works.'

'You can hardly chalk on hedges,' Pippa pointed out.

'No, but I could keep touching the right hand side. Never mind, I guess I'd better get down to work anyway.'

Together they walked back towards the house, and again Pippa felt a sense of ease in his company. In the vestibule she was reluctant to leave him. She hesitated, about to suggest that they looked through the papers together, when Mrs Purvis emerged silently from the kitchen quarters.

'Good afternoon, Mr Lorant. I have the key for you here,' she said quietly, offering him the key to the east wing. 'Was there a particular subject you wanted to cover today?'

'Yes, as a matter of fact, I wanted some details about Mr Korvak's leaving Hungary and coming to the States,' Stephen replied. 'Do you happen to know if there is a diary or something of the kind?'

The housekeeper thought for a moment. 'I think there is very little on that subject, so far as I remember, but what there is will be in the crate labelled number two. When you have finished perhaps you would be kind enough to return the key to me personally,' she went on, with the briefest of glances at Pippa. 'In the meantime, Philippa, perhaps you would care to iron your silk blouses — I've just washed them by hand for you.'

She was gone again, quickly and silently, before Pippa could demur. Stephen was already unlocking the double doors.

'Perhaps I'll see you later?' he said, and then he too was

gone and the doors closed behind him. With a sigh Pippa went to the kitchen. The ironing board was already set up and the iron heating, but Mrs Purvis was not there.

She came in some minutes later. Pippa looked up from her work. 'Did Mr Lorant bring a letter of introduction from Father?' she asked.

'He did, otherwise I would not have allowed him here?'

'May I see it?'

The housekeeper looked at her with a trace of annoyance on her normally serene features. 'Don't you believe me, child? Of course I don't have the letter now — it came to the London flat. I only stored and kept what was essential.'

'I see. Well, what exactly is he writing about Father?'

'A complete biography, I understand. You'd better ask Mr Lorant for yourself.'

'I shall.'

So it was that when Stephen Lorant eventually emerged from the east wing Pippa was waiting for him. 'Come and have a cup of tea with me,' she invited. 'There are questions I want to ask you.'

'Great idea,' he replied. 'Dusty papers have given me quite a thirst.'

'Now,' she said, as she handed him a cup from the tray Mrs Purvis had set ready in the drawing room, 'tell me who commissioned you, and to write just what.'

'Your father did. To write his life story.'

'How a penniless Hungarian emigrant became a renowned producer? But surely that's been done before.'

'Not the whole of it,' Stephen said quietly. 'His life in Hungary before he left, and much of his private life afterwards. Much of that has been kept quiet.'

'We all have parts of our lives we prefer to forget,' Pippa commented with feeling. 'So why should my father change his mind now and ask you to uncover it all.'

'He didn't exactly ask me — he challenged me,' Stephen replied. 'And I am a man who can't resist a challenge.'

'Challenge? Yet he laid all his private papers at your disposal? You expect me to believe that?' Pippa exclaimed.

'I can prove it. In my car I have a tape of a conversation with Korvak,' Stephen said quietly. 'Shall I fetch it?'

'Do.'

When he had left the room, Pippa remembered the dirty little yellow Fiat with the file on the seat about Korvak. That must have been Stephen's car. And the notes in the file had hinted at some unpleasant facts about Father. There was more she must ask Stephen Lorant.

He came back with a small tape-recorder in his hands. 'Wait a moment until I find the place,' he said.

Pippa poured more tea while he ran the tape back and forth and odd snatches of incomprehensible speech issued from the machine. More clicks and a whirring sound, and then suddenly the room was filled with the sound of a voice which made her start.

'That's Father's voice!' she murmured. There was no doubt of it — the lazy American drawl superimposed upon but not disguising the gutteral accent of his native Hungary. It was a rich, resonant voice, which latterly she had heard over the transatlantic telephone more often than in person.

'Listen,' said Stephen. 'Hear what he says.'

The rich voice rolled on. 'So you want to print my whole story from the beginning, do you, Stefan? From the start in Budapest to England and then to the States? The whole truth like it's never been done before, warts and all? Then go ahead, I won't stop you. You can check out what you will — it will do no harm to me. And when you've done, let me see it, to confirm that it is the truth. I want no distorted picture of me to go down to posterity.'

'You'll allow me to check any of your papers?' Stephen's voice on the tape asked crisply.

Korvak gave a deep, rumbling laugh. 'You are determined to prove me an *ördög*, aren't you, Stefan? Go on then, prove it.'

There was a click, and her father's voice vanished from the tape.

Stephen cocked his head to one side. 'Do you believe me now, Miss Korvak?'

'Yes, of course. And do call me Pippa. Tell me, what did that word mean that Father said?'

'You mean *ördög*? It means a devil in Hungarian.'

'You know Hungarian?'

'We spoke it as well as English at home. I think I told you

63

my father too was Hungarian.'

'Why does my father accuse you of wanting to prove he is a devil?' Pippa pressed him.

'He did not accuse me — he challenged me to do so. His life is a very eventful one, to put it mildly,' Stephen replied. 'And he himself is to vet the story when I have completed it. Are you satisfied now?'

'I suppose so,' Pippa admitted. 'Tell me, it has been suggested he was hated — have you uncovered any reasons why he should be?'

Stephen looked away, replacing the cassette in its case. 'I haven't yet done very much research. After the papers, I shall have to cover all the ground he travelled and ask many questions. Since I arrived in England I've been busy mostly on another assignment, about bats, for a naturalist magazine. Fascinating creatures, bats. Didn't know a thing about them until I started this assignment.'

Pippa was barely listening as he launched into an enthusiastic account of his meeting a couple in Hertfordshire who were bat experts and had convinced him that bats were not the sinister, repulsive creatures superstition had led people to believe. 'They're tiny, harmless creatures, very poor-sighted but with an incredibly efficient echo-location system, like radar. They can catch their prey in the dark and find their way unerringly — it's a fallacy that they get stuck in people's hair.'

Although she was not listening, Stephen seemed unaware. 'I never knew they were so interesting. Did you know that apart from living high under roofs like old churches, some bats burrow underground, like the Daubenton? I was given a baby Pipistrelle to hold in my hand.'

'Pardon?' said Pippa, her attention arrested by the word, so like her own name.

'You weren't listening,' Stephen accused her. 'It was such an appealing little thing, so small and helpless and vulnerable. I shall think quite differently about the genus *Chiroptera* from now on, and I hope my readers will too.'

Despite his smile and obvious enthusiasm Pippa had the distinct impression that she was being side-tracked, but before she could attempt to pick up the thread of her enquiries about her father, Mrs Purvis glided into the room.

'Mr Bainbridge is on the telephone. He wants to speak to you, Philippa.'

Pippa rose. 'Excuse me a moment,' she murmured.

Stephen rose too. 'It's time I was going anyway. Thanks for the tea.'

He followed Pippa out into the hall, where she picked up the 'phone.

'Hello?'

'Ah, there you are, Philippa,' Bainbridge's voice rasped. 'Now about that Dormobile on the edge of my land — is it yours? I want it shifted, otherwise trippers will get the notion they can all park there and I don't want my fields covered with litter.'

'Dormobile? Where? I know nothing about it,' Pippa remarked. Stephen paused in the doorway. 'Where is it anyway?'

'By the copse, where there's a handy stream. Just where your land reaches mine — that's why I thought it might be yours. Sorry. I'll have to go down and speak to them. Sorry I troubled you. And by the way, don't forget, my offer is still open.'

Stephen was still waiting when she turned away from the telephone. 'What was that about a Dormobile?' he asked. She told him. Stephen frowned. 'It wasn't there when I came by this morning. As he says, it's probably a cheeky camper.'

Pippa smiled. 'Well, I wouldn't like to be him when Bainbridge gets there — he'll make short shrift of the fellow.'

'I don't doubt it. Cheerio, Pippa. Be seeing you.'

Impulsively Pippa followed him out on to the doorstep.

'Stephen,' she called after him before she had time to think what she was saying, 'Why don't you move back into the Hall? After all, it would make your work so much easier and I'm sure Mrs Purvis hasn't stripped your room yet. Whereabouts was your room?'

Stephen was regarding her quizzically. 'Upstairs in the east wing. Are you sure you don't mind?'

'Not in the least, now I know you. I acted hastily when I

said you had to leave — I was just angry at the thought of a snooper. But now it's different — I'd be glad to have you back here.'

'That's very kind of you. I'll move my things back this evening, if you're sure.'

'I'll tell Mrs Purvis to expect you.' Smiling, Pippa was about to turn back into the house when a thought struck her. 'Upstairs in the east wing? Then it must have been you I saw at the window that morning I was swimming,' she murmured.

Stephen grinned. 'So you spotted me. I have to confess — I was prying then. It was a lovely sight — you looked like a water-nymph, Pippa, so graceful and relaxed in the water. You have a very trim and shapely figure, if I may say so.'

Pippa felt a blush of pleasure begin to tingle on her cheeks, and then another thought came. 'And it was also you who brushed past me in the dark that night in the east wing? Was that you?'

Stephen shook his fair head. 'I left that day and didn't come back into the Hall until you invited me.'

Pippa smiled. 'Well, one mystery is solved anyway. I daresay the other will be too in time. Shall we expect you after dinner?'

Mrs Purvis's thin eyebrows rose fractionally when Pippa announced the news to her. 'So you've changed your mind?' she remarked drily. 'You do not change, Philippa. Unpredictable and impulsive still, I see.'

Her tone was cool and Pippa wondered if she had annoyed the older woman. 'I'm sorry — does it inconvenience you, Mrs Purvis? I'll make up the bed again if that will help.'

'No, no inconvenience at all,' the housekeeper replied. 'The bed is still made up so Mr Lorant may return as soon as he wishes.'

It was curious, Pippa thought privately, how Mrs Purvis always said the right words yet at the same time managed to sound as if she meant the opposite. Her unsmiling expression and cold eyes made it clear she did not like Pippa's invitation to the young man but could not criticise her right to do so.

After dinner that evening Pippa heard Stephen's car pull up outside the Hall and his voice in the vestibule as he talked to Mrs Purvis. She kept her distance while he unloaded his belongings and carried them upstairs, glad he was here but reluctant to appear too eager for his company. To her disappointment, however, he remained upstairs for the rest of the evening, and when the housekeeper announced that she was going to bed, Pippa had no choice but to retire too.

Of course, she thought as she undressed, the footsteps in the night when she first arrived — he was still here in the Hall then. It must have been Stephen's footsteps she had heard. That was another small mystery solved. She went through to the bathroom and turned on the controls of the shower, then went back to the bedroom to fetch her robe.

On re-entering the bathroom Pippa let her robe fall to the floor and slid aside the cubicle door. Instantly she leapt and screamed — a myriad tiny red-hot needles seemed to be piercing and burning her naked flesh while a vast white cloud of steam enveloped her. Horror and disbelief swept through her. Another step and the skin would have been boiled away from her bones.

Incredulous, she switched off the control and then inspected the heat control knob. Stiff and resisting to her touch, it was clearly set at maximum. With an effort she managed to turn it down to cool.

She was shaken. It could be no accident, she thought as she stood under the cool, refreshing spray. Even the cleaning woman could not have moved the control by chance as she polished. Someone must have changed it purposely, using some effort to set it to high. But why? There was no reason for it — unless someone had wanted Pippa to be severely scalded. Surely not; no one had any reason to want to harm her. And yet — there had been many hints of the hatred for Korvak. Could it be that someone hated him so much they were malicious enough to transfer that hate from father to daughter?

No, she told herself firmly as she prepared for bed. There was some other, simpler reason for the near-accident, and she would doubtless find out in the morning when she told Mrs Purvis about it. She must be careful not to let the strange and subtle air of mystery in the Hall influence her, simply because it was night and she was slightly excited.

She had to be honest with herself and admit that it was Stephen Lorant's proximity which disturbed her. Pleasure filled her at the thought — and it proved she had driven all lingering desire for Clive out of her mind. She fell asleep and dreamt peacefully until suddenly, and for no apparent reason, she awoke. Pippa lay still, wondering, and then an uneasy sensation filled her that she was not alone. She sat up slowly, staring into the darkness.

'Hello? Who's there?'

No answer came. Pippa was aware only of a perfume, a heavy scent that filled the room. It was a strange scent, like none she had smelt before, and the silence in the room was oppressive.

'Hello?' she said again, in a whisper. Her fingers reached for the light switch. Before she could reach it she heard a click. The room filled with light, and there was no one there.

Pippa leapt from the bed and darted to the door. The corridor outside was in total darkness and not a sound disturbed the stillness of the house. For a moment she stood there, and then returned slowly to her room.

Either she had dreamt or imagined it, she told herself. But no, the lingering scent hovered in the room still. It must have been a woman, and so it must have been Mrs Purvis — who, to Pippa's knowledge, never wore perfume. And why on earth should the housekeeper visit Pippa's room in the middle of the night and not speak?

Purposefully Pippa climbed back into bed. Mrs Purvis would have several questions to answer in the morning.

6

Pippa was down in the kitchen early the next morning, anxious to put her questions to the housekeeper, but to her surprise it was Stephen's tall figure that stood by the stove, not the thin, angular figure of Mrs Purvis. He smiled at Pippa.

'Hi, there. Want a cup of coffee, Pippa? I've just taken the liberty of brewing up for myself since Mrs Purvis doesn't seem to be about yet.'

'I'd love some.' Pippa felt disappointed, not at seeing Stephen so early in the day but in having to contain her curiosity a little longer. It was a ridiculous question, but as Stephen handed her a steaming cup of black coffee she looked him straight in the eye. 'Did you by any chance go to my room last night, Stephen? I have a reason for asking.'

He showed no sign of shocked amazement, but only buttered one slice of the toast he had just lifted out of the toaster. 'Not guilty, but why do you ask?'

'Because someone seems to have tampered with my shower in an attempt to scald me, and someone came in while I was sleeping. I'm determined to find out who it was.' Her voice was as level in tone as his, betraying no sign of her eager curiosity. He placed the toast on a plate and put it before her on the table.

'I never moved from my room all evening or in the night,' he assured her. 'But I'm disturbed to hear about it. Perhaps someone does have it in for you after all, though Lord knows why. We'll have to keep a close watch from now on.'

She liked the quiet, possessive way he took her problems on to his own shoulders. It gave her a warm, comfortable feeling of being protected, a sensation she had never felt before. But then suddenly he shattered the reassuring feeling of closeness.

'Well, I'd best be off — a lot to do,' he muttered, and tossing off his cup of coffee he left the kitchen.

Shortly afterwards Pippa heard the front door close, and felt oddly disappointed. She had thought he was going to work on the papers, but he had evidently gone out.

Five minutes later the housekeeper appeared. She looked at the used cups on the table and then at Pippa. 'Is Mr Lorant up?'

'He's gone out,' Pippa replied. 'Mrs Purvis, did you alter the control on my shower?'

'Why on earth should I do that? Now, what will you have for breakfast?'

'I've already eaten. And did you come to my room during the night?'

The housekeeper stopped and looked at her curiously. 'During the night? Of course not. Now what is this, Philippa? Questions about your shower and midnight visitors — are you up to your imaginative games again? If so, I must warn you that I have no time for such nonsense. I'm much too busy with you and Mr Lorant to look after.'

'It's not my imagination, Mrs Purvis,' Pippa said firmly. 'Someone altered my shower to high, so that I was nearly scalded. Could it have been the cleaning woman?'

'She hasn't been in since you arrived. Dear me, at high that shower could have flayed the skin off your back. You must be more careful in future.'

Pippa could have throttled the woman. In her cool, detached way she was implying that Pippa herself had carelessly set the control too high. She had to resist the impulse to snap at her. Instead, she rose from her chair.

'I'm going to have a dip in the pool,' she announced.

Mrs Purvis glanced up. 'Ah, you haven't swum yet today. I thought you might have while I was out.'

Out so early? Pippa mused as she changed in her room. She and Stephen had both thought she was late getting up, and had overslept for once or had forgotten to set her alarm clock. The idle thought faded from her mind as she went out on to the terrace and felt the sun's warmth on her skin. She sat on the lip of the pool and lowered herself into the water, revelling in its cool caress. A water nymph, Stephen had called her, she thought with pleasure as she swam with leisurely grace. It was so warming and comforting to receive compliments from a man like him. It was a pity he was not here now, to share the pleasure of the pool. She must remember to invite him to make free of the Hall's facilities, and to ride the Korvak horses if he had a mind to.

She turned over to float on her back and was so relaxed, with her ears under water, that at first she did not hear the housekeeper calling to her. Mrs Purvis was standing at the open doorway, shielding her eyes with one hand against the sun.

'Philippa! Here a moment! I'd like a word with you!'

Pippa swam smoothly towards the shallow end of the pool. The housekeeper disappeared back inside the Hall. Pippa made for the steps in the corner of the pool and as she came to them, she put a hand on the highest step. Her fingers slid off, unable to grip the smooth surface. She tried again, curious, and again her hand slipped off. The surface of the step was unnaturally smooth and slippery, as though it had been coated with an oily substance.

It was far too unsafe to attempt to walk up the steps, but tentatively Pippa tried. The steps under the water were perfectly easy to climb, but the top three were impossible. Had she not discovered their state by touching them first, she could have come a nasty cropper. Pippa heaved herself up over the lip of the pool and put on her robe, then went in to the kitchen. Mrs Purvis handed her a large towel.

'I thought I would go into Reading for some shopping, Philippa. I shall need Carson to drive me and to carry the groceries, so I just wanted to be sure you'd be all right on your own and had no need of a car this morning.'

'No, I'll be fine,' Pippa assured her. With luck she might manage to have Stephen's company all to herself while they were gone. 'Oh, by the way, would you tell Carson the pool steps are very slippery. They could be dangerous,' Pippa remarked, and at once she saw the light that leapt into the housekeeper's eyes.

'Slippery? You didn't fall, did you?'

'Luckily, no. I found out in time, but they'd better be attended to before someone has an accident.'

The light in the older woman's eyes puzzled Pippa. After the housekeeper had driven off, Pippa went back to the pool. She had made no mistake: the top three steps were treacherous and the substance looked and smelt like engine oil. No one but she used the pool . . . and someone had tampered with the shower yesterday. Was it too ridiculous to believe that someone was trying to cause an accident? To Pippa, who had no enemy and had never hurt anyone in her life? Of course it was ridiculous. She must have been reading too many Agatha Christie novels lately. She ran back into the house and upstairs to dress.

The Hall seemed strangely quiet and empty now that Mrs Purvis, Carson and Stephen were gone. Pippa made up her mind to walk into Marlow and look around.

Going down the lane, she soon found the road that led into the little town. It was a pretty place, full of picturesque charm and items of interest. The grammar school, she noted as she passed its mellowed brick, bore a plaque which dated its origins in the seventeenth century, and next to it was a small row of Georgian houses, one of which carried another plaque bearing testimony to the fact that the poet Shelley once lived there. A little further along she came to a small obelisk marking the town centre, the old market square, and from it a busy high street leading towards the Thames.

Sunlight rippled on the river's surface, furrowed by the pleasure launches and cabin cruisers of the holidaymakers. Shrill cries of children filled the air as she leaned over the parapet of the suspension bridge to watch. It was a lively, bustling scene, far different from the calm, strange quiet of Cambermere. Girls in summer frocks giggled on the towpath below, watching with covert glances the passing youths evidently unaware of their presence. A dog leapt from a launch moored on the quayside and fell with a splash into the water, sending a squad of marauding ducks squawking away over the flashing waters. Pippa was so engrossed watching the ever-changing scene that she did not notice someone approach.

'Hi, there! Beautiful, isn't it?'

Pippa started, and then felt a rush of pleasure. She

responded warmly.

'Indeed it is. Have you seen the weir down there, and the lock? I think I'll walk down that way and take a closer look.'

'I'll come with you. There's a road down behind the church,' Stephen said, turning in step beside her. She did not ask why he was here or what he had been doing. She was content to have his company.

Crossing the green with its war memorial by the slender-spired church, Pippa and Stephen turned down towards the river bank. Stephen was in high good humour.

'It's a fascinating town, with quite a history. Did you know that in the Catholic church they had a relic claimed to be the mummified hand of St James the Apostle? The town was once surrounded by a ring of monasteries and nunneries and the Knights Templar and Knights Hospitaller had houses here — in fact, Spittal Street is a relic of the Hospitallers.'

They walked down a small street to the water's edge.

'This is the wharf,' Stephen went on. 'The old wooden bridge used to cross the river here before the suspension bridge was built.'

Pippa breathed a deep sigh of pleasure. From here she had a superb view of the weir with the water tumbling over it and a magnificent backdrop of woods on the Berkshire side of the river. Stephen was silent now, staring into the distance, the sunlight gleaming on his fair head.

'It's lovely,' Pippa said softly. 'And the pub there looks very old.'

'The Two Brewers? It is, and there's always been an inn there. Can't you imagine the Roundhead or Cavalier soldiers quaffing their ale there after a skirmish on the bridge?' He glanced at his wrist watch. 'Let's go and have a drink there too.'

Pippa was enchanted by the oak panelling and low raftered ceiling which gave atmosphere to the bar, and also by Stephen's words about the Cavaliers. It showed that he too was an imaginative person. Clive would never have thought of the past. But then, Clive was long ago and far away, part of the past now himself.

'There is so much more I could show you,' Stephen said

as he returned from the bar and set two glasses down on the table in the corner. 'I must take you to the two headstones in the graveyard, back to back. It seems a Marlow man who was a showman, some time in the eighteenth century, bought an African child for his show because the boy was piebald — part of his skin white and part black. He grew very attached to the little thing, possibly because he'd been born in a workhouse himself, and when the boy died as a result of the English climate, he had him buried in his own family mausoleum. Master and boy, they lie together back to back now.'

'Curious,' Pippa remarked. 'You know a great deal about Marlow, Stephen.'

He shrugged. 'Read it up in the local library. Journalist's training — learn about the background of your subject. I can't write about Alexis Korvak at Cambermere if I don't know something about the area.'

'You're very thorough,' Pippa said thoughtfully. 'Are you always so meticulous?'

He leaned back in the small wooden chair, his long body appearing far too large for it. 'I guess so. That's just my way.'

Inwardly Pippa approved of all she was learning about Stephen Lorant. Meticulousness showed professional pride and conscientiousness, yet he was not fussy and critical like Clive used to be. She was pleased with herself too. Already she could look back on the past with critical objectivity, and that argued well for the future.

'But tell me about yourself, Pippa. You hardly ever talk about your hopes and fears, your likes and dislikes. You interest me. Tell me about your job.' He was leaning across the table now, his bronzed forearms reflected in the high black gloss of the varnish and his blue eyes eager. Pippa found herself talking easily to him about Paris and the Sorbonne and Professor Garnier, but making no mention of Clive. Stephen's keen gaze never moved from her face as she spoke, and Pippa sensed herself blossom and come alive, feeling an unaccustomed sensation of being an attractive and interesting woman. A sudden breeze flicked her hair as the door opened and a group of strangers entered.

'Gee, that was fascinating,' a vivid blonde woman in her

forties exclaimed to her two men companions. It was evident from her accent and from the exotic shirts the men wore that they were American tourists. 'I'm so glad we decided to moor here overnight or we'd never have seen those fabulous caves.'

'Yes, they must have been quite some group, those Hell Fire men,' her balding companion drawled. 'What are you drinking, Ida — Scotch, or some more of that warm English beer?' He headed towards the bar, and the woman and the other man followed. As they passed under the low lintel into the inner bar, Pippa heard the second man's voice trail back over his shoulder. 'I reckon Korvak must have been forming a new club of his own to compete with Sir Francis, don't you, Ida? Remember all those stories?'

'I sure do, honey. Mine's a Scotch, Ben.'

Pippa looked at Stephen with wide eyes. 'Did you hear that, Stephen? They were talking of my father.'

Stephen leaned back. 'I guess so, but forget it. He was, and still is, always the subject of gossip and speculation.'

Pippa frowned. 'No one seems to have a good word for him, though, and that troubles me. Who is Sir Francis, anyway, and what was this club they mentioned?'

'Ah, now that I have read up, though somewhat hastily, I admit,' Stephen replied, and she could see his momentary stiffness relaxing instantly. 'Sir Francis Dashwood was an eighteenth century nobleman who had estates near here. He was your proverbial rake, wild as they come, and he and his group of rich, pleasure-seeking companions held their secret debaucheries in this area. At first they took over the ruined Medmenham Abbey and held strange rituals there — not black magic, you know, but certainly anti-Christian. They used to row up river to the abbey by barge from London. Then later they transferred their activities to Sir Francis's estate at West Wycombe.'

'West Wycombe?'

'A small village not far from here, just outside High Wycombe. Sir Francis had the grounds of his hall laid out specially, with underground caves where they conducted their rites. The Hell Fire Club's activities were the terror of the neighbourhood.'

'Terror? Why, what did they do?'

Stephen smiled. 'I didn't read all the details, but I gather the local peasant girls who were virgins were in demand for their destructive purposes. Sir Francis was a cruel, relentless man when it came to pleasure. The club's motto was "Fay ce que voudras." '

'Do as you please,' Pippa murmured. 'And was that their aim, then, gratifying their own pleasures?'

'Totally, and the villagers hated and feared them as a result. Peasant folk had no redress against the rich. Whatever the Hell Fire men wanted, they took.'

Pippa mulled over the information for a few moments. From what the American tourists had said, it seemed they were comparing Father to this historic villain, and the thought hurt. Suddenly she could tolerate the close atmosphere of the inn no longer.

'Let's get out of here,' she said abruptly, rising from her chair.

Stephen followed her out without question.

Outside, with the cool breeze fanning her face, Pippa found her tongue. 'Do they really believe my father is as wicked as Sir Francis was?' she asked quietly as they climbed the narrow street back to the church. 'Can they really believe he is such a monster?'

Stephen was silent for a moment, his sun-bronzed forehead furrowed in a frown. 'It seems from what I've heard that some people have reason to believe that, yes. He hasn't treated everyone as generously as he has you.'

'But he wouldn't deliberately hurt anyone either,' Pippa protested. 'He's a sick man, in hospital again now. You can't speak of him like that!'

'He may be failing now, but he was vigorous and active once and he too took what he wanted,' Stephen said quietly, but with a firmness that appalled her. 'I know of several instances of his misdeeds.'

'Like what?' Pippa stopped and turned to face him, her expression at once angry and challenging. Stephen's answering gaze was equally resolute.

'He has lied, cheated and stolen. As a young man he killed another man.'

'In self-defence, surely? There must be an explanation!'

'The evidence indicated otherwise, but in the event he

76

was acquitted. The fight was over a woman.'

'There you are, then,' Pippa said hotly. 'A *crime passionnelle,* and that's always been regarded leniently, in French courts at least.'

'The woman was a whore in a brothel,' Stephen said levelly, as though determined to spare her nothing. 'And women have figured largely in his life.'

'Who would attack an impulsive lover?' Pippa demanded.

Stephen's laugh was dry, ironic. 'Korvak love? He never loved anyone. He used women as pawns − charmed them, used them and abandoned them. Charmed money from the rich ones to further his career. He's an exploiter, Pippa, but I can't expect you to understand that. You don't know the man; you only believe in a fantasy picture you have built up of him.'

'He's my father, and he's always been kind to me!'

'Your family loyalty does you credit, my dear, but he has behaved cruelly to others nonetheless − cheated and deceived them, betrayed their trust and used them diabolically. This I know for a fact, and the more I learn of him the more I know it to be true, and there are many who positively hate him.'

'Like Walters, you mean, and Bainbridge? But why?'

Stephen sighed and took her elbow to lead her into the churchyard. 'He cheated one out of his land and the other of his sister. But that's all in the past now. Let me show you those two back-to-back headstones I told you about.'

Pippa's mind was racing with a confusion of tangled thoughts as they walked along the tree-shaded path of the graveyard. It was impossible to believe her father was as ruthless as Stephen said − a hard bargainer and relentless in business, perhaps, but then any man who reached the height of success he had achieved had to be so. And apart from her angry disbelief, she regretted too the shadow that had fallen on the warm closeness which had been blossoming between Stephen and herself until a few moments ago.

Stephen was pointing at the two headstones, but Pippa could only look on with disinterest. 'What did Father do to Bainbridge?' she persisted quietly. Stephen looked away as he answered.

'Bainbridge wanted Korvak land to extend his farm. Your father would not sell but in the end agreed to gamble a piece of land against an equivalent plot of Bainbridge's — he was like that, enjoying the danger of a gamble rather than a straightforward deal. However, the cards fell in Korvak's favour.'

'So why did Bainbridge object? He agreed to the wager, presumably?' Pippa asked in puzzled tones.

'Yes, but Korvak cheated, he said. He kept an ace up his sleeve. There was no way he could prove it, however, so he lost his piece of land. Years later Korvak let it out while drunk, bragging about his cleverness, so I know it was true.'

'Were you there? Did you hear him admit it?' Pippa challenged.

'No, but my father was.'

There was no retort Pippa could make to that. But Walters — what had father done to him? Something to do with his sister, Stephen had said. In the dappled shadows cast by the trees over the grey slabs in memory of the dead, Pippa looked up at him hopefully.

'And Walters? What of him?'

Stephen smiled ruefully. 'Worse, I'm afraid. Korvak caught sight of Geoff Walters' sister Nina and desired her instantly. He seduced her.'

'Is that so terrible? I imagine she must have wanted him to,' Pippa argued. 'I expect it was when he was still a bachelor, for I know he was devoted to my mother — his mementoes of her at Cambermere show he loves her still.'

Stephen's eyes were solemn as he looked down at her. 'No, Pippa. It was only ten or twelve years ago. Nina Walters gave birth to a child and shortly afterwards killed herself.'

A child! Pippa drew in her breath sharply. 'Robin? Is the boy Nina's child?'

'And your half-brother.'

For a few minutes Pippa could not speak. The revelation had shattered the last illusion about Father. 'Would he not acknowledge her — or the child?' she ventured tremulously at last.

'He cast Nina off. She never told him of the boy.'

'But surely Father knows now?'

'No, Geoff Walters is a proud man, but he will never forgive your father's heartlessness. If it had not been for him, Nina would not have committed suicide.'

Pippa could take no more. 'I've heard enough. I'm going back to the Hall,' she said, and turned sharply towards the gate. Stephen followed.

'My car is here. I'll drive you,' he said.

Pippa slumped in the passenger seat as Stephen negotiated the busy high street towards the obelisk and climbed the hill towards Cambermere. Maybe Father was not the perfect man she had always believed him to be, but time should have mellowed people's attitudes towards him, though it evidently had not. Even his daughter bore the brunt of his misdeeds, it seemed. She thought again about the shower and the oil on the pool steps.

In the front drive of the Hall, Stephen pulled up. 'Look, I'm sorry, Pippa, but you had to know the truth,' he said quietly. 'You could not go on living in a fool's paradise.'

There was compassion in his tone and she responded with a thin smile. 'Stephen, do you honestly think anyone would harm me because of Father?'

'Why do you ask?'

'Because, as I told you, someone tampered with my shower. And then today there was oil on the steps of the swimming pool. Only I use the pool, Stephen, and the oil couldn't have got there by chance, could it?'

His eyes narrowed and the frown reappeared. 'Oil? That's a mean trick. I'll go and see.'

He stepped out of the car, then paused before he closed the door. 'Don't worry, *dragam*, I'll see no harm comes to you.'

Pippa glanced up. 'What was that? That word you said?'

'Oh, *dragam* — it's Hungarian. It means my dear. No offence, Pippa, but endearments come more easily to the tongue for me in Hungarian. I'll just go and have a look at the pool.'

In a few strides he had disappeared around the side of the Hall. Pippa got out and went indoors.

As if by magic, Mrs Purvis materialised as soon as Pippa entered the vestibule. 'Ah, there you are, Philippa. Have you had lunch?'

'No, I'm not hungry,' Pippa said dispiritedly.

'I hope you're not becoming ill, Philippa, going off your food and imagining things as well. I'm not sure that I shouldn't call Dr Ramsay in to have a look at you.' The housekeeper's thin features registered doubt and disapproval and her proprietorial air irritated Pippa.

'I'm not ill and I don't imagine things, Mrs Purvis,' she said crisply.

'Intruders in your room and scalding showers?' Mrs Purvis replied in a tone of patent disbelief.

'Both were real,' Pippa exclaimed, 'and so was the oil on the pool steps. I could have fallen when you called me in this morning.'

'Oil? My dear girl, you don't really expect me to believe that,' the housekeeper said, her tone still cool and level but with an air of vexed impatience. 'You'll be telling me next that someone plans deliberately to hurt you.'

'And how can you be sure they are not? From what I have learnt it would hardly be surprising.'

Pippa and the older woman held each other's gaze for a moment, until the door opened and Stephen entered. He stood looking at the two women and Mrs Purvis turned to him.

'Some coffee, Mr Lorant? I have some bubbling ready in the kitchen.' She walked smoothly to the kitchen door.

Alone with Stephen, Pippa turned to him eagerly. 'Well?' she asked. 'Don't you agree those steps are dangerous?'

Stephen shook his head slowly. 'Pippa, there is not a trace of oil there. I inspected every step carefully.'

'What? But they were thick with oil this morning, I know they were!' She rushed past him to the french windows and out on to the terrace. The waters of the pool rippled with a limpid shimmer. The steps were dry, rough and so easy to gain a footing that even a toddler would have been safe there. Pippa squatted, looking at her dry fingertips disbelievingly, then slowly returned to the Hall. Stephen was sitting in the kitchen. He and Mrs Purvis fell silent as Pippa entered, and she knew she had been the subject of their conversation.

'It was there, I tell you,' she said sullenly. 'I don't know how it's gone, but I know I could have fallen on it this morning.'

'You see?' Mrs Purvis said quietly to Stephen. 'It's always been like this. Imagination working overtime. Philippa certainly is in need of a rest so that her nervous tension is relaxed.'

'I'm not imagining!' Pippa snapped. 'Not the oil nor the shower nor the person who was in my room in the night — someone wearing perfume too, an odd sweet perfume it was. I'd know it if I smelt it again because it was unusual. But I imagined nothing!'

'Imagination,' Mrs Purvis went on smoothly as if Pippa had not spoken. 'In her childhood days it was this imaginary friend of hers, Gwen, who kept getting up to mischief. Are you sure it isn't Gwen who is doing all these tricks now, Philippa?' She spoke to Pippa in an unusually gentle voice, as though humouring a sick child's fantasies. Pippa was angry and frustrated, knowing that the house-keeper presented an image of cool reason in contrast with Pippa's excitedly expressed statements which, in the cold light of day, could only appear paranoid.

'And as to perfume,' Mrs Purvis went on as she poured out the coffee, 'as I told you that was your mother's room. Her things in the drawers probably still retain traces of her scent — she always wore the same one. Come, I'll show you if you like, Philippa.'

She led the way from the kitchen and Pippa followed, angry with herself for appearing the chastened, now-dutiful child in front of Stephen. In the bedroom she watched while the housekeeper opened drawers, revealing layers of fine linen and silk underwear. 'Here,' she said.

Pippa came closer. As she bent to touch the fragile lingerie she caught the scent, and recognised it. 'That's it!' she exclaimed. 'That's the perfume I smelt last night!'

'I thought so,' said Mrs Purvis, closing the drawer again. Her smugly satisfied tone was infuriating. 'That explains away one of your fantasies, Philippa, and I'm sure the others have an equally simple explanation. Now let us get on with lunch, for we're late enough already.'

'What is the perfume?' Pippa asked as they made their way downstairs again.

'Californian Poppy, it's called. Miss Carrie always wore it. In fact, she began the vogue for it in the 'forties, and even years later when every shop-girl in the country was wearing it, she still would not use any other. Ah yes,' she murmured, pausing at the foot of the staircase and looking towards the doors to the east wing, 'just to catch a whiff of it recalls Miss Carrie clearly to me. So beautiful, so kind and gentle, the loveliest creature that ever lived. She didn't deserve to go the way she did.'

For a fleeting second Pippa could swear there was a mist in the black eyes of the normally imperturbable house-keeper, but the glimpse vanished instantly as she turned to the kitchen. Whatever Mrs Purvis's shortcomings towards Pippa, she evidently had one human streak in her love for her dead mistress.

Lunch was a belated and silent affair, neither Stephen nor Mrs Purvis being disposed to talk any more than Pippa. Carson must have been busy elsewhere, for he did not appear. Pippa's thoughts were confused and she ate little. Someone had been in her bedroom last night, despite Mrs Purvis's explanation of the perfume. Someone had altered the shower control – and put oil on the steps – but were they all one and the same person? And why? Was it because of Father, unreasonable as it might seem?

If so, was it Arthur Bainbridge, cheated out of his land? It seemed hardly likely. No more likely than Geoff Walters, whose sister Nina Father had betrayed, if Stephen's words were true – and Pippa had no reason to disbelieve him. After all, Stephen was an outsider; he had no axe to grind over Alexis Korvak, only a commission to fulfil.

Nina Walters. Her son, the young boy Robin, was Pippa's half-brother. It was a shock to discover a sibling she had never heard of until now. And more than that, he was an unacknowledged bastard, poor thing. Father should know of his existence and surely then he would do some-thing for the boy.

She must get in touch with Geoffrey Walters and apologise to him for her behaviour. Had she known the truth she would have been far more considerate and understanding. She made up her mind to telephone him straight after lunch.

Pippa declined the cheese and biscuits Mrs Purvis set on the table, saying she had eaten enough. Stephen was still munching thoughtfully when she excused herself and left. In the vestibule she found the local telephone directory, looked up Walters' number, and dialled it. Walters' voice crackled over the wire.

'Mr Walters? Philippa Korvak here. I just wanted to have a word with you . . . '

'Miss Korvak?' he interrupted in surprise. 'What a coincidence! I was going to ring you this afternoon to apologise. You were quite right. The horses are Korvak horses and you have a perfect right to ride whichever you choose, whenever you choose. I'm sorry I spoke so sharply to you. Very uncivil of me, and I hope you'll forgive me and call again soon.'

'That's very courteous of you, Mr Walters,' Pippa replied, warming to him for his gracious apology. 'As a matter of fact it's for me to apologise to you. I've since learnt that you had good reason to distrust the Korvak name and I'm truly sorry that I spoke so hastily.'

'Not at all, Miss Korvak. You held to your rights and one can only admire a young woman of spirit.'

Complimentary as well as gracious, Pippa thought. Her earlier dislike of the man faded altogether. Her response was equally gracious. 'Mr Walters, if you will forgive my touching upon what must be a painful subject to you, I think it would be fair that my father should know about Robin. I believe he knows nothing.'

'No.' Walters' voice was almost a bark. 'We want nothing from Korvak. It's best he should continue in ignorance, though I can't claim to want to spare him any discomfort or inconvenience. But no, I want him to have no part in Robin's life — he's better off not knowing about a father like that.' There was a pause, and then he added gruffly, 'I do appreciate your concern, Miss Korvak, but I'd rather you left things as they are.'

'But you don't see,' Pippa said as a fresh thought struck her, 'Robin is a Korvak, and is entitled to some share of Father's inheritance one day, just as much . . .'

She never reached the end of the sentence because a hand suddenly appeared in front of her and cracked down on the receiver rest. She turned to see Mrs Purvis's face, set and cold — so cold that her dark eyes glittered like icicles.

'What do you think you are doing, Philippa?' she demanded quietly. 'I did not know you knew about the boy but even if you do, why do you presume to interfere? He is your father's affair, not yours.'

'But Father doesn't know,' Pippa countered. 'I was only suggesting that he should be told so the boy can be treated fairly.'

'And by that you meant to apportion part, at least of the Korvak inheritance to him. How impulsive you are, child! And don't you realise that people could see you as a vulture, waiting to pounce along with the boy the moment your father dies? He is already a sick man, and appearances could be against you if he were to worsen.'

'Oh no, you couldn't think that!' Pippa cried. 'I don't want that at all! I was only trying to see Robin was fairly treated!'

'By giving away to him what is not yours to give,' Mrs Purvis pointed out. 'It is fortunate that I overheard. And you should know that the child is already well provided for, as his uncle's heir. He will want for nothing.'

'Maybe not, but in justice my father ought to know he has a son,' Pippa argued.

Mrs Purvis eyed her closely. 'And possibly disinherit yourself? No, Philippa, he must not be troubled with the news, not when he is already so ill too. Now come along, no more of your rash gestures, if you please. I know you meant well, but in your usual way you have allowed your impetuosity to rush you headlong into foolish actions. Let us talk no more of it, and with luck Mr Walters will forget it also.'

'He would have none of it anyway,' Pippa admitted lamely. 'He is too proud to want Korvak charity, he told me so.'

'There you are, then. That's the end of the matter,' the

housekeeper remarked with obvious satisfaction. 'Now if you'll excuse me I have matters to see to.'

She glided smoothly away. Pippa went gloomily out on to the front terrace. Mrs Purvis was probably right. She had no business to interfere, especially as Walters was so opposed to her suggestions. Gloomily she sat on the stone balustrade and looked out over the lake. Over the scent-laden air, heavy with the perfume of roses, she could hear the whir of a motorised lawn-mower. Carson must be cutting the lawns on the far side of the maze. A dragonfly fluttered up from the water's edge and hovered momentarily before Pippa, its azure wings irridescent in the sun's rays.

At that moment Pippa became aware that someone was standing close behind her and she looked up with a start. It was Stephen. His proximity, so close she could catch the scent of his sun-warmed arms, threw her off balance and she blurted out what was on her mind.

'Oh, Stephen, I feel such a fool! I misjudged Geoff Walters, I misjudged even my own father, and now you and Mrs Purvis both think I am lying about the oil. But I'm not lying, Stephen, and I'm not mistaken — it *was* there this morning! Someone must have cleaned it off, and that would be easy for anyone to do since you and I and Mrs Purvis were all out most of the day.'

He looked down at her gravely, his hazel eyes penetrating hers as though he could read her soul. Pippa looked away quickly. He seated himself beside her on the balustrade. Then, to her surprise, he covered her hand with his.

'I do believe you, *édesem*. I know you speak the truth.' His quiet tones thrilled her.

'You do? Even though the oil is gone?'

He nodded. 'Whoever it was, was able to remove the oil from the steps, but I've seen the detergent in the pool, and the thin film of grease on the surface. They didn't have time to empty and re-fill the pool to remove all traces of the evidence.'

Pippa digested the information. It gave her a degree of pleasure to be proved right and she returned the pressure of Stephen's hand. 'Then perhaps you will believe the rest too

— about the shower, and about someone coming into my room in the night? Oh, Stephen, I'm so glad! You can't know what pleasure it affords me to know I have a friend here at Cambermere, someone who believes in me! Until you came I felt so alone.'

His hands still lay over hers but the smile had faded from his handsome face. Pippa began to feel gauche. She had cried out with the unbridled lack of inhibition of a school-child. Perhaps she had embarrassed him with her clumsiness. Shyly she began to withdraw her hand, but Stephen's closed tightly over it.

'Pippa, let's go for a walk this evening after dinner,' he murmured. 'Away from Cambermere Hall where we can talk more freely.'

She looked at him, surprise in her eyes. 'Of course. I would enjoy that,' she replied.

'By the way, did you get your letter?' Stephen went on. 'I saw it in the vestibule this morning.'

'A letter for me? No,' Pippa said slowly. 'I wonder why Mrs Purvis didn't tell me. But how strange, since no one knows I am here.'

When at last they went indoors Pippa went to the vestibule. No letter lay on the hall table. It was at dinner that she remembered to put the question to Mrs Purvis.

'A letter? No, Philippa, there was no mail for you,' the housekeeper replied coolly. 'How could there be since you have told no one you were coming to Cambermere?'

Pippa would have been satisfied with the answer if she had not glanced up at that moment and seen Stephen looking in disbelief at Mrs Purvis, and the housekeeper's coldly challenging stare. Pippa was aware of the sudden hostility that screamed across the silent air between the older woman and her guest.

86

The sun had spread its last saffron rays along the western horizon and finally sunk from view. The low crescent moon had not yet gathered sufficient strength to illuminate the shadows of the wood where the figure of a tall young man bent attentively towards the slighter figure of the girl beside him.

They strolled in leisurely fashion, deeply engrossed in each other and with a strong bond of intimacy between them despite the twelve or fourteen inches that separated them. Suddenly the young man stopped and ran his fingers through his thick blond hair.

'I can't understand it, Pippa, any more than you can. There was oil there this morning but not this afternoon. Your housekeeper appears to know nothing about it, and yet who else can have cleaned it up? It must have been Carson or Mrs Purvis.'

'Don't forget they were out of the house all morning and so were we,' Pippa said dubiously. 'Anyone could have come up to the Hall while no one was there.'

'But who? Walters? Bainbridge? Or any one of a dozen or more people probably who hate Korvak. But why attack you, Pippa? That's what doesn't make sense to me.' Stephen shook his head, defeated by the bewildering enigma.

'Perhaps it wasn't aimed at me after all,' Pippa remarked, though she did not believe it even as she spoke the words. Neither did Stephen.

'No. Only you swim in that pool. Only you use your shower. They mean to hurt you, Pippa, though heaven alone knows why — unless it's to get back at your father. I'm still curious about Mrs Purvis — why did she lie to you?'

'About the oil, you mean? But it could truly be that she doesn't know . . .'

'No. That letter. There was definitely a letter for you. I saw it. It had a foreign stamp on it. It was lying in the vestibule this morning, and yet tonight she told you there was no letter. Now why should she say that, Pippa? Do you know? Have you ever offended her in some way that makes her want to get even with you?'

'Of course not!' Pippa protested hotly. 'We hardly ever meet and when we do she treats me civilly. And what's more, she makes it plain how much she loved and still misses my mother. If only for that she would bear no grudge against me, certainly not to the extent of wanting to harm me!'.

'No, perhaps not as strong a dislike as that, but there's something that makes her less than honest with you if she denies the existence of that letter.'

'Are you sure about it, Stephen? That it was for me? Perhaps it was for her. After all, no one knew I was here.'

Stephen shook his head decisively. 'I saw the name Korvak clearly, and the foreign stamp – French, I think, though I'm not sure. Perhaps a friend in Paris was writing to you.'

A friend? Pippa started. The only people in Paris who would write to her would be Professor Garnier and Clive. The Professor was unlikely to contact her when the vacation had barely begun, and she could not believe it was Clive, after what had happened. She looked up at Stephen's darkly thoughtful face.

'I shall find that letter,' he said quietly, 'if only to prove what I say.'

Pippa smiled, touched by his concern. 'Don't worry about it, Stephen. It can't have been important. Let's not talk about it any more, but talk about you instead. I know so little about you and yet I feel you know all there is to know about me.'

He grinned broadly. 'This is likely to take some time. Shall we find ourselves a comfortable spot?'

The night hung in the sky like a magnificent deep blue tapestry scattered with glittering points of starlight. Stephen selected a grassy knoll in a clearing where the moonlight threw latticed shadows, and sprawled nonchalantly on the grass. Pippa sat beside him, drawing up her knees to her chin and clasping her arms around them to listen attentively.

Stephen's expression grew serious. 'I was joking, Pippa. There isn't really a lot to tell. My father died when I was still young and my mother worked hard to keep the two of us.

She was a wonderful woman, always optimistic and never complaining, determined to do the best she could for her only child. She used to talk to me, I remember, about how clever I would be when I was grown up, how famous and admired, and that would be all the reward she wanted. But she too died young.' There was a catch in Stephen's voice but he went on quickly. 'It was an orphanage then for me, and after that working on a farm out west. I loved the country life — the animals, riding in rodeos — but always there was this thing, this feeling deep inside me. I knew that somehow I had to get to college.'

Pippa nodded but did not speak. She could understand. He had a deep need to fulfill his dead mother's dream for him, and that was commendable.

Stephen sat up. 'Well, to cut a long story short, I got to university in the end, working nights in a drugstore and early mornings in an automobile showroom cleaning the cars, and finally I made it. I graduated from college with a degree in English studies and managed to get a job as a journalist on a local newspaper. From there I moved on to one of the big papers and finally I broke away to freelance. And here I am. Story complete, Pippa, up to today, that is.'

Pippa noticed that he made no mention of a wife or girlfriend. Presumably he had pursued his career so single-mindedly that there had been no room for that. She shied away from the thought.

'And today you are working on my father's story,' she said quietly. 'Where do you go from there?'

'After the Korvak story? I haven't really planned that far ahead. You see this one is going to be big — the most complete, exhaustive story of Alexis Korvak from the cradle — ' He stopped suddenly, as though aware of his maladroit choice of words. 'The definitive work on Korvak, Pippa. It'll sell to the syndicated newspapers and in book form to the publishers both here and back home in the States. It'll make me a fortune. After that, I can choose what I do, if I want to work at all.'

Pippa's feeling of easy closeness with him faded instantly. He no longer sounded like the warm, sympathetic Stephen she knew but a cold, calculating stranger. She glanced up at him.

'You sound as though you mean to exploit my father's story to your gain and profit,' she challenged.

Stephen nodded. 'It's no more exploitive than what he did to others,' he replied coolly. 'Notorious people are fair game.'

It was true. Famous people were open to fair comment, but would a journalist's account be fair, she wondered? Stephen had played the tape which proved that Father knew and approved of this venture, but Pippa felt uneasy, nonetheless. Nothing that Stephen said about Alexis Korvak gave any hint of sympathetic treatment of his subject. To her surprise, Stephen stretched out a hand and laid it gently on hers.

'It's something that's got to be done, Pippa, and after that the future is our own.' His voice was low, his tone sombre, but it was his words that puzzled Pippa. The touch of his hand on hers, however, awoke such a vibration in her that she could not think clearly what it was that puzzled her.

And then a cold tingle shivered in her spine. Pippa darted a quick, backward glance over her shoulder, certain that someone stood watching. But amongst the shadows under the trees nothing was to be seen, nothing moved except, perhaps, a badger or a mole on its nocturnal prowl. Stephen felt her shudder.

'What is it, Pippa? What's the matter?'

She conjured up a smile to reassure him. 'Nothing. I just had a feeling that we were being watched, that's all. You know that feeling that someone's eyes are boring into your back. It's just the darkness and the moonlight stirring my imagination. Mrs Purvis says I'm full of that.'

Without a word Stephen got up and looked about, then strode to the edge of the clearing and paced slowly round it. Pippa watched him, then got up.

'It's time we went back anyway, Stephen. It's growing chilly now.'

Stephen took her arm to guide her down the grassy slope beyond the wood, and Pippa welcomed his warm, comforting touch.

Nearing the Hall Stephen began to talk again of Mrs Purvis. 'Odd how she keeps slipping off. I wonder what she does? She's a very private, even secretive person.'

Pippa remembered the eggs, the way the housekeeper said she had to go out for more eggs when there was already a stack in the larder. 'Yes,' she agreed cautiously. 'Once I tried to follow her, but she vanished in the lane. But honestly, Stephen, what's so odd about that? You're getting as bad as me, looking desperately for a culprit, but I'm certain she's not the one. After all her years of loyalty to the family, why, it's laughable to think so!'

'I guess you're right. Okay, then, let's leave the subject for the moment.' He paused to look across the fields to the stream alongside the woods. 'I see the Dormobile has been moved — it's over there now. Bainbridge must have made them shift. Is it Korvak land they're on now?'

Pippa shrugged. 'I don't know, and if they are I don't think it matters. There's no litter or fire burning. So long as they cause no harm I don't see why they shouldn't be left in peace to enjoy the place.'

Stephen smiled down at her and she felt the pressure of his hand on her elbow. 'You can't tell how glad I am to hear you say that, Pippa. It proves you are not possessive like your father. You're a very gentle soul without a trace of malice in you.'

Pippa was about to retort in defence of her father, and then held her tongue. In the light of all she had learnt recently it began to seem that she really did not know him at all. This tall, handsome man at her side knew him perhaps better than she did. At the top of the long lawn, where the beech trees shaded a gravel walk down towards the Hall, Stephen suddenly stopped and let go of her arm. Pippa stopped too, looking up at him questioningly. Without a word he drew her to him and kissed her lightly. Pippa did not resist, nor did she respond, but when he bent his head to kiss her again, longer this time and with fire, she felt herself react with warmth, sliding her arms about his neck. Over his shoulder she could see the moonlight flickering through the branches of the trees and she began to feel dizzy, intoxicated with the fever he stirred in her.

Suddenly he broke away. 'I'm sorry, Pippa,' he muttered. 'I had no right to do that. Stupid of me. It must have been the moonlight, the magic of the woods, and your warm personality. Forgive me. I won't do it again.'

He was walking on and she had to hurry to catch up and fall in step with him. She felt ashamed and embarrassed. How could she tell him there was nothing to forgive, that she was enjoying it until he stopped so unexpectedly? He did not speak again, striding along with a set, almost savage expression on his face until they reached the terrace.

'I'm sorry,' he muttered again. 'Forgive me.'

'There's nothing to forgive,' Pippa murmured.

'But there is. I promised myself long ago that I would not become − well, involved with anyone − until I had done what I set out to do. There's no excuse, only that I found you too great a temptation for a moment. Goodnight.'

He vanished inside the Hall while she was still standing there bewildered. Forlornly she let herself in, locked the door, and went up to her room. Well, at least he had found her tempting, she consoled herself as she undressed for bed. She had stirred the man in him, however involuntarily, and far from being angered by his uninvited kiss, she was flattered. The first gentle kiss had blossomed into fire, no less ardent on his side than on hers, and for that she was grateful and glad. She could not help nursing a secret hope that perhaps, in spite of his protestations, he might be tempted again . . .

The next morning Pippa was greeted in the hallway when she came downstairs by an eager-eyed Stephen. He brandished a key before her.

'Guess what, *babam*,' he said with an air of triumph. 'Mrs Purvis was ready to go out when I came down. She said she had to go up to London to see to something to do with the redecoration of the flat and before she left she gave me the key to the east wing again.'

Pippa was surprised. Now she would be free to explore in peace. 'Odd she never mentioned she was going away,' she remarked to Stephen. 'Did she say for how long?'

'Only overnight. She'll be back tomorrow.'

Stephen declined to come into the kitchen and drink coffee while Pippa breakfasted, so she ate alone, savouring both the bacon and the prospect of freedom and the next twenty-four hours alone with Stephen. When she went to join him she found him in the first room in the east wing, sitting cross-legged on the floor amongst the packing cases. As she entered he looked up and smiled.

'By the way, Pippa, I forgot to tell you that I found your letter this morning, in the cutlery drawer in the kitchen. I was right; Mrs Purvis must have forgotten she left it there.'

From his pocket he produced an envelope, a crisp, thin airmail letter, and handed it to her. He had been right. It bore a French stamp and Clive's neat handwriting. The address of the London flat had been crossed out and the Cambermere address added in untidy thick felt-tip handwriting — the janitor's, no doubt. Pippa thrust it in her pocket.

Stephen, apparently immersed in a yellowing magazine, glanced up. 'Not going to read it now?'

'No, later.'

He gave a wry smile. 'From which I deduce it is either from a boring correspondent or a matter too personal to be opened in public.' Pippa darted him a sharp look, which he acknowledged with a shrug. 'I'm sorry, I shouldn't have said that,' he apologised.

Pippa allowed her expression to relax into a smile. 'You're quite a student of human nature, Stephen. But I shan't satisfy your curiosity as to whether you were right on either count. Tell me instead what you have found.'

She settled herself on the floor beside him, both enveloped in the pool of golden sunlight that fell across the carpeted floor from the high window. This was going to be a wonderful day, Pippa thought contentedly, and no intrusive letter from Clive was going to spoil it. Excuses, explanations, an apology even — that was all the letter would contain and she was in no hurry to reawaken the hurt.

Stephen laid aside the magazine and picked up a sheaf of photographs. Leaning close to Pippa, so close that his shoulder touched hers, he looked at the first one. It was a studio still of Carrie Hope, wide green eyes and half-open mouth betraying a childlike innocence despite the clinging black gown, so filmy it revealed the flesh beneath. The Titian hair cascaded in lustrous curls on her bare shoulders and long jet earrings were suspended from her ears.

Stephen looked curiously from the photograph to Pippa.

93

'You have your mother's eyes,' he remarked.

Pippa laughed. 'And there the resemblance ends, I'm afraid. She was beautiful.'

He was still staring at her closely. 'You have the same gentle air of innocence, and that is where the beauty lies, *szerelmem*.'

Pippa felt her heart flutter at his praise, but she did not know how to answer. Instead she looked over his shoulder at the next photograph. It was Father with a child on his knee in a sunlit garden. The dark child, not herself.

'Is this your sister?' Stephen asked.

'My half-sister, Irma.'

'Ah yes, I remember. Your mother had been married before, to a businessman, hadn't she? And he was eager to get her into films so he introduced her to Korvak.'

'She was a very talented dancer,' Pippa said hotly. 'Her talent and beauty were what got her into films.'

'Added to her husband's ambition. But that was his mistake,' Stephen said quietly. 'He did not allow for Korvak's weakness for beautiful women.'

'What are you saying?' Pippa demanded.

'Only what any gossip column of the time would tell you. Your father wanted her, and Jacobs, her husband, agreed to a quiet divorce in return for a consideration. Don't look so angry, Pippa. It's no reflection on you if your mother's first husband was an opportunist.'

Pippa sat silent. She had known of Mother's first marriage and of the child Irma, but she had never heard before how the first marriage ended.

Stephen was peering at the picture. 'Your half-sister looks decidedly like your mother here,' he commented. 'Did she still resemble her when she grew up?'

'I don't know,' Pippa answered briefly. 'I don't remember. She left home when I was still very young; I haven't seen her since.'

He looked at her in surprise. 'Not seen her since? In how long?'

'Oh, about twenty years. I think she ran away to marry someone Father didn't approve of and no one spoke her name after that. In fact, I rather think she must be dead.'

Pippa rose and walked to the window, vaguely irritated

by his questions. It was unkind to subject her to a form of interrogation about things which the family never discussed. Even now she could recall the way Mrs Purvis's always-reserved expression became decidedly withdrawn, almost melancholy, whenever Mother or Irma were mentioned. And once, when Pippa had chanced to mention Irma's name to Father, his gaiety had momentarily fled, to be replaced a second later with animated conversation about another matter altogether. She had been astute enough to recognise that this subject was one he preferred to ignore.

'Hey, I guess this must be yours.' Stephen's tone was surprised and pleased. Pippa went across to him. In his hand he held the dog-eared scrapbook she had cherished through all her schooldays. Even now she could remember lying face-down on the dormitory floor while the other girls were out on the games-field, lovingly pasting the latest magazine picture of Mother into place. To see it in Stephen's hand seemed an invasion of her youthful privacy. She snatched it from him impulsively. Unperturbed, he reached into the packing case for more papers.

Turning away from him Pippa stood by the window, leafing through the now rather dilapidated pages. The lovely, gentle face of Carrie Hope appeared again and again, once in the arms of a smiling Tyrone Power at a film ball, once at a banqueting table seated between Father and Edmund Purdom. In another David Niven smiled down at her while Ronald Reagan looked on benignly. The illustrious stars of her day were always admiring companions and often Father too looking proud and magnanimous.

'I can see the resemblance between you and your mother here,' Stephen remarked, holding out a glossy film-still he had taken from the case. 'The same long, slender legs.'

Pippa took the photograph from him. It was Mother in fishnet tights and a leotard with a feather boa about her neck, and alongside her the blonde, voluptuous Betty Grable.

'She was a superb dancer, you know, Stephen. She danced with Gene Kelly in one film.'

'Do you inherit her talent? Do you dance?'

Pippa laughed, the first time she could remember laughing in weeks. 'No, not really. I learnt ballet as a child, but I had no aptitude for it. A little ballroom dancing now and again, that's all.'

She stopped abruptly. Formal dances and balls at the Sorbonne were a thing of the past now, a part of a life so far removed from Cambermere that it already seemed like another planet in another time-scale. Stephen did not appear to notice her sudden change of mood. He was engrossed in reading a small notebook. Then he suddenly stuffed it in his pocket and got to his feet.

'Pippa, I've got to go out for a while. Will you be all right by yourself? I should be back by lunchtime. Tell you what, we could take a picnic lunch out into the countryside if you like.'

'Good idea,' Pippa said. 'I'll get it ready while you're out.'

He left her, without saying a word about the key or locking up the east wing. Now she could explore further.

The corridor and indeed the whole house seemed to ring very hollow once Stephen had gone. Pippa would have welcomed his company longer, but he had work to do and in any event there was the picnic to look forward to.

Putting down the scrapbook, Pippa went out into the corridor and walked along it. The first room, the Victorian parlour, looked even more desolate than before with its deepening layer of dust. She closed the door and went on. The Mississippi gambling saloon looked sombre despite its crimson plush, the sunlight outside Cambermere Hall hardly penetrating the small circular portholes. Pippa closed the door.

The third room took her breath away. It was oriental in style, with marble floor and pillars and rich drapes of tapestry and satins. Scattered cushions of rainbow colours trailed up a flight of marble steps to a dais, where a gilded throne bedecked with peacock feathers overlooked the pool in the centre of the marble floor. The water lay placid now, but Pippa could see that the miniature figure of a nymph in the centre was probably a fountain.

The court of an Indian prince or the suite of a sultan,

Pippa concluded. She could not recall any such film in which Mother had appeared but then, as Mrs Purvis had told her, these were sets from Father's films. Perhaps it was from *The Slave Girl and the Sultan,* an exotic picture made in his early years in Hollywood.

The fourth door revealed the set of yet another of his exotic eastern triumphs. It was a jungle setting, with synthetic liana vines hung from ceiling to floor and dense plastic undergrowth. A rubber python lay draped around the foot of a thick tree trunk. If Pippa remembered aright, it was Dorothy Lamour who had slunk sultrily among the scarlet hibiscus in her sarong to Father's directions.

She moved on, curious to discover what the next room would disclose. As the door swung open she saw a scene as sombre and gloomy as the others had been colourful, so dark that she had to switch on the lights. Stone walls and a heavy nail-studded door with an iron grille revealed that it was a prison, and the iron sconces set in the walls bearing unlit torches told her it was a period set. The dungeon of an old castle, no doubt. On a thick oak table lay a metal ring hung with heavy keys. Around the wall stood a variety of metal contrivances, which she gradually realised were instruments of torture — thumbscrews, a bed of nails, a rack, an iron maiden. A torture chamber. Pippa shivered. She could not remember this film, but even on a summer day the air felt cold and clammy in here. She closed the door quickly and retraced her steps to the vestibule.

Back in the main block of the hall Pippa began to feel at ease. Sunlight streamed in between the marble pillars of the hallway and flooded the shining kitchen, filling the house with cheerfulness. The shiver induced by the cardboard stone walls of the dungeon was gone, or was it simply Mrs Purvis's absence that gave her this welcome feeling of freedom? Whatever it was Pippa sliced tomatoes and cheese and cucumber to prepare a picnic lunch as she had promised, humming to herself as she worked. It was only as she wiped her hands clean on a towel that she remembered the letter still unread in her pocket.

'*Dear Philippa,*' the neat, clear handwriting read. '*I do so hope your journey home was pleasant.*' Pippa snorted. What a lame wish after giving her an abrupt brush-off!

She read on.

Clive made a few more statements about his doings since she had left, and then added, as if as an afterthought, that Joyce had decided after all not to disturb the even tenor of her life by uprooting herself and going to live in Paris.

'*So on your return, presumably when the Sorbonne re-opens, perhaps we could arrange to meet,*' he had added coolly. At once Pippa felt angered by his presumption. Now that Joyce was not going to clutter up his life after all, he evidently saw no reason why he and Pippa should not carry on where they left off. What impertinence! After all the pain he had caused her! Pippa crumpled the letter and thrust it back into her pocket. It had been an effort to shut this man out of her mind, and she was not going to let him reassert his domination over her. Clive was finished, and that was that.

It was with a positive leap of pleasure that she heard a car-horn tooting outside and knew that Stephen was back. She hurried out and climbed into the passenger seat of the dusty little Fiat beside him, her face aglow in a smile. Stephen looked thoughtful as he put the car into gear and drove off.

'Here we are,' he said at last, turning off the road down a narrow track. 'Temple Lock. It's a pretty spot for a picnic.'

Indeed it was: a serene stretch of the river where willow trees bent languidly over the water and a group of ducks paddled at a discreet distance from a majestic white swan. Stephen opened a blanket under the shade of a willow and Pippa laid out the food. Stephen returned to the car to fetch a bottle of wine and two glasses. After the meal Pippa lay back on the grass feeling utterly relaxed and content.

Stephen rolled over to look at her. 'More wine, Pippa?'

'Just a little. I'm feeling sleepy as it is. How's the work going, Stephen?'

He refilled her glass and regarded her soberly. 'From my point of view it goes well, thanks.'

She squinted up at him. 'You say that oddly. What do you mean?'

'I mean I've been reading a diary your mother wrote in the year before she died. It proves to me once again what a bastard your father is, so for me it's good but I don't expect you to feel so happy about it.'

Pippa thought for a moment. He was right, of course, but at the same time her curiosity tingled, and within seconds it got the better of her. 'So that's the little book I saw you put in your pocket. What did Mother say in it?'

Stephen looked at her closely. 'Are you sure you want to hear? Wouldn't you rather treasure your illusions, Pippa?'

She sat up sharply. 'You're going to shatter them all when you finally publish your findings, so why be reticent now? Do you have the diary here? I'd like to hear how my mother felt about Father.'

Stephen took a deep breath. 'Well, at the time she was writing this diary she didn't think too highly of him. It seems she could not keep the peace between Alexis and your half-sister, Irma. Irma was sixteen and something of a handful, by your mother's account, and your father had no patience with her.'

'She was fiery, I remember,' Pippa remarked. 'There was always tension and anger. That frightened me.'

Stephen nodded. 'Your mother wrote that she was afraid that her little one would be upset by the frequent rows. She obviously loved you deeply, Pippa.'

'I never doubted it.'

'And Irma too. She tells how beautiful but how tempestuous the girl was, and says she thinks perhaps Alexis had no time for her because she was not his child. There's a part where Carrie comments how much he spoilt you yet was hard with Irma, in an effort to tame her. It's clear Carrie began to hate him for that, and as the diary goes on that hate deepened, especially when she discovered Alexis was carrying on with other women.'

'She must have had a hard time,' Pippa said sadly.

'Harder than you know. The terrible tension came to a head when Alexis not only said he was willing to let Irma go off with the young man she fancied, but insisted she left. He wasn't prepared to shelter her in his home any longer; he told Carrie she must part with Irma or with him.'

Pippa buried her face in her hands, unwilling to believe it. 'Lord, I did not think he could be so cruel,' she murmured between her fingers. 'Poor Mother.'

'Yes, poor Carrie. It seems she had never been well since your birth; not really ill, but on the other hand not in robust health. There are frequent references in the diary to the doctor visiting her. It's obvious that the whole business of Irma made her go into the decline which killed her.'

Pippa could not speak for the lump in her throat. Stephen took the diary from his pocket. 'Would you like to read it, Pippa? She speaks very touchingly and lovingly about you.'

Pippa pushed his hand away. 'No. Tell me no more, Stephen. Whatever else you unearth, please don't tell me about it.'

He put the little book away in silence and then began gathering together the remains of their meal. Pippa sat numb, not offering to help until everything had been packed and put back in the car. Then she got to her feet.

'Let's go home. I feel cold.'

The sun still beat its fierce rays on the roof of the car as they sped homeward. In the driveway Stephen pulled up.

'Look, I'm sorry, Pippa, but I've got my work to do and I can't let sentiment get in the way. I won't talk about it if you prefer.'

'Thank you, I'm glad you won't say any more.' She got out stiffly and mounted the steps to the front door. 'Have you got the key?'

He came up beside her. 'Pippa, I'll take you out to dinner tonight. Dino's in the High Street is a very good Italian restaurant, they tell me. We'll eat and drink and talk about everything except Alexis. Okay?'

'No,' said Pippa sharply. 'I don't want to see you any more today. I want to be on my own.'

Stephen opened the door and stood back. As Pippa passed him he put something into her hand. 'Here, in case you change your mind,' he said quietly. 'I'll stay out for the rest of the day.'

He turned and left. Pippa looked down at the little brown notebook in her hand, then slammed the door and ran upstairs to her room. Through the window she could hear the sound of the car receding down the drive. In a turmoil of rage and frustration she flung herself on the bed and wept.

Life was going crazy again, getting all out of hand and unruly just as it had been beginning to sort itself out in the most pleasant way. A warm and significant relationship seemed to be blossoming between her and Stephen — why did he have to destroy it all with his unwanted revelations. It was bitterly cruel. If she let him go on telling her more and more unpleasant facts about Alexis Korvak, she would have no one left. How could he, knowing she had lost her mother, try to rob her of her father too?

Pippa sobbed unrestrainedly. More than anything she needed someone to love and trust, and she was not going to let a young man, however personable, destroy her faith in her father.

She reached for a tissue on the bedside cupboard and caught sight of the diary. She picked it up and flicked over the pages. The spidery handwriting blurred before her misty eyes, but gradually she began to focus.

'*My poor baby Pippa, I fear she is more disturbed than anyone realises by all that is going on, poor lamb. She hides away in the nursery for hours at a time and I sometimes find her holding conversations with a creature who is not there — Gwen she calls her.*

'*And the nightmares too. Alexis does not understand that he himself causes them, the way he thunders up the stairs to remonstrate with Irma. The baby has been long asleep, but soon I hear her scream in terror. I ran to her again last night, and she told me of the bogey man chasing her in a cellar. Poor darling. I'm sure it's Alexis' footsteps she hears in her sleep. She is terrified of the dark and I put a night light by her bed, though Mrs Purvis often removes it because she fears a naked candle is dangerous in a child's room. She too does not understand the baby. Despite her very evident affection for me and Irma, her patience and conscientiousness in her care of Pippa, she really does not seem to understand or to have time for her childish fears.*

'*It is strange that a woman can bear two daughters so unalike — one wild and beautiful, the other timid and withdrawn. It must be having different fathers, though one would have expected Alexis' child to be the fiery one and not my gentle Pippa.'*

Tears filled Pippa's eyes again as she read her dead mother's words, and she cast the diary aside and lay down on the bed. In spite of a jumble of confused thoughts about the insensitive, selfish father and the loving, helpless mother, she finally drifted off into uneasy sleep.

Dreams filtered in and out of her sleep, disturbing her mind so that she found no repose. The final dream was claustrophobic. No clear figures emerged in it, only a terrifying sense that something was trying to choke her, to rob her lungs of air. Some thick, nauseous fog seemed to be clawing its way into her nostrils so that she could not breathe.

Gasping, terrified, Pippa awoke with a start. The room was filled with a heavy, cloying scent, a perfume so powerful that it was sickening. That was what had caused her dream and made her waken. Pippa sat up, sniffing.

The square of the window framed a patch of darkness now, not sunshine. Her watch showed it was after eleven — she had slept the whole evening away. But it was the perfume that puzzled her.

She recognised it as the scent on Carrie Hope's underwear, but far more lavishly spread than the subtle scent in the drawer, as if someone had just sprayed it there. Californian Poppy, that was it.

Pippa shivered. It was as though her strong emotions about her mother had conjured her spirit to return, shrouded in her favourite perfume. She got up off the bed. That was silly thinking. There must be some more rational reason for the scent.

In an effort to dispel the clammy, pungent atmosphere which made her feel so uneasy, Pippa went across to the window and opened it. A low, lambent moon hung over the trees, bathing the grey stone of the Hall in a sombre light. Pippa looked down into the shadows, and suddenly caught her breath.

A pale wisp of light drifted across the terrace, miasmic and tenuous, and slowly came to a halt beneath the window. Not a sound stirred the stillness of the night, and as Pippa's eyes became accustomed to the dark she began to make out the shape of a human figure, clad in a pale, diaphanous robe. The figure began to move again, slowly and deliberately, like a slowed-down film-clip, and the light of the moon grew stronger. It was a girl, her pale face turned upwards and her arms held aloft as she moved in a slow, graceful dance. Her hair, dark in the pearly light, streamed about her shoulders. There was no mistaking that beautiful face, and she knew that the hair was only dark because of the feeble light. In the sun it would have shone fiery and red, for the face with its wide eyes and parted lips was unmistakably that of Carrie Hope.

Mother! Pippa gasped, her fingers gripping the window sill and the scent of Californian Poppy choking in her nostrils. Disbelief and horror froze in her veins. The figure below pirouetted in a gauzy swirl, a grey vision that blurred at the edges into the darkness, and drifted as if suspended toward the bushes. In another second it had vanished from sight.

Pippa turned away from the window, the thick miasma of perfume still choking in her throat. Alone in this great Hall, with no one near but the vision outside in the darkness, she felt a chill of dread seeping into her bones.

Was she ill, or had the ghost of Carrie Hope really returned to Cambermere? And if so, why had she come? To protect her child? Or to warn her? Fearfully Pippa slid under the bedcovers, and wished desperately that morning would come.

8

Pippa, shaken and disturbed by her inexplicable experience barely slept for the rest of the night. Stephen did not return and it was strangely frightening to be alone in the Hall, its air of mystery now charged with menace and the fragrance that lay heavy on the air.

She wondered if indeed she had really seen the figure on the terrace and not just imagined it. She had been disturbed at the time by the dark and the loneliness and Stephen's words, and above all by that heady perfume. But not disturbed enough to hallucinate, surely.

So if the vision was real, what did it mean? Was it truly Mother, drawn back to the scene of her death because her beloved child was in need of her? Or was it some omen, a portent of evil? Pippa shuddered. She had a strange sense of foreboding, and she wished with all her heart that she were not alone in Cambermere Hall. If only Stephen were here, or even Mrs Purvis. If only the welcome sight of dawn would streak the eastern horizon.

When at last daybreak began to spread pale fingertips of light over the trees Pippa rose. Still there had been no sound of the car returning. Stephen had evidently stayed out all night, presumably at the inn he had used before. She dressed shakily and went downstairs to make coffee. As the full light of day began to flood the bright kitchen her fears of the night began to fade. Strange how darkness could breed fear and exaggerate tremors into terrors, and then the sun could banish them all in an instant.

By mid-morning Stephen had still not appeared. Pippa made up her mind to go out, far from the Hall and its claustrophobic atmosphere. But where? Not to the stables, she decided. Walters hated her father, and for that reason alone she would not go near the stables. She needed to get away from anyone and everything which had any connection with the Hall and its occupants.

West Wycombe. Those historic caves the American woman in the pub had mentioned — that's where she would go. A visit to the haunt of those eighteenth-century rakes was just the thing to divert her mind from Cambermere for a few hours. It could not be far from here, and Mrs Purvis would only have taken one car from the garage.

The keys. A quick hunt through the kitchen drawers unearthed two sets of car keys, and in the garage the little Fiat stood waiting. Mrs Purvis had evidently taken the saloon to London. Pippa climbed in, and the engine sprang to life instantly at the turn of the key.

Pippa pulled up in the high street to ask a woman traffic-warden the way. Her instructions were clear and precise, and fifteen minutes later Pippa found herself in a charming old-world village, a cluster of thatched cottages nestling beneath a village church and a rippling stream. She breathed a sigh of pleasure. On such a summer day, warm and balmy although for once the sun was not actually shining, the peace and tranquillity of the hamlet was just what Pippa sought.

Leaving the Fiat in the car-park, she climbed the steps to where the signpost indicated the caves. The way was steep, and at the top she could see a wall of rock facing her and a terrace with scattered tables and chairs, a long low shed which housed a souvenir shop, and a turnstile at the opening into the face of the rock. Intent on savouring the leisure of the day, Pippa went first into the shop and bought a guide book, then sat on the terrace to acquaint herself further with the affairs of the Hell Fire Club before going into the caves. Here, in the peace of the village, she could afford to smile at the account of the ridiculous, often obscene, antics of a crowd of rich eighteenth-century rakes who had little better to occupy their idle minds. Dressing up in monks' habits and coming here with great ceremony to the accompaniment of organ music just to feast and revel and indulge in orgies with maids both willing and unwilling — it seemed so ludicrous and unreal that the whole idea reminded her of a fantasy film-script. Alexis Korvak would have done justice to the theme. Hastily she put her father out of her mind. Nothing to do with Cambermere was to spoil today.

People passed by her table, some British and some European, for she caught snatches of French and German behind her as she flicked the pages of the guide book. The caves were evidently popular with tourists. As she looked up, she glimpsed a dark head in the crowd and caught her breath.

Geoffrey Walters — and he had Robin with him. Swiftly Pippa rose from the table and made for the pay-kiosk. If she stayed at the table he would be bound to see her, but with luck she could get away into the caves unnoticed.

Beyond the turnstile a vaulted passage in the rock curved gently downwards. The instant she set foot in it she felt cold air encircle her, and the further she hurried along the colder and damper the air became. After a moment her eyes became accustomed to the gloom, for the passage was only dimly lit at intervals. Behind her she could hear voices chattering in Spanish, and breathed a sigh of relief.

The passage broadened out suddenly into a chamber. To Pippa's surprise a voice announced, mechanical and tinny, that this was the robing room where the Hell Fire monks used to don their scarlet habits before proceeding. She hastened on to where the passage narrowed, leaving the voice to continue its tale to an empty chamber until the Spaniards arrived.

Even the walls were damp, she realised, as she put out a hand to steady her steps on the uneven ground which still sloped downwards. And there were carvings in the rock walls too. She peered closely. A demon's face leered back at her from the chalk rock. Pippa went on, catching up with a group in the next chamber who were pointing through a steel grille and talking in broad, north-country accents. Beyond the grille Pippa could see wax figures in eighteenth-century costume: two gentlemen standing by a table.

A small boy tugged his mother's hand. 'Come on, Mam. There's a skeleton somewhere I know because Jimmy told me. Come on, let's find the skeleton, Mam.'

Pippa left them behind. A little further on, the passage-way spread itself out into a series of tunnels. She followed one which twisted and looped, intersecting with other passages. She went on, as far as she could from the entrance and Geoff Walters. Another mechanical voice described the labyrinth as 'the catacombs', and shortly after that the passages joined into one again. Presently it opened out into a huge chamber, where twenty or so tourists stood looking about them at the waxwork effigies contained in many small cells which ran around the walls of the huge cavern. From yet another taped voice Pippa learnt that this was the banqueting room, and the cells used to be screened by curtains when the 'monks', sated with gargantuan meals and copious wine, indulged in their lascivious orgies. With

106

a squeal of delight the little north-country boy found his waxwork skeleton beyond the grille in a cell.

Pippa shivered. It was extremely cold and damp down here in the bowels of the earth. She must have walked a quarter of a mile underground, downhill all the way. She tried to visualise silent figures in blood-red robes filing down here in candlelight procession, organ music reverberating through the great subterranean hollow, but it was not easy with so many chattering folk in modern dresses and sandals and shirtsleeves. It must have been eerie once, terrifying even, for those unwilling maidens brought here to be ravished. But she could sense no chill of fear here now, only the cold darkness. Nevertheless she gave a start of alarm when a voice suddenly spoke her name.

'Hello, Philippa.'

She turned to see Walters looking down at her gravely, no hint of a smile curving his lips. She stared in amazement. How could he have caught up with her?

Robin's excited little face broke in on them. 'Aren't you glad I made you run, Uncle Geoff? It's super down here, isn't it? And there's that skeleton, come and see.'

'Say hello to Miss Korvak, Robin,' his uncle reproached him.

'Oh, I'm sorry. Hello, Miss Korvak.'

'Hello, Robin. Show me the skeleton, will you?'

He took her hand and almost dragged her towards the grille. Pippa was aware of Walters coming to stand behind her, and wondered how she was going to get away. Robin was chattering happily, and she could see Walters' face soften at the boy's evident pleasure. When Robin had finished telling her his somewhat garbled version of the Hell Fire Club's activities, he looked up at her thoughtfully.

'Do you like spooky things too?' he asked.

Pippa nodded and crossed her fingers. She did not, and especially the strange happenings at Cambermere Hall, but she could not cloud his happiness by appearing a wet blanket.

Robin was approving. 'I thought you did. I told Uncle Geoff you were a nice lady the day you came to ride Alouette. Are you really going to ride Copper too?'

She glanced at Walters, who looked away. 'Perhaps,' she said. 'We'll see. I'm rather busy at the moment.'

'He can be a bit awkward at times, but I bet you could manage him. Uncle Geoff doesn't think so but I heard him say you were a Korvak and used to having your own way. So you probably could ride Copper, couldn't you?'

'Come on, Robin. Don't forget we've got to get to the dentist this afternoon,' Walters cut in. 'I told you we wouldn't be able to stay here long.'

'Oh, just let me see the river before we go,' Robin pleaded, and the cunning smile on his young face jolted Pippa's memory. *Alexis Korvak:* He wore exactly that look in some of his photographs, a smile calculated to charm and cajole. She felt suddenly sick. Until this moment she had forgotten Robin was her father's son.

Robin skipped away towards the far end of the chamber and Walters strode after him. Pippa began to hurry back the way she had come.

Very few visitors were coming downhill towards her. It was lunchtime, she realised. Her hurried footsteps began to slow after a time, for the return route was all uphill. The way was clear until she reached the labyrinth. Here she hesitated, then chose one passage.

'The reason for Sir Francis' construction of the catacomb is not clear,' the mechanical voice was saying. Pippa turned from one passage to another, and began to realise she was lost. 'Possibly it was meant to confuse intruders, but more likely he was endeavouring to imitate the catacombs of Rome which he had visited.'

The taped voice was growing fainter. She had evidently gone further into the labyrinth, and she began to feel alarmed. Down here, alone in the chill, damp atmosphere, it was eerily frightening. At yet another intersection of the low passageways, she paused.

Suddenly the spotlamps overhead went out, plunging her into utter darkness and Pippa gasped. Don't panic, you fool, she told herself fiercely, they'll come on again in a moment. She reached out a hand to find the clammy rock wall and moved forward cautiously. Seconds passed and still the lights did not come on. Sweat began to break out on Pippa's brow. Suddenly it came to her that this situation was her lifelong nightmare realised: lost in impenetrable darkness, shut in underground. All it lacked was the thud of approaching footsteps.

Even as she thought it, the sound of footsteps came to her ears, distant and hollow but closing rapidly. Recognition that this was the nightmare complete made the perspiration begin to trickle down her neck and fear choked in her throat. Then she heard a voice calling.

'*Philippa!*'

It was Walters! Unreasoning terror made Pippa hurry forward, away from the sound, until her foot caught a rock and she stumbled. Dear heaven, don't let him catch me, here alone in the black void and helpless, she prayed, but at every step the sound of the pursuing footsteps came closer. Pippa leaned back against the clammy rock wall, panting.

'Philippa! Where are you?'

At that second light splashed out, revealing the face of Walters within yards of her. Pippa's fear vanished when she saw he was leading Robin by the hand. With the boy he would hardly dare to harm her.

'So there you are,' he said. 'I guessed you'd get lost and then when the lights went out . . . Well, anyway, now they're on again we'll show you the way, won't we, Robin?'

Walters spoke little after that as they retraced their steps up towards the entrance. He had little opportunity, it was true, for Robin was talking eagerly all the way about his earlier visit to the caves. Once outside the turnstile the heat of the day, although it still remained sunless, struck Pippa forcibly. It was wonderful to be warm again, out in the air where she could breathe and away from the nightmare of the dark. Unwilling to speak to Walters, ashamed now of her earlier panic, she thanked Robin instead for his guidance.

'You will come and see us soon, won't you?' Robin asked shyly. She nodded.

'Yes, I'll see you soon. Goodbye, and thanks again. I couldn't have managed without you.'

The boy was still smiling with pride but Walters' expression remained impassive as she turned away to go down to the car-park. She had been stupidly alarmed by the dark, she thought as she drove away out of the little village, but the doubt still lingered in her mind about Geoff Walters. Had his intentions really been chivalrous, trying to find her to lead her out, or might events have taken a different turn if the lights had not suddenly come on again, and if Robin had not been there?

Speculation was idle, she knew, but she still remembered with a shiver how terrified she had been for a few minutes down there under the chalk rocks of the Buckinghamshire countryside. As she sped away through the lanes thick with elm and beech trees on either side, she realised she was hungry. She would drive into High Wycombe and buy something to eat.

In the town centre she managed to find a parking meter and walked through the Hexagon, the indoor shopping arcade. Here she purchased some rolls, fruit and a carton of apple juice, feeling happier now that she was surrounded by people busily pursuing their errands. For a time she sat on a bench, munching a crisp roll, then went back to the car. She would continue her lunch in the countryside, for the sun was at last beginning to shine.

Nearing Marlow, she swung the car off to the right, in the general direction of Cambermere and the river, to find a pleasant spot on the river bank. The lattice of interlocked branches overhead spattered sunlight on the windscreen in sporadic bursts, momentarily dazzling her, and she realised with a start that there was a figure on the road in front of her. She slammed on the brakes before she recognised it was Arthur Bainbridge waving his thick arms. As the car stopped, he came alongside the open window.

'Recognised the car and saw it was you,' he grunted without even a greeting. 'Wanted to see you anyway. Come along up to the house and I'll get us a drink.'

He turned to go up a drive, which Pippa could see led to a long, low house. He had given her no opportunity to refuse, so she pulled the Fiat up on to the grass verge and then got out and followed him. At the top of the drive she saw a long, rambling farmhouse, whitewashed and neatly painted. Bainbridge stood in an open doorway and beckoned her in.

She found herself in the kitchen, which was large and

110

airy, with a stone-flagged floor and a deal table in the middle surrounded by several wheel-backed chairs. Genuine old farmhouse-style, she thought with admiration, even to the copper pans gleaming on the wall and the Aga range.

'What will you have to drink, Philippa?' Bainbridge asked. His red-veined eyes rested on her in a way that made Philippa feel uncomfortable. 'Sherry? Gin?'

'I'd rather have lemonade or some orange juice, if you don't mind, Mr Bainbridge.'

'Arthur,' he corrected. 'Remember, I told you to call me Arthur.'

So he had, in an attempt at familiarity which had led to an instant proposal of marriage. Pippa hoped he was not going to mention that again. He took a bottle of orange juice from the refrigerator and poured two large glasses, then plopped in several ice cubes.

'Let's drink it in the parlour,' he said, leading the way out of the kitchen. The parlour was an equally pleasant room, sunlit and airy, with chintz curtains and chair covers, a pretty Pembroke table by the wall with an inlaid tracery of brass, a long sideboard which looked decidedly seventeenth century and a lovely brass carriage clock on the mantelpiece and above it a flintlock of ebony and silver. In the passage beyond she glimpsed a grandfather clock, which even now was whirring like an ancient bronchitic as a prelude to striking the hour.

'It's a lovely house,' she commented to Bainbridge. He nodded his thanks of her approval. 'Have you collected all this furniture?'

'Aye, and it's all genuine antique, none of your reproduction stuff. Some of the pieces were here when I bought it. That's why I wanted you to come.'

'I don't understand. You wanted me to see your house and furniture?'

'Aye, I wanted you to see what you'd be getting if you agree to my proposition. You'll have a good home, nowt artifical or make-shift — but the real thing. You can see over the rest of the house before you go, and if there's owt else you want I'll see you get it. I'm a man of my word, Philippa, and for you there'll be only the best.'

111

Pippa put her glass down. 'Now look here, Mr Bainbridge, you must realise – '

'Arthur,' he interrupted.

'You must realise that a proposal of marriage at one's first meeting is not really something one can take seriously.'

'I meant it seriously, as you should well know. Tell me, has anyone bothered you up at the Hall yet?'

'Bothered me?'

Bainbridge slapped his glass down on the table testily. 'Have you forgotten already? I warned you you'd need protection if you was to stay in Cambermere, and I was willing to offer that protection in return for marriage. Are you telling me that you've been here above a week already and no one has yet shown you how much you Korvaks are hated? Hasn't anyone harassed you or even threatened you?'

Pippa looked away from his challenging blue gaze, reluctant to admit what he wanted to hear. 'So far as I can gather there are a few who had cause to dislike Father,' she replied slowly. 'Is it true he acquired your land by cheating at cards?'

'Who told you that?' Bainbridge's fresh complexion reddened even more. 'Look here, I gave you time to consider my proposal and you've kept me dangling. I'm not used to being messed about, particularly by a chit of a girl. I've shown you you've everything to gain by marrying me and nowt to lose, now give me my answer. Will you marry me?'

'No I will not.' Pippa rose purposefully, angered by his threatening, domineering tone. 'Now good day to you, Mr Bainbridge. Thank you for the drink.'

He stood glowering in the open doorway as she retreated down the drive. 'You'll be sorry, mark my words,' he called after her. 'God help me, you'll be sorry!' Pippa leapt into the Fiat and drove off at speed, angry with Bainbridge and with herself. It was high time she stopped letting people affect her so deeply. Once it had been Clive, now she was letting suspicion and distrust of her new acquaintances lead her into fear.

The intended picnic by the river completely forgotten,

she drove into the grounds of Cambermere Hall, its stately grace imposing in the afternoon sunlight. Funny, she thought, she had left the Hall behind so as to forget its occupants and the threats it seemed to hold out to her, only to run into Walters and Bainbridge. It had not been a very successful outing, to say the least.

The Hall was strangely still and silent when Pippa unlocked the door and let herself in. Then she remembered she had left the remainder of her picnic rolls and fruit in the car, but she simply shrugged. She was no longer hungry anyway. For a time she lingered in the vestibule, noting the way the shafts of sunlight fell between the seven marble pillars grouped in a circle and played vividly on the mosaic pattern in the floor between them. She eyed the door to the east wing, and then crossed to try it. It was locked, and Stephen had the key.

She went first to the kitchen and then called his name up the great staircase. She remembered there had been no sign of his dusty little Fiat when she had driven round to the stable yard. He was taking her at her word and keeping his distance. Pippa began to regret her hastiness. She would have liked Stephen to be here now, to hear his opinion of her exploits. Now, after the way she had spoken, he would be in no hurry to seek her out again.

Suddenly, and for no apparent reason, she had a strange, unpleasant feeling and a tingling at the nape of her neck; the feeling of someone walking over one's grave. Or of being watched. She spun round quickly, the shafts of sunlight between the pillars dazzling her for a moment but not blinding her entirely to the tall black figure at the top of the staircase. With a quick intake of breath she stepped forward, shading her eyes.

'Who is that? Who's there?'

A smooth voice rippled down the stairs, calm and almost sepulchral in the great void: 'Philippa, my dear girl, it's only me.'

It was Mrs Purvis, dressed in black as she almost always was, and looking far taller than usual from this angle. Pippa breathed a sigh of relief as the figure began to glide down the stairs. 'Oh, Mrs Purvis! I didn't know you were back. I didn't see the car.'

'I left the car in the village because the battery seemed to be going flat. I walked up,' the housekeeper explained, her keen eyes inspecting Pippa closely. 'What have you been doing with yourself today?'

'Oh, I went out. To the West Wycombe caves.'

There was something different about her, but at first Pippa could not place it. Then she realised: the housekeeper was wearing a pair of pendant black earrings. It was unusual for her to sport something so feminine, but to Pippa's mind they only added to the woman's funereal starkness. They were long and thin, just like their owner, and with a glittering brittleness about them. Pippa could not help remarking on them.

'I like your earrings, Mrs Purvis. Did you buy them in London?'

For a second the housekeeper's searching eyes were veiled by fluttering lashes. 'In London? Ah, no. They were a gift, from a friend.'

'They're very pretty.'

'Jet, my dear. Real Whitby jet. Victorian, I believe. I've always wanted some although I don't go in for jewellery as a rule. Still, a treasured gift from a treasured friend. My Miss Carrie used to have some just like them.'

That was it, Pippa realised. Mother was wearing long black earrings in that photograph. That was why Mrs Purvis admired them so, because her adored mistress had once worn ones very similar. Pippa softened towards her.

'They're very pretty, and tasteful,' she commented.

'Of course. Miss Carrie always had perfect taste,' Mrs Purvis said with a touch of asperity. 'I'll put the kettle on now if you would like a cup of tea.'

Pippa followed her to the kitchen. Mrs Purvis rattled the kettle under the kitchen tap. 'Did you enjoy the caves, Philippa? I've never been there myself.'

Pippa smiled. Her fears of the afternoon now seemed unreasonable and childish. 'Not really. I got lost in what they call the catacombs, and if it hadn't been for Geoff Walters and young Robin I might have been there still. They led me out.'

'Walters?' the housekeeper repeated. 'I hope you

weren't too friendly towards him. It would be foolish to encourage him, knowing how he feels about the Korvaks.'

'He feels no more strongly against Father than Bainbridge does,' Pippa pointed out.

'Did you see him too?' Pippa could see disapproval shaping in her face again. 'He's an even less desirable character.'

'He asked me again to marry him so as to protect me,' Pippa asserted. 'He can't dislike me too much.'

'He wants Korvak land, that's all. And do you think you need protection Philippa? Against what, and whom?' The housekeeper's cold eyes challenged hers.

Pippa stammered, confused: 'You've just said — Walters hates the Korvaks, and someone *did* put oil on the pool steps. Someone does want to harm me.'

'Nonsense. Imagination, as I said. You must be careful, Philippa, or you'll become paranoid, imagining someone is out to harm you. Paranoid, what your father kept accusing Miss Carrie of being.' She bit her lip suddenly.

'Did he, Mrs Purvis? Why, what did Mother think?'

'Nothing. Forget it. It's all long ago now.'

'But you said it, Mrs Purvis,' Pippa insisted. 'Are you saying my mother's nervous condition was brought about by Father? And if so, how? What did she think he was doing?'

'Nothing, I told you! It's true he was hard on her, true she suffered from her nerves as a result, poor lamb. But she didn't imagine things; she wasn't paranoid or schizophrenic or any of the dreadful things he said. But he wanted her to think she was going crazy so he could get his own way. All I'm saying is that you'd better guard against being driven the same way with your wild dreams of being threatened and all. There was no oil in the pool, no one in your room at night — it's all your fancy, Philippa. Rest and quiet, that's what you need.'

There had been no one in my room at night, she had said, and Pippa remembered suddenly the perfume and the vision in the garden last night. Perhaps the housekeeper was right and she was simply overwrought. But that perfume? The memory of it choked Pippa's nostrils even now.

The housekeeper was standing at the stove with her back to Pippa, waiting for the kettle to boil. The question came unbidden to Pippa's lips and before she could think she had spoken it. 'Mrs Purvis, I keep smelling Californian Poppy in my room. Strongly, and always at night. Did you know how it comes to be there?'

She saw the housekeeper's back stiffen slightly before she answered. 'I showed you the drawer where your mother's things are . . .'

'It's much stronger than that. Almost as if someone sprayed it freely in the air.'

'Well, yes, I do spray it sometimes, but not often. I haven't done it since you came.' The woman's voice was almost defensive. Pippa was curious.

'Why do you do that, Mrs Purvis? Is it because it reminds you of Mother?' she asked gently. Mrs Purvis turned quickly, her dark eyes glittering like her earrings.

'Because it was her room and because for me she will always be there. Because I have to cleanse the air and purify it, the way it was when she was still here. It has to be sanctified after strangers have been in her room, alien, unclean presences who defile her memory! I do it for Miss Carrie, my pure and saintly mistress!'

Pippa stared at her, stunned. 'Alien presences? Unclean? Do you mean me, Mrs Purvis? For heaven's sake, I'm her daughter!'

The housekeeper's eyes blazed from a white face, 'Anyone who invades her room defiles it because no one else can hope to attain her purity and goodness. Oh yes, I know some may say she too was defiled by the way her first husband prostituted her beauty and sold her to Korvak. They both used her shamelessly, exposing her to the lustful eyes of men, but whatever they did to her my Miss Carrie stayed untouched, pure in heart and soul as only an angel can be.'

Her words were quietly-spoken but venom glittered in them like an icicle. Pippa stared at her aghast. Mrs Purvis's fierce loyalty and devotion to her mistress were hysterical to the point of blasphemy.

'But you didn't spray her perfume last night because you weren't here,' Pippa went on quietly. 'But someone did.

Either that, or my mother came back — but why?'

'Came back? What makes you say that?' Mrs Purvis demanded.

Pippa regarded her levelly. 'Because I could swear I saw her, down in the garden, dancing in the moonlight.'

The housekeeper stared hard at her for a moment as though she were trying to lay bare Pippa's soul, and the look in her dark eyes made Pippa quail. 'She did come back, didn't she?' Pippa persisted. 'She did come back — but why?'

The housekeeper's angular face appeared hazy through the cloud of steam as she poured boiling water into the teapot, and Pippa could see a faint smile curving her thin lips. 'You think she too wants to protect you, like Mr Bainbridge?' Mrs Purvis asked, and Pippa could detect the edge of irony in her tone.

'Why not? She would not wish to harm me,' Pippa said defensively.

'You think not? I would not be too sure.'

'Mrs Purvis! What on earth makes you say such a thing?' Pippa was shocked. The housekeeper put down the kettle and eyed her coldly. Pippa rushed on. 'I've seen her diary! I know she loved me!'

'So she did, until your father forced her to part from her elder daughter.' The words were icy.

'Irma? You mean when he made Irma leave? But Mother would not stop loving me just because she lost her!'

Mrs Purvis shrugged. 'Oh, she never said as much. She was too gentle and kind to hurt anyone, but could you blame her if secretly she came to hate the child she was obliged to keep in place of the one she was forced to part with? The child of a man who was a brute to her? If she came back to you, Philippa, I should be concerned if I were you, not too ready to believe it was a sign of good.'

'You're wrong!' Pippa cried, ignoring the cup of tea the housekeeper held out. 'You say that, yet you profess to love her!'

'Profess?' The housekeeper put down the cup and drew herself upright. 'I do not *profess* to love, Philippa. I worship her now as I worshipped her then, with the kind of love you will never know or understand.'

Pippa could only stare at her. She was mad, inhuman, to be so obsessed by a dead woman, and Pippa resented the way she seemed to try to exercise some kind of proprietorial right over Mother. It was no use arguing with her, carried away as she was with her idolatry. Angry and sickened, Pippa rushed from the kitchen.

Tears pricked her eyelids and her first impulse was to rush to her room, but in the hallway she hesitated. It was Carrie Hope's room, not hers, and no doubt when Mrs Purvis had appeared suddenly at the top of the stairs she had just been to that room to tidy it and perhaps even, as she put it, to purify it. Pippa would not go there, not yet.

At that moment the front door opened and Stephen strode in, his handsome face set and unsmiling. Pippa felt a rush of warmth and moved towards him.

'Stephen! Oh, Stephen!'

He stood in front of her, stiff and erect. 'Pippa, I want to talk to you. Come into the music room.'

She followed him, glad at heart to see one sympathetic person at last. Once inside the music room he closed the door and turned to her; afternoon sunlight from the high window surrounded his tall silhouette.

'Pippa, it's no good. I've been allowing myself to be diverted from what I came here to do. Now I've made up my mind to ignore everything else.'

'Of course you must, Stephen, and I won't prevent you. Indeed, I'll help all I can, so long as you don't expect me to hurt my father.' She said the words gently, persuasively, anxious for his friendship at least. He jerked away from her and leant on the grand piano.

Pippa watched him, as anxious premonition leaping in her. The great white piano with its gilt candelabra and the Aubusson carpet seemed to lose their colour and fade as Stephen spoke.

'You don't understand. I must hurt your father – I *want* to hurt him. It's been my plan for so many years, and it kept me and my mother going when times were hard. It was her dying wish that I should carry this thing through, and I will. Pippa I'm going to expose him utterly. He was, and is, a bastard, an *ördög,* and now I think I can prove he was a murderer too. I must and will do it.'

Pippa was dismayed. 'But we knew of that — he was tried and acquitted! And it was years ago, when he was a youth.'

Stephen turned slowly. 'Not that, Pippa. I think he murdered again — and I aim to find the proof. I aim to clear my father of the shame that was attached to his name, and to blacken Alexis Korvak's name in revenge. I'm sorry. There's nothing you can do to stop me. My mind is made up.'

Pippa's fingers flew to her lips. 'Oh no! Stephen, no, you can't! You must not! Does our friendship mean nothing to you?'

He smiled wryly, but there was no trace of humour in his face. 'Friendship or any other commitment must give way to justice.'

Fury rose in Pippa. 'Do as you feel you must, Stephen Lorant, but I hope I never set eyes on you again! I never want to see you as long as I live!'

She turned and fled from the music room, tears of rage and frustration blinding her now. Like a crazed thing she ran from the house, down the drive and away, not knowing where she was going nor caring. Flight was instinctive, essential, to escape what her mind refused to accept. Mrs Purvis's declaration, so closely followed by Stephen's insistence, were facts Pippa yearned to disown, to deny, and since that was impossible, to escape.

She ran madly, unseeing and uncaring, until a white gate suddenly appeared before her: Walters' riding stables. She pushed open the gate and rushed up the drive. Ride, that was what she would do, ride in wild, headlong flight where the dizzying sensation of excitement and exhilaration would drive all else from her mind and bring peace, for a few moments at least.

Panting, she reached the stable yard and saw Robin standing outside a stall, his young face full of concern.

'Oh, Miss Korvak! Copper seems to be upset and Uncle Geoff's gone out. I think there must be a mouse in his stall or something.'

She looked through the open upper half of the stable door. Copper, already saddled, was snorting and moving around in agitation, every now and again snorting and

119

whinnying.

'Uncle Geoff was going to ride him, but Mr Bainbridge called him away,' Robin said. 'I don't know where he is now.'

'Telephone Bainbridge. Leave Copper to me.'

The boy ran off obediently towards the house. Pippa laid a hand on the lower door and began murmuring words to the horse.

'There now, boy, take it easy,' she said soothingly. 'There's nothing to get excited about.'

He seemed to grow calmer, and Pippa opened the door cautiously and moved towards him. He backed away nervously, smelling that she was a stranger, but Pippa knew that he must sense that she was calm and in control.

'There boy, there,' she murmured and reached up for his bridle. He let her take it, regarding her with curiosity and distrust. There was no sign of a mouse or a rat, or anything which could have alarmed him. As she peered about in the gloom of the stall, the door suddenly slammed shut and she heard the sound of a bolt.

She turned in dismay, resisting the temptation to shout angrily lest she alarm Copper again. Whoever it was, it was a damn fool trick to shut her in the dark with a capricious, temperamental horse like Copper in his present mood. Any second he could decide to dislike her and start to rear up, and in this confined space she could not escape being trampled. Then alarm leapt in her. Perhaps it was the same person who had put oil on the pool steps . . . Copper pawed the ground restively and Pippa tried to slow her thundering heartbeat as she crooned soft words to him. It was not easy with the anger that blazed in her.

Suddenly she heard the bolt slide back and daylight streamed in again. With a surge of relief she saw Robin's head peer over the stable door.

'Who locked the door, Miss Korvak?'

'I don't know. Let me out, will you, Robin? Is your uncle coming?'

'Mr Bainbridge's housekeeper said he's not there, so he must be meeting Mr Bainbridge somewhere else.'

'Never mind. Copper only needs exercise,' she said as she led the horse out. 'I'll ride him for a while and then bring him back.'

She adjusted the girth and shortened the stirrups and then mounted Copper smoothly, still speaking softly and confidently to him. She saw the boy watching her as she rode away across the cobbled yard.

Once out in the fields she gave Copper his head, both animal and rider eager to give full vent to their emotions. Pippa forgot the horse as she galloped, bursting only with her own anger and frustration. Walters, Bainbridge and Mrs Purvis had all conspired to enrage her, but Stephen was the last straw. Even the ill-wisher who had locked her in the stable with an animal half-crazed with fear seemed of less importance than Stephen's disloyalty. She had come to trust and even to − to like him, she told herself angrily − and he had betrayed her just when she needed him most.

The breeze fanned her cheeks as Copper sped along, tossing her long hair wildly about her, but even the summer wind could not cool her anger. *I hate him, I hate him,* she muttered savagely to herself, and she was so choked with her own fury and sense of betrayal that she did not notice that Copper was heading straight for the wall.

At the last second before he jumped, he suddenly whinnied and reared. Pippa saw the ground flash past her face and then the blue sky racing past her. She knew that she was sailing through the air, clear of the stirrups and over the wall. It all happened with the same slow-motion clarity of a delayed film-run. She could even see, on the far side of the wall, the scattered rocks and pebbles and realised in that instant that there was nothing she could do to avoid falling on them. A million sparks of multi-coloured fire scorched across her brain, and then utter darkness enveloped her.

9

As consciousness returned, Pippa lay there, un-comprehending, and then wished desperately that she could turn back to the womb-like comfort of oblivion.

Voices murmured quietly about her, but at first they were no more real than flickering ghosts in the empty corridors of her mind. Where her head should be there was just one enormous ache, and for a time she lay, eyes closed, trying to overcome the pain and reorientate her disordered brain.

There were also confused sounds of footsteps and metallic clinks. With an effort she sought to remember where she was. Not Cambermere Hall, she thought hazily, for the sounds were wrong.

'Miss Korvak?' a quiet voice interrupted. 'Are you awake?'

Even more puzzling. The voice was totally strange. Pippa nodded, without opening her eyes.

'That's good. There's someone here to see you.'

More footsteps, the ring of a bell, someone coughing, and then at last a remembered sound.

'Philippa? How are you now, my dear?' It was Mrs Purvis's voice, and Pippa's confusion began to slow down from a whirl of something more like normality.

'Where am I?' she murmured.

'In hospital. But don't worry. The doctors say no bones are broken. A spot of concussion, that's all, but you had a nasty fall. It was lucky Mr Walters found you so quickly.'

Walters. Copper. The fall at the stone wall — it all came back. She shuddered as she remembered those strewn rocks on the ground. No wonder her head ached. She heard the sound of a chair being pulled forward, then Mrs Purvis spoke again.

'It gave us all quite a turn, I can tell you, but as I say, you were lucky. You could have lain up there by the woods all day and all night, hidden by the wall, if Mr Walters hadn't gone out to look for you. He warned you that horse was too big and powerful. He got worried when the boy told him you'd gone out on Copper and you weren't back. Very lucky. The doctors say they only need to keep you in overnight for observation. That's the usual procedure for concussion.'

Pippa lay silent, barely listening and only wishing that Mrs Purvis would stop talking and let her fall asleep again. Consciousness brought with it only returning worry about Walters and Stephen – and that vile headache.

'Was there anyone with you when you fell?' Mrs Purvis asked. Pippa moved her head from side to side slowly, and even that hurt.

'Had you been with anyone before? Was anyone in sight?'

'No.' Even that was a tremendous effort.

'So you saw no one after you left the stables until you fell?' Oh, why did the woman persist so.

'No.'

'And do you know how you came to fall? Did the horse refuse, or was it your own clumsiness?'

Pippa hated her. The housekeeper could be cruel in her choice of words, and why on earth should it matter to her how the accident occurred?

'Something startled Copper, I think. A rabbit or something, that's all.'

The effort of replying had cleared the last of the fog from Pippa's brain. She was fully awake now, troubled only by the thudding ache, and slowly she opened her eyes.

'Is it night?' she queried doubtfully. 'Is the room in darkness, Mrs Purvis? I can see nothing.'

She heard the scrape of the chair on the floor. Mrs Purvis's cold fingers touched hers. 'Are you sure, Philippa? Can you see nothing?'

'Not a thing. Is it night?'

Mrs Purvis breathed a slow sigh. 'No. It is full daylight. I'll fetch the sister.' Pippa lay stunned. Whatever fears she had felt before, they were as nothing to the panic that leapt in her now. Full daylight, did the housekeeper say, and yet for Pippa there was only impenetrable blackness? Something was wrong, terribly wrong, and before swift footsteps pattered to the bedside the full horror of the situation had crashed in on her: the fall had robbed her of her sight. *She was blind.*

'Now, Miss Korvak what's this I hear?' It was the pleasant, unruffled woman's voice which had first awoken Pippa. 'Can you see me?'

Pippa groaned.

'Can you see the sunlight at the window?'

Pippa turned and buried her aching head in the pillow. Distantly she heard the nurse's voice. 'Don't upset yourself, my dear. There's probably a very simple reason after that fall. I'll ask the doctor to have a look at you. Until he comes, just lie still and rest.'

Retreating footsteps pattered away down the ward, and Pippa heard Mrs Purvis's murmured questions, then silence. Evidently the Sister had made the housekeeper leave the ward, and for that at least Pippa was grateful. It was terrifying enough to recognise her plight without that thin voice rattling on. Blind panic rose in her. How on earth was she going to cope with life, sightless? The prospect was too horrifying to contemplate, and she felt herself begin to shiver uncontrollably.

More footsteps, and then a deep, masculine voice spoke. 'Let's have a look at you, Miss Korvak. Tell me about it.'

Pippa muttered garbled words and heard a click. 'Look up, towards the ceiling,' the voice commanded gently. She did so, wishing with all her heart that the ceiling would magically appear, but it did not. It was like being back in the catacomb when the lights went out.

The masculine voice was murmuring quiet words at the foot of the bed now and the nurse was answering, but Pippa could not catch their words. She clenched her fists in fear, then a cool hand pushed up her sleeve.

'A little prick, Miss Korvak. It will make you feel better.'

She felt the needle slide into her arm. Of course, they were sedating her to counteract the shock, but that was useless. She felt angry and helpless. Even if she became unconscious again she would only have to face the horror once more when she awoke. It was only delaying the terrible truth. She seized the cool hand as it was about to withdraw.

'Am I blind, nurse? What did the doctor say?' She could not help the fear, the childish tremulousness in her voice.

The Sister's reply was meant to be reassuring. 'He cannot see any reason for your condition so he'll ask the ophthalmic consultant to have a look at you. Now you just lie and rest. That's the best thing you can do right now.'

No evident cause, Pippa thought, as the nurse went away up the ward again. She digested the information, trying to extract a gleam of hope from it. If no physical evidence was visible, perhaps the darkness was only temporary, perhaps a shock-reaction, like a black-out, which would pass. It was only a glimmer of hope, but it was something to which she could cling. Her whole mind rebelled against submitting to perpetual darkness — for darkness was where all terrors lurked for her, and always had done.

Sleep came uninvited, but when Pippa awoke the terror returned. Open or closed, her eyes still saw only deep black velvet. Everyday noises around her told her that life was continuing as usual for others, and she felt desperately lonely. She pulled the bedcovers over her face, trying to find comfort in the warm haven of darkness as she had as a child, but the terrible feeling of fear was not so easily banished. Inwardly she prayed for someone to turn to, and for a moment her thoughts rested on Stephen. His low, vibrant voice and gentle touch would have been reassuring. But he too was an enemy now. There was no one left to calm the way and chase the nightmare.

'Tea, Miss Korvak?' Pippa emerged from the sheets. 'Do you take sugar?'

She must make an effort to behave like a human being, however terrified she was. She nodded in the direction of the cheerful voice. 'Thanks. No sugar.'

Cold china pressed against her hand and she groped for the handle while the nurse waited patiently.

'Bread and butter? There's raspberry jam today. I'll do it for you.'

Moments later she heard a plate being placed before her

on a surface, and her fingertips revealed to her that it was an overbed table. Carefully she placed her cup on it. Metallic sounds came to her ears — a trolley where the tea was poured, she guessed.

After the tea things had been cleared away the nurse came back. 'Mr Hunter-Price, the eye-specialist, is on his way to see you, Miss Korvak. He'll be here in a moment.'

Pippa heard the deep voice at the end of the ward and the firm tread as he approached. His words to Pippa were few, his examination of her eyes brief — almost perfunctory. He breathed deeply.

'I'll need to do some tests. Send Miss Korvak to the ophthalmic department right away, will you, Sister?'

A few minutes later Pippa was transferred to a wheel-chair. The journey from the ward, along corridors and then downwards in a lift was confusing, like being hurtled along in a car at night, without headlights, on an unlit road. Then she was moved from the wheelchair to a seat and asked if she could see lights flashing. Electrodes, the technician told her, would now be placed on her head and face while further tests were done and readings taken. One set of the electrodes were placed on her eyeballs and though not painful, it felt unnatural not to be able to close her eyes. The whole proceedings had an unreal quality about them and Pippa wished heartily that any second she might awake to find it had all been a ghastly dream.

When the tests were at last concluded, the technician told her cheerily that Mr Price would see her again.

Once more the specialist spoke little, and as she rose from the examination couch Pippa could contain her anxiety no longer.

'Well?' she asked timidly. 'How bad is it?'

'I can't tell you yet. I've still to see the results of the tests when the calculations are complete. Don't fret, my dear. We'll let you know in the morning.'

The morning? A whole long night still to endure the agony of not knowing whether this fearful darkness was only temporary? Pippa could hardly bear the thought of it. The nurse, helping her out of the wheelchair and back into bed evidently noticed her stricken face.

'Cheer up, love. It's nearly visiting time and your friend

will be back to see you then.'

Mrs Purvis. The thought of her spare, angular frame and unsmiling face did little to cheer Pippa, and with a sudden return of panic she realised that she might never see the housekeeper's unattractive appearance again. Never see Mrs Purvis again — or Stephen. With a sickening lurch in her heart Pippa recalled her last words to him: '*I hope I never see you again.*'

It was almost as though destiny had heard and ironically obliged. Then a new thought struck her. By now Stephen must have heard of her accident. Perhaps he would forget those words and come to see her in hospital, perhaps even this evening.

Pippa sat up, running her hands over her hair. There were sticky lumps adhering to the strands — the adhesive used to secure the electrodes, no doubt — and they were decidedly stubborn to remove. Bit by bit she picked them off, tidying her hair as best she could.

Visitors began to trickle in. Pippa heard their steps passing her bed. There was no mistaking the slow, deliberate step of Mrs Purvis.

'Good evening, Philippa. I hope you are feeling better. I've brought your own nightclothes and toothbrush and all I think you'll need. I'll put them in the locker and you can ask the nurse later to give you what you want.'

'You're very thoughtful. Thank you.'

Stephen was not with her, evidently. Perhaps he would come later. There was the scrape of the chair again and the housekeeper's cool voice.

'Has the consultant given an opinion yet about your condition, Philippa?'

'Not yet. I've had tests. They'll know tomorrow.'

'I see. Well, let's hope for the best.'

Unbidden, the thought leapt to Pippa's mind, and she was instantly ashamed of it. Hope for *what* best? That Pippa should remain blind? But it was unkind of her to suspect Mrs Purvis, however cold and distant she was, of wishing her harm. She had always cared dutifully for Pippa over the years — and yet, along with Walters and Bainbridge and latterly, Stephen, she had not proved herself an ally or a friend recently. But she was no secret enemy either. In any case, no one had caused Copper to throw her. That was the result of her own carelessness. She had ridden wildly, irresponsibly, and all because of that wretched scene with Stephen. If only he were here now.

Tentatively she put the question to the housekeeper. 'Where's Mr Lorant? Does he know about me?'

'He's gone. He left a note to say he had completed his work at Cambermere and was leaving the district. Most likely he's in London by now, or flown back to America for all I know.'

'Did he know about my accident?' Pippa asked incredulously. Surely he, of all people, could not be so hard as to leave her at a time like this? But he had spoken harshly at that last meeting, disowning all feeling for her because his work came first.

The housekeeper coughed and cleared her throat. 'No. He had gone by the time I got back from the hospital. That is, he didn't know from me, but Mr Walters might have told him, if they met.'

No, Pippa argued inwardly. He did not know or he would be here. Lost in this confusing darkness it was one reassuring belief she was determined to cling to.

The visiting hour dragged interminably. Mrs Purvis made small-talk about the amount of work still to be done on the London flat and the difficulty of her supervising the work in the present circumstances. Pippa barely listened. Her mind was far away, wondering just where Stephen was now and wishing that he knew she needed him.

After the bell rang and the visitors filtered out, the rest of the evening and the long night passed with inexorable slowness. Night in its dark mantle was no different from the day, save for the silence in the ward, interspersed only with snores and the rustle of papers where a nurse sat on duty. As she lay, restless, the same word kept hammering in her brain: *blind, blind, blind*. She longed for sleep and escape from the insistent horror of the word.

Pippa slept at last, a sleep of tangled dreams, no doubt due to the pills they had given her, but when the clatter of teacups awoke her, the same sudden alarm at finding herself still blanketed in darkness assailed her again. It was no awful nightmare, banished in the light of day, but a never-ending nightmare to accompany her for the rest of her days. God, but it was unthinkable to waken every morning for the rest of one's life in such a desperately lonely void!

'How's your head today, dear? I heard as you had a fall off a horse.'

It was a warm, motherly voice Pippa had not heard before, presumably either a nurse or another patient. Pippa sat up slowly, hearing again the chink of teacups. Her head no longer ached.

'Fine, thanks. It's just this not being able to see I can't get used to.'

The woman gasped. 'You mean you've gone blind, dear? Oh Lord!'

A nurse intervened. 'Miss Korvak must rest, Mrs Philips. Don't bother her with talking now. Here's your tea, Miss Korvak.'

Pippa took the cup gratefully and sipped. Distantly she could hear Mrs Philips, apparently now in conversation with another patient. 'Gone blind, would you believe! And her so young, too. What a shame!'

'Poor soul,' another voice murmured, and Pippa grew irritable. They were discussing her as if she were a child or as if blindness meant she was deaf too. Dear God, if she remained blind she would probably have to put up with even more humiliating treatment.

The blind man on the train; suddenly she remembered him, and his dog Shula. He had said something about able-bodied people not knowing how to talk to the disabled, about their embarrassment and often well-intentioned clumsiness. She remembered feeling uneasy at his words, recognising herself in the accusation. Grimly she realised that perhaps now she too was about to experience what he had spoken of, today, tomorrow — possibly for the rest of her life. Oh God! Would she have the strength to endure it, and alone too?

The ward routine of medication, temperature and pulse-taking preceded breakfast. Interspersed with the sounds around her, Pippa could hear snatches of Mrs Philips' conversation with some other patient, evidently also a newcomer, for Mrs Phillips was describing the recent extraction of her appendix in detail. By now she had evidently lost interest in Pippa's misfortune. By chance, Pippa's hand encountered the plastic headphones by her pillow, and she placed them over her ears. A radio announcer gave the time and said that the news would follow.

Pippa lay with closed eyes, feeling unaccustomedly weary. Suddenly the sound of her own name over the air arrested her attention: *Korvak*.

'He is at present in the Espirance Clinic in Los Angeles in a critical condition and fears for his life are mounting. Alexis Korvak made his name in the film industry in the 'fifties and was at one time husband of the film star Carrie Hope. His most recent films include *The Lorelie Legend* and *Passport to Frenzy*.'

Pippa started upright. As the newsreader moved on to other items she tore of the headphones and called out, '*Nurse! Nurse!*'

Measured footsteps came at once, swiftly but with calm authority. 'What is it, Miss Korvak? Is something wrong?' It was the cool voice of Sister.

'My father — he's dying in America! I must go to him!'

Pippa was already swinging her legs out of bed but Sister restrained her. 'Now what's this all about, my dear. Whatever the crisis, you're in no fit state to go anywhere yet. Your father dying, you say?'

'I've just heard on the radio — Alexis Korvak, the film producer — he's critically ill in Los Angeles! I must go to him!'

'Just you get back into bed, Miss Korvak. You've had nasty concussion and we've still to see about your eyes. You're not fit to go home yet, let alone to America. Critical doesn't necessarily mean he's dying, you know. Now Mr Hunter-Price will be along to see you soon, so just you settle back into bed until he comes.'

Sister tucked in the sheets so tightly that Pippa felt constrained and loosened them again as soon as her steps died away. She was right, of course; Pippa could be panicking unduly, and flying to the States was hardly feasible in her state. Nevertheless, Father must learn about Robin — before it was too late.

Hearing the young nurse with the warm manner at the next bed, Pippa called to her. The nurse came over. 'Yes?'

'Please, would you do me a great favour if you've got a minute to spare? I must write a letter to my father — he's desperately ill in America.'

The nurse hesitated. 'Do you think it's wise to tell him about your accident then if he's so bad?'

'It's not that — it's another terribly important thing he must know in case — in case anything happens to him. Please help me. It's very private and I can't ask anyone else.'

'All right, then, if it's urgent. I'll be back in a moment.'

Until the nurse returned Pippa sat thoughtfully, mentally phrasing, rejecting and re-phrasing how she should tell him. By the time the nurse returned she was ready. Five minutes later the letter was done and the nurse addressed the envelope to the Espirance Clinic, Los Angeles.

Pray heaven Father is not about to die, thought Pippa fervently, but if he does please let the letter reach him first. Perhaps by now he would be too ill to understand or to act upon it, and she blamed herself for her delay.

It was not long before heavy male footsteps told Pippa that the eye-specialist had arrived. She sat tense, eager for his verdict.

'Good morning, Miss Korvak. Now let's have a look at you. Drops, please, Sister.'

Pippa felt the cool liquid drip into her eyes. Hurry, oh hurry and tell me the worst, she prayed inwardly, but the specialist took his time, lifting each eyelid in turn and breathing deeply while he examined her. Then there was a brief, murmured consultation with someone else before he came back to sit on the edge of Pippa's bed.

'Well, you really set us a poser and no mistake, Miss Korvak,' he remarked. 'I can see no damage whatsoever, no detachment of the retina, no lesions or haemorrhage or any other injury. Moreover, the results of your tests show that everything apparently functions perfectly normally.

Quite a mystery.'

Pippa held her breath, unable to decide if what he said was good or bad news.

Mr Hunter-Price went on: 'My colleague here and I are somewhat baffled, I have to admit. We can only advise you to be patient and take things easy.'

'You mean it will clear by itself? That my sight will come back? How soon?'

He sighed. 'I cannot promise that, I'm afraid. I can only say that there have been cases of blindness with no apparent physical cause, such as yours, though they are infrequent.'

'But what causes it, doctor?'

'It's hard to say. It's always of a psychological origin, usually a bad shock of some kind. Did you have such a shock, Miss Korvak?'

Stephen – that was it. The shock of finding he cared nothing for her. She remembered her rage and bitterness, how she had stormed out and gone off to ride Copper.

'Well, in a way, I suppose I did. You say it's psychological – you mean the brain shuts off sight, as though it didn't want to see whatever it was that caused the shock?'

'In a manner of speaking, I suppose that is it.'

'But what happens then, doctor? Does the blindness last only as long as the shock does? Do people recover their sight eventually?'

'Sometimes. Sometimes not. There is no clear prognosis, I fear. I'm sorry I can't offer you more encouragement than that, Miss Korvak, but your sight could suddenly return spontaneously just as swiftly as you lost it. It might return, or it might not. Another traumatic event could trigger it or it could happen while you're at rest. All I can advise is that you return home to Cambermere and live as normal a life as possible. Trying not to be too anxious – that wouldn't help.'

He rose from the bed. 'I'm sorry not to be able to promise more, my dear, but you are young and resilient and that is in your favour. Even if you do not recover you have the weapons to adapt more easily than the old. I'll see you again – we'll have you back for a check-up very soon.'

Pippa felt limp and empty at the prospect of facing

eternal darkness without Stephen, and perhaps with Father gone too.

Within an hour Mrs Purvis, summoned by Sister on the telephone, appeared to take Pippa home. Pippa refused help and dressed alone, but it was surprising how weak her legs felt as she stood by the bed. What was more, she ached all over but then she realised that she must be bruised after such a fall. No wonder she felt so tender and stiff.

'Let me lead you,' said Mrs Purvis when at last Pippa was ready, and Pippa felt her thin, cold fingers take hold of her hand to lead her from the ward. Pippa's instant reaction of resentment grew as the housekeeper turned her sharply left, then pushed her into the lift, and finally guided her down the steps out of the hospital. The steps were terrifying to Pippa. It was all very well to be told firmly, 'Here, now there are four steps,' but actually putting one's foot out into a void and the sensation of downward movement felt as if one was about to plunge into an abyss. Once inside the car she felt safe, and almost began to yearn for the security of the hospital bed again.

She must stop thinking about herself and examining her sensations and emotions all the time, she reprimanded herself. Self-absorption was not healthy. Blind people were capable of thinking about others beside themselves.

If only Stephen would be at the Hall when she arrived — then she felt she would be better able to cope with the frightening day ahead. But Stephen was the cause of her present plight and she ought to hate him. Indeed, because of his intention to torment her father even on his deathbed, she did hate him. But still she longed for him. The homeward journey passed in silence as Pippa battled to reconcile the two warring halves of her mind.

Mrs Purvis, driving the car with smooth dexterity, at last broke the silence. 'Mr Walters was most disturbed about your accident, Philippa, especially when he learnt that you were blind.' Pippa could not help noticing the way the housekeeper used the word boldly, with no attempt to spare her feelings. 'He rang to say he would like to visit you, and I suggested he should wait until you were back at Cambermere. Mr Bainbridge too was shocked and said he

133

would call to see you.'

Oh no, thought Pippa. She had no desire to meet either. Hesitantly she asked about Stephen. 'Do you know whether Mr Lorant too came to hear about it from Mr Walters or someone else?'

'Not that I know of. Someone in the village may have told him if they learnt of it before he left Marlow. I really couldn't say.'

The tone of her voice seemed to Pippa to indicate that she really did not care either. Still, Pippa clung to the hope that someone had told him and that, despite everything, he would come to her. A chill thought struck her: she had no address either in London or America where she could contact him. He could be gone from her life forever. She shut the thought from her mind.

'I guess you'll have heard about Father,' she said to Mrs Purvis. 'About his illness, I mean.'

'Of course. I told you he was in hospital some time ago.'

'But I only heard today how critically ill he is. In other circumstances I'd have gone straight to him, but as it is . . .'

'Who told you?' The housekeeper's tone was crisp.

'I heard it on the radio. Didn't you?'

'Yes. But I didn't intend to alarm you in your condition. The doctor says no stress of any kind must be allowed to slow your recovery. It's a pity you had to learn about it yet.'

Pippa kept silent about her letter to the clinic. Some instinct warned her to hold her tongue. Poor Father, if he had never known about his illegitimate son it might be hard to accept on his deathbed; but it was possible that the news could bring him pleasure. In silence she prayed that Father would recover and that he would forgive her for her disclosure.

The sound of crunching gravel under the car wheels told her that they had reached the drive to Cambermere Hall.

'I'll drive round to the stables and then we can go in by the kitchen door,' said Mrs Purvis. She parked the car and came round to open the door for Pippa. 'Here, I'll take you inside.'

Pippa felt her fingertips under her elbow guiding her towards the door. One step, and she was inside. A succulent smell of roasting meat filled the air.

'Goodness, just in time,' said Mrs Purvis, and Pippa heard her open the oven door. Cautiously she moved forward, felt the arch of one of the wheelback chairs, and sat down.

'Shall I make some tea?' Mrs Purvis asked. Her tone was cool, polite rather than inviting.

Pippa shook her head. 'No thanks. I feel rather tired. I think I'll lie down.'

'Of course. Give me your jacket.' As she took it, Pippa heard her gasp with surprise. 'Philippa! Your arms are covered in bruises! Black and blue you are, and some of them turning yellow. What a sight!'

Pippa smiled ruefully. 'I imagine I have bruises all over judging by how tender I feel. Maybe a hot bath would ease the ache.'

'A hot bath would be the worst thing. But what about a spot of infra-red heat? That couldn't do any harm.'

'Is there a heat lamp in Cambermere?'

'Of course. Mr Korvak had a solarium installed as well as a sauna. It's on the same corridor as your room — come, I'll show you.'

Pippa rose and felt her way round the edge of the table. Mrs Purvis was evidently waiting by the door, watching. This time she made no attempt to take Pippa's arm and Pippa reflected that probably the housekeeper was right — she must learn to be independent, and after all, she was on familiar territory now.

Out of the kitchen she moved with care and along the short passage to the door leading to the vestibule. She knew when she had passed through the open door by the sound of her own footsteps, now ringing on the mosaic floor in the high-vaulted area. The marble columns — she must take care not to collide with them. She held out an investigating hand and eventually felt the cool smooth surface of a pillar. Here she paused.

'Which pillar is this, Mrs Purvis? I know there are seven here. Which one is it, counting from the left to the front door?'

'The fourth.'

Pippa moved forward a few steps. 'Then the door to the

135

east wing is about there? Between the second and third pillars?'

'That's right. And the staircase opposite.'

Pippa nodded. 'I'll soon learn. I remember meeting a blind man once, on a train, and he said the secret was to count everything. He knew what station we had reached because he counted every stop. I'll learn too.' And inwardly she resolved that she would. Blindness was a terrible blow, but it need not be the end of the world. God knew what she was going to do with her life now, how she would earn her living and act like normal, sighted people, but the first hurdle was to learn to fight back, to adapt and not to let tragedy and self-pity beat her down.

She turned and walked firmly in the direction of the stairs, but Mrs Purvis suddenly snatched at her arm and pulled her to one side.

'You'd have had yet another bruise, on your nose this time,' she said. 'You were heading straight into the pillar.'

She set Pippa squarely at the foot of the stairs, and as Pippa went up, hand on balustrade and counting, she reflected how easily one's sense of direction became confused in the dark. She could have sworn she had turned a full hundred and eighty degrees from the east wing to the staircase. The balustrade suddenly flattened out, just in time to warn her that she had reached the top step. Twenty-two.

The corridor was easy. Running her fingers along the wall she could count the doors until she reached her own room.

'Two doors further along to the solarium,' Mrs Purvis remarked. 'I'll show you how to use it and then leave you. Afterwards, you can rest in your room until dinner if you wish.'

She opened the door and Pippa followed her inside. There was carpet on the floor underfoot but the room had a hollow ring when Mrs Purvis spoke.

'It's a sunbed with an overhead lamp,' she explained. 'The lamp has both infra-red and ultra-voilet settings. I'll lower it to the right height for you and switch on. Then you can undress — there's a chair alongside to put your clothes on — and lie down. The infra-red is very soothing and relaxing so you might even doze there instead of on your bed. It won't do any harm.'

Pippa ran her fingers along the smooth surface of the sunbed and heard a mechanical noise as the housekeeper lowered the lamp. Pippa felt that too, long and smooth like the bed surface.

'Show me how to switch it on,' she said.

'There's no need. I'll switch it on and you can leave it when you've finished. I'll see to it later.'

The first surge of independence rose in Pippa. 'Show me just the same,' she said firmly. 'I'll have to learn to cope with everyday switches and things, or I'll end up useless.'

'Very well.' The housekeeper's cool hand took hers and raised it. 'Feel the large circular knob here? Turn left for infra-red, right for ultra-violet. Back to vertical to switch off.'

'And this knob?' asked Pippa, feeling another switch alongside.

'That's the timer. It's only used for ultra-violet, so you can forget that one. There, it's switched on now. Will you be all right?'

Pippa assured her that she could manage, and she left. Already warmth from the machine was caressing Pippa's bare arms. She undressed quickly and lay down on the sunbed's surface.

Despite its hardness she found the sunbed remarkably comfortable and after about ten minutes she began to feel drowsy. Above her there was a faint click, but she took no notice. Eyes closed and a velvety warm darkness all around her, she would have been asleep within seconds but for a sudden sound that made her jerk awake. A telephone bell was shrilling insistently in the solarium.

Pippa listened. It was probably an extension line and Mrs Purvis would answer it downstairs. But the demanding sound persisted, over to her right, and at length Pippa swung her legs cautiously off the sunbed, stood up, and walked carefully towards the sound. A smooth surface met her questing fingers and sliding along it, she found the telephone. Even as she lifted the receiver, however, the caller decided to hang up.

Retracing her steps towards the sunbed Pippa found it

easily and was about to extend her stiff limbs on it when a sudden, irrational impulse seized her. Reaching up towards the overhead machine which housed the sunlamps, very carefully so as not to burn her hands on exposed radiants, she found the switch on the edge. It was turned to the right. The right, surely, was ultra-violet if she remembered the housekeeper's words accurately. The switch should be turned to the left. Could she have remembered it wrongly?

Irritably she switched the knob off and began to dress. Mrs Purvis must have gone out, since she had not answered the telephone. Insidious suspicion returned. If the machine was set at ultra-violet, she would have been badly burned, especially if she had fallen asleep. Alarm seized her. It could have been accidental, of course; but if it was deliberate then someone, heedless of her disability, was still out to do her harm.

But why? What had she done?

10

All afternoon, lying on her bed, thoughts chased through Pippa's mind. Could Mrs Purvis have set the machine wrongly and if so, was it by accident or design? Or could she or someone else have come into the solarium surreptitiously, knowing Pippa could not see, to alter the setting? There had been a click, she remembered, but she had attached no importance to it at the time.

Mrs Purvis must have been out of the house or she would have answered the telephone. Then who else had access to Cambermere Hall? Carson was on holiday. None of the casual staff from the village appeared to be here today, though one of them could have a key. But why should he or she try to burn Pippa? The whole thing was so irrational and stupid that Pippa feared to mention the subject to Mrs Purvis when at last the housekeeper came to say that dinner was ready. Nevertheless Pippa told her hesitantly.

'Set to ultra-violet? Nonsense! I set the switch myself,' Mrs Purvis said shortly. 'You must be confused.'

'It was turned to the right, Mrs Purvis.'

'Indeed? I shall see for myself.'

'It's no use looking now. I turned it off.'

'I see. Then I only have your word for it. Will you come down before the soup gets cold?'

The soup could be no colder than the housekeeper's voice, Pippa reflected as she made her way downstairs.

Seated at table she mentioned the lamp again, politely but firmly: 'It was set to ultra-violet and I did not imagine it. If you did not set it so, then someone else did.'

She heard the sound of liquid being poured into her bowl. 'Someone else?' Mrs Purvis queried. 'Who, for goodness sake, when there's no one else here but you and myself? I tell you, Philippa, you are confused, that's all, and it's not to be wondered at after your concussion. You'll be all right in a day or two.'

Pippa fumed as she sipped the soup. The woman still had a maddeningly cool way of always putting Pippa in the wrong, making her seem stupid or forgetful, just as she did long ago in her nursery days. It was useless to argue with her.

'Did you go out?' she asked the housekeeper instead. 'The 'phone rang.'

'Did you answer it?'

'Eventually, but whoever it was hung up as I got there.'

'I expect they'll call again if it's important,' Mrs Purvis said smoothly. It was moments later that Pippa realised she had cleverly avoided answering whether or not she had gone out. Her next words drove all thoughts of further questioning from Pippa's mind. 'Oh, by the way, Philippa. I forgot to tell you earlier that I found a letter addressed to you in the hallway, presumably left by Mr Lorant.'

'From Stephen?' Pippa's heart leapt in hope. 'Where is it?'

'There, alongside your plate. To the right.'

Pippa felt the crisp paper under her fingertips, an

139

envelope but not sealed. It was both saddening and annoying that she could not take it away to peruse its contents alone. She was forced to forget her pride and ask the housekeeper, 'Would you read it to me, please?'

Mrs Purvis took it and cleared her throat.

' "*Dear Pippa, I am sorry that we must part with angry words but I want you to know that despite everything, I shall always think of you tenderly and wish you well. Though we may never meet again, God speed and bless you. Stephen.*" '

Mrs Purvis handed the letter back across the table. 'There's a foreign word I can't say at the end. Otherwise, quite a charming note, wouldn't you say? I didn't know you two had words.'

'It's not important now.' Pippa's reply, murmured and spontaneous, made her realise how much she missed him. It was ridiculous really. Only two weeks ago she was swearing to forget men and tackle life alone, and now here she was desolate because of a man she hardly knew. The words in the letter implied he had gone forever — and gave no address where she could find him. She curled her fingers tightly about the letter in her pocket. The word Mrs Purvis had not been able to pronounce — that must have been one of the many Hungarian terms Stephen used to use, endearments which had sounded sweet to her ears though she could not understand. Now he was gone, she felt alone and cold inside.

Mrs Purvis refused her help with carrying the dishes to the kitchen, so Pippa made her way to the music room, the last place she and Stephen had been together. As she closed the door behind her, she felt tears begin to prick her sightless eyes. The room was still and silent, as though still shocked at the harsh, cruel words they had flung at each other.

'*I never want to see you again!*'

The tears sprang unbidden now, and she was conscious of the cruel irony that fate had taken her words literally. Even if Stephen were to walk in the door now, she would never see his broad shoulders, his blond head and gentle smile again. As Pippa lowered herself into the velvet seat of a large armchair, an indignant squeak met her ears. Puzzled, she reached behind her and found a cat, small and furry and with outstretched claws, half squashed beneath her weight. Pippa picked it up gently, murmuring comfort and apologies and stroking its back. It was only young, judging by its size, but its anger quickly vanished and it walked on to her lap, arching its back against her trustingly. Pippa's self-pity melted and vanished.

The touch of the cat, its soft fur and its bony little head cradling under her chin, began to ease her pain and she felt her coldness thawing. The kitten, so slender and fragile, forgot its vulnerability in its evident trust of her. Its tiny, rapid heartbeat in the warm, resilient little body stirred in her a sense of being alive, and of hope and trust, and she sat peacefully stroking the little creature until he went to sleep, purring contentedly.

Mrs Purvis found her later and expressed some surprise when, switching on the light, she saw the kitten on Pippa's lap.

'How on earth did that creature get into the house?' she exclaimed. 'It's a stray — I've seen it in the grounds. I'll bet it was because Mr Lorant made a fuss of it that it thought it was welcome here. Give it to me, Philippa, and I'll put it out.'

'Oh no!' Pippa's determination to keep the kitten was redoubled, if only the housekeeper knew it, by hearing that Stephen had fondled it too. It was one last link between them. 'He's not to be put out, Mrs Purvis. If he's a stray then I shall adopt him. I'll take him down to the kitchen and give him some milk. Would you please find a piece of blanket or something for a bed for him?'

'Keep him!' Mrs Purvis exclaimed. 'But Mr Korvak doesn't like animals in the house. And besides, it might have fleas.'

'No matter. I've made up my mind he is to stay, so please don't let's discuss it any more.'

She rose and made towards the door, aware that the housekeeper was obliged to step aside to let her pass. The kitten sat hunched under her arm, its little claws unsheathed in alarm at the sudden interruption of his sleep.

It was not difficult to find a saucer and the milk in the refrigerator, but less easy to pour the milk for there was no way of knowing when the saucer was filled. She put the kitten and the saucer on the floor and listened to its dainty, rapid lapping. Mrs Purvis brought a piece of blanket, sniffing her disdain audibly before leaving, saying she was going to bed.

The kitten seemed disinclined to settle in the spot she chose for him by the boiler, preferring instead to chase her as she moved about and to attack her ankles with its tiny claws. Pippa's heart swelled with affection for him, his obvious happiness and joie de vivre. She did not want to be parted from him. Managing to catch him at last when he pounced, she carried him up to her room.

This empty world of hers was always dark, and, it was unnaturally still in the old Hall at night, but the kitten's warm little body purring away like a miniature motor-bike on her pillow gave Pippa a measure of peace and reassurance. Its warmth and welcome friendship were just what she needed. A reminder of Stephen, she thought sleepily, before things went wrong.

The succeeding few days passed slowly; with no definition between night and day it was not easy to recognise the difference at first. Normal daytime sounds like birdsong and the distant clatter of dishes in the kitchen were clear signs, but the night with its deep silence and only the occasional hoot of an owl or bark of a dog was a nebulous, unnerving time. Cambermere Hall by night had been an eerie place even when Stephen was here, but now it was distinctly ominous. Whoever wished her harm was here still, and there was nothing Pippa could do to protect herself.

By day she kept to a normal routine, with the additional task of learning her way about unaided. Steps, doors, even paces across a room — everything had to be counted and memorised. It was an adventure, she told herself firmly, not to be compared to riding out on the fields, but that would come. She should be grateful that her handicap did not deprive her of all mobility; she was lucky compared to a paraplegic.

The housekeeper gave her grudging approval. 'You're doing well, Philippa. I'm so glad you didn't sit down and feel sorry for yourself as you might well have done. Now, what will you do while I'm out shopping this morning?'

'I think I'll go for a swim — is the sun shining?'

'No, but it's bright and warm. A swim will do you good. By the way, Marion is here to clean the bedrooms, so you can call her if you want anything.'

Marion was a woman from the village who 'obliged' twice a week. Pippa could hear her humming in the vestibule just after Mrs Purvis had gone out and Pippa was about to mount the twenty-two steps to her room to change.

'Oh, the postman's late this morning,' Marion commented. 'There's a letter for you, Miss Korvak, and it's got an American stamp on it.'

From America? Pippa's heart leapt in anticipation. It must be from Father! She took it eagerly, and then fingered it helplessly. She had not told Father of her accident so he could not know that she was unable to read. Someone would have to read it for her — but who? Not Mrs Purvis, she decided, and since no one else was available she had no choice but to ask Marion.

'I hate to trouble you,' she explained, 'especially as I think it contains matters which are confidential. Do you think you could read it and then forget what it says? I know that sounds silly but I really need to know what it says, and I don't want Mrs Purvis or anyone else to hear of it. If you'd rather not, then please say so and I'll find someone else?'

But who? Bainbridge and Walters were out of the question, Stephen was gone, and young Robin could not be allowed to see. To Pippa's relief Marion patted her arm.

'Don't you fret, miss. I can be as discreet as anyone. Of course I'll read it for you.'

She took the letter and Pippa heard her tear the flap. For a moment she paused. 'It's from a firm of lawyers in San Fransisco,' she said.

'Lawyers? Not Alexis Korvak?'

'No. But the letter mentions him.'

'Read it, please.' Pippa's heart was thudding. Pray heaven she had not written too late.

Marion began to read:

' "*Dear Miss Korvak, My client Mr Alexis Korvak instructs me to write to you on his behalf to say that he was both surprised and pleased to receive your news. Far from wanting to contest paternity of the child, as we advised, he is pleased and eager to recognise him. Though weak and seriously ill, Mr Korvak is perfectly lucid and instructed a new will to be drawn up at once and its contents to be notified to you.*

"Accordingly, the new will now instructs certain substantial bequests to his housekeeper for many years, and to one other legatee, the remainder of his estate to be divided in equal parts between yourself as his legitimate daughter and the boy, the latter's inheritance to be held in trust by you until the child attains his majority.

"We enclose a brief note from Mr Korvak, being all that he could write in his present circumstances. We look forward to hearing the name of your lawyers in England with whom we can process the matter in due course. Leo J. Engel." '

Marion sighed. 'There's a half-sheet of paper attached with a few scrawled words. It says, "*Thanks, honey. You've made me a happy man. Father.*" '

A lump came unbidden to Pippa's throat. It was clear her father was very ill, perhaps dying, yet the knowledge of his illegitimate son had brought him joy. Whether he was the wicked creature people said or not, he deserved to die happy.

'Thank you, Marion. I'm very grateful to you.'

'You're welcome, miss. And not a word to a soul, I promise.'

'Bless you.' At least the solicitor's letter had not mentioned Robin Walters by name, so perhaps even Marion did not realise the meaning of what she had read — though it was possible that it was common knowledge who fathered poor Nina's child.

At that moment the telephone rang. Marion picked it up. 'Hello? Yes, she's here. It's Mr Walters, Miss.'

A curious coincidence, thought Pippa as she took the

receiver. She would have some good news to tell him.

'Philippa? How are you now? I didn't know whether you were home yet. Are you all right?'

'Well,' said Pippa cautiously, 'I've recovered from the concussion, but perhaps you know from Mrs Purvis what happened?'

'I haven't seen her since that day. I did ring the hospital but they would only say you were comfortable, nothing more. What did happen?'

'The blow to my head — it did something to my eyes. I'm afraid I can't see.'

She heard his gasp, then there was a pause. 'You don't mean — that you're blind?' he said incredulously.

'They say it may go right again of its own accord, with care.'

'Oh, God! Oh, Philippa, I'm so sorry.' There was dismay and sorrow in his tone that she felt sure he was not feigning.

'But I've something to tell you that you may be glad to hear,' she hurried on.

'No, listen. I must tell you something,' Walters interrupted. 'I wasn't going to tell you, but in the light of what's happened . . . Listen Philippa, someone *is* out for your blood, I'm sure of it. Robin told me about someone locking you in the stable.'

'Well, yes, I'd almost forgotten that. Copper was very restive.'

'And no wonder. After the ambulance had taken you to hospital I unsaddled Copper. There was a thistle-burr under his saddle and his back was raw. That's why he was irritable, and no doubt that's why he threw you at the wall.'

'Oh!' Pippa digested the information slowly. 'But no one expected me to ride him,' she said reflectively. 'It was you who planned to ride him.'

'But someone locked you in with him, knowing he'd be in a vicious mood. Listen, Philippa, if you feel you should tell the police, I wouldn't blame you.'

'Too late now,' she replied. After all, the harm was done, she had lost her sight and the ill-wisher would leave her alone. And how could she be sure it was not Walters himself?

'It wasn't Bainbridge,' Walters was saying musingly. 'He

145

was with me and anyway, it's not like him to be devious. Whatever his faults, he's straightforward enough. Well, what was it you wanted to tell me?'

'My father has acknowledged Robin as his son. Robin will not lose out now.'

There was a silence at the other end of the line, and Pippa could sense that Walters was not pleased at the news. Then he asked, 'Who told him? Was it you?'

'Yes. I thought it only fair. You've probably heard on the news that Father is critically ill.'

'Yes. But Robin is my ward. I don't want Korvak to lay claim to him. He's mine, and he's all I have left. Now look, Philippa, I'm sorry for what's happened to you but I wish you'd kept your nose out of my business. I know you probably meant well — '

'Of course I did!'

'But Korvak has caused enough misery in my family. I won't have him giving orders to send Robin away to school or fetched to America. I won't have it! Nor do I want the boy to learn who his real father is — a man the world knows for a villain! How could you inflict that on Robin?'

His voice was so cold that Pippa felt wretched. Unintentionally she had hurt him and he would continue to believe that Korvaks always brought trouble. 'I'm sorry,' she faltered, 'I didn't think . . . '

'No more than your father did,' he snapped, and she heard him hang up abruptly.

About twenty minutes later, the telephone bell began to call insistently again. Knowing that Marion was now busy running the vacuum cleaner back and forth upstairs, Pippa felt her way out into the vestibule to answer it.

'Philippa? It's Arthur Bainbridge. God, what a terrible thing to happen! You wouldn't listen to me, would you?'

Pippa sighed. 'I take it you've been talking to Geoff Walters,' she remarked.

'He rang me just now and told me. Hell, I guessed someone would try something on, but I never guessed it would be that bad. Tough blow, that. I just wanted you to know it wasn't me — and I doubt it were Walters either.'

Pippa could not resist a smile. Her two neighbours were

gentlemanly enough to vouch for each other. 'I didn't think it was you, Mr Bainbridge.'

'Arthur,' he interrupted.

'In fact, whoever put the thistle under Copper's saddle could not have known I was going to ride him. I didn't know myself till the last minute. So if someone was being threatened, it wasn't me.'

'But Walters said someone locked you in with that horse in a nasty mood. You can't tell me that person wasn't gunning for you? You're a hard woman to convince, but I just wanted to let you know that, er, with your eyes, er, being the way they are now . . . ' He paused, obviously finding it difficult to phrase his words without hurting. Pippa decided to help him out.

'I know, Mr Bainbridge. In the light of my present circumstances you wish to say that you will not press me again with a proposal of marriage. I'm grateful to you, truly.'

'Nay, lass, that's not it at all!' Bainbridge bellowed. 'Just the other way about! Now that you must believe me at last, perhaps you'll admit that you need a protector! I'm your man, Philippa. I'll marry you as soon as you like. There's not a soul in Buckinghamshire or in all England for that matter as will dare to bother you once you're Mrs Bainbridge. Now, what do you say?'

Pippa swallowed hard. 'Mr Bainbridge, I'm very grateful to you, honestly, but I'm afraid the answer is still no, and will remain so. After all, I've lost my sight – why should any persecutor need to attack me now? Thank you, but I've no wish to marry, and especially now this has happened. That's my last word on the matter, Mr Bainbridge, and I'd be obliged if you would never mention it again. Goodbye.'

She hung up firmly before he could protest. He was a kindly man despite his roughness and she hoped she had not offended him. It was only as she was counting her way up the stairs that she remembered his proposal was not entirely altruistic, for he still wanted Korvak land. But marriage was not essential for that – he could always buy it. Then when the unwelcome thought suddenly leapt on her that perhaps soon the land might be hers, she thought

147

fiercely that he need not buy the land — she would give it back to him.

On the landing a small, furry body suddenly thrust itself between her feet and began polishing her ankles with its arched back. She smiled and bent to pick up the young cat, cradling it tenderly. It purred loudly, pushing its bony head against her cheek. The distant hum of the vacuum cleaner stopped and Pippa heard Marion's quick footsteps approaching.

'Hello, miss. The bedrooms are all done now. Shall I give pussy the meat Mrs Purvis left for him before I go? It's ready in the kitchen, and she told me it was for him.'

'Oh, thank you.' Pippa handed over the kitten reluctantly, feeling its claws fasten into the sleeve of her shirt as if he too was unwilling to go. She was mildly surprised that the housekeeper had had such concern for him.

'She's left your lunch ready too,' Marion added. 'Would you like me to bring it up on a tray?'

'Oh no, don't trouble to come up again — I'll come down,' Pippa replied quickly.

'No trouble, miss. I've got to come up again to collect the polish and dusters and that. I'll bring it to your room.'

She was a cheery soul, a shaft of light in an otherwise cheerless day, thought Pippa. A pity she was on her way home now. She brought up the tray, but Pippa left it untouched on the table and sat instead in the window, feeling the sunlight on her face and staring out into the same blank void that confronted her wherever she looked.

Nothing. Black velvet. She sat alone in the Hall. Marion was gone and the place was deserted. Pippa longed at that moment for sight, to be able to gaze out over the tranquillity of Cambermere's grounds in the warm afternoon sunlight, to gain peace from just looking . . . Never to see sunlight again, or moonlight, never to see the tall grace of trees and the vibrant colour of flowers — it was too terrible to conceive. If only one knew, when sighted, just how fortunate one was. People felt no gratitude for sight, or health, they just took it for granted, as she had done. If only she could see now, she would never take it for granted again.

The dark night of the soul enveloped her for a few

148

seconds, and then angrily she thrust the feeling of self-pity aside. She must think positively, she reminded herself, not allow herself to wallow in negative gloom.

As she held out her hands to cross the room towards the table for her lunch tray, she heard the sound of the telephone once again. She would have to answer it herself. Groping her way out of her bedroom to the top of the staircase took time, and then she remembered the extension in the solarium. By the time she had retraced her steps to the second door beyond her room the bell had ceased its shrill call.

A sudden thought leapt to her mind: Walters and Bainbridge had already rung, so the caller was unlikely to be either of them. It could have been Stephen, anxious to make peace at last now sufficient time had passed for tempers to cool, or simply giving an address or number where he could be found. She went into the solarium, found the telephone and stood anxiously over it for several minutes, willing it to ring again, but the instrument failed to oblige. Disappointed, Pippa turned to go back to her room.

An unexpected sound arrested her. Down below, in the hallway, there was the sound of a light cough.

'Marion? Is that you?' Surely she had heard the door closing earlier as Marion left. There was no reply. 'Who's there? Is it you, Mrs Purvis?' she called.

Still there was no answer. Pippa felt her way along the wall until she reached the head of the stairs. Leaning over the balustrade she had a clear impression that someone below was looking up, watching her, but there was no sound.

'Who's there? Why don't you answer?'

She was positive she faced an intruder, but perhaps he might not know she was sightless. She walked with apparent poise to the stairs and began to descend slowly, her heart thumping inside her. What she would do when she reached the bottom she had no idea.

He was lightfooted, but she caught the quick sound of movement, and he could not disguise the click of the door closing. She recognised it as the door to the kitchen. Resolutely she went towards the hall telephone. An emergency call to the police would either deal with the intruder or, if he heard it, frighten him away.

Receiver in hand, Pippa had to search her memory to remember the order of the numbers. Did nought come first or last? Last, after the nine. Her fingertips felt for the last hole, then moved back one to the nine. Twice she dialled nine when the front door suddenly opened.

'Philippa! Who are you calling?' asked Mrs Purvis's surprised voice. Pippa replaced the receiver.

'Oh, Mrs Purvis! I'm so glad you're back! There's someone in the house — I heard a cough here in the vestibule.'

'Marion, probably. Had you forgotten it was her morning?' the housekeeper replied smoothly. 'You mustn't let things excite you so, Philippa.'

'No, it was after she'd gone. And then I think he went through to the kitchen — I was just about to ring the police.'

'The kitchen? Wait here.' Pippa was amazed at the woman's calmness as she walked past and opened the kitchen door. A click, and she was gone. Dismayed, Pippa made to go after her, fearful lest the intruder should attack. But when she reached the kitchen she could hear only the rustle of paper.

'I've got some lovely tomatoes from the nursery,' Mrs Purvis remarked. 'Just feel how firm they are.'

'But the man . . .'

'There's no one here, my dear. You heard something you *thought* was a cough, that's all. Don't worry. It's probably just your highly fertile imagination working overtime — I shouldn't have left you alone in an empty house knowing how excitable you are. I won't leave you again.'

'I'm not excitable, and I didn't imagine it! I heard the cough, and I heard the door close. Mrs Purvis, there *was* someone here! Hadn't you better check that nothing of value is missing?'

'If it makes you feel happier', the housekeeper replied, and Pippa grew angry. It was evident she was humouring her charge. Pippa moved across to the door leading to the stable yard. The key was still turned in the lock.

'Satisfied, my dear?' said Mrs Purvis smoothly. 'Now, how about a nice cup of tea?'

Pippa shook her head forlornly. Whatever she thought was going on here she could not understand it. Now she knew only too tragically what being in the dark meant. She felt confused, disorientated, and in need of closeness and companionship.

'Is my kitten here? Marion brought him down to feed him?'

'No. He's not here. Perhaps he went out with her. I shouldn't rely on him coming back, Philippa. He's only a stray, remember.'

That was true, but he had seemed to welcome her friendship just as she had his, as though they sensed the need and loneliness in each other. He'd be back soon, she was sure.

'He's eaten all his dinner anyway,' Mrs Purvis remarked as she clattered dishes in the sink. 'Not a scrap left. He's probably sleeping it off somewhere. Did you eat your lunch?'

'No. I'll eat it later.'

'Too highly spiced for you, perhaps. I made the pâté myself.'

'I wasn't hungry, that's all. I'll eat it for dinner and you won't need to cook.'

The housekeeper sighed and went out. She returned a few minutes later and Pippa heard her clatter the tray down on the counter. Then she heard the sound of scraping. Mrs Purvis was throwing the meat away in the waste-bin. She was evidently annoyed at what she considered was Pippa's rejection of her cooking.

'I said I would eat it,' Pippa ventured.

'Not after it's been exposed to flies all this time,' the housekeeper snapped. Pippa bit her lip. There was no point in trying to apologise in her present mood. Pippa's best plan was to leave her alone.

Out in the vestibule again, Pippa lifted her head, her ears caught by a faint sound. It sounded like the kitten's mew, muted and distant.

'Here, pussy, here,' she called persuasively, but no little body brushed against her legs. For several minutes she called, opening the door to the music room where she had first found him, eager for the warm soft touch of him, but to no avail.

Dinner was a dismal affair. Mrs Purvis was still in a taciturn

151

mood, only replying to Pippa's attempts at conversation with monosyllabic answers. As soon as she decently could, Pippa escaped from the table. Aimlessly she made for the music room. Perhaps it was the memories that this room held – of Stephen, and the kitten – that brought her here. Perhaps it was the piano. She found the stool, raised the lid and let her fingers drift over the keys in a haphazard collection of half-remembered chords from days long ago.

It was no use. Sombre music only served to enhance her loneliness and sense of isolation. In this dim no-man's-land she inhabited alone it was frightening to have no means of measuring time or space, a blankness without borders or definition. She shut the lid sharply and reached for the deep arm-chair.

There was something hard under her. Pippa stood up again to investigate. Her fingers encountered something hard and furry. She probed further.

A cry escaped her lips. At first her mind rebelled, refusing to acknowledge what she had discovered. It was the kitten – not warm and resilient any more, but stiffened and cold, its legs outstretched and neck arched from frail agony. It was the kitten, lifeless as a piece of stone.

11

It was not only the saddening recollection of the kitten's death that troubled Pippa as soon as she awoke next morning, but also the sickening thought that its death was unnatural. It had been lively and healthy earlier in the day, so its sudden death surely could not be the result of illness. It was an unnatural death, but whether by accident or design, that was the question.

The poor little thing had evidently chosen the armchair to lie down in when it began to feel something strange happening. It might have chosen her bed, where it usually slept if the door had been open. The thought of finding the stiff little body in her bed was even more heartrending than the shock of discovering it in the chair.

Tears filled her eyes, her heart swelling with compassion for the creature. Yesterday it had been so lively and capricious, completely ignorant of its approaching end. She was suddenly convinced that it had been poisoned — what other explanation could there be? But was it an accident, or had someone killed it deliberately?

Surely it was not yet another means of punishing her? Surely no one would be so petty as to try to get at her by killing an innocent kitten? A prickling fear tingled in her spine. If someone could be so inhuman, he was a deranged creature and the more to be feared.

But no, she was being silly, she reproached herself. Any such person, if he existed, must know she had already been punished, if that was what he sought. To harm her kitten gave him no advantage at all; it only robbed her of something she had treasured.

Pippa was reluctant to go down to breakfast. Instead she took a leisurely shower and examined her thoughts. She was disinclined to face Mrs Purvis, that was the truth of it, because the housekeeper was the only person who knew of her attachment to the kitten, the only person who knew how deeply its death would hurt her. It was stupid, Pippa told herself angrily. Mrs Purvis, however detached and cold she might be, had no reason to want to hurt her, none at all. And besides, Mrs Purvis had been out of the house most of the day. Pippa dressed and went downstairs at last.

Resolutely she pushed open the door to the kitchen, expecting the usual sound of dishes and the smell of cooking. Both were absent. The kitchen was deserted. Returning to the vestibule and calling the housekeeper's name had no effect. Pippa was alone.

The telephone rang. Pippa's heart thudded. Could it be Stephen ringing at last? As she lifted the receiver to her ear she heard Walter's voice and could not help feeling disappointed.

'Philippa? I just wanted to say I'm sorry. I shouldn't have snapped at you like that. You did the honourable thing and I should have thanked you.'

'That's all right. And if you've forgiven me for interfering, I'm happy. Incidentally, the news made my father happy.'

There was a pause before Walters spoke. 'How is he? Have you heard?'

'No, nothing, but I'm cabling the clinic to keep in touch. By the way, can you give me the 'phone number of your vet, Geoff? You must know a good one.'

He gave a number and the name Fletcher without query, and then went on: 'Would you like to go out for a drive with me this morning? Just to show there's no ill-feeling?'

She smiled. 'I'd be glad to.'

'I'll call for you at eleven. Okay?'

'That's fine, thanks. Goodbye.'

As soon as he had rung off, the idea flashed suddenly into her mind that she ought to check that the kitten's body was still there. She pushed open the music room door and groped for the chair. Its smooth fabric met her touch, but the seat was empty. Nonetheless, she decided, she would speak to the vet.

'Well, from the condition of the body as you describe it I would certainly suspect poisoning.' Mr Fletcher's voice said cautiously in reply to her query, 'although of course without actually inspecting the body it would be impossible to say for certain.'

'I understand. Thank you all the same, Mr Fletcher.'

That done, Pippa made another call, this time to the operator. Two minutes later she had sent her cable to the clinic where Alexis Korvak lay ill. The receiver was still in her hand when the door opened and Mrs Purvis entered. Pippa recognised her quick, light step.

'Telephoning someone, Philippa?'

Pippa was flustered. 'Geoff Walters has invited me to go out for a drive with him this morning,' she said hastily.

'Do you good to go out for a change,' the housekeeper remarked. Pippa wondered why she made no objection, when not so long ago she was warning Pippa not to encourage his friendship. Curious.

'My kitten is dead, Mrs Purvis. I think he was poisoned.'
It took an effort to say it so coolly, and for a fraction of a second she could hear the housekeeper's silence, as though searching for a reply.

'Dead, my dear? How do you know? He went missing yesterday, strayed again, no doubt.'

'He was dead in the music room last night, all stiff and stretched out. I found him there.'

'Indeed? I know nothing of that — why didn't you tell me? I'll go and see.'

'It's no use because he's gone now. Did you move his body?'

There was silence for several seconds before Mrs Purvis spoke again. 'Gone, you say? Are you sure he was ever there? You know how you've been lately, Philippa, imagining all manner of things. Are you sure it's not just your concern for him that made you imagine it?'

'*Imagine.* That's all you ever say, Mrs Purvis! No, I did not imagine such a terrible thing, and I'm not ill. Why do you persist in trying to make me think I am? What have you got against me, Mrs Purvis? I want to know!'

'Oh, my dear child, you really are overwrought,' the housekeeper murmured in a maddeningly soft voice. 'I have nothing against you, you poor thing, and I never have had. But you really are ill, whether you believe it or not, when you say such things. And if the creature really is dead, you apparently imply that I had something to do with it. What nonsense! You prove my point, Philippa — you are ill and have no hope of a cure until you stop having all these silly paranoid ideas. I'll ask the doctor to come and see you. Perhaps he'll prescribe a sedative that will help.'

Infuriated, and knowing it would be useless to argue, Pippa turned, wishing madly that she could race up the stairs instead of being obliged to grope her way ignominiously. Her hand on the balustrade, she had a sudden change of heart. Anger and flight were useless. She must not let the housekeeper continue to treat her as a child; instead, she must challenge the woman's cold air of superiority. She turned slowly.

'Mrs Purvis, have you had breakfast? I haven't, and I fancy I'd like some bacon and egg today. I'll cook it myself

155

— shall I cook some for you too?'

She was already heading towards the kitchen as Mrs Purvis answered. 'Thanks, no, I've eaten. But I'll get the bacon and pan for you.' Pippa's ear could detect the tone of mild surprise in her voice.

It was not easy, although Mrs Purvis fetched all the materials she needed to fry the bacon and egg. Firmly she refused the housekeeper's offer to take over, but it was not pleasant trying to chase elusive bacon around the pan or to gauge when the egg was done. The fat spat every now and again, and she could sense that the housekeeper was keeping a wary eye on her. No doubt she feared the fat might catch fire.

'I've got to learn to do things for myself,' Pippa muttered defensively, but when at last the bacon and egg had been persuaded to leave the pan to sit on her plate, the resulting greasy bacon and half-raw egg made it clear she needed a lot more practice. Still, she told herself grimly, it might be necessary to fend for herself in the dark permanently. Sooner or later she had to begin to learn.

'I'm glad you seem so much calmer,' Mrs Purvis remarked as she poured tea. 'You had me worried when you flared up like that.'

'I was upset about the kitten,' Pippa replied levelly. 'Poisoning is a cruel fate. It was just my feelings showing, that's all.'

'Yes,' the housekeeper murmured, 'we would all welcome the opportunity to give vent to our feelings sometimes, but the years teach us it is often wiser to learn how to hide them.'

Pippa looked up, across at where she imagined Mrs Purvis's face to be. She was curious about her remark but before she could ask her what she meant, Mrs Purvis spoke again.

'You're looking at my neck, Philippa. I know you can't see, but it's most disconcerting. I feel as though I have a dirty neck or something. Look up a little higher.' Pippa did so. 'That's better. Now you appear to be looking at me directly. It's something you'll have to practice so as not to draw attention to your disability. Odd how blind people always look down.'

156

Her tone was polite but her words hurt. Blind was a bare, brutal word, but what she said was true. One's instinct was to look down, as though watching warily for steps one could no longer see. Even seated and reasonably safe, one's eyes only rose half-way to the normal direct line ahead. Pippa reflected. Actors in films, supposedly blind, almost always stared up over their companion's head or looked as if they were inspecting the roofs of houses across the road. How false that was, she now realised, and then she recalled the frank gaze of the blind man on the train. He had stared fixedly at the direction of her belt, though his expression had been mobile. Practice, much practice would be needed, she thought sadly.

She was ready when Geoff Walters's car pulled up in the drive promptly at eleven o'clock. She opened the front door and called out a greeting, then heard his feet crunch on the gravel.

'Mind the steps,' he warned and taking her hand, he counted them slowly as her toe felt for each in turn. 'That's right. Hop in.'

The car sped smoothly down the drive. 'Any preference for where you'd like to go, Philippa? Reading or Maiden-head? Henley?'

Pippa suddenly remembered the letter from her father's lawyers. 'Can you take me first to a solicitor in Marlow, Geoff? I've got some business to see to.'

'Okay. I'll take you to mine.' He asked no questions, for which she was grateful. She was grateful too for the smooth way he persuaded the receptionist to allow Pippa to see Mr Hobbs there and then, without an appointment. Walters took her by the arm and led her into the solicitor's office, then murmured, 'I'll wait for you at reception.'

Pippa handed over the letter and explained. Mr Hobbs read it in silence, then agreed to handle the matter, and made a note of Pippa's name and address. If he knew the name Korvak he made no comment.

'There's just one thing I should add,' Pippa said as she rose to go. 'I'm afraid I can't see. I'd be obliged if you would ring me rather than write if the need arises.'

'To be sure I will.' Suddenly he was by her side, his hand

157

on her elbow, and a moment later she was back with Walters. She felt a warm glow. People could be so kindly and unobtrusively helpful.

As she came out of the solicitor's office with Walters, she felt the sun's rays on her face. Walters sighed. 'Heavens, it's hot. Shall we head for the river somewhere? Maidenhead is very pretty at this time — ' He broke off suddenly. Pippa realised he was embarrassed at his clumsiness.

'Please,' she said quietly, 'don't worry. If you keep trying to pick your words with care you won't be able to speak at all. I'd much rather you spoke naturally, as you would to anyone else.'

'I'm sorry. You're right,' he muttered.

She thought again of the blind man on the train. He had said something about handicapped people wanting and needing to be treated like normal people, and here was an instance of it. But at the same time she was aware of being jostled by passers-by who, unaware of her predicament, expected her to give way a little on Marlow's narrow pavements. Walters did his best, guiding her by the arm, but the pathway was barely wide enough for two.

As Walters unlocked the car, Pippa raised her head and sniffed. The heavy, sickly scent of brewing beer filled the hot, narrow street. Walters must have noticed her expression.

'That's the brewery just behind the shops,' he remarked. 'Powerful today, isn't it?'

There was another scent too, equally strong and more attractive. It was the delicious aroma of newly-baked bread. Pippa commented on it.

'That's the bakery along at the end of the high street,' Walters told her.

'I remember, at the corner where we turn off to Cambermere.'

'That's right, then turn right again at the pub.'

Pippa had a sudden idea. 'Geoff, would you mind very much if I asked you to leave me here? I have a sudden urge to try to find my way home alone. I'm sure I can do it. Would you mind?'

She was gazing eagerly at him, at where she believed him to be by the car. She heard his deep, contemplative sigh.

'Philippa, I can understand you wanting to fight back, to accept a challenge,' he said slowly, 'but are you sure this is the best way to start? There are roads to cross and you haven't even a white stick.'

'I've got my sunglasses in my pocket,' Pippa countered. 'I'll put those on. Oh, let me try, Geoff, please. It's the first time I've felt willing to try. You carry on, and let me do it alone, please. It's only half a mile or so.'

Walters was reluctant. He offered to follow and watch her, but Pippa refused. As she set off along the hot pavement she felt excited and only the least bit afraid. Around the corner she would have to cross the road but there was a pedestrian crossing outside the supermarket — it would not be too difficult.

She moved slowly and with great caution, and now passers-by seemed to recognise there was a difficulty and let her pass. When she reached the bakery the succulent smell of fresh bread was overpowering. Only a building society to pass now and the corner would be there.

She felt foolish running her fingers along the rough brick of the wall to discover the angle of the corner. But so long as one did not mind appearing foolish, independence would not be so hard to attain. The next problem was to judge how far to walk before trying to find the post which would indicate the pedestrian crossing.

She was lucky. Ahead of her she could hear a young woman's voice admonishing a child.

'Richard, hold on to the pram like I told you. We've got to cross here to go and get our shopping for tea. Hold on tight now. Wait till this car has gone.'

Pippa stood behind the voice and waited until she heard the pram wheels thud down on to the road. Then she followed. At the far side her ears again told her the pram was mounting a step. Judgement was needed to guess the distance to that step, but once on the pavement Pippa felt elated. She had crossed a busy road alone, unaided, with not even a stick to help.

She used her nose to discover the pub at the next turning. That was easy. The pub was open and laughing voices were coming out as she passed, and the open door emitted a powerful smell of beer and tobacco smoke. Beyond the pub, on this quieter road, the pavement became uneven and the scent gave way to petrol fumes. Of course, she remembered now, there was a garage on the far side of the road with a row of petrol pumps. The smell gave her an instant mental picture of the road. The lane up to Cambermere was not far now.

She discovered the lane by walking into an obstruction on the pathway. Rubbing a bruised knee, she explored the object with her hands. It was the post box on the corner of the lane. She turned up the lane with a growing feeling of achievement, and as she went she heard the faint purr of a car engine fading behind her. Curious, she had not heard it appoach. Then she smiled. She guessed Geoff Walters had been following her at a discreet distance after all, and now that the worst part of the journey was over, he had left her to it. Funny, she thought, only a few days ago she had believed him a threat to her, and she smiled to recall her terror in the labyrinth. Out here, in the warm sunlight, one could afford to laugh at one's foolish terrors in the dark.

She was still in the dark, in a sense, but climbing the last stretch of the lane towards the Hall she felt a quiet glow of triumph. She was not yet ready to accept blindness as a permanent state of affairs but as a temporary handicap she knew she could cope with it. It would have been easier with Stephen's encouragement, but there was gratification and pride in knowing she could do it alone.

Stephen. She wondered whether she kept penetrating his thoughts the way he constantly recurred in hers. She walked carefully along the edge of the grass verge, thankful there was no traffic, until the curve of the grass edge indicated the entrance to Cambermere Hall.

A tall stone pillar beneath her fingertips confirmed the gateway, and the crunch of gravel beneath her sandals kept her in the right direction. It was important to follow the snaking line of the drive with care and not wander off over the lawns, or she could end up in the lake. The sweet scents of wild flowers in the hedgerows gave way now to a drift of woodsmoke. It was the gardener, no doubt, making a bonfire of the hedge clippings. The drive seemed to go on endlessly, far longer than she remembered. Odd how one's sense of time and distance was distorted in the dark.

At last the drive curved sharply left to where the front steps mounted to the terrace. Pippa, remembering she had no key with her, decided to go round to the kitchen door rather than make Mrs Purvis answer the bell. She found the kitchen door at last, half-covered by the ivy on the walls. It was open, and there was no answer to her call of 'Hello' when she went in.

She crossed the kitchen and made her way out into the vestibule. She was about to call again, when her ear caught the sound of voices coming from the direction of the music room. Feeling her way cautiously around the marble pillars Pippa approached the door.

'I'm glad you came all the same,' she clearly heard Mrs Purvis's voice say. Her fingers told her the door was closed, and she hesitated. 'I must confess I've been worried about her. Not the accident so much — she seems to be coping with that very well — but her behaviour is decidedly odd.'

Pippa flushed. The housekeeper was evidently talking about her — but to whom? Hope leapt in her — could it be Stephen?

'Odd? In what way?'

Hope died again. It was a masculine voice but not Stephen's low-pitched, resonant tone. It was the higher pitch of an elderly man.

'Well, she seems convinced that someone is out to harm her, strange as it may seem. She thinks someone tried to trip her into the swimming pool and then burn her with a sunlamp — really, doctor, there's no end to what she's determined to believe. Why, I'll bet she even thinks the fall from the horse was no accident.'

'I see. That is rather unusual, I must admit. There really is no reason for such beliefs, you think?'

'Oh, I'm certain there's no foundation! Philippa has always been rather strange and secretive, but lately it seems to have become far more pronounced. Like yesterday, for instance — a stray cat appeared here and later it went. Philippa would have it that the creature had been poisoned on purpose to upset her! Really, doctor, I am beginning to become very worried over her, especially when one remembers her mother's last illness.'

'Ah yes — Miss Hope. Not my patient, but I recall the case-history. Paranoia and nervous debility, wasn't it? Yes, I can understand your concern and thank you for talking to me about it. As I was Mr Korvak's doctor while he was here, perhaps Miss Korvak will agree to see me. Would you ask her to arrange a convenient time for me to call again?'

'Of course, Dr Ramsay. She has been getting me very alarmed and it's a relief to talk to you about it. I mean, all this imagining there's someone in her room at night and even thinking she saw her mother's ghost in the garden. And talking to this imaginary friend of hers . . .'

'Dear me, yes, I must see the young lady as soon as possible and see what we can do for her. In the meantime, don't worry, Mrs Purvis. I'll make arrangements for a social worker to call.'

Pippa stood there, stunned. Her first impulse was to cry out, to deny Mrs Purvis's accusation. But it was quickly replaced by fear. What Mrs Purvis had relayed was true, but the way she told it made Pippa sound crazy — and a furious outburst on her part would only confirm that view.

Pippa backed away from the music room as the doctor and Mrs Purvis came out. She felt for another door. As she opened it and hurried in, she realised it was the door to the east wing. Evidently Mrs Purvis no longer considered it necessary to keep it locked.

The voices in the vestibule faded away and Pippa heard the hum of a car engine. She emerged and called, but Mrs Purvis did not answer. She headed for the kitchen, and still Mrs Purvis did not answer. She must have gone out when the doctor left. Anger simmered in Pippa. She must indeed meet Dr Ramsay and endeavour to set him straight, but in her own time. He must be made to see that she was rational, not warped in any way, and that strange things really did happen here in Cambermere Hall.

It was in the vestibule that the frisson of fear tingled in her spine, the certain knowledge that she was being watched, just as once before when Mrs Purvis had stood watching from the head of the stairs. Pippa looked up.

'Who's there? Mrs Purvis?'

No sound disturbed the late afternoon stillness but the

162

song of birds in the garden. Pippa walked firmly to the bottom step. 'I know you're there. *Who are you?*'

Again, no answer, but seconds later Pippa could almost swear she heard a distant door close somewhere in the upper regions of the house. Pursuit was useless. At that moment the doorbell rang and Pippa hurried to the front door.

'Miss Korvak, Uncle Geoff sent me with these for you, and he told me to say congratulations.'

She recognised Robin Walters' clear young voice and felt the brush of foliage against her hand. He was offering her flowers. She took them and stood back to let him enter.

'Come in, Robin, and thank you. They're lovely.'

'How do you know? Uncle Geoff says you can't see. That's why he sent the flowers.'

'I know because I can smell them. There are carnations, aren't there, and roses?'

'That's right.' There was admiration in the boy's tone. 'We picked them in the garden because the ones in the shop are too expensive.' She could not resist a smile at his innocent candour. 'I took all the thorns off the roses so you wouldn't prick yourself,' he added.

'That was very thoughtful of you,' she replied gravely. 'Will you come and help me find a vase so we can put them in water?' She led the way to the kitchen, conscious of his curious gaze, and set the flowers down on the table.

'Tell you what,' she said brightly, 'we'll have a look in all these cupboards to find a vase — I'm sure there'll be one somewhere. And while we're looking, perhaps we can find some glasses so we can have a drink of orange juice. Okay?'

'Oh, yes,' he said eagerly, and she heard the cupboard doors open and close as he scrabbled in search. At last she heard a clink.

'Here are the glasses,' he said. 'I'll find the vase in a minute. That's a funny place to put a letter.'

'A letter?' she repeated. 'What letter?'

'This one here. It's not even been opened.'

'Whose name is on it?'

'Miss P. Korvak. That's you. Had you forgotten about it? Waiting for someone to read it for you?'

She recovered her wits quickly. It was not a letter from

163

Clive — that was upstairs and it had been opened. This must have been intercepted and held by Mrs Purvis. It could be from . . . She bent to the boy eagerly.

'Yes, that's it. I was waiting for someone to read it. Would you do that for me, Robin? Tell me the postmark first.'

'London. Seven-thirty p.m. Dated the fourth.'

That was last week, soon after Stephen had gone. 'Open it, then, Robin.'

She heard him tear it open and felt her heart thud in hope. London — it must be Stephen. Robin drew a deep breath and read:

' *"Dear Pippa, You meant what you said and so did I. But I hate to recall the angry words of parting and can't bear to think the cord is snapped forever. You must know why I have to go on. The enclosed may help to explain. If, after reading it, little pipistrelle, you feel you want to contact me, I shall be at the hotel until the tenth. If I do not hear from you, I shall know you truly meant what you said. Take care. Yours, Stephen."* '

Robin stopped. 'I'm not sure if I said that word pipistrelle properly,' he said thoughtfully.

'You did. You read beautifully,' Pippa said absently. *'Meant what you said,'* Stephen had written. That was about never wanting to set eyes on him again — she must ring the hotel and tell him she spoke in haste, in anger.

'There's a newspaper cutting here too,' Robin said. 'Shall I read that to you as well?'

'What is it about, Robin?'

'It's very old and yellow. It's from an American newspaper dated 1953. The headline says: "MORE DENUNCIATIONS IN McCARTHY TRIALS." '

Pippa was puzzled. Why should Stephen send a cutting of a rather unpleasant American episode of thirty years ago? There must be a reason. 'Yes, please Robin.'

' *"Yesterday further denunciations were made by Senator Joseph McCarthy's powerful Permanent Sub-Committee on Investigations of un-American activities.*

164

Those accused of Communist leanings included several well-known film actors and actresses, and the eminent physicist J.R. Oppenheimer, who directed the A-bomb project.

"Public interest was particularly aroused by the arraignment of Jan Loran, Loran . . ." '

Robin paused. 'I can't say it. Too many s's and z's. Somebody has underlined it and written the word "Father" in the margin.'

'Call it Lorant,' said Pippa. 'Go on.'

' *"Jan Lorant is not himself well-known — he is a technical operative in the Shearing film studio — but the fact that he was denounced by Alexis Korvak has stirred considerable interest. Both Korvak and Lorant are of Hungarian origin and were known to be close friends at one time. Someone close to Lorant claims that his denunciation was an act of vengeance on Korvak's part, in retaliation for an affair between Lorant and Korvak's beautiful wife, the actress Carrie Hope. Neither Korvak nor Lorant will confirm or deny the story." '*

Robin paused. 'That's it, Miss Korvak. There's another cutting too, dated 1955.'

'Call me Pippa, Robin. Read that too, will you?'

'It's a shorter one. It says:

' *"Jan Loran — Lorant died, suddenly yesterday at his home in Los Angeles. His widow, Helen Lorant, told our reporter that she would never forgive Alexis Korvak, the film-producer, for bringing about her husband's death. It may be remembered that Korvak denounced Lorant in the McCarthy trials some time ago, and Mrs Lorant claims that Korvak's persecution led to her husband's excessive drinking, his loss of position in the film studio and his subsequent decline in health. Besides his widow, Lorant leaves one son, Stefan." '*

'That's the end, Pippa.'

'Thank you, Robin. Here's your orange juice.'

As he drank thirstily Pippa thought of Stephen. He was right, she could see it now. His mother's determination to avenge her persecuted husband was a strong enough motive for Stephen to want to expose her father. But was Father really so ruthless? Had Mother really taken Jan Lorant as her lover? If so, Father too was to be understood, if not pitied. But it was cruel that passions so long dead could influence the present and drive her and Stephen apart. It was more than cruel — it was wrong, and she would not let it happen. She must get in touch with Stephen at once. When did he say he was leaving London? The tenth? Heavens! That was today! She might be too late!

'Robin, on the letter, is there a telephone number after the name of the hotel?'

'Yes, here it is.'

'Come into the hall with me and dial it for me, will you? Then you can have some more juice.'

Obediently he followed her out and dialled the number. Pippa took the receiver from him.

'The Argosy hotel? Is Mr Stephen Lorant there, please?'

There was a pause before a dispassionate voice replied. 'I'm sorry. Mr Lorant checked out this morning.'

'Oh.' Disappointment thudded like lead in her stomach. 'Do you have a forwarding address or a telephone number?'

'I'm sorry, madam. Mr Lorant left no instructions to that effect. We cannot help you, I'm afraid.'

She hung up dispiritedly. He had given her a chance to make peace and she had failed. Now he would believe she wanted no more to do with him. And she had failed because someone had hidden the letter — and that someone must have been Mrs Purvis. But why?

Obviously she must want to prevent Pippa and Stephen from continuing their relationship — out of jealousy, perhaps? Or did she know about Jan Lorant and her beloved Carrie all those years ago? And if so, why should that colour her attitude to Pippa and Stephen now?

Did she know and connive at that old affair, or did she hate Jan Lorant for it and so wish to prevent a relationship between his son and Carrie's child? The thought crossed Pippa's mind that Jan could almost have been her own father, but for the fact that she was not born until after his death. If she *had* been his child, it might help to explain the housekeeper's attitude and even some of the strange happenings. Silly, thought Pippa, pushing the thought from her mind. All this wild speculation in the light of what the cuttings revealed was making her imagination work over-time again.

'I'll have to go home now, Pippa. It's nearly time for tea and I have to help Uncle Geoff to peel the vegetables and things.'

'Of course, Robin, and tell him I'm very grateful for the flowers. And thank you too for your help.'

'I like helping you. I put your flowers in the vase while you were on the telephone. They're on the kitchen table.'

'Thanks, every time I go in there and smell them I shall think of you. It'll remind me how glad I am of your friend-ship.'

She could have hugged his small frame, but instead she contented herself with ruffling his hair as they walked to the front door. Peel the vegetables, he had said. There was not enough money in the Walters household to afford domestic help, evidently. She wished she could assure the child that he would not always be poor, that one day, after Father's death, he would be a rich man in his own right.

'Flowers from your own garden mean far more to me than flowers from a shop, Robin,' she said impulsively. 'And one day you will reap your reward, I promise. You'll never want for anything, and especially not love.'

'Bye, Pippa.'

He was gone, his feet crunching rapidly down the drive in a hurry to return home. He was a delightful child, a source of much comfort to Geoff Walters, she was sure.

Before Mrs Purvis returned, Pippa had time to think. The McCarthy witch hunt of the 'fifties was something she had only read about in books. The senator's manic pursuit of all those he suspected of Communist sympathies at the height of America's cold war with Russia — intellectuals, writers, actors, scientists — had led to many of his victims losing their careers, even after they had been cleared. Stephen's father had evidently suffered and the family's hatred for the

167

man who had denounced him unjustly was understandable.
Had Father hated Lorant that much? And hated Mother
too, for betraying him? He must have forgiven her, for
Pippa was born later. Or had Father sought consolation in
mistresses of his own? Pippa thought of Nina Walters, and
the child Robin.

It was a curious coincidence that Mrs Purvis's conversation over dinner turned to the subject of Alexis Korvak's
illness and his disappointments.

'He always wanted a son, you know, Philippa. It was a
grudge of his that Miss Carrie never bore him a son.'

Although she could not see, Pippa could feel the housekeeper's bright eyes boring into her. Firmly Pippa kept her
lips shut.

12

Pippa lay in bed wondering just how much Mrs Purvis knew
about the past, and its effect on the present. Did she know
that Stephen was the son of her cherished Miss Carrie's
lover? The name Lorant bore some resemblance to the
original Hungarian spelling Jan had used. And if Stephen
looked like his father, Mrs Purvis had probably recognised
him long ago. She must have known about Jan and Mother.
Pippa could imagine the thin-lipped housekeeper moving
heaven and earth to contrive secret rendezvous for her
beloved mistress and her lover.

Strange, thought Pippa. If she had smiled on Jan Lorant
all those years ago she certainly did not grant his son the
same favour. In fact she had behaved very coolly towards
him, apparently only receiving him on her employer's
orders. Pippa had a sudden recollection of the openly
hostile glare she had darted in Stephen's direction the night

168

Pippa and he had challenged her over the missing letter. Yes, Pippa remembered, she was lying then, denying the letter's existence when all the time it lay in the kitchen drawer.

Just as Stephen's letter lay there, unopened, until today. It would appear that once again the housekeeper was interfering with Pippa's mail — but why? What had she to gain by keeping back a message from Stephen? Why should she attempt to keep them apart? What had she to gain by alienating Pippa who, before long, might well become her mistress? And then only today she had been trying hard to convince the local doctor that Pippa was mentally unbalanced. It just did not make sense. And added to that, she had seemed to derive malicious pleasure from telling Pippa that her mother had not loved her but the other child, Irma, the one she had been forced to give up. Thank God Stephen had made Pippa read Mother's diary, which proved beyond doubt that she did love her younger child. Stephen had found that diary in a packing case in the east wing, the wing Mrs Purvis had tried to prevent Pippa from entering. The reason for that at least was clear — to prevent Pippa from reading of her mother's love for her.

Mrs Purvis must hate Pippa deeply to want to hurt her so, Pippa reflected. Was it because she really hated Alexis Korvak for his cruel treatment of Miss Carrie, and in his absence the hatred was diverted to his daughter? That was feasible. The housekeeper herself had reasoned that the local villagers would dislike Pippa simply because she was her father's daughter.

Well, then, if one accepted that reason, was the next step that the housekeeper should attempt to harm her? Pippa thought back over the now lengthy list of mishaps — the overheated shower, the oil on the pool steps, the ultraviolet lamp, the burr under Copper's saddle, and the agonising death of the little cat. Mrs Purvis had been around and could have made some of these furtive attempts on her life, but not all — and certainly not the thistle burr. That, Pippa decided, must be pure coincidence. The burr must have been accidentally transferred from a horse blanket to the horse's back and somehow overlooked when he was saddled. Since no one, not even she herself, had known she was going to ride Copper that day, no one could have planned that way of harming her. Mrs Purvis was certainly not to blame for that, reflected Pippa. Nor, surely, for any of the other mishaps. Then who could it be?

It was a double mystery to solve — both the identity of her attacker and the reason for Mrs Purvis's evident hatred. The latter, Pippa felt sure, was due to Father's behaviour over the years. It was sad to admit that he was less than the perfect gentleman she had always believed him, but in recent weeks a very different picture of him had emerged. Stephen had reason to speak so strongly of his hardness, his ruthlessness. Father had exploited his wife's charms, spurned her for many mistresses, and then punished her for her infidelity by ruining her lover's career and indirectly causing his death. That was why Stephen had called him a murderer. And he had raped Nina Walters and cheated Bainbridge. The truth, ugly though it was, had to be faced and admitted. Father was far less than perfect, but he was a dying man.

Pippa was grief-stricken. It seemed such a futile way to die, of alcoholism, just as Jan Lorant had been doomed to die. She was glad Father found comfort in knowing about Robin — the son he always wanted. But her heart was heavy. With Father so ill, Stephen gone perhaps for ever, and Mrs Purvis obviously resenting her so bitterly that she wanted to brand her a neurotic, the world was a dark place. She was alone, with no one to whom she could turn. Lying there in bed in what was once Mother's room, Pippa began to feel apprehensive. With night and blackness all around, she felt as though she were marooned on a tiny island in a sea of limitless gloom. She had a strange sensation of being completely disorientated, disembodied almost, and the atmosphere of Cambermere Hall cloaked her in claustrophobic silence.

That scent: it was there again, faint at first to the nostril but growing in intensity every second. Pippa lay still, tense and fearful. If someone was there in the room, they moved in catlike silence. Not a sound reached her straining ear except the whisper of the trees in the grounds. The sweet fragrance of Californian Poppy forced its way into her lungs, nauseous and powerful. She could bear it no more and sat upright in bed.

'Who's that? Is that you, Mrs Purvis?'

No answer came, and somehow she had expected none. No one had opened the door and there was no movement in the room, only that insidious scent growing now so powerful that it made her feel sick. And more than that, frightened, for if that perfume was being spread by no human hand, then it must be supernatural . . .

'Mother?' she ventured softly, half-afraid and half-annoyed with herself. 'Mother?'

There was the tiniest sound, a flutter which could be the echo of a laugh or the brush of curtains against the window sill in the breeze, then the perfume began to fade. In a few moments it had gone, only the least suspicion of it still lingering in the cool night air. Pippa lay still and sleepless, wondering fearfully whether she had imagined the menacing potency of the scent and that mocking, lilting laugh, or whether the housekeeper's suspicions regarding her sanity were indeed well-founded.

She must have slept well after all, for she awoke at last to the sound of china clattering on a tray and the dull, insistent patter of rain against the window. Whether it was Marion or the housekeeper bringing the tray Pippa could not be sure until, with a swish of curtains, Mrs Purvis spoke.

'It's a perfectly dreadful morning, Philippa. Raining cats and dogs. Not a day for going out at all. Did you sleep well?'

The question was posed in her normal cool and detached manner, but Pippa felt herself draw back, on guard. Whatever she told the housekeeper, she seemed to be able to use the information against her. She answered warily, 'Quite well, thanks. Did you?'

'Indeed, yes. I must have been exhausted, I think, for as soon as my head touched the pillow I went out like a light. As a result I'm all fresh and prepared for today's routine.' She sounded just as she used to in nursery days. 'Early to bed, early to rise, makes a girl healthy, wealthy and wise,' she would say, always in the admonishing tone of a governess. But, it struck Pippa, she was being more than usually chatty this morning. Was she trying to discover something?

171

'You were tired last night, then?' Pippa asked. 'Had you been extra-busy yesterday?'

'Oh, no more than usual, though it takes some effort to run a house this size. No, I think it's just the pure country air down here after the fumes of the city. It makes one sleep well.'

She poured out tea. Pippa could hear the gurgle and smell the refreshing aroma even before she handed her the cup. Then she still hovered in the room, as though curious. Pippa made a sudden decision. One thing she had learnt from this wretched blindness was that it sharpened the ears — failure of one sense seemed to heighten the perception of the others. She found it easier now to read people's intentions, their meanings, not so much in what they said but in the way they said it. Falseness or sincerity, decision or hesitation were far clearer. And added to that, a new kind of intuition came into play. Once she had watched a person's facial expression as they spoke to try to gauge their true intention, but now the voice revealed far more.

'Tell me, Mrs Purvis, I know how attached you were to my mother. You were with her before she married Father, weren't you?'

'Oh, yes, long before.' Already the housekeeper's voice had lost its sharp edge and softened with affection.

'Then you remember the days before she was a star. Did fame change her?'

'Not fame, nor wealth, nor adulation nor anything else. However sordid the world became she remained true to herself.' The voice was almost reverential now, the subdued tones of a tourist in a cathedral.

'Even in the dreadful days of the McCarthy witch hunt? Many famous film people lost their reputation and their jobs then, I understand. But a slur was never cast on her?'

'Good gracious, no! She never dabbled in politics. Others around her were tainted, but never my Miss Carrie! People like John Garfield were driven out of the studios, Joseph Losey the producer went into exile in Europe — many did fade into obscurity, but there was never a whiff of scandal about her.'

The indignation in the housekeeper's voice was threaded with a hint of anger, as though she was reluctant to expand on this theme. Pippa could guess why. Hints of scandal might be attached to Carrie Hope's name because of her affair with another man, who had been denounced as a Communist by his former friend. It was evidently an incident in her idol's life that Mrs Purvis would prefer to forget.

'I heard some of those discredited people were in despair afterwards,' Pippa went on as she sipped her tea. 'Driven to drink, some of them, and even suicide, I'm told.'

'I don't know about that,' the housekeeper said snappishly. 'Garfield certainly died young from alcoholism but I heard of no suicides. That's a morbid subject, Philippa. Don't let a miserable day like this throw you into a depressed mood. It's not healthy. What will you have for breakfast?'

Ignoring her question, Pippa challenged her. 'That's one advantage in my position, Mrs Purvis. Not being able to see the state of the weather I am hardly likely to be influenced by it. Only the sighted feel gloomy on a grey day.'

There was a pause for a moment, a silence in which the housekeeper's displeasure was evident. Pippa felt a small glow of achievement. For the first time in her life she had contested the older woman's unspoken domination, and the housekeeper seemed to be aware of her power slipping rapidly away.

'Will you have boiled eggs? Or bacon?' she asked quietly.

'Both, please,' Pippa replied calmly.

It was only after Mrs Purvis had gone downstairs that Pippa had time to consider whether she had been a little reckless. If the woman had been determined to have her classified insane and perhaps put away, she would be even more determined and more cunning, now battle had been openly declared. Her motive was still not clear, but her intention was.

Mrs Purvis denied that she had sprayed Californian Poppy in Pippa's room before, but Pippa suspected she had lingered in the bedroom this morning, slightly more affable than usual, waiting for Pippa to tell her that she had been almost overpowered by the choking perfume again. Then she could relay that information to Dr Ramsay as yet another sympton of Pippa's paranoid condition. 'Why, Philippa actually believes her mother's ghost returns to her,' she could almost hear the housekeeper tell him, 'to warn her that harm is about to befall her.'

No, thought Pippa firmly as she set the cup aside and got up out of bed, I shall not give her that satisfaction. Whatever happens now I must stay cool and in control and above all, not tell Mrs Purvis what thoughts are in my head. She had completely forgotten to tax the housekeeper about Stephen's letter being hidden in the kitchen, but on reflection she decided not to mention that either. Mrs Purvis must be curious to know where the letter had gone.

Stephen — if only he were here, the darkness would be so much more bearable! In his letter he had even called her pipistrelle, little blind bat — how ironic, in the circumstances. Stop that, Pippa told herself fiercely. You must shut him out of your mind, as you did Clive. You must not think of him again. He hated the name Korvak, and he was gone for ever. Forget him.

Yes, she could do it. Even if he telephoned now, she would not talk to him — would she? Uncertainty hovered. She might, just briefly, to clear up one or two things, but that was all, just to say she now understood the force that drove him on even if she could not condone it, that she would do the same in his shoes . . . But, that done, she would let him go.

It was the following day Pippa decided to test her position with Mrs Purvis further. In the meantime the housekeeper had remained distant but polite, not exactly subservient but certainly less positive than she used to be. If Pippa was to establish her new-found independence she must assert herself.

'That east wing,' she remarked casually as she helped the housekeeper fold the washing she had just brought in from the garden, 'the disused wing, I found that quite interesting.' She made no reference to the key and how difficult it had been to lay hands on it. Mrs Purvis made no answer. 'I should like to have another look around there. Will you come with me and tell me about the sets I have not seen?'

The housekeeper drew a deep breath. 'I am surprised it

interests you, Philippa, but for my part I do not care for it much. Apart from being busy, I would prefer not to go in there. Would you mind very much exploring on your own?'

That was progress. Instead of condemning the proposal and forbidding Pippa to go, she was actually excusing herself and allowing Pippa to go by herself.

'Very well,' she conceded. 'Then at least tell me what sets there are. I've seen a steamboat set, a Victorian drawing room and what seemed to be a sultan's palace.'

'Apart from those, there's only a medieval banqueting hall and a dungeon,' Mrs Purvis said coolly.

'Ah yes, I saw the dungeon. Then there's only the great hall left,' Pippa remarked. 'I can visualise that — straw-strewn floor, trestle tables, high slit windows and perhaps a minstrels' gallery.'

'That's right. Now, shall we take the laundry upstairs?' The housekeeper's tone had taken on an abrupt edge again. Pippa was curious.

'It all seems rather odd to me, either nostalgic or just plain egocentric, maintaining those sets for all these years. It seems almost like a mausoleum.' She was following the housekeeper up the stairs, one arm laden with linen and the other hand following the bannister. 'Downright unhealthy, in fact. Those sets ought to be stripped and the house brought back into use again. Rooms should be filled with living people, not become shrines to the past.'

'Not while your father lives.' The housekeeper's quiet voice drifted back down the stairs. Pippa caught her breath, angry with herself at her clumsiness. With Father so desperately ill it did indeed sound as though she were anticipating her inheritance already. It was not only stupid of her, but sounded callous too. Mrs Purvis had won that round in the battle.

In the afternoon the housekeeper declared that she was not going to stay indoors on such a glorious day but would take a pair of secateurs and go out in the garden. Some of the rose bushes could do with having dead blooms cut off, she said, and without inviting Pippa to join her she went out. She was probably glad to be free of her company. Pippa was debating what to do when she heard footsteps on the gravel outside and then the doorbell rang.

'Hello, Pippa,' said Robin's cheerful young voice. 'Can I read for you or something?'

Pippa's heart warmed. 'Thank you, Robin, no. Not reading, but you can take me for a stroll round the grounds if you like and see I don't fall into the lake.'

She loved the way his small, firm hand took hold of hers and guided her along the path below the terrace. Sunlight fell like a blessing on her upturned face. It was good to be alive, despite everything.

'Have you had a visitor today?' Robin asked. Pippa shook her head.

'No. What makes you ask?'

'Oh, I saw a lady by the gate. She asked me my name. And she asked if I knew you.'

'A lady?' Pippa was puzzled. She knew no woman except Mrs Purvis in Cambermere. 'What was she like?'

'Oh, quite pretty, really. She had lovely hair, all curly and shining in the sun, like our dog Rusty.'

A canvasser, perhaps, sounding out the lie of the land, Pippa guessed. 'Did she ask about me by name, Robin?'

'She said did I know Miss Korvak, that's all. I said yes. Then she went away.'

Curious, but not important. Most of the locals would know by now that she was Korvak's daughter. Robin let go of her hand, and she knew he was bending down. Then she heard him grunt with effort. A distant plop told her what he was doing: he was throwing gravel into the lake. She smiled. Such a simple action, and yet it rolled back the years for her. She could still recall skimming stones across the surface of the pool in the gardens of their Kent home, and Mrs Purvis jerking her arm and telling her to stop. Conduct unbecoming to a young lady, she had said. On an impulse Pippa bent and picked up a handful of gravel and began throwing pieces in the direction Robin seemed to be throwing.

'Further left, and throw harder!' he exclaimed, pleasure gleaming in his young voice. Obediently she changed direction and length and was rewarded with a gratifying plop. Robin cheered. 'Well done! That was clever, Pippa.'

After a while they moved on, around the house and across the lawns towards the woods. Robin was recounting

176

how Uncle Geoff could throw a ball the length of a cricket pitch and knock down the middle stump at least twice out of every three goes, and Pippa derived great pleasure from his evident adoration of his uncle. Father would have revelled in this son if only he had known.

They came to the edge of the field. 'There's a fence here but we can climb over,' Robin said, and she could hear his shoes grate on the wooden rail. Suddenly he gasped. 'I think we'll wait a bit,' he said in a small voice.

'Why, what is it, Robin?'

'It's that lady. She's over there by the woods.'

'No matter, we can go on.'

'No, wait. She's talking to Uncle Geoff and he looks cross. He's all red and waving his arms. There, she's going — she's got into the van.'

'Van? What van?'

'A sort of caravan you can drive. She's gone in the back. Uncle Geoff is walking away. He hasn't seen us, but he looks very cross.'

So she was the owner of the Dormobile, Pippa thought. But what connection had she with Walters, and why were they arguing? The van was on Korvak land, not his. However, as the boy said, it was best to let him go without becoming aware of their presence, especially if he was angry about something.

She touched Robin's arm. 'Come on, let's go back. It's hot and we could get a nice cold drink from the fridge. There might even be some ice cream.'

Retracing their steps they approached the Hall from the back and made for the kitchen door. As they crossed the stable yard Pippa felt Robin's hand tighten on hers.

'There's a black lady by the door.' She recognised instantly whom he meant. 'I've changed my mind, Pippa,' he hurried on. 'I think I'll go home now and come and see you again soon.'

He relinquished her hand and fled. From his graphic description, she could visualise Mrs Purvis by the door, dark hair gleaming, black-gowned and probably still wearing proudly those jet earrings she treasured. She made no sound as Pippa approached until she was close to the door.

177

'I didn't know you were out, Philippa,' she said crisply. 'Was that the Walters boy with you?'

'Robin, yes. He took me for a walk. Do you know him? A delightful child.' Pippa was probing, and she sensed that the other woman knew it.

'I've seen him, that's all. Come along in and we'll have some iced tea.'

She led the way indoors. As Pippa entered, her nostrils were filled with the glorious, heady scent of roses. At first she thought Mrs Purvis must have cut some to bring into the house, but then she remembered Robin's gift of flowers. They filled the kitchen with their beautiful perfume, and her heart swelled for him again. She was lucky to have him as a half-brother.

Ice rattled in a glass. 'Philippa,' the housekeeper said calmly, 'I've been meaning to tell you. A letter came for you, from Mr Lorant, I believe. I kept it because I did not consider it good for you to continue the relationship with him.'

'What?' Pippa was astonished, not only by her admission of guilt but also by her presumption. 'By what right do you presume to make decisions for me, Mrs Purvis? As it happens I have the letter, but may I remind you it is an offence to interfere with the mail. And in any case, I am quite capable of making my own decisions.'

'I know, but I still think you naïve and unused to the ways of the world. I wanted to protect you.'

'Protect me? From Stephen?' Pippa's breath was taken away.

'Yes, from Stephen. He had more reason than most to hate you, though you could not know it. I know who he really is.'

But she was evidently unaware that Pippa knew too. Pippa decided to lead her on. 'Who was he, that you should think it safer to part us, Mrs Purvis?'

'He is the son of your mother's lover, the only man she ever loved. His name was Jan.'

'I see. But why should that make Stephen hate me?'

'Jan Lorant was a passionate man who adored your mother, and Miss Carrie adored him. I used to see to it that they met in safety. Though I did not approve at first, I had

178

to see my Miss Carrie had what gave her happiness — she had too little with Alexis Korvak. For a time they were blissfully happy.' The housekeeper's tone mellowed to gentleness at the memory.

'And then?' prompted Pippa.

'Your father found out. He had Jan Lorant hounded and persecuted — those McCarthy trials you spoke of — and the man was ruined. He might have been competition to Alexis in the studios, so his dismissal was a double triumph for Alexis Korvak. Jan Lorant, a failure and ostracised by everyone, took to drink. Miss Carrie was whipped away to Europe and she never saw him again. She pined and became ill. When he died she almost lost her reason.'

There was bitter anger, quiet and controlled, in Mrs Purvis's voice. She stopped speaking, re-living the horror of those days. Pippa prompted her again. 'So you believe Stephen hates me for what my father did to his? I can't believe that.'

'Oh yes, he does. At first I did not know who he was when he came here with a letter of introduction from your father. But the American accent, the similarity of his name to Jan's — it soon dawned on me. Not that he looks like his father, but I knew.'

'And you did nothing? You did not tell me?'

'Why should I?' Mrs Purvis's tone was fierce. 'It was obvious he wanted to discredit Alexis Korvak, and why should I stop him? Korvak had made Miss Carrie's life a misery, and I'd be glad for anyone to punish him. He's a vile, callous man, a man everyone hates and no one loves!'

'You haven't explained why you intercepted my letter from Stephen,' Pippa said quietly.

'I thought I'd made it clear. He hates you because you're Korvak's daughter. He set out to harm you. He must have been the cause of all those events you told me about — the sunlamp, the pool, the shower. He was here in Cambermere when all those things happened.'

'No, no, that's monstrous!' Pippa protested hotly. 'He wouldn't stoop to devious things like that!'

'No? Then why is it that nothing has happened to you since he left?' the housekeeper retorted calmly. 'You're a very gullible child, Philippa, as you always were. And for

179

that reason and because you're Miss Carrie's child, however unwanted, I feel it my duty to look after your interests. You should be grateful, though I don't expect you to be able to realise that. I'm going out now, down to the village. In the meantime, think over what I have said.'

The door closed sharply behind her and Pippa was left clutching her glass and shaking with anger. Not for a second would she entertain the dreadful suspicion the housekeeper was trying to plant in her mind. Not Stephen, no, emphatically not Stephen!

It was curious the way the shrewd housekeeper could turn her own deceit in the matter of the letter into a seeming virtue, claiming it was protection. She was a cunning creature indeed, one to be watched warily. Somehow, once again, she had made their encounter into a victory for herself. But whatever she did or said, she was not going to poison Pippa's mind against Stephen. If she had known the contents of that letter she delayed, she would have known its tone showed his concern for Pippa, not hate.

After supper Mrs Purvis referred to the subject again.

'Philippa,' she said tentatively, 'whatever he has written to you, I hope you are not going to see Stephen Lorant again. I honestly believe it will do you no good.'

'Then you can set your mind at rest,' Pippa retorted before she took time to think. 'He's left the country. I don't know where he is.'

She could hear the housekeeper's sigh of satisfaction and could have bitten her tongue. She should have kept silent and played a wary game just like Mrs Purvis, instead of blurting everything out. In that at least Mrs Purvis was right — she was naïve.

As Pippa stretched her arms and made a move to go to bed, Mrs Purvis chose that moment to hurl her final salvo — but carefully disguising it as concern.

'Never mind, Philippa, my dear,' she said soothingly as Pippa reached the door, 'although it's hard to acknowledge that you're alone and friendless now with your young friend gone abroad and everything, don't be too downhearted. We have to find inner strength at a time like this. I'm sure your solution will be to talk it over with Gwen. Sleep well, Philippa.'

Controlling her irritation, Pippa left. It was not easy to retort when one could find no words of defence. She lay sleepless far into the night, fighting to keep at bay the feeling of loneliness and disorientation that threatened to swamp her. It was bleaker than ever, now that warfare with the housekeeper had been tacitly admitted on both sides.

Lonely, vulnerable, fearful again of the night's silent menace, Pippa yearned for Stephen. Then, forcing herself to recognise that he was gone from her life, she curled under the blanket and chewed her fingernail. Half-asleep, she found herself murmuring, 'I don't believe her, Gwen, she's lying because she resents my friendship with Stephen. I'm sure it's envy, Gwen, truly I do. I won't believe evil of him — he was so gentle and understanding and, Lord, how I wish he were here!'

Troubled, she rolled over. It was hot and sticky in bed. She stretched her arms out of the blanket and up into the black void, vast and limitless and empty of hope.

'Stephen!' she called softly. 'Oh, Gwen! Where are you? I'm so lonely!'

She stretched her fingertips into the still night air, groping for hope, for release from this terrible isolation. There was a movement, and then a million volts seemed to crash through Pippa's body as she leapt in terror. Her hand, outstretched before her, was held in the cold grip of another hand.

13

Pippa lay rigid, shock and fear combining to render her speechless and unable to move. The seconds seemed to stretch into an eternity as cold sweat broke out all over her, then Pippa felt the hand slide away from hers. She lay there, numb and terrified, waiting for a sound to betray that the hand was human and not the cold touch of a spirit from beyond the grave.

No sound came, only the rustling of the trees, but just the faintest trace of that familiar perfume came to her nostrils. Could it really be Mother, come back again as she did the night she danced by moonlight? Pippa trembled. No, no, it could not be. There was no love or tenderness in that cold touch.

Minutes must have passed. Pippa shook from head to foot, then as no sound or further movement disturbed her, she began to grow calmer. It was a living creature, no ghost, she told herself firmly. Someone was here; someone who wanted to frighten her. She sat up quickly and reached for the bedside lamp. Even if it could not illuminate the room for her it would cause the intruder to start in surprise.

The switch clicked. Still there was no movement in the room.

'What do you want?' Pippa demanded sharply. If it was a stranger, he would not know she could not see. No answering sound or movement came. She swung her legs out of bed, trying to look confident despite her thudding heartbeat. The bed creaked as she stood up, and it could have been her imagination that there was the faint click of a door closing.

The room was empty. Pippa felt angry with herself for her recent fear. Some living person was playing a trick and she was foolish to allow it to terrify her. She groped for her robe and put it on, then marched firmly to Mrs Purvis's room. She knocked sharply on the door. Instantly she heard movement inside and then the housekeeper's voice.

'Philippa? Is that you?'

Grasping the knob Pippa turned it and went in without waiting for an invitation. A pity she could not see, she thought, for there was no way of telling whether Mrs Purvis was already dressed or genuinely disturbed by her knock.

'Mrs Purvis, are you up? Were you in my room just now?' Pippa demanded. 'If someone was trying to play a prank on me I am not amused. I've had about enough of someone's idea of a joke. Was it you, Mrs Purvis?'

There was a rustling sound which could have been the

housekeeper pulling on a dressing gown. 'What are you talking about, Philippa? No, of course I wasn't in your room. And what do you mean by joke? What happened?'

'Never mind that. Come with me and we'll see if there is anyone there now, though I doubt it.' Pippa walked out, hands outstretched before her. Mrs Purvis followed.

'This is nonsense, Philippa. It's not the first time either.' She opened Pippa's door. 'There, you see, there's no one here.'

'Then he's somewhere in the house. We'd better check.' Pippa was turning to go but the housekeeper barred her way.

'Now look here, there's no one in the Hall but you and myself and I have no intention of getting into a state of hysteria like you over some imaginary intruder. What happened, anyway, that you look so pale?'

Pippa hesitated. If the housekeeper continued to insist that the house was empty then the story of a hand in the dark would sound insane. But Pippa's fingers could still feel that cold, hard touch. It had been no dream or hallucination.

'I shall call the police and ask them to come and check,' Pippa said, but she could sense the housekeeper's thin body still blocked her way. 'Will you move aside, please? I'll ring from the solarium.'

Mrs Purvis hesitated and then moved. 'Very well, but remember this, Philippa. You are going to look very foolish indeed once they've spent an hour investigating the house and grounds and find nothing. Very foolish indeed.'

She was right, of course, Pippa had to admit. And the tale of the night's incident would be strong confirmation to Dr Ramsay that his patient was indeed paranoid. She heard a door close and knew that Mrs Purvis had returned to her room. It angered Pippa to think that the woman was so sure of herself, but what could she do?

All right, if there was no intruder in Cambermere Hall it could only have been Mrs Purvis who took her hand. But the hand, cold as it was, was not so bony as the housekeeper's. Slim-fingered, yes, and ringless, but not angular. It was smooth and supple, more the hand of a woman than a man.

But what woman would come to the Hall — except Carrie Hope? Puzzled and unwilling to believe anything so superstitious, Pippa returned to bed.

In the morning she awoke to the distant sound of church bells drifting across the fields. Pippa realised she must have slept late. She lay listening to the sound, so distinctly English and summerlike, visualising sunsoaked meadows and cricket on a village green. It all seemed so serene and secure after the fears of the night. Sunday. There was something reassuringly normal about an English Sunday with all its connotations of morning service and then a family stroll or a drink at the local pub before the roast beef. How could one believe in nightmares and ghosts on a day such as this, so steeped in tradition and normality?

The day passed quietly. Mrs Purvis decided to spend some hours on bringing her accounts up to date. Monday, as if having made up its mind to start the week with activity, proved more eventful. It was still only mid-morning when Mrs Purvis found Pippa in the music room and announced that she had a visitor.

'Miss Fenton, from the Social Services Department to see you, Philippa,' Mrs Purvis said. 'Do sit down, Miss Fenton.'

The door closed and Pippa knew she had left them alone together. She felt ill at ease, unable to determine whether the other woman was old or young, and knowing she had been sent by the medical authorities.

Miss Fenton spoke first. 'Miss Korvak, I understand you've recently had an accident. I've been sent to see if we can help you in any way. How are you coping?'

The voice was young, cool, capable. Pippa guessed her to be thirtyish, poised and efficient at her job. 'Quite well, thanks, in the circumstances,' she replied.

'Problems with cooking and so on, I expect?'

'Not really. Mrs Purvis sees to all that.'

'Yes, now I'm not quite sure what your circumstances are here, Miss Korvak. According to my papers you live and work abroad. Is that so? What do you do?'

'I'm secretary to a university professor in Paris. That is, I was until . . . ' It was the first time it had occurred to her

184

that now she could not possibly go back to Professor Garnier at the Sorbonne. She would have to hand in her resignation, and then what would she do? Miss Fenton's cool voice was speaking again.

'So you will probably remain in England, I take it. Is this your home?'

'My father's — Alexis Korvak. He's in America and my mother is dead.'

'So you're here alone. And Mrs Purvis?'

'She's my father's housekeeper, both here and in his London flat.'

'So she is taking care of you until your father returns to England,' Miss Fenton surmised. She had evidently never heard of Alexis Korvak or of his illness.

'So your own income will of necessity be stopped,' she remarked. 'You're not married?'

'No.' Pippa could see where she was leading. No income, no supporting husband — she might be in financial need. 'But there is no need to worry,' she went on quickly. 'My father is wealthy and I am in no need.'

'I see.' Pippa could hear the sound of her pen on paper. 'Still, I'm sure we can help you. You must not allow your disability to turn you into a recluse, you know. We can arrange classes in mobility for you, to learn how to use a long white cane to get around alone. And when you're ready you can have lessons in braille-reading and — well, I was going to say touch-typing, but you were a secretary.'

Pippa could not help the angry lump that constricted her throat. *Were* a secretary, in the past tense? The implication was that her useful life was over. From now on she could be taught merely to endure life by means of braille dots or basket making. The thought made her bristle.

'Thank you, Miss Fenton. I don't want to learn braille or how to use a long cane,' she began tartly.

'Well, a collapsible white stick then, and you can keep it in your handbag. Just to enable you to get out and about, you know, and not feel cut off,' Miss Fenton said cheerfully. She was clearly accustomed to the natural hostility of the newly-handicapped and knew better than to react angrily.

'I do get out and about,' Pippa snapped. 'I walked back

here from Marlow unaided, and I can do it again.'

'That's splendid, Miss Korvak, and shows the right spirit. I can see you've come to terms with your problem already and are going the right way about meeting it. I'm very glad But if there is any way in which you think I can be of help to you, don't hesitate to contact me. I'll leave you my card and telephone number. Good day, Miss Korvak.'

She left the room, brightness and competence radiating about her. Pippa felt deeply sorry that she had treated the young woman in such a bad-tempered way, making her the butt of her own anger and resentment and fears. It was too late to hurry after her to apologise and thank her for her good intentions. Pippa slumped in the chair. Dr Ramsay and Miss Fenton might treat her blindness as a permanent condition but she herself was never going to admit that it could dog her all her days, or the fight would be over. White stick? Never! To carry that stick would be for her tantamount to an admission of defeat, a white flag of surrender.

It was useless to stay in the music room, idly picking out chords on the piano as she had been doing before Miss Fenton came. Pippa made up her mind to go for a swim – in the pool, at least, one could move about without a cautious hand to ensure that the way was clear. As she came through into the vestibule she was surprised to hear that Miss Fenton was still there. Her silvery voice, though gently modulated, echoed in the marble vault.

'I see, and thank you very much for the information, Mrs Purvis. It does help so much to have a clear picture of the situation. Good day to you.'

Suspicion leapt into Pippa's mind. What had the house-keeper been telling her, she wondered. No doubt the same exaggerated picture of Pippa's mental imbalance that she had drawn for Dr Ramsay. But before Pippa could question her the telephone rang. She could hear Mrs Purvis's quick, light step as she came from the door, and Pippa hurried to reach the telephone before her.

'Hello? Who? Hobbs, Sharp and Ridler? Ah yes, the solicitors. Yes, Miss Korvak speaking.'

Mrs Purvis's footsteps lingered close. The lawyer's voice sounded warm and Pippa remembered it – Mr Hobbs, whom Geoff Walters had taken her to see.

'I have some details now from your father's solicitors in the States,' he told her. 'There's just one question — two other beneficiaries are named — Mrs Purvis, who I understand is your housekeeper?'

'That's right.'

'And a Mrs I. Starkey, last known address in Nottingham. Can you tell me that lady's present address, Miss Korvak?'

'Starkey?' Pippa repeated slowly. 'No, I'm sorry, I can't help you, Mr Hobbs. I'm afraid I don't know the name.'

Mrs Purvis was instantly at her elbow. 'Who is that, Philippa? What do they want?'

Pippa spoke into the receiver. 'Just one moment, Mr Hobbs. Perhaps Mrs Purvis knows.'

'Knows what? What's this all about?' The housekeeper's voice was cold, demanding.

Pippa covered the mouthpiece. 'The solicitors dealing with my father's affairs. They need to know the address of a Mrs Starkey, last heard of in Nottingham. To do with Father's will, I believe.'

'Give the 'phone to me.' Mrs Purvis snatched it unceremoniously from Pippa's hand. 'To whom am I speaking? Ah, Mr Hobbs.' She paused for a moment, obviously listening. 'I see. Yes, well as it happens I do know the address. Yes, 32 Yewtree Close, Bramley, Nottingham. Not at all, Mr Hobbs, glad to be able to help. Goodbye.'

A click indicated that she had replaced the receiver and she began to move away quickly. Pippa hastened after her.

'What was that about? Who is Mrs Starkey?'

Mrs Purvis began to hum to herself quietly. Pippa persisted, 'Who is she, Mrs Purvis?'

Mrs Purvis sighed. 'Oh, no one of importance to you, my dear. She was a member of your father's household years ago, long, long ago.'

Of course, thought Pippa. Housekeeper perhaps in the days when Mrs Purvis's position was nanny. Another faithful servant whose service Father wanted to acknowledge at the end. He was not so thoughtless after all, to remember two of his employees in his will. Satisfied, she went to her room and changed into a swimsuit and robe.

Out on the terrace she had to feel her way gingerly around the sunchairs and tables. She was quite unaware that she was being watched until she heard the housekeeper's voice calling out, 'A swim will do you good, Philippa, but I should take care not to hang about afterwards. There's a chilly breeze about now. You could sunbathe on your balcony though, where it's sheltered.'

Pippa stepped forward carefully, feeling for the edge of the pool with her toes. Having found it, she sat on the lip and slid into the water. She was taking no more chances with slippery steps. The water was cool and caressing and it was a comforting sensation to abandon herself to it, gliding and floating, freed at last from the tension of walking. It was only now that she could realise just how tense she had been, her muscles permanently flexed and her brain always alert for signals of danger. It was bliss to lie on her back, supported by lapping water and feeling the sun's warmth on her face. After twenty minutes or so Pippa swam to the edge, felt her way round to the steps and climbed out.

Mrs Purvis was right, there was a nippy breeze blowing. Pippa shivered. It was too chilly to lie on a sunchair to dry off so she wrapped the towelling robe about her and went indoors. Perhaps a sunbathe on the balcony, out of reach of the breeze, would be pleasant.

As she crossed the vestibule she heard voices coming from the direction of the music room, so subdued that it was unclear whether a man or a woman was speaking. She hesitated, and then made for the staircase. It could be no one who wanted to see her or Mrs Purvis would have called her, and in any event she was not dressed to receive guests. As she reached the top of the stairs she heard a door open. Mrs Purvis must have caught sight of her.

'Ah, finished your swim? There's a deckchair on your balcony, Philippa, and a rug over the balustrade if you should need it.'

'Thank you. Is there someone with you, Mrs Purvis?' Pippa called out.

'With me? No — why do you ask?'

'I thought I heard voices.'

'Ah, the radio probably. I was listening to a play. I'll

make tea in an hour.'

The door closed, and Pippa went on to her room. She could feel the sunlight streaming across to her before she reached the open french window. Facing south and out of reach of the breeze, the balcony was a suntrap.

All the same, before the hour was up Pippa decided to dress. The deckchair was not so comfortable as a sunbed, and it was growing cooler. As she struggled up out of the deckchair she felt something brush her arm. Alarmed, she stretched out a curious hand, and then smiled. It was only the rug Mrs Purvis had spoken of, draped over the rail of the balcony. No wonder she had felt cool — its shadow had lain across her.

For a moment she stood there, her hand lightly resting on the rail while she looked out unseeingly across the grounds. She felt calmer now, though no less lonely than before. Calm acceptance, that was what she must cultivate — the ability to resign herself to destiny and not be frustrated by her limitations. At the same time, she must fight back and make what she could of life, with or without Stephen Lorant, and find the strength to be complete within herself.

She gripped the rail firmly as she made this private avowal, and turned to go inside. As she did so, there was a crunching sound as the rail slithered down from her hand and the rug fell across her feet. Then there was a metallic clang. Startled and mystified, she stood stock-still, and then heard running footsteps on the terrace below.

'Philippa! My God! What happened? Are you all right? Mrs Purvis's voice rang out. 'What on earth did you do?'

'Nothing. Why, what is it?' Pippa moved a foot cautiously forward and held out her hand. Nothing was there, no balustrade, only the rug on her feet. She stood, tense. 'Mrs Purvis? Has the balustrade fallen?'

'Yes, it has. You'd better go inside carefully.'

Pippa turned, puzzled. How could a whole metal balustrade just fall away like that, with no pressure to speak of? It didn't make sense — but then, nor did any of the other strange incidents which had occurred since she first came to Cambermere Hall. And the footsteps running just before Mrs Purvis called out — now she thought about it and heard

189

the sound again in memory, she could swear there had been more than one pair of feet. If so, who was the second person, and why didn't she speak? Pippa remembered hearing the voices in the music room, and Mrs Purvis's denial.

She dressed quickly and went downstairs. Her nostrils had distinctly detected the smell of toast and she was led to the kitchen.

'Philippa, there you are! Tea's just brewed and I've got some lovely hot muffins for you, you used to love them on Sundays in the nursery.'

'Never mind the muffins, Mrs Purvis,' Pippa said firmly. 'Just tell me what's going on here, and why.'

'I don't know what you mean, my dear. Oh, the balustrade. Yes, I must get that seen to tomorrow. Such a mercy you weren't hurt. The railings can't have been checked for ages, since your father never gave orders to do so. Redecoration, yes, but maintenance is another matter. Perhaps I should have thought of that myself. So much for one person to do alone, you know, caring for two homes.'

'You're being evasive again,' Pippa persisted. 'That balustrade must have been tampered with, just like the pool and the sunlamp. No,' she went on as the housekeeper tried to interrupt, 'don't tell me again it's paranoia. I may be incapacitated in one way but I'm not stupid. Slow, yes, but I can see now that someone is out to harm me, even if I don't know the reason. But I suspect you do.'

'You think I would try to kill you?' The older woman's voice was harsh, challenging. Pippa tried hard not to subside before her cold strength.

'You are the only person around, so far as I know, and I know you lie to me.'

'Lie? What about?'

'You say we're alone, but I swear I sense another presence. That's one thing about blindness, you know, it gives you sixth sense, and I'm certain there's someone else. The door to the yard there closes when I come in, footsteps on the terrace beside yours just now, and I know I heard voices in the music room.'

'I explained that,' the housekeeper said with a patient sigh. 'The radio, remember?'

190

'And you interfered with my mail — twice. That too is deception. So is trying to convince the doctor I'm mad. I do not trust you, Mrs Purvis, though I cannot for the life of me understand why you do it. Would you care to explain?'

She heard the housekeeper draw a deep, quiet breath. 'Philippa, I could explain though I doubt you would appreciate my concern for you. The letters I thought would only unsettle you when you were in a sensitive enough condition already. I felt the doctor should be made aware of the chance you might inherit your dear mother's instability . . .'

'You always swore she was perfect, faultless in every way,' Pippa said angrily.

'So she was,' the other woman retorted icily, 'until your father drove her mad. Quite mad. She killed herself because of him.'

'*Killed herself?* You never told me that!'

'Killed herself, here at Cambermere, out of her mind after all he'd done to her. And how do I know you won't do the same?' the quiet voice went on. 'You're just as unstable now.'

'*No, no!* You're still doing it, Mrs Purvis! Either it's you who threatens me, or you're in league with someone else who is! And now you're trying to plant the idea of suicide in my mind, lying about my mother, but it won't work. It's you who are mad.'

'And you're not? Then why do the doctors call yours a hysterical blindness?' she asked mildly.

Pippa flared at her. 'For God's sake tell me why you hate me so!'

Despite the vow of calm confidence, Pippa could not help her outburst.

'Shall I pour you more tea, my dear? I think this first cup has gone cold. Help yourself to the muffins — I've already buttered them.' The swift change in Mrs Purvis's tone from icy rage to cool politeness was breathtaking. This time Pippa was not going to be thwarted so easily. In equally controlled tones she addressed the housekeeper. 'Why should you hate me so, Mrs Purvis? After all, I am Carrie Hope's child.'

'That's so, but Alexis Korvak's too. Her first child, Irma,

inherited all her looks and temperament, but her second child had the bad blood — the evil that was in Korvak. Irma was to be loved, but Philippa to be feared and hated.'

She spoke the words in such a sunny way, referring to Pippa in the third person as if she were not there, that Pippa recoiled in horror. There was no doubt of it — robbed of her adored mistress and first baby, the housekeeper was demented, but in a way that was not obvious to the world. So much the more dangerous, thought Pippa, and it was impossible to reason with a mad woman. She would have to think about how to handle this situation.

Over the rest of tea, Mrs Purvis made polite conversation as though nothing had happened. And Pippa found that even more sinister.

Later that evening the telephone rang. Pippa waited, but no one seemed to be going to answer it. Mrs Purvis must be out again, she thought. Pippa walked quickly from her room to the solarium, but as she picked up the receiver she heard a click.

'Hello?'

'Oh, Pippa! I was about to ring off.' She felt her heart thud in surprise and delight — it was Stephen's voice. 'Listen, Pippa,' he said urgently. 'I know you have no time for me but I'm at the airport now and I couldn't leave without speaking to you when I heard the news.'

'News?' she repeated, wondering if he could have heard about her blindness. 'What news?'

'You haven't heard? It was on the radio — Alexis is sinking fast. I'm sorry, Pippa.'

'I should go to him,' were Pippa's first words, a choke in her throat.

'Too late, I fear. You wouldn't make it in time. Listen, Pippa. There's little time — my 'plane leaves very soon. I know you never want to see or hear of me again — '

'Stephen, I — '

'No, listen. I had to contact you, just once, to tell you I'm not going to do that book.'

'You couldn't find all the material you needed?'

'On the contrary, I found it all. I found he did let your mother die — '

'You said he was a murderer.'

'So I believed, for he was there when she killed herself and he did not try to stop her. Now I know. He was mesmerised, horror struck. He did love her, despite her instability and unfaithfulness.'

'So you've forgiven him,' Pippa said acidly.

'I had no choice. From his sick bed he wrote me a letter, clearing my father's name, explaining he had acted out of revenge, and giving permission for me to publish the letter or use it any way I pleased. I'm afraid I under-estimated him. I just wanted to say I'm sorry, *galambom*. I know you hate me, but I was very fond of you. Forgive me. Be happy, little one — let things flow over you and you'll be happy.'

She grew alarmed for he sounded as if he was about to hang up. She could not let him go like this, believing she still hated him and unaware of her plight. 'Stephen, listen a moment,' she began.

'Oh, and one thing more — I nearly forgot. Your half-sister, Irma. She's not dead, after all, as we thought — '

There was a sudden crackle on the line and then total silence. Pippa rattled the receiver rest anxiously. 'Stephen? Stephen, are you there?' It was no use; the line was completely dead.

Replacing the receiver, she returned to her room and sat on the edge of the bed, numb with disappointment. She could not even ring the airport back since the line was dead. She did not even know which airport he was at. In minutes he would climb into an aircraft and disappear from her life, and there was nothing she could do about it.

And Father was dying. He too was cut off from her. Mrs Purvis was out, and Pippa could not drive. She was helpless to reach or contact him. Tears pricked her lids and began to flow. Poor Father, so maligned and reviled. Thank heaven at least Stephen's view of him was happier now and that dreadful book would never be written. Father had un-doubtedly committed many sins, but he had done his best at the last to atone, admitting Robin as his co-heir with Pippa and clearing the name of a man he had dishonoured all those years ago.

She climbed wearily into bed, determined not to think any more about her problems. Tomorrow she would feel

193

fresh and more able to plan how to cope. Right now, with Father and Stephen about to leave her life, she would prefer to sink into the oblivion of sleep.

But sleep would not come readily. For an hour she lay, trying not to think, but small insidious thoughts kept creeping into her mind. The news about Father was on the radio. Mrs Purvis had been listening to the radio, or so she claimed. Could it be that she already knew the end was near and had deliberately kept the news from Pippa?

She pushed the thought aside and tried to concentrate on pleasant things — light and flowers and butterflies — oh, why did one's thoughts always have to centre on the visual?

Mrs Starkey. For no apparent reason the name of the legatee in Father's will came to mind. Mrs I. Starkey. What could the 'I' stand for? That was a good exercise to send one to sleep, like counting sheep. Ivy, Ingrid, Irene. There weren't very many female names beginning with I. Isabel, Ida, Iris — and that lovely but unusual one, Imelda.

Sleep was still not approaching. Work through the alphabet, she told herself, like doing a crossword. Imogen, Inez, Isadora.

Irma! She sat upright in bed. Of course, Irma Starkey. Stephen had told her that Irma was not dead after all. Irma Starkey was her sister, alive and in Nottingham.

14

Irma — Pippa was sure of it. The name Starkey had meant nothing because she had never known the name of the man her sister married.

Yes, it fitted. Mrs Purvis had been quick to supply the Nottingham address to the solicitors because she had kept in touch with her mistress's child. What was it she had said when Pippa asked who Mrs Starkey was? A 'member of the household', she had said, 'many years ago'. Pippa's lips curved in an ironic smile. It was a part-truth, at least.

But why did the housekeeper lead Pippa to believe that her sister was dead? Why so many lies and subterfuges? There must be a reason, and yet for the life of her Pippa could not see it.

Mrs Purvis was undoubtedly in touch with Irma; after all, she had made it clear that she loved Miss Carrie's first child and hated the second. Pippa wondered if she had told Irma about the accident.

In the morning Mrs Purvis knocked and came in with the tea tray, which she set down on the bedside cabinet. She crossed to draw back the curtains: Pippa heard the swish.

'Good morning, Philippa. Another beautiful day,' the housekeeper said in her usual crisp, confident voice, as though they had never crossed words.

Pippa sat up. 'Is there a radio here? I know my father is nearing the end.'

'There's no change,' Mrs Purvis said crisply. The sound of liquid tinkled into the china cup.

'Has there been a message? A 'phone call?'

'No. The telephone appears to be out of order. I shall have to go to another telephone to report it.'

'Then how do you know?'

'It was on the news earlier.'

'Mrs Purvis, why didn't you tell me that Irma was alive and that you knew where she was?'

'Do you ask out of concern for her? You hardly knew her and haven't seen her in twenty years. Life has not been easy for her, if you care to know. Far from it, with a faithless husband who finally left her.'

Pippa sipped her tea, wondering. 'But caring for her as you evidently do, Mrs Purvis, why didn't you go to her instead of staying in my father's employ? You've made it clear you cared nothing for him.'

'I told you once. I know which side my bread is buttered. Your father gave me a free hand in managing his two houses and from his allowance I could see to it that she never starved. She's been good to me too, bless her.

Always a little gift when we meet, like these earrings she knew I longed for.'

The jet earrings; Pippa remembered how pleased Mrs Purvis was when she came back from London. A gift from a friend, she had said.

Without being prompted further, the housekeeper began talking again, softly, as if to herself. 'Yes, she's had a raw deal, poor lamb, just like her lovely mother. It's a cruel trick of fate, the two of them alike as two peas, beautiful and yet doomed to hardship. But I wasn't going to let it happen again. I promised my Miss Carrie I'd see to her child. All these years I've bided my time to see she gets what she deserved. She'll come into her own yet, or my name's not Emily Purvis.'

Pippa heard her move to the far side of the room, to the dressing table. 'Don't you fret, Miss Carrie,' the house-keeper was murmuring, 'I'll not fail you. I'll keep my vow, my angel.'

Pippa was stunned. It was clear the woman was in a private reverie of her own, talking to her dead mistress, still bearing an unhealthy obsession for her and her child and a heart full of hate for Korvak and his child. There was no doubt of it now, she was plainly mad.

In a moment Mrs Purvis picked up the tray and left the room. Pippa sat hugging her knees, deep in thought. Mrs Purvis had promised to care for Carrie's child — but which child? It was more likely Mother had begged her to look after little Pippa than the grown girl who had already fled the home. It was Mrs Purvis's deranged mind, probably, which had in its own strangely twisted logic transferred the vow to Irma.

As she showered and dressed Pippa's mind was racing. How did the housekeeper propose to see that Irma came into her own'? An inheritance from Father, no doubt. She had been quick to supply Mr Hobbs with Irma's address. But the legacy, however generous, would be unlikely to be so vast that it warranted twenty years of planning and hatred. It was all very puzzling.

So were the accidents, mishaps, attempts to harm or even to kill her that had happened since Pippa came to Cambermere. A sudden stab of apprehension pierced her.

Was it possible that there was a connection, that Mrs Purvis was indeed behind all those accidents, attempting to kill Pippa so that Irma could benefit? Pippa hated to admit it, but there was a kind of cruel logic in it — kill off the hated child in order to benefit the beloved one.

Pippa trembled as she finished dressing and put on her sandals. Loth though she was to admit it, she knew that Mrs Purvis's insane devotion to Miss Carrie and Irma could render her capable of anything. A mind warped by hate and revenge, fostered over so many years, was desperately dangerous. From now on Pippa realised she must tread warily, taking even more care than just counting the steps and measuring the paces. She must treat the housekeeper in her normal manner, without showing her suspicion, but it would not be easy. It still gave her a shiver to think of her addressing the empty chair at the dressing table as if her cherished mistress still sat there. For Mrs Purvis that bedroom was a shrine, and while she adored her idol she was unaware of any other human presence. It was sick, unhealthy — crazy.

Halfway down the stairs Pippa remembered Stephen's call, and realised that there would be no more calls from him — or anyone else — if the 'phone was dead. She crossed the vestibule and lifted the receiver. Total silence. Then, her fingers followed the curled length of the cable until it reached the wall, she discovered why: the cable had been wrenched clean out of the wall. Mrs Purvis had obviously been listening in and had heard Stephen tell her that Alexis was dying and that he had found out about Irma. Then she must have decided that he'd said more than enough.

The first thing Pippa decided to do was to have the telephone line restored. Geoff Walters was the nearest person with a 'phone so that was where she would go, now. But stealthily as she descended the stairs, the housekeeper's ears must have been alert; as Pippa was crossing the vestibule, arms outstretched to avoid the pillars, a voice made her jump.

'Where are you going, Philippa?'

'For a walk, Mrs Purvis. I'll be back soon.'

It did not take long to reach the riding stables. Pippa felt the rough wood of the five-barred gate warm under her fingertips. Before she reached the cobbles of the yard Walters' voice hailed her.

'Hold on, Philippa! There's a bale of hay and a fork in your way.' Running footsteps, and then he was beside her. 'What brings you down here?' he asked.

'The 'phone's out of order. Would you ring in and report it, please, Geoff? My father, you know . . . '

'Oh, yes, of course. There's no more news then?'

'Not yet.'

'Do you want to ring the hospital from here?'

'You're very kind, but no thanks. I'll hear soon enough. But you could do something for me — find out the times of trains to London.'

'You're leaving?' His tone of surprise was genuine, but then, he did not know of all the strange happenings at the Hall. Or did he? For some unaccountable reason she thought of the woman in the Dormobile and Walters together, apparently in heated argument, according to Robin's description. She decided to take the bull by the horns.

'Geoff — what connection do you have with the woman who has been camping near here in a van? You seemed to be arguing with her the other day about something. What was going on?'

'The redhead? What do you know about her?' Walters' tone was decidedly on the defensive. Something clicked in Pippa's brain: *red hair*. A lot of lovely shiny hair, Robin had said. Like Carrie Hope? No — wait! Like Irma — with whom Mrs Purvis admitted she was in touch? It could not be — it was far-fetched in the extreme. She must learn more.

'Yes, the redhead. Why were you quarrelling?'

Walters grunted. 'I didn't know you knew. Well, the truth of it is, she wanted me to help her drive you away. Because of Nina, I agreed at first. Then I began to feel uneasy. I didn't like the gleam in her eyes — she talked wildly and I thought the whole thing might get out of hand and I honestly didn't wish you any harm, Philippa. So I told her it was off. I'd found out by then that despite being a Korvak you were really quite nice. Robin was getting fond of you too — that was another thing. Then you told me about writing to your father and getting Robin acknowledged as his son. She tried again to get me to help in some madcap scheme and I refused point-blank. That's all.'

'What madcap scheme?' Pippa asked. Daylight was beginning to dawn: Irma, with or perhaps without Mrs Purvis's help, had been behind some of the recent events — but which?

'She didn't spell it out because I wouldn't listen. I said I had no interest in avenging Nina now because you had made everything right. She seemed furious at that.'

'It was Irma, wasn't it, Geoff? Irma Starkey?'

'That was the name she told me. She said she was your half-sister, not a Korvak, and that she too had a grudge to settle against Korvak, just as I had. I must have been choked with hatred for your father even to listen to her, but when I saw the way things were going . . . ' His voice tailed away.

'I think my father hurt several people once, but he's a dying man now,' Pippa pointed out gently. 'Forgive him, Geoff.'

'I can, but only because of your generosity of heart, Philippa. You have more than atoned,' Walters replied quietly. 'Anyway, she's gone now. The Dormobile is no longer in the woods.'

Pippa felt a surge of relief. Nevertheless, she knew she must get away from Cambermere and the strange housekeeper. She told Walters of her plan to find a hotel in London for the time being and leave word with the solicitor, Mr Hobbs, where to find her. She added casually to Walters, 'And if anyone should come looking for me or want to reach me, tell him to contact Mr Hobbs. He'll know where to find me.'

Just in case, she thought. It was foolish to hope, but wilder dreams had come true. It would be terrible if, some time, Stephen did decide to try and trace her and found only a dead end. She walked back down the track to the lane and up towards the Hall.

She only stumbled once on the homeward journey — a pothole in the lane she could swear was not there before. By the time she reached the Hall steps her ankle was beginning to ache and she realised she must have given it a worse wrench than she had thought.

Mrs Purvis made no attempt to hide her concern. She was waiting in the vestibule. 'Where did you go for your walk, Philippa?'

'To Geoff Walters. He'll arrange to have the 'phone fixed. And you tell me something, Mrs Purvis — has Irma been here in Cambermere Hall? And whereabouts did my mother die, and just how exactly? Why didn't you want me to know about Irma? What harm have I done to either of you?' Pippa realised she was blurting out far more than she had meant to say and wished she could learn to control her impetuous tongue.

The housekeeper seemed not a bit disturbed. 'Shall I pour your tea? You do ask a lot of questions, don't you? Your curiosity about your mother is understandable, but Irma is no concern of yours at all.' How possessive she was, thought Pippa, about Irma as much as her beloved Miss Carrie. 'So I shall tell you what you want to know about your mother. She died in the east wing, in one of the film sets. She stabbed herself.'

'*Stabbed herself?*' Pippa was shocked. 'But you led me to believe my father was responsible?'

'So he was,' the housekeeper went on imperturbably. 'His treatment over the years had quite unbalanced her poor little mind. After he broke up her affair with Jan she was distraught, but after Jan's death she was overcome with a feeling of guilt. Her poor brain confused it with a role she had played in a historical drama some time before, until it became so muddled she could not distinguish between real life and fantasy. She would spend hours in the east wing, saying her lines over and over on the set.'

'What set? What part was she playing?' Pippa's question was no more than a whisper. She did not want to remind the housekeeper of her presence, for the woman was evidently only remembering aloud.

'The great banqueting hall. She played the medieval lady of the castle, the beautiful Lady Alys, whose lord has been away on a crusade for years and is now at last to return. Lady Alys is forced to part with her lover Peiral before he comes. Nevertheless she is torn by the conflict of love for

200

Peiral and loyalty to her lord, knowing she had betrayed him. As Lord Hubert enters the castle, eager to see his lovely wife, she takes a dagger and kills herself.'

There was love, compassion and pride in the housekeeper's voice as love for her dead mistress combined with proud recollection of how well she played the memorable role.

Pippa was sickened, horrified. 'And Alexis?' she asked.

'He came into the great hall looking for her, just as my Miss Carrie took up the knife. She had acted it out a hundred times before and I never dreamed she would really plunge the knife into herself. He watched, and did not stop her.' The hard edge of hatred crept back into Mrs Purvis's voice.

Poor Father. He had no more expected it to happen than the housekeeper had. The fading, forgotten actress, out of her mind with grief and the knowledge of her infidelity, probably never planned to do it at all. As Mrs Purvis had said, she was no longer able to distinguish between real life and dramatic fantasy.

The housekeeper suddenly averted to everyday practicality. 'I'll go up and change the beds while you finish breakfast, Philippa.'

There was a clatter of dishes, a brisk movement, and she was gone. Pippa pushed her plate aside. She had lost interest in eating. How she hated Cambermere Hall, she thought; outwardly it was so gracious and beautiful, but its whole atmosphere exuded sadness and grief. It was haunted by tragedy; suffering permeated its very stones and marbled magnificence. She would be glad to leave it behind. One day, perhaps, it could be exorcised and cleansed by other people and happier events, but not yet . . .

Yet it was not wholly evil, she reflected. There had been love in this house. Father undoubtedly loved Mother despite his lapses, and Mother had loved her children. Mrs Purvis's strangely twisted adoration of her mistress was love of a kind too. And it was here that Stephen had brought a new, stirring, wildly intoxicating sensation to Pippa — she knew now, beyond a flicker of doubt, that she loved him as she could love no other man. So much love in this house — it had an element of redemption in it already.

There was a tap at the yard door. Pippa rose and felt her way around the table, wincing at the throb in her ankle. She expected the caller to be a delivery man with groceries or on some similar errand, and was surprised to hear Bainbridge's gruff voice.

'Ah, Philippa, I'm glad you're here. Hoped it wouldn't be that housekeeper woman. Funny soul, she is. Can I come in — only for a moment?'

Pippa sighed. One more proposal from Arthur Bainbridge would be the last straw. 'Come in. Would you like a cup of tea?'

'No thanks. I only came to say as I'm sorry. I realise now I was harassing you. I learnt how you'd been stricken and I shouldn't have pressed you like I did. So I've come to say — forget all about it, and I'm sorry if I vexed you.'

His speech, evidently carefully rehearsed, was gruff and stiff but Pippa was quick to recognise his magnanimity. She smiled. 'There's nothing to forgive. I appreciate your concern and I value your friendship, Arthur.' She could feel his tension ease as she used his first name. 'And what's more, I shall see to it that your land is restored to you, very soon now.'

He cleared his throat, understanding her unspoken words, and groped for the right phrases. 'Ah, yes. I heard about your father. Very sorry, Philippa. If there's aught I can do . . .'

'You're very kind. I shall be leaving Cambermere soon, but I'll be back. I look forward to seeing you again then.'

She felt her hand seized in a strong grip. 'And I look forward to that too, lass.' Abruptly, he was gone. Pippa felt a sense of warmth. One old axe was buried at least — two, she corrected herself, now that Geoff Walters' ancient hurt over his sister Nina was healed. She could be satisfied that her visit to Cambermere had achieved something after all.

It was time to pack. Pippa left the kitchen and went up the stairs. Twenty, twenty-one, twenty-two. She turned the corridor where her bedroom lay, and then stopped short. There were voices. As she strained her ears, she recognised it was one voice — the housekeeper's, but in a lower, softer range than she was accustomed to speak — and the sound was coming from Pippa's room. Pippa approached the door quietly.

Mrs Purvis was murmuring soothingly: 'There now, my lovely, there is no more need to fret. Alexis Korvak is nearing his end. There is not much time left, then all will be well. Oh, how your hair gleams in the sunlight! Glorious hair, so soft and abundant!'

Despite all her dislike and distrust of the woman, Pippa could not help feeling compassion for her. There she was, in her dead mistress's room, addressing her as though she still lived. It seemed almost sacrilege to disturb her, alone with her prayers in her shrine. Pippa turned to move away unobtrusively and heard the last quiet words: 'Are you ready, my precious? There is so little time.'

Poor thing, thought Pippa. She was trying to prepare her Miss Carrie for Alexis's arrival in the other world. It was all so sad and distorted. Pippa left her to her orisons.

For a little while Pippa walked in the rose garden, savouring the heady scent of the blooms until her aching ankle forced her to sit. She sat on the terrace, the sun warm on her face, and reflected how vastly her life had changed over the past few weeks. A month ago — was that all it was — she had still been busy working for Professor Garnier, unaware of Clive's imminent departure from her life, unaware of the details of her mother's tragic death and of her own half-sister in Nottingham, unaware that she was soon to lose her sight, and unaware of the existence of the man she loved with a hopeless longing. Who would believe that life could change so dramatically in so short a time?

A sound like a distant voice distracted her from her reverie and she looked up sharply. An ironic smile curved her lips; it would take a long time yet to grow used to being sightless. The voice, high and shrill like a woman's or a child's, did not come again. She could have been mistaken; it might have been the squeal of a rabbit or a startled bird.

Pippa was never able later to pinpoint the moment that day when she began to be filled with a growing sense of unease, the kind of inner sixth sense that warned that all was not quite as it should be. It might have been when Geoff Walters appeared in the gardens looking for her to tell her that the London trains ran hourly, except on Sunday.

'By the way, have you seen Robin?' he asked. 'He hasn't been around since breakfast.'

'No. He hasn't been here.'

'Just thought he might, knowing how fond he is of you. I wonder where the little monkey's got to.'

Or the unease might have originated with Mrs Purvis's non-appearance at lunchtime. Normally so meticulous in seeing that there was at least a snack, today she was nowhere to be found. Pippa made good use of her absence to limp upstairs to pack. The task took far longer than she had anticipated. It was not easy to gather all one's belongings by touch. The drawers were a simple matter − it was easy to distinguish her own things from Mother's because the scent of Californian Poppy lingered in Miss Carrie's. Finding her suitcase gave rise to some delay until her fingers encountered it in one of the cupboards in the dressing room.

As she packed, she thought of Irma's promise to Walters that Robin would benefit, in return for Walters' help in driving Pippa away. But Irma herself only stood to inherit a limited sum. Perhaps she thought she and Pippa were joint legatees. That would certainly account for Mrs Purvis's promptness in supplying Irma's address to Mr Hobbs. And by getting rid of Pippa, Irma could inherit it all. Pippa blanched. Getting rid of someone could mean driving them away or, if they proved stubborn, taking more drastic measures. Was that what all the recent strange happenings here at the Hall had been aimed at? Had Irma been making those attempts on Pippa's life, with the help of the half-crazed housekeeper?

But Irma was gone now, according to Geoff Walters. Either she had given up, or some other factor had changed her mind. Was Father already dead, perhaps, and they were keeping the truth from her? Or, more likely, had Irma learnt that she had little to gain by Pippa's death or disappearance?

It was only when the doorbell rang that the new fear entered her mind. She opened the front door to hear Geoff Walters' voice.

'Philippa, have you seen anything of Robin since I saw

you? He still hasn't come home and it's almost teatime. I wouldn't have bothered you but your 'phone's not working yet.'

It was then she felt the sick feeling. 'He hasn't been here, Geoff, so far as I know. Has he got a friend he might be with?'

'I've tried them. No one's seen him today. I'm worried, Philippa. He's not a secretive child; he hardly ever goes off alone. He's usually with the horses, but the stable lads haven't seen him since breakfast either.'

She could hear the deep concern in Walters' voice. 'I'll go and call around the grounds and up to the woods if you like,' she ventured. 'Do you think you should ring the police?'

'It's a bit early for that, but I am worried. Okay, you go uphill and I'll look down towards the village. Someone must have seen him.'

Walters hurried away. Pippa had forgotten about her wretched ankle until she began crossing the lawn and the throb returned to remind her.

'Robin! Robin!' she kept calling. 'Where are you?'

Her way was suddenly barred by something which pricked her face. Her hands told her it was a hedge, and further groping along it revealed a gap. Of course, it was the maze. She hesitated. If Robin had gone in there he could have become utterly lost, but surely he would have called for help? Suddenly she remembered the sound she had heard earlier in the day from the rose garden, the sound she had taken for the cry of a bird or animal. Could it have been Robin? Was he still in there, possibly asleep from exhaustion?

'Robin! Are you there?' she called loudly. 'It's Pippa — can you hear me?'

She listened intently but heard no answering sound. She hesitated. If she were to go in there in search of him, she too could become lost. Stephen flashed into her mind. What was it he had said about finding one's way through a maze? Something about marking the right hand wall with chalk. It would lead one to the middle and out again, if she remembered rightly. Perhaps if she kept her right hand on the hedge, following it continuously wherever it led her, the result would be the same.

'Robin! Robin! Are you in there?' Her cry echoed and died away across the grass. No, she decided, she would not venture in. The whole process could take an hour or more, and that hour could be better spent searching elsewhere. She cupped her hands around her mouth and drew a deep lungful of air for one final call.

'*Robin!*'

As the sound died away she caught her breath. Was it her imagination, or was there a faint, far-away cry, just like the one she'd heard in the rose garden? She turned slowly. If there was, it came from behind her, from the direction of the Hall and not from the maze or beyond.

The nearest point of the Hall was the east wing. Pippa limped towards it as quickly as her ankle would allow. Nearing it she felt the sun's warmth on her face suddenly turn cool and knew she was in the shadow of the wing. She stopped.

'*Robin!*'

This time there was no doubting it: it was an answering cry, high-pitched and shrill — the sound of a frightened child. Poor little thing! He must have got himself accidentally locked in, in one of those bewildering film sets.

Pippa hobbled along the front terrace until she reached the front door and went inside. To her surprise the double doors to the east wing were unlocked. He must be hurt, she thought, and was calling for help. Pippa hastened along the corridor calling his name, but this time there was no response.

She flung open the first door. 'Robin?' Hearing no answer she limped quickly to the second door. That room too only echoed her voice hollowly. Then she heard a whisper much further along and hurried towards it. At the fifth door, the set she hazily remembered was the dungeon, she hesitated and listened. There was clearly a muffled sound within. She opened the door.

'Robin, is that you? I've been looking for you everywhere!'

A sound like whimpering or subdued sobbing came to her ears and she moved towards it anxiously. At the same time a vaguely familiar aroma came to her but she took no notice. 'What is it, Robin? Are you hurt? Come now, it's me, your friend. Don't be frightened.'

She was holding out her arms towards the sound, concerned lest he was injured, but no small hand met hers. Instead she heard a click behind her and recognised the sound of a key turning in the lock. Bewildered, she turned.

'Robin, are you playing a trick on me? Come on, Robin, you have me at a disadvantage, you know. Tell me what you're up to. You're not hurt, are you?'

The whimpering sound returned, subdued at first and then growing gradually in volume — until she realised it was no whimper but a laugh. And it was not Robin's laugh. It was not the laugh of a child at all, but that of a full-grown woman.

'Mrs Purvis? Is that you? What are you playing at?' Pippa demanded.

The chuckling subsided. 'Oh yes, it's me, Philippa. And your precious Robin is safe — for the moment. We haven't done anything to him yet, have we, my precious?'

The tinkling laugh resumed and Pippa wondered whom the housekeeper was addressing. Her words were sinister, and Pippa's bewilderment suddenly gave way to tingling fear when she recognised the haunting perfume of Californian Poppy.

15

Pippa was momentarily bewildered. Mrs Purvis and that perfume, now associated in Pippa's mind only with darkness and menace, combined to fill her with fear. The housekeeper spoke to her beloved mistress as though she were here, and Pippa was convinced that the woman had finally lost her reason completely. Then another thought came to her. Up to this moment she had not wondered which film set was in this room. Now she could guess: it must be the one where Carrie Hope took her life — the banqueting hall of the medieval castle.

Pippa had no idea of the room's layout, so she remained stock still. It must be next door to the dungeon set. Mrs Purvis was making purring noises like a contented cat, but there was no sound of Robin. Yet she could swear it was a child's cry she had heard from the gardens.

'Mrs Purvis, Robin Walters is missing. Do you know where he is?' she asked timidly.

Amused laughter rippled round the room, and Pippa realised with horror that it was not the housekeeper's voice but that of a much younger woman. She clenched her fists, feeling the perspiration damp in her palms.

'Robin?' the housekeeper echoed. 'He's not missing, my dear. He's here, safe with us in the next room.'

With *us*, thought Pippa? But something in her refused to accept that the spirit of Carrie Hope really was there. She existed only in Mrs Purvis's warped mind, didn't she? Then whose was the soft laugh?

Realisation dawned even before the housekeeper spoke: only one other person claimed Mrs Purvis's loyalty — a woman who might have reason to keep Robin Walters from his uncle.

There was patent pride in Mrs Purvis's tone. 'Really, Philippa, you really are rather slow just as you always were. Not like my quick little Irma, so like her lovely mother. If you could see her now, Philippa, the same glorious hair and figure. A pity you never reached stardom, Irma, like Miss Carrie did. The whole world had an opportunity to adore her.'

'It's not my fault if I never graduated from repertory to the West End,' a woman's mellow voice answered snappishly. 'I did my best.'

'I know, my love. You just didn't have luck on your side, that's all,' Mrs Purvis soothed. 'You had none of the advantages that were showered on Philippa. But your time is coming, my precious. We've waited and planned for years and soon the world will be yours.'

Pippa listened in horror, taking in the full implication of her words. Irma had been cheated, she believed, by Korvak, but she could still inherit his wealth if — and it was this thought that appalled and frightened Pippa — if Pippa was not in the way. They meant to do her harm, to remove her permanently from the scene, and she was like a powerless, fragile butterfly in their hands. And Robin — he too stood between Irma and the inheritance. Pippa realised with dismay that it was she herself who had put him in danger when she told Geoff Walters he was to inherit jointly, and Walters in turn had passed the information on to Irma. What a blind, stupid fool she had been!

But was her half-sister really so obsessed with this crazy idea as Mrs Purvis was? There was a chance she had only been coaxed into the scheme by the doting housekeeper. It was worth trying to appeal to her better nature.

'Irma? Is it really you, after all these years?' she asked quietly.

That musical chuckle again. 'Oh yes, it's me, Pippa. Twenty years older and wiser, but it's me. You haven't changed since I last saw you in the nursery. Still mousy and insignificant. I recognised you at once when I came to your room. I was curious, but I needn't have bothered.'

'So it was you who came to my room in the night — soon after I arrived here?' Pippa breathed.

'As I said, I was curious, so I came at once when Mrs Purvis told me you were here. I couldn't stay here, of course, because you had that young journalist fellow here.'

The van. And that was why Mrs Purvis kept coming and going quietly from the Hall, to see Irma. Things were beginning to become clearer.

'The perfume — that was you too?'

'Yes. Mrs Purvis likes me to wear it constantly because my mother did. And to be frank, I liked the way you reacted to it and thought it was Miss Carrie's ghost, so I continued to use it.'

Pippa shivered, remembering how that perfume had terrified her, choking in her nostrils to the point of nightmare. She was wrong about Irma: she had evidently enjoyed tormenting Pippa as only a cruel, twisted person could.

'You had to go, there was no doubt of that,' Irma's pleasant voice went on smoothly. 'You stood between me and comfort, and after the wretched life I've had I deserve some comfort now. I'm thirty-six, you know.'

'The same age as your dear mother was,' Mrs Purvis murmured, 'and you look just as magnificent as she did. How that husband of yours could walk out on you passes all comprehension.'

'He was slow and stupid, just like Pippa here, and anyhow that was a long time ago,' Irma remarked. 'What matters now is getting her out of the way before Korvak dies — and the boy too.'

'Everything is ready,' Mrs Purvis said. 'I've only to fetch the boy.'

Pippa's mind raced. Whatever they planned, there was little time. She spoke to her half-sister again, playing for time. 'Then it was you who changed the sunlamp to ultraviolet and oiled the pool steps?' she asked.

'Oh yes, in an effort to drive you away. And later it was I who loosened the balcony rail.'

'And the hand in the night?'

Irma chuckled. 'That was funny. I hadn't planned that but it appealed to my sense of the theatrical. You couldn't see I was standing there watching you, feeling just a little bit sorry for the silly, helpless creature lying there so completely in my power, and then suddenly you cried out for Stephen and then for Gwen and held your hands out. I couldn't resist it. It was hilarious to see the expression on your face!'

'It was cruel, and you know it,' Pippa retorted.

'But you ask for it with your blind trust and simplicity! You're a fool, Pippa, and easily taken in, so it serves you right if people trade on it. I learnt long ago to trust no one and care for no one, then you can't get hurt.'

'Except for me, my precious,' Mrs Purvis interjected. 'You always trusted and cared about me. You bought me these lovely jet earrings only the other week, remember. You do love the one person you know cares for you.'

'As you're so fond of saying, Mrs Purvis, I know which side my bread is buttered,' Irma snapped. 'But we're wasting time. That Walters fellow will be back by dusk when he hasn't found the child.'

'And it was you who locked me in the stable with Copper?'

Irma laughed shortly. 'That wasn't planned, just an opportunity I couldn't miss. I'd seen Walters leave before you arrived, then I saw the boy go into the house, and no one else was around.'

'One more thing,' Pippa burst in. 'You say you look very like my mother — was it you, then, who danced in the garden one night by moonlight? You had me completely fooled then, I confess; I really thought it was her.'

There was a momentary silence and Pippa sensed that the two women exchanged looks. 'Danced in the garden?' repeated Mrs Purvis. 'When?'

'Soon after I arrived, before I fell off Copper. Irma does look exactly like those old stills of Mother, doesn't she?'

'She does,' Mrs Purvis admitted slowly.

'But it wasn't me,' Irma cut in. 'I have many talents, but dancing isn't one of them. I inherited many things from Mother but not her talent for dancing. Sorry, Pippa, but it wasn't me you saw. That must be your imagination. Mrs Purvis, give me the matches and fetch the boy.'

Alarm leapt in Pippa. She could see it all now — they had somehow brought or lured Robin here and used his cry deliberately to lure her to this set too. Matches — did they really plan to set fire to the place and leave her and Robin to perish? Irma was right. They were completely at her mercy. The set, no doubt composed mainly of chipboard and hardboard, would go up like dry kindling.

'Pippa!' Robin's thin little voice echoed across to her.

'Robin? Come here to me.'

'I can't. My hands are tied up and Mrs Purvis is holding me.'

She could hear the bewildered fear in his voice and she grew angry. 'Let him go, Mrs Purvis! He's done nothing to you,' she commanded.

Irma's laugh rippled out again. 'Let him go? And lose all we've worked and waited for? You're crazy, little sister. I won't tie you up — there's no need. You can't see and the door will be locked. There's no other way of escape. I believe it's quite quick really. You'll know nothing once the smoke has made you unconscious.'

She talked as calmly and coolly as though she were an anaesthetist reassuring a patient, and Pippa could visualise Mrs Purvis standing by with an approving smile. They were demented, the pair of them, planning to execute a woman and a child so cold-bloodedly. Impractical ideas for escape tumbled into her brain and out again. The door was locked; she had heard the click. She could not rush at the housekeeper to grab Robin because she could not tackle Irma at the same time, especially as she had only a hazy idea of where they stood. Irma was moving about now, her shuffling footsteps mingling with metallic clangs. Then there was a splashing sound, and moments later an even more pungent smell overlaid Irma's familiar perfume. Pippa lifted her head and sniffed. *Petrol!*

She rushed forward impulsively towards the sound. 'Irma, what are you doing?' she cried, groping wildly to find the woman and restrain her. 'The set is inflammable enough already — you'll only succeed in burning down the whole wing, maybe the entire house!'

'What do I care?' the voice taunted. 'I hate this house, these loathsome sets, and you! I don't want Cambermere Hall! If I know Alexis Korvak, he has the place heavily covered with insurance and the money will be of far more use to me! Keep still, you fool — out of my way if you don't want to be soaked in petrol!'

'Take care where you're flinging it, Irma my love,' Mrs Purvis said anxiously. 'You don't want to splash yourself or me.'

'I know what I'm doing. Now stand back, near the door, Mrs Purvis. I'm going to strike the match.'

Pippa held her breath. If Robin was still being held by the housekeeper, then he was near the door — but where was the door? She had lost her sense of direction.

'Robin! Where are you?' she cried.

'Here, Pippa, by the door!' Even as she turned towards his voice she heard the scrape of the match behind her, and she hesitated. Should she leap for Robin and the door, and face the housekeeper — or should she turn back to try to stop Irma throwing the match? A click told her that Mrs Purvis had unlocked the door, ready for escape.

A hiss and a crackle behind her made up her mind. The pain in her ankle forgotten, she leapt forward, her hands outstretched, and encountered the boy's shoulders. Pushing him sharply to one side she groped for the housekeeper's angular body, but met only thin air.

'Watch out!' Irma cried. 'Don't let her reach the door!'

Instantly bony hands seized hold of Pippa, and with amazing strength Mrs Purvis forced her back. At the same time the housekeeper cried out: 'Take care, Irma! You've spilt petrol on your frock! Edge round the blaze towards the door!'

Pippa wrestled with her, trying to release herself from the woman's vice-like grip. Close behind her, so close, she could feel the heat, flames sizzled and roared. Pippa heard Robin cry out: 'Pippa, the pillar's on fire! The balcony above you is all in flames!'

With every ounce of her strength Pippa tore at the housekeeper's hands until she finally broke free, then sent the older woman flying. The crackling heat all around her made her break out into a sweat and at that second she heard a rumbling sound overhead.

'*Pippa! Jump!*'

Robin's warning came too late. She felt a sharp crack on her head and stumbled forwards, momentarily dazed by the blow. Then suddenly Mrs Purvis began screaming: '*Irma! Oh, my God! Irma!*'

It was then the miracle happened. In the black void before her Pippa suddenly saw a glow, a dull red glow which began to grow and gather colour. Then she saw a strange and terrifying *tableau vivant*: a thin, gaunt figure in black staring with wide, terrified eyes at a column of flame: and a small boy crouched with his hands behind his back beside a long trestle table. She stared, transfixed. It was not her imagination − she could see. Only hazily, but she could see.

Mrs Purvis screamed again and leapt forwards, directly into the column of flame. And then Pippa realised that the flame was not static but veering wildly from side to side. With a sickening rush of horror she saw red hair flying and hands beating at it, and Mrs Purvis beating her bare hands against the body. It was Irma, completely engulfed in fire.

'Irma, my precious! I told you to take care with the petrol!' Mrs Purvis was shrieking. 'Oh, my darling! What have you done?'

Pippa stared around. There was no water, no drape to quench the flame, only straw on the floor — and that was burning fiercely. She raced to Robin and seized his shoulder.

'Poor lady,' he was whimpering. 'Poor lady.'

'Outside, Robin,' Pippa commanded. 'Mrs Purvis, out! Get blankets!'

But the housekeeper seemed deaf, crazed with hysterical sobbing and feverishly tearing at Irma, who screamed and fell to the floor. Mrs Purvis crouched over her, still shrieking and sobbing. Pippa wrenched the key round in the lock and flung the door open wide. Robin scuttled out.

'For God's sake, Mrs Purvis!' Pippa yelled. 'Get help! Fetch blankets!' The figure of Irma screamed and then lay still. Mrs Purvis stared for a second and then, straightening, she turned a look charged with hate towards Pippa.

'You bitch!' she cried, unaware of the flame licking around her. 'You'll die for this!'

Like a cat she leapt, black and sinuous and swift as an arrow. Her slender body felt like a ton weight when it cannoned into Pippa, and they both fell heavily on the floor. Over the housekeeper's shoulder Pippa caught a flashing glimpse of Robin's terrified little face through the smoke.

'Go — fetch help!' she gasped, but as she rolled over and struggled to rise she could not see whether he obeyed. The housekeeper leapt on her again, her dark eyes glittering and her nails outstretched to rake Pippa's face. They were enveloped in smoke now, in the centre of the great hall, and Pippa was choking and gasping for air. The draught from the open door was fanning the flames and the minstrel's gallery overhead was blazing fiercely. Soon it must fall, and perhaps the roof too.

Mrs Purvis's hands found a hold on Pippa's throat. Pippa kicked and lashed out as hard as she could, but the older woman was amazingly powerful, and her adversary out of condition after spending so long as an invalid. Pippa was growing desperate. Air no longer reached her lungs. She

214

was choking and the world was going black again. Irrationally it flashed into her mind that it was her nightmare all over again — darkness, and the perfume choking her nostrils, only this time the smell was petrol and smoke, not Californian Poppy.

But this time the nightmare was not going to defeat her. As Pippa gathered the last ounce of her strength to fight back she felt the vicious grip about her throat begin to loosen. Encouraged, she battled even harder. The hands let go, and she gulped in a lungful of smoke-filled air. Dimly she was aware of the housekeeper scrambling to her knees and then she vanished into the smoke. Pippa too began to scramble up, filled with determination. Mrs Purvis must be caught and dragged to safety. Just as she stumbled upright, there was a rumbling, wrenching sound and something hit her, sending her flying. It was not Mrs Purvis making a renewed attack, she realised, but a great beam, charred and smouldering, which pinned her helplessly to the floor, like a butterfly pinned to a display board. She lay there, unable to move, desperate with fear. A blackened, immobile figure lay beside her. Inches from her head, a tower of flame was consuming the trestle table. Its heat was singeing her hair.

It was ridiculous, she thought. Suddenly and for no accountable reason she could see again, only to watch helplessly as she and her sister were burnt to death. The incredibly magnificent colours dazzled her. The blue and grey of the smoke, the scarlet and vermilion flame, were a garish kaleidoscope of colour which seared her eyeballs so long accustomed only to blackness, with an intensity no less than the fire. To behold a world of beauty in colour as she was to die was unbearably tragic. She struggled with every muscle to move, but it was hopeless. She was trapped. Smoke was filling her lungs, burning and choking — was it the nightmare realised at last? The hissing and spitting flames came nearer. Pippa choked, gasping for life, but she could feel the blackness of oblivion beginning to close in on her . . .

'*Pippa!*'

It was a dream, an overwhelming nightmare. It seemed to her dazed mind that a powerful male voice rang through the smoke-eddying rafters — Stephen's voice. Dimly she wondered whether she had already crossed the threshold to the life beyond. She was aware that the crushing weight across her body was suddenly gone, and then strong arms held her close. She felt herself being lifted and carried and then moments later there was pure, sweet air. Coughing and gasping, she gulped it in with desperate gratitude.

'Pippa, Pippa *babam,* are you all right?'

Unbelievingly she stared up into anxious blue eyes and her heart swelled with happiness. It was Stephen, alive and here and holding her tightly as he hastened along the corridor.

'Irma — and Mrs Purvis,' she managed to gasp.

Stephen shook his head. 'Too late for Irma. Mrs Purvis has gone — she was running out as I came in. She's all right. Let's get you out now.'

Over his shoulder Pippa could see smoke billowing from the room they had left and flames licking round the door. Stephen was running, and she could see the ash in his blond hair. Suddenly they were out in the open, and the air had never smelt so clean.

'My God!' she heard Stephen mutter. Dazed though she was, she could not fail to note the horror in his tone.

'What is it?'

'Mrs Purvis — oh, my God!'

With effort Pippa turned her head to look. At the foot of the flight of steps from the front door of Cambermere Hall lay a black, prostrate figure with a crimson halo.

'What happened, Stephen? Is she hurt?'

Stephen turned away so that Pippa could see no more. 'She's dead, Pippa. Stabbed in the neck.'

'*Stabbed?*'

'Yes. Her earrings. One of them has pierced her neck. It must have severed a carotid artery.' He strode quickly away from the building. 'Ah, thank God! Here comes the ambulance and the fire engine.'

Afterwards, Pippa could remember dimly being carefully lifted into the ambulance, the murmured, soothing words, and Stephen's hand in hers as she lay numb and stupefied. After that she must have sunk into oblivion.

Later, how much later she had no way of knowing, Pippa came slowly to her senses. For long moments she lay there, staring into the darkness and trying to recollect the nightmare that had so recently overwhelmed her mind. Gradually she began to recall taunting voices, a child's cry of fear, flame, blood . . . The isolated images that drifted back were so terrifying that it must have been a nightmare more hideous than she had ever experienced before. The only memory of it that filled her with disappointment was the belief, in the dream, that she had somehow miraculously regained her sight.

But was it a dream? Even now it seemed as if she could discern a faint light some yards away — and yes, beneath it a head wearing a white cap. Was she dreaming now of hospital after she fell from Copper? After all, even blind people probably dreamed. As she lay there, perplexed, the white cap rose and came towards her.

'Ah, you're awake, Miss Korvak. How do you feel?' It was a young nurse, but not one she recognised. She stared at her hazy face. 'Still a little sleepy, are you?' the nurse went on. 'Don't worry. That's the sedative the doctor gave you. Quite a nasty shock you had, wasn't it? Still, you were very lucky. Only a sprained ankle and your hair will soon grow again.'

Pippa raised a hand to her head and felt the short, crisp ends of hair. It had been no dream; dreams don't singe one's hair away. Her heart leapt. Then if it had all really happened, what had become of Robin and Stephen?

'Stephen . . . ' she murmured. The nurse smiled.

'Is he the young man who sat by your bed all night? He's still here. I don't suppose Sister will mind if he comes in — it's nearly time for the morning bell.'

Suddenly he was there, tall and broad, his fair head surrounded by a halo of golden light, and as he bent to kiss her cheek Pippa felt warmth and life flow in her veins. 'Stephen — '

'Don't speak, my love,' he whispered, laying a finger to her lips. 'I'm so glad I listened to the promptings of my heart and not my head or I'd never have reached you in time.'

'The 'plane to New York . . . '

'I let it go. There was something in your voice on the 'phone when I rang you, nothing you said, just a tone of helplessness, fear even. I stayed the night at the airport hotel trying to decide whether to go, or to defy you and come back. Thank God I came back. I should never have left you. I'll never leave you again, Pippa.'

He was covering her hands with kisses, muttering brokenly, 'I've thrown away the book. My father's name was cleared and I realised I wanted you more than I wanted revenge. I didn't realise how much danger you were in, that Irma was crazy. Oh, my little pipistrelle, I was nearly too late!'

'Robin?' Pippa murmured.

'He's safe, and unhurt. Irma died, I'm afraid. And Mrs Purvis. Strange thing that, being stabbed by her own earring.'

Strange, and ironic, thought Pippa, since the earrings had been a treasured gift and a memento of her beloved Miss Carrie. Ironic too that her pet child Irma had died in the same spot as her mother.

'Cambermere?' she asked.

'The fire's out. The east wing was gutted but the rest is safe. Don't worry.'

She was not worried. Indeed, she was glad that the east wing with its grisly film sets and unhallowed memories was gone forever, and with it the reminders of Miss Carrie's tragic death and Father's past misdeeds.

Stephen said in a low voice, 'I've only just learnt of your blindness, Pippa, and I'm amazed at your courage. You never told me or cried out for help. And yet, as I carried you out, I could swear you looked at Mrs Purvis as she lay there. But never fear, my darling, I'll always be here now to love and guide you.'

She would tell him the glorious news later, once the memory of that dreadful night and the two sprawled black figures circled in scarlet had begun to fade. There was time enough, she knew, to tell him of the miraculous blow on the head in the midst of the fire which had restored some hazy sight: and time to tell him she had never meant to blaze at him, to banish him forever, because she too loved him with all her heart. With his hand tightly gripping hers and his gentle voice murmuring words of love, there was all the time in the world.

'I discovered how your mother really died from the coroner's inquest, poor soul, and how your father kept the truth a secret so that her fans would never know she had lost her reason. Instead he put it about that she had gone into a decline and died in a sanatorium. Then I traced Irma to Nottingham,' he was saying softly. 'She was not there, but her talkative landlady told me a lot. She took me for a relative, I think. She said Irma had expectations of great fortune once she had got rid of an importune sister. That worried me. I kept thinking of the things that had happened to you — the oil on the swimming pool steps and all that — but I couldn't bring myself to believe that she could be behind it. Now I see she must have been, probably with Mrs Purvis's help. Forgive me, *galambom*, for not taking your fears seriously and for leaving you to face danger alone. I see now that all those odd things must have been her doing. I should have stayed by you, whatever you said.'

Pippa stroked his bent head. His hair too was singed. Yes, my beloved, she thought. All those strange events have at last been explained away — except one.

Irma had sworn, in that great hall which was to become the blazing inferno where she was to die, that she had not danced in the gardens of Cambermere Hall by moonlight. Who, then, had been the enchanting, ethereal figure that glided from the trees and dipped and curtseyed with such lissom grace? Pippa raised Stephen's face and cupped it between her hands, seeing dimly the gentle curve of his lips and the tenderness in his eyes. She might never speak of it to him, but deep inside she was convinced that figure was the shade of the woman who wrote so lovingly of her child in her diary, the doomed, unhappy Carrie Hope. From her grey limbo world she had come back to ensure that child's safety and escape from darkness into the bright world of love and hope.

219